Buried Beneath the Light

THE SOUL BOUND REALMS
BOOK TWO

CARLIANN JEAN

Copyright © 2025 by Carliann Jean

All rights reserved.

No part of this publication may be reproduced, distributed, or transmitted in any form or by any means, including information storage, retrieval systems, photocopying, recording, or other electronic or mechanical methods, without the prior written permission from the author, except for the use of brief quotations in a book review. For permission requests, contact Carliann Pentz.

This is a work of fiction. The story, including all names, characters, organizations, and incidents portrayed in this production are either products of the author's imagination or are used fictitiously. No identification with actual persons (living or deceased), places, buildings, and products is intended or should be inferred. Any similarities between characters, settings, and situations in this book and real people, places, or events is purely coincidental.

Cover Design by Melania Guarnieri from Miss Pink Coconut

Chapter Illustrations by Melania Guarnieri from Miss Pink Coconut

Maps by Lexie from Selkkie Designs

Editing by Maddi Leatherman from EJL Editing

Final Proofreading by Rachel Yanan

First Edition: January 2025

Independently published.

Amazon Paperback ISBN: 9798303956490

Table of Contents

Also by Carliann Jean — vii
Playlist — xi
Mental Health Warning — xiii
Themes to Consider — xv
Prologue — xix

1. Athena — 1
2. Eira — 15
3. Nyx — 28
4. Athena — 39
5. Hadwin — 50
6. Astira — 61
7. Eira — 70
8. Tryg — 85
9. Nyx & Eira — 92
10. Astira — 106
11. Eira — 116
12. Athena — 136
13. Hauke — 153
14. Tryg — 160
15. Hadwin — 171
16. Astira — 191
17. Tryg — 207
18. Athena & Nyx — 215
19. Eira & Nyx — 233
20. Astira — 252
21. Eira & Athena — 269
22. Hauke — 296
23. Astira — 300
24. Eira — 315
25. Tryg — 333

26. Nyx	353
27. Hauke	366
28. Athena	369
29. Eira	392
30. Astira	408
31. Tryg	418
32. Hadwin	430
33. Nyx	435
34. Hauke	439
35. Unknown	442
Thank You for Reading!	445
Note from the Author	447
Acknowledgments	449

PART ONE

A GUIDE TO THE REGIONS ON FUTURE EARTH & MAJIKAERO

Regions on Future Earth	455
New Africa Territories	457
New Antarctica Territories	461
New Asia Territories	463
New Europe Territories	465
New North America Territories	469
New Oceania Territories	473
New South America Territories	475
Regions on Majikaero	477

PART TWO

GODS & GODDESSES, COUNCIL MEMBERS

Gods and Goddesses Worshipped	481
List of Council Members	483

PART THREE
CHARACTER NAMES & PRONUNCIATIONS

Main Character Names & Pronunciation Guide	489
Main Character Names & Pronunciation Guide	491
Main Character Names & Pronunciation Guide	493

PART FOUR
COMMON MAJIKAERO TERMS

Common Majikaero Terms & Pronunciation Guide	497
About the Author	501
Let's Connect!	503

Also by Carliann Jean

The Soul Bound Realms

Book 1: The Light Within

Dedication

*For those who have hidden their darkness
beneath the facade of light.
I see you.
Your darkness and the light you project are both beautiful.*

Playlist for *Buried Beneath the Light*

Listen to the complete playlist on Spotify.

Mental Health Warning

Special Note, as written in the first book of this series: It's important to me on a deeply personal level to share the darker mental health themes and trauma that my characters endure and grow through. Some of you will read these trigger warnings and be absolutely okay continuing through the story. Others might believe they'll be okay, yet a scene will trigger an emotion or memory within them.

As a therapist, I can't emphasize this enough: If you become triggered or upset, please seek the appropriate support. Whether it's a typical self-care plan or talking with a therapist or needing crisis support, please take care of your mental health.

For those needing suicide and crisis support in the United States: You can call 988 or go to www.988lifeline.org/chat. There are also local and international hotlines, depending on where you live.

Themes to Consider

Dark Themes
Mental Health Disorders
Impact of Trauma
Explicit Language
Suggestive Language
Violence
Gore
Manipulation
Suicide
Sexual Assault
Rape
Murder
Emotional and Physical Abuse
Torture
Mention of Kidnapping
Mention of War
Scenes of a Sexual Nature
Other Heavy Themes

Discretion is advised.

Future Earth

- Kopania
- Kyazssia
- Kyazssia
- New Taszealia
- Swean
- Swean
- Kyazssia
- Hungatia
- Kossnia
- Iktlekstan
- Griclin Edinaees
- Belauy
- Urama Arglia
- Saihocg O
- Nax Tyaxiff
- Urnia Abagopea
- Guinegalia
- Kunia
- Stryaka Nassion
- Sbogon Sigollin
- Torinarry
- Torinarry
- Torinarry
- Torinarry
- Ongollies
- Zonargwa
- Gulizaeras
- Gulior Pakdoar
- Bochentuay
- Torinarry
- Hlavia Calaska

Antarctica

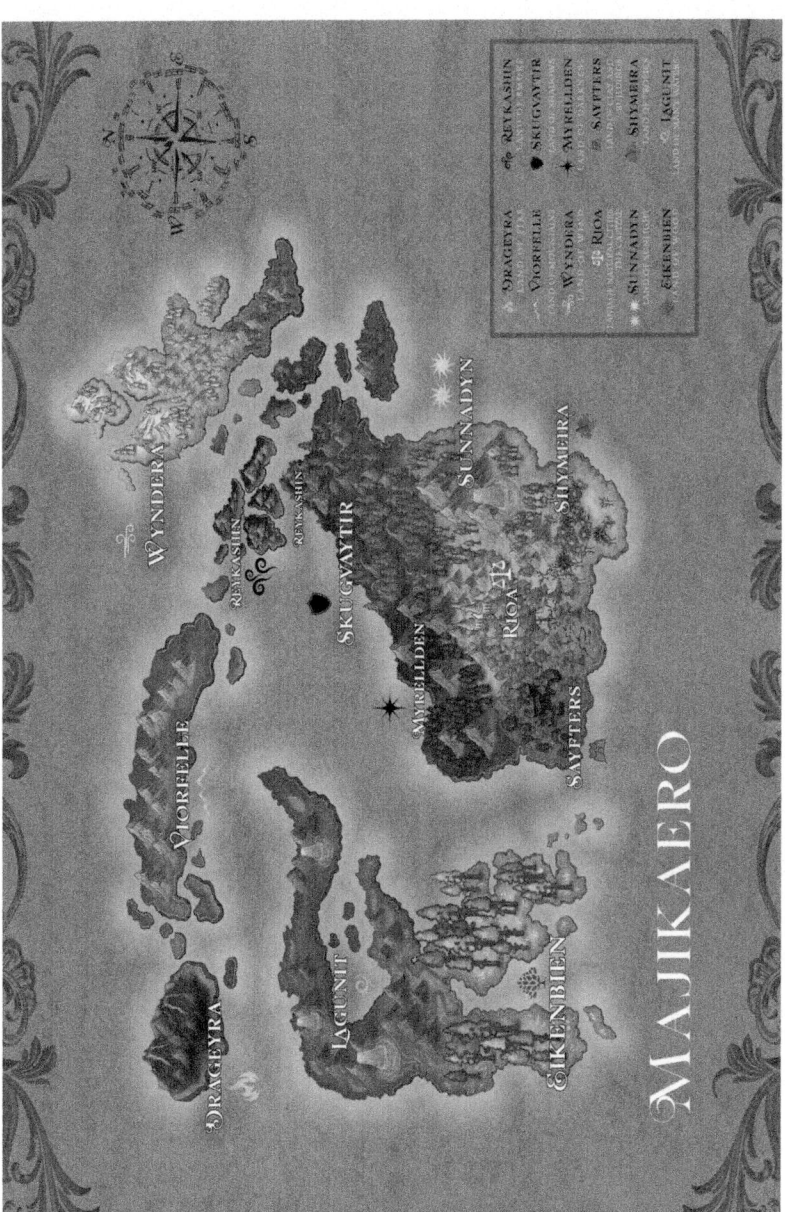

Prologue

With my breath caught in my throat, I roll further down the hill of damp soil until my famished body bangs against the base of the hidden tunnel. My head bounces back and rattles from the impact. Blood seeps out of my left ear, and the purple bruises framing my collarbone like a lurid necklace throb. I allow myself a whole minute to readjust to the pain, and then I'm pushing off from the earth again, racing down the pitch-black tunnel.

There are no candles to light the way as I scramble across the bumpy surface of the ground. I have no expectations that I'll survive this next part of my journey. It's either escape or be thrown into the flames of a hell I didn't ask to be in. I've accepted I might trip or fall into a pit of raving monsters as easily as the rest of my family did.

Those monsters are always watching, always eager to feast on the flesh of the innocent.

My heart is hammering, beating as fast as a hummingbird's wings, except my heart is nowhere near as colorful or exuberant. No, no, any splashes of color that still existed after being captured were bled out of me drop by miserable drop. Now my heart is just an organ, operating on pure adrenaline.

I sprint harder, pumping my arms and legs as high as they will go. A sigh of relief deflates out of me when a cool draft laps at my skin. *I'm close to the other side.* One more step, then the next. My right foot scrapes the exterior of a new object that grinds against my ears like sandpaper. I make the mistake of looking down, thinking I'll catch a glimpse of what I'm now running on. That's all it takes for me to tumble to the ground and split my scabbing wounds open.

No, not the ground.

I've fallen headfirst into the open jaws of the enemy, my insignificant life coming to an end as I choke on the way my body burns in agony.

ONE
Athena

We're only as broken as we allow ourselves to be.
-Liv Tyonela, Lead Therapist at Arms of Healing Love

Thick grasses tangle in the wind in front of me, twisting together like my knotted emotions. They're long and iridescent, reflecting the light from the two blazing suns peaking above the forest. Tufts of fluffy bulbs sit on top of each strand, as soft as a kitten's neck. My fingers twitch with the need to touch them. To feel anything soft and neutral and innocent when my world has been turned upside down in the worst way possible.

I breathe in the summer breeze and burrow my toes into the moist soil beneath me, grounding myself. Silky black coverings wrap from my shoulders down to my ankles in a sleek jumpsuit. I purposely didn't select any shoes from what some of the other healers created. I *want* the soles of my feet to make contact with the dirt. I'm begging the earth to swallow my legs and intertwine its roots with each inch of my scabbed skin, and hoping for a fool's dream that it'll bury my body so deep, even I won't remember who I am.

The *solliqas* here talk about trauma and darkness taking over the realm. A plague ripe with tainted shadows and fresh pain that'll consume the soul from the inside out. It doesn't matter the age of the soul—the disease slithers in the shadows until it finds you. It starts small, hiding in the crevices of the soul and heart, until you're bathed in nightmares and vines of darkness glide up your skin. Until you're lashing out with razor-sharp teeth and even sharper words at the ones you love, at yourself, at anything that offends you. Until you're well on your way to turning into the very monster you told yourself you'd never become.

I hold back a snort at the thought, not wanting to disturb the relative peace that swirls around me. These *solliqas* have every right to fear such a disease. Who wants to turn into a monster, dripping in poison and agony? Yet I can't help but smile at their reactions. As if they're the only ones to come across such a plague. *As if I'm not weighed down with my own trauma and pain and warped thoughts that I carefully bury deep, far away from prying eyes.*

No one would guess that about me. I'm as sturdy as the pink and blue tree trunk that towers behind me. Its roots bubble over the ground and weave in intricate patterns through the white grass. If I look up, my neck stretches all the way back as I search for the tips of the branches. Each of them are tall and far out of my reach. I can barely make out the last of the blue leaves. The only indication this tree is tired and old beyond any soul in this realm is the way its bark chips and withers away against my shoulder blades. Pieces of it crumble to the ground, sprinkling the tops of my feet with colorful shards of the tree's skin.

Yet I don't allow myself to chip away or to crumble. At least not on the exterior. *No one* sees the rolling waves of melancholy lapping away just under the surface. Not even Eira with her ability to read nearly everyone we interact with. She's incredibly sensitive to the energies around her, and it can send her down a tunnel of panic that consumes her. As we've walked side by side through life, I've been careful about how much of my own tunnel I allow her to see. My own spiraling thoughts of disgust and despair. My urge for destruction—to end the constant influx of emotions that are *so* heavy.

If I'm able to keep this from my best friend, my soul sister, then I know each fragmented feeling is stuffed away deep enough.

When I first met Eliina in her spacious tent by the other healers, I was sure that her *maji* would sense how torn up I am on a daily basis. A small part of me was almost counting on it, so I could finally be free of this burden I've kept locked down in my heart. But my own damn *maji* was completely out of my control. It slithered up and around me when Eliina's hands connected with my own. The power brought the sweet scent of the earth through my whole body until I was coated in a layer of protection from any *solliqa* around me. Almost as if it sensed my secret desire to conceal the darker parts of myself and bent to my will immediately.

I can taste the slick power of my *maji* at this moment. How strong it already has its hold on my soul, similar to the tree's roots weaving around and surrounding me, but it's learned that I can be even stronger. I expected to need more time to learn the intricacies of my magic, that it would be too good to be true to land in some magical realm and have the ability to bend my power how I please. But like a fairytale, I've been able to play and experiment with the earth *maji* without any consequences. Yet, unlike a fairytale, I'm waiting for chaos to erupt and show me true happy lives and endings are not possible.

The destruction from what happened at the Moons Cycle Festival is thankfully proof that nothing is perfect. And my *maji* is just *waiting* to be released upon this realm. I've kept its abilities close to me, not wanting any other soul to know what I've discovered about my powers. And I've succeeded.

Mostly. No one knows the extent of what I can do, but *he* knows how much power flows through my veins now.

Fucking Hadwin.

I bristle at the thought of his stupid face while my heart spasms uncontrollably at the thought of his name. I'm still reeling from the fact that I'm in a magical world full of souls, let alone that my *maji* called to him the moment we stepped through that archway on the way to Eliina's quarters at the Council building. His own powers flared as bright as my own, with the same colors of green. Colors of the forests back on Earth. They swirled together in a seductive dance and pulled me flush against his soul, even though we were standing on opposite ends of the room.

Parts of my *maji* slink in coy movements, thinking about the moment we connected with one another. But a much larger part of me will never forget the harsh surprise in his golden eyes. Shadows of disgust curled within their depths, subtle enough that no one else would notice unless they were lost to our staring contest. There was a flicker of desire, *oh yes*—a fleeting second where that gold melded into me with a possessive force that shook my soul to the core.

But it was only a second. A mere inhale of air. And then that liquid gold hardened into stone and a disinterested mask had set in place on Hadwin's idiotic, beautiful face.

Naively, I tried to talk to him. I *knew* Eira noticed what happened between us and had told her to let me figure it out. I've never been one to be shy around men—or women, for that matter. I thrive and my soul comes *alive* when I'm tangled up with the body of another. Telling someone how I feel? Easy as the warm wind that currently drifts through the strands of my hair. I don't need to bare my inner turmoil to form a connection with someone. It's part of what's made me good at being a therapist. That and being able to communicate clearly. It's a strength I've honed over the past few decades, from the moment I learned from my family that not communicating meant broken relationships—which meant having to endure even more years of suffering.

Does Hadwin communicate? *Nope.*

Does Hadwin remove that fucking mask of indifference for me? *Never.*

Does Hadwin even show up when he says he'll finally meet me to simply talk about our similar powers? *Of course not.*

He didn't even make eye contact with me in the library when I had a million questions about this world and using earth *maji*. I'm fucking fortunate that I'm a quick learner and love to read. The books Eliina gave to me about our shared earth *maji* have taught me a significant amount about what I'm capable of doing with my powers. Who knew I'd be able to use plants to strip away trauma sticking to a soul? Or that I can bend trees, those gentle giants, to my will? When I'm ready, I can even shift into a number of different creatures of the forest. There are healers that Daya introduced me to that offered their own insight. Although, they're insisting that I need to start the process of healing any stored trauma in my soul, similar to Eira and Nyx, if I want to make more progress with understanding my powers.

Don't make me laugh. They're sure as hell not digging up my pain if I won't even let Eira see it. I'll squirm my way out of the healers' grasps until I'm good and ready to open up to them.

Until I can open up to *myself*.

The only time Hadwin ripped off that dreaded mask, the one set in place for everyone, was a few nights ago during the Moons Cycle Festival.

I saw the first crack in his mask when we made eye contact at the beginning of the night. His eyes sparkled, their gold as bright as sunlight, when he raked his gaze over my body and gauzy white-green dress. Its sheerness hugged my curves and left little to the imagination with the way it stopped just under my ass—even more so with how exposed my sides and back were under the flimsy lace. My maji *thrummed under the surface, practically begging to play with his own.*

As soon as the bells rang out and Eira transformed into her crystallized fox, I gave in to my powers. Beds of purple and blue flowers, a whole spectrum of these colors that matched the moons rising above us, surrounded my feet. I allowed myself to laugh as pure exhilaration flooded my veins. It was as if the trees and soil and grass and every soul in the forest called to me and breathed life into my skin. I followed the trail from the bustling market stalls through the flourishing forest all by myself until I found myself dashing under the trees and floating orbs of maji. *Dazzling flowers and plants wove around me midair until I was a part of the earth itself.*

That's when Hadwin threw away his broken mask, the one that's tangible and real to me even if it's metaphorical. I thought I was alone in that part of the forest until his luminescent snake form slithered around my legs, black smoke blending with my colorful leaves. Death dancing with life. I thought I would be afraid, except how could I? Even filled with shadows and darkness, Hadwin's maji *calls to my own. A missing piece of my soul I didn't realize I had lost. One a best friend can't quite reach.*

Those golden eyes bled into my own as we danced under the illuminated night sky. A smile tugged at his lips, soft at first, until I coaxed a boisterous laugh from him when I tripped over a tree root. The movement caused a burst of glittery insects to erupt, and I went flying wildly to the ground. Hadwin's shadows contorted and writhed until they caught me before I could hurt myself, and they cradled me in a dark embrace. We didn't exchange many words, but we didn't need to. Our eyes told their own stories, and our maji *sent hushed messages through the earth to one another. We were so in tune and deeply rooted in the world around us, and a sad part of me knew that I couldn't count on this side of him sticking around.*

So, I didn't ruin it. I didn't speak. I took whatever he was willing to give me, even if it only appeared as amused smiles and deep belly laughs influenced by the maji *tricks floating around us.*

Much to my surprise, Hadwin's enormous, sinuous serpent coiled its tail tightly around my legs, forcing my feet to burrow deeper into the rich soil. I thought I would cringe as he wound up my thighs and hips, considering I'm not the biggest fan of reptiles or scales. His body molded perfectly to me, though and was a mixture of smooth softness, lustrous gold, and steel wrapping me in a layer of protection. It felt like him: *strong, dangerous, and intense.*

When his snake's head swung around to face me with those golden predator eyes, each one the size of my face and assessing me as prey, a quiet calmness settled over me. Hadwin swiftly transformed the upper half of his body into his humanoid form in a flash of sparkling light, keeping his bottom half as a python. One calloused, tawny hand wrapped around my hip, grounding me further, and the other traced the outline of my jaw. His fingertips trembled, as if he was terrified I would disappear from his grasp. I felt treasured and desired in a way I still can't describe. It was the single most intimate moment of my life.

Yet, of course, fairytales don't exist. I knew something was wrong, terribly *wrong, the moment his scales shifted into mere shadows, and they stuttered around my waist. Hadwin's grin fell in one vast sweep of emotion, his liquid gold eyes turning so rigid and sharp they could be weapons. The muscles rippled along his bare back until he was as still as the trees around us, made sturdy from his tension. Gold irises twisted into empty black shadows until I was staring into the eyes of a demon. A scream lodged in my throat when he bared his fangs at me and sprinted off in the opposite direction in a blur of smoky darkness.*

I'm not sure how I convinced my body to move, but I ran after him with everything I had. I flew past many solliqas *enjoying their time under the full moons, bathing in the navy and lavender light. All of them were clueless that Hadwin, a powerful* solliqa *in this realm, was acting deranged—that they should be afraid of the swift change in his behavior from mere moments ago. I let the flowing grass absorb into my feet and legs and willed it to carry me faster after Hadwin. Faster and faster and faster. I didn't know what was happening, but there were alarm bells rattling in my head. They warned me that if I didn't get to him in time, his soul would be lost forever. Some message sent to my* maji *from the earth itself that I had to* hurry.

When the other part of your soul gives you even a piece of their love, you don't let go. You hold on until they see how enchantingly you thread together. I couldn't—no, I wouldn't—*let him out of my grasp until he saw what we could become.* Together.

Gasping, my lungs on fucking fire, I finally caught up to him. I nearly choked and fell backward when I saw what he was gaping at—absolutely mesmerized and lost in a spell cast upon him. Hadwin seemed to be hovering near a black and purple swirling portal that floated in the night air, some kind of vortex that oozed in ominous shadows. The edges of it flickered against some of the tree branches, the bark crackling in distress. It had a sickly sweet scent and nearly suffocated me with its power.

My maji *shook in waves of alarm and forced itself up through my legs, propelling me forward. I lunged at Hadwin before he could take a step into the portal's thick, glossy, whirling colors. I was convinced that it would devour his soul, and my hands wrapped around his hips in a desperate attempt to make him stay. Hadwin hissed at me and grabbed my fingers with a grip of iron and sharp black nails. I won't ever forget the urge I had to shrink back from those demonic eyes of pure evil, the terror that wrapped around my whole body.*

But I couldn't let him go. My maji *shuddered with how terrified I felt, but it flared to life when Hadwin's hands touched me. It didn't care that his green aura was dim and mostly shadows slinked out to meet us. My magic homed in on Hadwin and coiled like corded rope around his darkened wrists until he was falling on top of me, the weight of him forcing us into the tall grass. I clawed at his tanned skin with a desperation I hadn't felt in a long time. He fought against me and* snap—*my wrists cracked, breaking in the midst of his struggle. I couldn't stop the bloodcurdling scream that flew out of my mouth when the pain rocked through me.*

That scream of suffering made his shadows stutter, made him blink at me in confusion for a brief second. Yet again, it was only a second. Barely lasting a breath this time around. Not enough time for his soul to crawl back to me before one of the Council's protectors rammed into his side and wrapped glowing chains around his entire body. They throbbed with bright light that was almost blinding. Hadwin was consumed by his shadows again while he thrashed against the throbbing chains and the overwrought protectors holding him down. All their yells were muffled as I fell back against the blanket of grass, only mildly aware that I was picked up off the ground, as if I was a limp rag doll. My body was draped over a set of thick arms like a winter coat. In a blink, I was unconscious, momentarily free of the pain latching onto me.

I remember peeling my eyes open and blearily looking around me. It had taken me a while to gather my bearings. The sharp sting in my wrists had dulled to a low throb at that point, my healing magic helping me recover quicker than most. I was curled up in the corner of a stony dungeon cell. The freezing rocky floor sent shivers up my body, and I struggled to find a place against the wall and ground that wasn't uncomfortable. There was no window near me, and I was bathed in darkness. Trickles of liquid dripped around me, sounding way too loud to my sensitive ears amid the smothering silence. I could only hear that drip, drip, drip *mixed with my ragged breaths.*

My attention shifted down to my body. Horror smacked me right in the face as I took in the still bleeding scratches that littered my arms and legs. My gauzy coverings were ripped in too many places and barely stayed attached to my shaking body. I brought a trembling hand to the fabric, moving it over a deep gash near my hip to cover it from my sight. Right as I did this, a body moved in the corner of my eye.

Fuck, I wasn't alone.

I groaned as I shifted my body to face whoever I was thrown next to in this cell and squeaked when I realized it was Hadwin. Even in the dark, I'd recognize his body and presence anywhere— the way his soul was damaged in the worst way. His golden hair hung in tangled webs over his face, but I could see the outline of his body as my eyes continued to adjust to the dark room. I gasped when I realized the dripping sound was actually his blood trickling onto the ground.

"Hadwin?" *I whispered.*

His body twitched, and within seconds, the chains weighing him down flared to life with a brightness that mimicked the stars. They provided enough light that I could see there were other cells and solliqas *around us, and it was nauseating how many gashes painted Hadwin's body.* There were puddles of blood everywhere.

While I was thrown into a cell with him, a decision that was still unclear to me, I could see I didn't have chains attached to my arms and legs. Perhaps the protectors associated me with him but didn't deem me as a threat. *The next moments of my life in Majikaero passed by simultaneously slowly and quickly, a dragging speed that made my stomach churn. I wanted to slow everything down even more to change what happened next, but at the same time, the slow motion made the agony even worse.*

Hadwin's gold eyes flashed to mine, our maji *making a momentary connection. Flecks of black swirled in his gaze as he looked upon me with what could have been* hope, *but that all came crashing down. His eyes hardened again, and he growled at me, loud enough to shake his chains.*

"You *can't be here," he hissed.*

I scowled. "I certainly didn't ask to be thrown in a cell. I couldn't let you run off to whatever the fuck that swirling portal was."

Hadwin glared so hard at me, it went spearing right through my soul. "Perhaps that's exactly what you should have done, zamia."

My eyebrows furrowed in confusion at his tone and what he called me. He didn't give me time to ask questions. Hadwin screamed out in agony as his feet shifted into a snake tail, only partially able to use his maji. *He slashed with thunderous strength at the bottom of the cell door. Shards of what could have been metal shattered on the ground in piercing sounds.*

Gaping at him, I was going to ask what the fuck he was doing when protectors were surely near us, when his tail of broken scales coiled around my feet. It was tight enough to cut off my circulation, and I already knew there'd be bruises painted onto my ankles. Hadwin yanked with a groan and shoved my battered body through the bottom of the door. It was too small of an opening for me to fit comfortably, which resulted in the ends of the door slicing through my shoulder blades.

Sobbing, I half glared, half snarled back at Hadwin. There was too much pain skating down my arms to lift them, weighed down by figurative chains that matched the strength of Hadwin's literal ones. Before I could do anything else, Hadwin muttered some words under his breath that had the door piecing itself back together with dark shadows.

"No!" I screamed, the sound raspy and strained. "What are you doing?!"

Hadwin narrowed his eyes at me. "I told you that you can't be here," he rasped. "Now you have a chance of surviving."

My heart fluttered at his words, at his concern about my safety. I scooted my body along the floor until I got to the cell door and begged any maji *in me to help me kneel. It took ages to get on my knees, and by the time I did, I managed to reach my quivering hand through the door toward Hadwin's bleeding head. He surprised me by bringing his hand up to mine, a look of longing flinging back and forth between us.*

I became vaguely aware of Eira and Nyx arriving at the dungeon. Parts of me wanted to throw myself at Eira, at my best friend who's always been a second home, but I couldn't look away from Hadwin. Not when that longing in his eyes dimmed to a pit of nothingness and that fucking mask *fell right back into place. Cracks and all. A wail of heartbreak and confusion and fury broke from my lips.*

Now, as I continue watching the grasses sway in front of me, basking in the light of a new day, I can't stop thinking about what happened with Hadwin. I know I should fear whatever is going on in this realm—the potential portal, what's happening to the other *solliqas* in the dungeon, Eira being engulfed in her fire. I should fear so many situations right now. But all I can think about is that *damn mask* settling into place again, the one I thought he discarded for me the night of the festival.

Nature breathes all around me. The wind continues to tickle my skin, caressing the scars puckering everywhere that haven't been able to fully heal since I was found. I'm mentally sick enough to refuse additional healing, to keep them on my skin as souvenirs. They're a reminder that Hadwin does have a fucking heart, and it's something to be treasured.

Movement in the distance catches my attention, barely noticeable to the naked eye. My *maji* is different, though. It's healing and earth-based and allows me to communicate through the world of nature in a way others can't. Based on what I've read about earth *maji*, I know this to be true. Sunlight shines on what I now understand is a *canielor*. It lurches near a tree a good mile from where I'm standing. Sparkling pink and turquoise eyes flick around its leathery face, the beauty of them at odds with the rest of the torn creature. Its worm-like body is made of a wrinkly, shriveled skin. Hunks of dirt and white grass are stuck to its gaunt form, as if it has spent time rolling around underground.

Hm, is its pain related to the earth? I inhale deeply, and on my exhale, I imagine sending a flash of my *maji* out toward the *canielor* through the roots under the grass. My power travels through my veins and bleeds into the soil beneath my feet. I'll have to tell the others about this creature, just in case any of the healers or manipulators want to peer into what's left of its soul or put it out of its misery before it attacks any *solliqas*. *I'll take a minute to inspect it, to gather intel.*

Breathing in and out in steady movements, I watch as my *maji* travels along each root and patch of grass until it winds its way around the *canielor*. I don't let myself blink and my breathing might have stopped. My *maji* swaddles the creature in a compassionate glow of healing magic, and I'm blown away by the scraps of information I learn in such little time.

This unfortunate soul. The soul worked with crops and would use magic to create remedial drinks and dishes for those in pain. They wished to provide nourishment and a way to ease emotional distress. I catch a scent of masculine and friendly energy, yet now there's only a throbbing ache in its place. The reason the solliqa *became a* canielor *is unclear, but the taste of desperation and anguish is unmistakable. Those eyes are the beauty they find in their pain, yet I won't learn why unless I work with them directly. They felt there was no other way than to cave into their grief, but what or who were they grieving? Why are they vaguely familiar?*

The unsettling presence of a *solliqa* behind me presses down on my senses. As I gently place the *canielor* back onto the ground, not sensing the petrifying alarm I felt from the monsters I saw the night of the festival, I call my magic back to me. It ripples through the soil as tiny streams of healing light. One of the healers is approaching, and with my luck, they'll want to give me an update about Hadwin. My jaw ticks in agitation as I pivot to face the nearing healer. Their name and face are already forgotten as I wade deeper into my emotions and prepare myself to return to the healing quarters. If I'm going to refuse treatment, the least I can do is try to help the other souls who are still recovering from the attack during the Moons Cycle Festival.

In a mere second, I imagine that same infuriating mask Hadwin wears sliding into place on my own face.

A barrier of protection.

A shield against the parts of myself I don't want to face.

A way to hide from the terror and brokenness and confusion of what will come next.

TWO

Ceira

Flames have no limits. Only the restrictions we force around them and on ourselves.
-Edan, God of Fire

"Next time, I won't go as easy on you." Nyx huffs out a laugh. His gray and blue coverings billow in the humid breeze floating around us. The lightweight material of his long-sleeved shirt hangs loosely around his corded muscles and cinches at his wrists.

I swipe at the haze of smoke still wisping past me in waves of darkness. As soon as my vision clears, Nyx's amused face comes into view, as well as a small group of healers walking a few yards away—Athena in tow. Nyx and I are in a flat clearing, the normally white grass seared down to dirt, that's surrounded by a now-scorched garden. It sits to the right of the healing quarters and south of the Council building, stretching the length of the now-razed structure. I've been told that it's typically used for special events or for *solliqas* to stroll through. In our case, since most *solliqas* are either in the healing quarters or have fled the city, it's a space to practice wielding my fire and light *maji* in preparation for another attack.

Smirking, I let my *maji* thrum louder until sparks fly across at Nyx's arms, wiping the laugh clear off his handsome face.

"You shouldn't," I say, throwing one last flame licking at his shins for good measure. "You won't find the word 'easy' aligns with my personality."

Nyx arches a dark eyebrow and snorts. "Yeah, that's certainly the truth."

The breath gets knocked out of me in a *whoosh* as his tendrils of shadows snake around my wrists and drag me right into his chest. His biceps contract slightly as he slides his hands up my slick arms until his fingers interlace with mine. Those corded muscles might be distracting me a little bit.

"Good thing I've always loved a challenge," he breathes into my parted lips.

I lick my lips at his dark tone, at the way his breath bleeds into my own. Nyx's crackling brown eyes track the movement, and his shadows slink down and around my waist, pulling me impossibly closer. I swear I see a flash of red flame spark at the ends of each tendril dancing along my skin.

Nyx brings his chiseled face to my neck, his curved nose tracing a spot just below my ear. He lightly kisses the area with petal-soft lips before skimming his teeth back and forth. I shiver, still not quite used to the immediate and overwhelming way I can't help but respond to him. Nyx applies more pressure until a few of his front teeth turn into sharpened canines, and he bites down gently. I moan and turn my head slightly to the side, giving him more access to do whatever the hell he pleases. His bite turns from sweet to piercing, and the sharp sting sends a delicious tremble down my spine.

"Mmm," Nyx hums. "You relish in being devoured, don't you, sweetheart?"

Words and coherent sounds aren't available in my brain; it's filled to capacity with thoughts and sensations tied only to Nyx.

"You *love* some pain with your pleasure."

Nyx squeezes my hip tightly enough to bruise and winds his other hand into my braided ponytail. He pulls my head further back in a harsh movement, causing prickles of pain to flare along my scalp, while he gingerly presses a finger against my still covered clit. My hips buck involuntarily, and my knees go weak as I press myself closer to him.

He fucking chuckles. "No, you love *a lot* of pain with your pleasure. And lucky for you, I have no qualms about giving that to you here in this very field." Nyx brings his lips to the shell of my ear and flicks his tongue. "And maybe you'll even enjoy it if a *solliqa* watches us. Because I know there's something filthy hidden in all that dazzling light of yours."

"I see the training session is going well," Stefanie chirps with a smirk.

Startled, I instinctively break away from Nyx in response, but his shadows simply pull me flush against him again. I'm nearly gasping for air, but he keeps his eyes calmly locked on mine as he responds, "As they always do."

Rolling my eyes, I huff out in annoyance until Nyx snickers, letting me go. I almost fall back on my ass and give him a growl before I turn to face the red-headed healer. A *solliqa* who's already become my friend. Her thick hair is pulled half up out of her face today and wound into a small bun. Streaks of natural highlights glimmer in the sunlight, and her green eyes pop like gemstones, resembling the matching light green skin-tight top and bottom she's wearing.

"Isn't she cute when she's irritated?" Nyx asks with a wicked smile.

Irritated. I'll show him irritation. I'm not sure which I hate more: how riled up he's got me or that he's absolutely right about what I'm secretly into. Perhaps I should find a mirror and hold it up to him; that should be all it takes to give him a dose of his own medicine. I mock him under my breath and settle my gaze on Zaya. My deceptively innocent-looking cat is lounging under the shade of a blue and pink tree. She's watching me with bright gold eyes while her tail swishes wildly behind her—ready to pounce on her next victim.

"Go wreak havoc on him," I whisper to her. Zaya hisses silently before lunging at Nyx's low, leathery boots. She curls around them in a ball of fur before slicing her pointy little teeth into his ankles.

"Fuck, that comment doesn't deserve *this* kind of attack," Nyx mutters while trying to shake her off him.

"But she's *so* cute when she's irritated with you," I say, a wide smile overtaking my clammy face.

Stefanie throws her head back, cackling up at the orange and blue sky. She hooks her arm with mine and leads me away from Nyx, letting him find a way to deal with my favorite little demon cat locked around his feet. The black and green backless coverings Stefanie made for me fit me like a glove, zig-zag lines of gauzy cloth weaving up and down my arms and legs. I still have yet to learn how to make my own coverings. The very concept of me designing my own clothes is baffling to me, even if there's magic to help the process. It's a skill set I've envied since I was a young girl. I'm unfortunately not one who should be trusted with a thread and needle—or whichever *maji* tools I'll need—and I have a strong inkling I'll be trading my *maji* with anyone who can make me intricate coverings.

There's magic and then there's the impossible. Expecting me to make coverings that won't fall apart at the seams if I bend over the wrong way is definitely the latter and won't be fixed by sticking me in a magical realm.

"Are the training sessions actually going okay?" she mutters to me.

I heave a sigh, not knowing how to answer. It's been an

impossibly long and insufferable past week here in Rioa. Most of the Council members scattered throughout the realm after the disaster that was the Moons Cycle Festival. I was confused and traumatized enough as it was with Eliina disappearing. Then, I learned that a bunch of powerful *solliqas* I've never met before left for other regions with their own agendas. Most of the healers were fortunate to survive the attacks and, a fact that disturbs me, are apparently accustomed to storing up their *maji* to be ready to help at a moment's notice ever since the plague started. *It is just like healers, no matter the world, to always be ready to respond and expected to be on call.* They were able to jump into shuffling many *solliqas* to designated areas of safety within the healing quarters and parts of the Council building that had a protection spell over them. Some, such as Stefanie, used her *maji* to find me. She insisted that Eliina had made her promise that if anything bad were to happen during the festival, Stefanie would prioritize protecting and healing me. But I saw the sly glint in her eyes when she told me—she would have found me regardless of the chaos and high demand.

That's what true friends do. Our souls find one another when we're lost and in pain. And somewhere between our first introduction and having her *maji* search my soul for traumatic memories and holding me as I sobbed for my friends, we've officially become friends.

After Stefanie found me and Nyx in the dungeons, she realized that I was too engulfed in my flames of rage—unable to settle down until my friends and the other *solliqas* were freed from their cells. She sent for more healers and trusted protectors. I had burned large portions of the metal cells to the ground, but they assisted in breaking everyone free from the starlight chains and started the elaborate process of their soul healings.

Everyone except Tryg, who's officially caught the plague. My heart spasms at the thought of him still sitting in the frigid dungeon cell by himself—a forgotten thought, an emotion that doesn't matter. I *know* that isolation is only going to make what he's going through worse. It's no better than what was done to Nyx, but the healers insisted that we couldn't talk to him for another few days, not while the worst of the darkness is overtaking him. Nyx even agreed that it would be futile and what we do after his demons have settled their foul claws into his soul would matter more.

I've been throwing myself from one injured *solliqa* to the next, doing what I can to assist the already practiced healers and collaborate with anyone deemed trustworthy by Stefanie to figure out our next steps. Nyx asked me what I needed the most right now. I originally told him to let me be the Queen of Light everyone keeps saying I'm supposed to be. He had merely arched an eyebrow and curled me into his arms, wrapping us in a pillow of his shadows.

"You were never a traditional queen. And even if you were in a past lifetime, you can't lead as a queen when you never learned how to," Nyx had murmured in my ear. *"We'll work on honing the skills that you already have. Your obvious leadership capabilities, the aptitude to think on your feet, a never-ending supply of empathy and healing skills, the way other souls drift toward your light. Everything else will eventually fall into place, my firefly."*

Rolling my eyes, I pushed back against his firm chest. "That's quite easy for you to say. You already have the training from being a prince. I need to help these solliqas *now."*

Nyx smirked at me. "Exactly. Allow me to take the reins with figuring out the Council members, how our friends and other solliqas *ended up in the dungeon, and the impact the attack is having throughout the rest of the realm. You focus on what you do best—healing and connecting with souls right now."*

The conversation involved a lot of push back from me until Nyx eventually growled in annoyance. He said I could join him when he talks to trusted *solliqas* in Rioa, such as his long-term friend Jade. He said I could also accompany our friends as they have their memories sifted through by healers and manipulators, or perhaps by me. The second part of his offering was of little significance. *Obviously* I'd be a part of these conversations with our friends. He might have been raised as a fancy prince, but who is he kidding? Those smoky shadows of his aren't exactly inviting, and I sincerely doubt each *solliqa* is going to react kindly to his haunting eyes and his emotive and short-tempered personality.

Only *I'm* that wildly obsessed with a soul half-consumed by the plague and find his darkness eerily comforting. *Surprise, surprise, going for this type. A deranged enough soul to match your own, Eira.*

The training sessions, as Stefanie calls them, are a whole other story. An infuriating, annoyingly helpful, physically draining story. Nyx got the idea in his thick head that in between meeting with *solliqas* and our friends, we should do exercises with our *maji* that he learned back on Drageyra. We essentially spend time connecting with our breath and communicating with our *maji* and practice using our powers as weapons and forms of protection. I initially argued that weaponizing our *maji* seems pretty damn negative and a degrading way to interact with it. Nyx countered that by utilizing our powers for both good and bad, especially for a *solliqa* like myself who hasn't caught the plague yet, I'll be able to protect myself and those I love during future inevitable attacks.

I absolutely will *not* admit that it's a great idea. I don't need to make his ego bigger than it already is around me.

Stefanie nudges my side when I don't answer right away, giving me a playful smile. I nearly trip into the ocher-colored flower bed next to us, causing us to break out in a fit of tittering laughter.

"They're... going as well for a *solliqa* with my levels of exhaustion as they can," I say after catching my breath. "If you were to ask Nyx, he'd say they're a new form of foreplay."

Stefanie snorts. "That sounds like him. It's been forever since I last saw Nyx in Rioa. You're bringing out his more flavorful sides."

"Lucky me!" I chirp. She laughs while steering us into the healing quarters. Stone doors with glittering stones and winding vines are already held open by a few azul boulders. Cracks that weren't there a week ago weave their way down each door from the attack. Perhaps from the use of *maji* or from *solliqas* trying to claw their way into safety before the healers could get to them.

If I wasn't used to the unwelcome tide of chaos that comes with being a therapist, there's no way Stefanie could convince me to enter the healing quarters right now. The normally tranquil environment is drenched in the scent of sickness. Each step I take is the same as pushing through a wall of dark magic, and I have to fight the urge to physically brush each soul's aura off my arms. They linger as close as the shadows I see around Nyx and his friends. Everywhere I look in here, there's a *solliqa* being immersed in one of the rippling pools or trying to talk through the attack with muffled sobs. Most are being physically repaired by a healer, their own *maji* only going so far to heal them. A handful of *solliqas* are gathered in one of the back corners. By the looks of their gnarled faces and pallid yellow eyes, I can tell they're close to becoming *canielors*. The healers who found them must have deemed their souls still salvageable, but it'll depend on if they even want to be saved at this point.

Sometimes, a soul sees too much to believe living is worth it.

I'm waiting for the glass and stone ceilings above us to cave under the building pressure. It's like invisible hands are pushing up against the walls, straining and twisting with the goal of collapsing the stones outside on top of our bodies. As if the hands choking everyone in here aren't doing enough damage.

My gaze snags on one of the shifters I saw chained up in the dungeon cells. I thought they didn't have as much physical destruction compared to our group of friends, but getting a closer look, I can see how wrong I was. Two horns that should curl up naturally from their head are broken at odd angles, with one of them cracked down the middle. Dark pink stripes frame their bright blue eyes and travel down their face and shoulders in intricate patterns. Elongated fangs dip below their top lip, the bottom half ripped off completely, and deep gashes litter their dark patterned skin. I can't see a smooth patch of skin anywhere on their exposed body. They have *misn* energy radiating off them as they yell out in pain when one of the healers pushes them gently under the water.

Murky shadows leech out of the shifter's body and lunge for the healer. Another healer jumps into the pool with their hands raised. A small wave of water drenches the plants near us, and a glowing red light pulsates from their hands in time with the way the shadows move. Light is sent toward the shifter and hits them right in the chest. *Hard*. I can't stop the strangled sound I make when the shifter falls back into the water, knocked unconscious.

"That's Panjan," Stefanie murmurs. Her voice is tight and sad. "He's a talented shifter that previously worked closely with Hadwin. I can only imagine what sort of damage was done to him for being associated with our friends."

"Our?" I whisper.

"Of course," she insists. "There's no place for isolated groups of *solliqas* right now. We're all on the same side."

I drag my weary eyes away from Panjan's limp body and stare into Stefanie's green orbs. They're almost duller from being inside this building and surrounded by so much suffering. "How do you know we're on the right side? That we're all good?"

She doesn't break the stare. "No soul is entirely good or bad —it's their actions that define them. It's us against whoever is driving this plague and forcing pain into our world. It's us against the disease. No matter how good or bad some might deem Nyx's companions."

"Thank the gods for that," Nyx murmurs from behind us.

His shadows snake around my waist in a form of greeting, not able to keep his hands off me for long. I turn back to peer at him and find he's a number of feet taller and on top of Zaya.

One of the first things we did after getting everyone out of the dungeons involved Nyx portaling us to Eliina's quarters. While the building was falling apart with stone crumbling down on top of us, I *had* to be there. Panic crushed my lungs while we called out for Zaya and searched under every crevice for her. My heart had beat at a maddening pace and grief was about to push me over the edge when Nyx yelled out that he found her. Zaya, my poor baby, was cowering behind a ripped purple cushion under one of the broken windows. When she spotted me, she dashed out from her hiding space, almost taking the fluttering curtain with her. I had seen her grow larger in spurts, but when she landed in front of me, Zaya grew at least three feet taller than me.

No longer a ferocious house cat but rather a vicious feline beast. Her fur stood upright in different places while she bared her teeth around the room in fear. I had reached up to stroke her fur until her golden gaze found my own and she looked less on edge. Her size didn't diminish though, not for a few days. I rode her out of the deteriorating room with Nyx traveling by our side in his shadows. We made our way to check in on the *drekstri* and *alklen* that we came here on. Fortunately, they were sheltered in one of the parts of the building that had a spell of protection over it. Just because they were sheltered from the worst of the danger doesn't mean these creatures were any less restless, though, and it took us hours to get them all settled.

Zaya is this same size yet again. Nyx must have gotten her worked up outside before they entered the building, or perhaps it's the screams and pain coating her fur that have her ready to fight. Nyx peers down at me from his seat on top of Zaya with such sorrow, it physically reaches out for me. He jumps down to join us, and his arm quickly replaces where his shadows were touching my body. Zaya shrinks to a slightly smaller size but still looks like a fluffy mountain lion when she steps next to me.

"Are you both ready?" Stefanie asks us. Her tone is laced with that same sorrow in Nyx's eyes. None of us want to be here or face what we're about to encounter. I force any flighty feelings down as deep as I can before raising my chin at her.

"We'll do what we must," I confirm. Nyx nods his head and remains uncharacteristically silent by my side. I have to keep my focus on the task at hand, even if there are a million and a half thoughts spinning around in my cluttered head. We can typically only heal a handful of *solliqas* at a time if we don't want to risk burning out. My mind drifts to the additional support Nyx needs, what Stefanie might be experiencing, and the panic-inducing topic of my friends still on Earth.

One step at a time, or I risk not taking any step at all.

Stefanie sighs deeply. "Let's go, then. You too, kitty cat."

Zaya nudges Stefanie's hand with her wet nose before we continue walking. It warms my heart that she approves of Stefanie. The four of us weave through healers and *solliqas* with haunted faces before entering a back room. It's large enough to hold at least twenty solliqas. There are no healing pools back here, only four wide walls made of a dark, shiny stone with a low ceiling that curves outward. Colorful woolen rugs have been thrown across the smooth floor, and vivid plants are nestled into each corner. It's dimmer than the rest of the healing quarters from only having a few floating orbs of light and from the amount of darkness seeping out of those being healed in here.

This room is reserved for the ones who faced the worst of the pain. Which would be our friends, *of course*.

Ivar. Odin. Fraya. Ulf. Hadwin. Daru. Those who had to physically be mended like threading the skin of a corpse back together. Those who were already pushed so close to the edge, perhaps with the exception of Daru. It'll be a miracle if the healers can pull them back to where they were before the night of the festival. If *my* powers will be enough.

Of all of them, I can barely stand to look at Daru. A stabbing pain sluiced through me when I saw each of them near death. When I now settle my gaze on Daru, a throbbing ache etches itself into my chest. Some of our last words weren't kind. The defensiveness I felt when he insulted Nyx was staggering. After physically opening up to my *almaove*, one of my only reactions was to crush anyone or anything that would slander what we have. It still doesn't make sense to me how I could become feral that quickly, and even more so, how I could shut Daru down when he clearly felt a connection to my soul. The version I know of myself wouldn't do that to someone.

Then again, the version I know of myself is long gone and might as well have stayed on Earth.

Athena sits on her knees in the corner, keeping a close eye on our companions and refusing to go elsewhere until we have more answers. Her vacant stare meets mine—so lost on her drained and tattered face, it makes my breath hitch. My best friend is detached from our new reality, and she's next on my list to heal and speak with. *If she'll finally meet with me, that is.*

"We'll start here before I take you to see Mayra," Stefanie says to me. A withered look passes between us. Manipulators I've never met before, Esen and Riker, are tending to Mayra right now in a separate space. They're doing everything they can to gently open her mind and get a glimpse of how one of my clients from Earth is even here in Majikaero.

Nyx grabs my hand and squeezes tightly. The strength of his hand matches the vise forming around my heart as I take in our friends before us. *And not even all of them.* We still don't know where Erika, Daya, and Del have gone. I've both avoided this room and have been eager to speak with them, desperate to learn more about what happened a week ago. Fresh fire blooms along my palms, and I take a slow step forward, basking our group in blue light. My eyes meet Stefanie's, and she nods slightly, letting me know she's ready. She and I have discussed and practiced a few ideas with other harmed *solliqas* over the week in preparation for today—for my first time using my healing powers on a whole group of souls, friends at that.

I face all six of them, seven, including my best friend. Terror sluices its way through me at the single thought that's plagued me for the past week: Did Tryg's darkness stain my healer soul? Has my *maji* been tarnished, smeared with the sickness that's taken over my friend?

I still don't know. Assisting Stefanie and the others with one-on-one healing sessions seemed to go okay. My blue flames and shining light flared out of me with ease. Approval had radiated out of my friend's eyes, and I trust that she would have caught it if my *maji* was tainted.

But I can't push away the thought that Tryg changed *something* deep within me. It's hiding. Waiting with bated breath. When his darkness shoved image after cruel image of how much suffering my friends on Earth have endured into my already vulnerable mind... they were shards of ice ripping through my soft skin. The kind of cut that doesn't heal over nicely. No. It's the kind that festers from an infection with black pus oozing out of it. The type of wound that makes you doubt if you'll ever truly recover from it.

I manage to inhale a deep breath. These doubts can't be my focus. My new friends are hurt and my best friend is barely holding on. As disgustingly self-righteous as it makes me, I want to be the one to help them heal.

And now the next nightmare begins.

THREE
Nyx

*Numbness is easier than the never-ending
rage felt during a soul war.
Even if it means you're no longer your true self,
lost to the wrong kind of darkness.
-Wrathiala, Goddess of Manipulation*

Beginnings fall into endings the way flames drift into the sky. There's a flurry of frantic movement until nothing is seen at all. At least, that's what my father would tell me when I'd become anxious about a plan or strategy presented to the Council, only to have the finicky members rip it apart in front of me. He would tell me this phrase every single time as a reminder that their reaction, blustering and unnecessarily antagonistic, was only the beginning of my next plan. Of my next step. Their behaviors would fade into nothing, just as my own emotions would do the same. Until we were balanced once again.

As I watch Eira's flames lick up her arms in flickering gusts, the same unbidden phrase comes to the front of my mind. The words of my father are the *last* thing I want to hear right now, that piece of *alklen* shit. But I suppose they're embedded deep in my memories for situations I'm forced to face, such as the one right in front of me. In this dark room with warm-colored cushions and a handful of orbs glowing faintly, all twelve hollow eyes stare into the distance. All six bodies that should *not* have been able to heal with the states they were in. It's a testament to these healers' abilities that they're all still alive and their souls weren't scattered to another world.

It's also, much to my surprise, an indicator of their will to keep living.

They're all leaning up against plush cushions against the back wall and are looking at Eira, Zaya, and me with such emptiness, I can barely fucking take it. My shadows shudder away from the darkness for once, not wanting to get wrapped up in what's still overtaking their souls. Especially not when I'm standing this close to Eira's healing light. *But all the dark gods of Cudhellen, I don't know if her light will be enough to save them.*

Ivar. *His shoulder blades are still reforming into his shredded back.*

Odin. *His forearms are twisted as if someone wrung them out like a towel to dry. Erika, his twin sister, is still missing. A fact that makes my heart ache. I miss her sibling energy, the way she made me feel like I'm needed as a brother, and how she disguised her love as snarky comments.*

Fraya. *Her entire abdominal area still has pieces of skin seared off and her pelvis is wound tight in a blanket.*

Ulf. *His body finally appears more human, but there are patches of fur almost melted into him. He has claws instead of fingernails.*

Hadwin. *His torso has deep indents where he was stabbed straight through to his back and scars in the shape of talons.*

Daru. *His fucking neck. It's a miracle it's still attached after nearly being mauled to death.*

Their pain was a flurry of frantic movement the night of the festival and will drift into the sky as a flame until what they're experiencing fades into nothing. I'm begging the gods who still listen that *all* of this will fade into nothing. It's better to go numb than to endure the shit they experienced.

Will they shift, breathe, laugh, walk, function, *fucking trust* ever again?

Eira drops to her knees in the middle of the room and falls forward on a multicolored rug in front of our friends. The flames spread from her arms to her back and match the few blue, purple, and white orbs floating above us. Her palms push into the chilled ground outside the edges of the woolly rug, and I can see a deep breath rattle through her stretched body. Zaya pads forward and grows larger, enough for her to wrap herself around Eira's kneeling form. I hesitate, struck with the realization that Eira's pet knows more about how to support her than I do. I have no idea how to help at this moment, and it causes a plume of smoke to rise out of me in agitation.

Stefanie slinks over from where she was checking on our friends to where I'm standing near the doorway, utterly frozen in place by my frustration and battling emotions.

"Settle your breath, Prince," Stefanie quips next to me. "Eira knows what to do because we've discussed this throughout the week. The handful of *canielors* slinking along the demolished buildings have been captured, and she was able to practice some of her healing *maji* on them. There's been *solliqa* after *solliqa* brought to the healing quarters' doors who've been traumatized in one way or another from the night of the festival. Eira has learned a significant number of techniques in a short amount of time, but with enough strength and determination, she'll be okay. And remember, Nyx, she's not alone. We're both here, and Zaya has a special bond with her. That mysterious feline has known her for many human years—of course she'll know what to do when she sees her owner distressed."

I throw her an irritated glance. "And I've known Eira for many *lifetimes*."

Stefanie simply raises an eyebrow. "Who's to say the same doesn't apply to Zaya?"

I scoff and go to respond, but she cuts me off. "Don't worry so much about a cat, Nyx. Focus on slowing your breathing. You'll be needed when Eira works her way into each of their souls. We need someone to collect the necessary information."

Clenching my fist in time with each heartbeat, I try to follow what she's saying. It's a little hard to do when I'm watching my *almaove* now spread a wall of thrashing fire in a circle around our friends. It reaches the back wall and goes up another few inches.

"I don't see why Eira has to be the one to do this," I mutter. A surge of protection churns around me. Even my inner beast—his agitation really fucking clear from the dark feathers sprouting up and down my arms—wants to claim her. "She's still learning about her *maji*."

"That may be so," Stefanie agrees. "But her powers are still stronger than the other healers' abilities. And she has a special soul connection to each of these *solliqas*, which should allow her to break through their walls of darkness easier than the rest of us. Eira also didn't want anyone else talking to them. She said it should only be those of us they might have trusted with their souls." She squeezes my arm with a surprising level of tenderness and glides over to Eira.

Stefanie drops down to her knees behind where Zaya is curled around Eira. She places her hands right through the fire on Eira's back and mumbles a chant that I can't make out from where I'm standing. White light flares to life under her hands and mixes with the ring of blue fire. Under other circumstances, I'd be in awe of how dazzling the mixture of healing lights looks in this room. I hear Athena make a small gasp from the other corner, clearly on the same wavelength as I am right now. For a second, I'm watching the sun mix with the moon and the sparkling stars and the heart of a flame. *Mesmerizing, just like my firefly.*

Eira takes another deep breath and cries out as more fire spreads in a line in front of her. Her hips twitch, and I have to force myself to stay where I'm at and not go to her. My shadows can sense from here the tension radiating off her body, especially along her abdomen. She's described how the chronic illness has felt throughout her human years and the, often daily, torment she endured. I can't help but worry she's feeling it now, as if her own pain is calling out to the ones she's trying to heal, and it'll strike her down mid-healing. Give her those horrible, wretched sensations that slither inside her soul, their own special form of poison. At least Stefanie must be aware of this issue. One of her hands repositions closer to Eira's hip, and it gives me hope that she's sending Eira strength there.

Hope. What is my firefly fucking doing to me that I'm even thinking that word?

A stream of fire winds its way to each of our friends in a river of blue flames. A tiny part of me wonders if it'll burn their healing forms or if that dreaded snake from the pools will make another appearance. But Eira's fire only coats each of them as a blanket, and I can physically sense their collective sighs of release. Nothing changes with their skins, but that empty gaze in their eyes disappears for a moment. *Thank fuck.*

Eira's crystalized fox leaps from her shoulder blades and prances in between each of our friends. She stops next to Athena and nuzzles her neck before darting back and forth around the room again. Worry seizes me when I consider what her fox might do to me again, but she only glances in my direction. I swear she winks at me before settling near Fraya, a blue light pulsing out of her.

My attention diverts to Daru. He's the first to tremble with awareness. His neck muscles strain against the fresh scars etched across his skin, and his back arches off the floor. He thrashes, eyes wild with unspoken emotions, until he gapes at Eira. But she can't see him. *Fucking Cudhellen*, she isn't even looking at him. Her forehead is flat against the floor, and Stefanie is bent at an angle between her and Zaya, still chanting and sending whatever *maji* she can into Eira.

Gods. Why are these healers so damn confusing? Or is it a *fim* thing? Stefanie assumed I'd figure out this is the moment I'm needed?

I shake off my fury at these *fimmes* and walk in quick strides toward Daru. I don't give a damn if the fire will burn me and force myself to continue through the ring of flames. Not even a flicker of pain reaches me. *My talented firefly*. I fling myself to the ground next to Daru and grab onto his arm, bringing his focus to my face. He must be in serious agony if he's relieved to see *me*.

"Nyx," Daru gasps. "I... where am I? Is Eira safe? I see... she's a living flame."

"Yeah, she's using her *maji* to bring you enough relief to speak and is taking away some of the darkness that is smothering you," Athena says quickly next to me.

Startled, I nearly jump out of my skin. *The fuck?*

"Nice of you to join me," I grumble at her.

Athena shoots me a no-nonsense glare. I'm taken aback by how quickly she shifted into healer mode from the detached being I saw in the corner of this room moments ago. "Where else would I be?"

"How did you even know to do this?" I ask.

She rolls her eyes at me—fucking *rolls* her eyes. "Gods, Nyx. Because I'm not stupid. Eira is stressed. She dove right into healing and doesn't always know where her *maji* will take her. Stefanie is doing what she can to guide her, and it's obvious she's taking some of the pain out of their souls. What? Don't look at *me*. Take a gander at the shadows slithering from their bodies under her fire."

Sure enough, Eira's *maji* isn't just coating their bodies. It's pressing deep into them and dark splotches of shadows are curling out from under them. *Huh*. I turn back to Athena with an incredulous expression on my face.

"How did you even see that in this dark room?" I ask.

"Nyx. I'm struggling emotionally, but that doesn't make me stupid. Or blind. Or unable to function. My soul has many pieces to it and the rest of them are working fine. And honestly, I'm a healer. I was born to understand the healing process and catch on quickly to what different souls do," she bites out.

She whirls back on Daru, her face softening. "It's going to be okay," she whispers, brushing back a few strands of his hair.

Mood. Swings. *Should I say something?*

"Athena—"

"Stop talking," she barks at me.

That would be a no.

"Daru, what are you feeling right now?" Athena asks.

His eyes roll back slightly as he drags his face toward her. Purple bruises splatter across the side of his face and down his neck and shoulder—a grotesque picture of what he is experiencing on the inside.

"I'm so... weak," he mumbles. "It hurts to swallow. My skin is heavy. Nothing like... when I'm a bird and free. I don't feel free."

Athena grabs his hand and rubs her thumb against it.

"I'm sorry you're having to experience this right now," she whispers. "And you're not weak. Farthest thing from it, hun. You've managed to stay alive despite what happened to you."

Daru's eyebrows furrow as he peers up at her. A thin black line that matches the outline of a vein crawls up his throat. My heart sinks unbelievably fast. It's the first official sign of the plague, which shouldn't surprise me. He was dealt a serious dose of trauma the night of the festival. But even though it's *him*, that doesn't mean I wish this fucked-up plague on his soul. *Fuck*.

"Do you remember what happened to you?" Athena asks. I know she told me not to speak, but even if she didn't say that, I still wouldn't be brave enough to ask this question. I've been able to navigate a bunch of political shit this past week, train with Eira, meet with Jade to start the search for our other friends, among other important tasks. But sitting in this dim room with our companions who have been *so close* to fading away from us? This is fucking torture.

His eyes blink a few times before the green in them lights up briefly, a darker version of Athena's.

"I had to go to them," he mumbles.

"Them?" Athena asks, creases lining her eyes in concern.

"Yeah," Daru coughs. "I heard everyone's voices calling for my help. You were all tied up and cried out for me to come for you. I... I saw you. And Eira. She was tied to a chair, naked, and black and blue blood was smeared across her skin."

Athena searches his eyes for a moment. "Where did you see us?"

"It was really dark," he rasps. "*Dark!* Black and purple and that smell... It was disgustingly sticky. And I had to get it off you and Eira and the others."

"Did it smell sweet?" Athena asks with narrowed eyes.

Daru's eyes bulge slightly. "*So* sweet. And you were all crying out in distress. But when I reached for you, all I saw were glowing eyes. They were red and white and yellow. And then I felt my body break into pieces. Too many pieces..." He continues to mumble incoherently to himself. But I'm not paying attention—I'm staring at Athena.

"Sweet?" I ask her.

Her eyes meet mine, startled and nervous. "Remember that portal I thought I saw? The one you said you'd never heard of before and didn't make sense? It was also black and purple, matching Daru's description. And it smelled *disgusting*—a sickly sweetness. It reminded me of these candy shops on Earth that would be crowded with little kids." She scrunches up her nose and pats Daru's arm. "You take a deep breath and let your body relax now."

He struggles against her hand for a second before falling back into the layered cushions. His eyes are still moving under his closed eyelids, but he's no longer mumbling to himself and looks to be lost in his internal world.

Athena pulls me out of my racing thoughts. "Come, let's check in with the others while we can. Eira can only hold her fire for so long."

Guilt stabs at my heart that I didn't consider how Eira has been doing these past moments, the time ticking by slowly. She's usually wrapped around each of my thoughts, but this past week has made my brain a jumbled mess. Jade and the others were waiting outside of the Council building as soon as Eira and I left with Zaya and had checked on the *drekstri and alklen* in the stables. She landed on top of my shoulder, on edge, and her talons sunk straight into my flesh.

Her *maji* powers extend beyond just shifting, a gift that I've kept a secret, even from my current companions. Eira will be the only one to soon learn about it when I take her with me to meet Jade tomorrow, unless my friend wants the others to know, too. Jade has the ability to pass her memories to another, either through a collage of images, sounds, or imprinted words. This has especially come in handy when she wants to share a visual of a specific Council member and doesn't dare breathe an actual word about it.

I could see why Jade didn't want to speak of the horrors she needed to share with me this week. She leaned her tiny head against mine and in a blur of colors, I was traveling through memory after graphic memory. Horror hurtled through my entire body, and if it wasn't for Eira calling my name, I wouldn't have remembered to breathe. Images of *solliqas* being taken by monstrous creatures, soaked in darkness even worse than my own. Souls of all kinds, even the young ones, were ripped and filleted into thousands of pieces. Their bones snapped in too many ways to count, as if their souls and existence didn't matter in this realm. Picture after picture slammed into me—different shades of blood, a cacophony of screams threaded through each scene. I've never seen that many monsters with Ulf's same ability to kill a soul before, and it formed a deep pit of dread in my stomach. *Fuck*.

Jade switched to other types of images of the capital. Some of the buildings remained intact, simply hollowed out and empty of souls. Others crumbled as each *canielor* and larger creatures barreled into the Council building, businesses, and homes —clearly searching for *something*. Relief whooshed through me when I saw healers, protectors, and other *solliqas* in the background moving souls to safety. At least not all hope would be gone. Just a huge portion of the fucking capital would be destroyed. The healers would have way too many souls to work on. *Solliqas* would experience nightmares for weeks to come. The Council members the realm is supposed to depend on scattered to other cities as the attack happened.

Yeah, not all hope is lost. Only most of it.

And it kills me that I still can't pinpoint what in Cudhellen is going on. I had never seen those creatures before, nothing larger than the *canielors*. I don't know where they're from or where they're going. Athena had shared with Eira and me that she'd seen a huge black and purple swirling entity that floated above the ground in the forest. She's convinced it is some kind of portal. I, of all *solliqas*, am very familiar with portaling and how to travel from one location to another. But what she described is a lot bigger than what I or anyone else can do. No soul in Majikaero would need to create a portal that large to transport anyone or even lure another *solliqa* into it. This feels *other-*

worldly. Unfamiliar. Strange. Undecipherable. And I don't understand which *solliqas* were drawn toward this portal and why. Who or what is searching for souls here? What were those monsters searching for in the buildings that warranted breaking everything down in their paths until they found it? *Why* demolish our world when we're already going through a plague? Or is that the fucking idea?

Everything is warped at this point, and it's taking what little restraint I have not to fucking scream with the way it's stretching my skin way too thin.

FOUR
Athena

*The unknown is often more
frightening than our current reality.
Until we look inside ourselves once again.
-Dabria, Goddess of War*

Thin air, that's what this sensation must be. The reason I can't take a full breath, like someone is strangling me from the inside. I make myself walk past Hadwin, the shapeless gray coverings I chose to make for myself today dragging across the floor as I hurry forward. My brain pretends that he isn't the *solliqa* directly next to Daru. *No, he's not this close to me. I cannot look into those eyes right now. I won't.*

I walk straight to Ivar and hope Nyx is still behind me with his smoke and shadows. He certainly won't hear it from me today, but I *need* him to stay next to me. The base of my strength is cracking the longer I'm in this room, and I'm not even sure what the hell I'm doing here. I saw Eira and Stefanie heading this way earlier. As empty as I am right now, as I've felt the whole damn week, I can't abandon other healers when they're faced with impossible clients. And that's what this situation is—

impossible. I've only started to learn how to connect with my earth *maji* and have nowhere near the level of control Eira already has. The magic itself is a feral entity pulsing through my veins. I know I'll catch up with Eira soon, but hopefully my training as a therapist will get our friends to talk in the meantime.

And then I can get back to the task I prioritized before the festival: finding our friends on Earth.

I drank as much *einral* as I could this morning, guzzling it down as if it was a fresh pot of coffee. *If only*. One of the healers insisted if I have both that and *lipva*, I'd stay awake for days without any issues. Little do they know that I'm craving a drink I'll never get my hands on again, and nothing dampers my mood more than remembering my version of home is gone.

As I approach Ivar, he blinks slowly up at us. His blue-gray eyes remind me of the windy sky, even in this dark, isolated room. The black vein markings that peek out of his loose cream and tan coverings and bloodied bandages are the only things keeping him tethered this close to the earth right now. I imagine that even being stuck inside of this room, if he didn't have more trauma weighing him down, he'd be soaring free.

"Hey, Ivar," I murmur.

He blinks a little quicker now. "I can feel Eira's light," he croaks. "It's foreign. I can't say I hate it, but my shadows might disagree. She's bright and all-consuming and it's beautiful."

I give him a wry smile. It's reassuring that he's talking more coherently than Daru. "That's my best friend."

"I can also sense your aura," he murmurs. "I bet it'd be similar to hers."

Snorting, I shake my head. "Doubtful right now. That's very doubtful. I'm strong in many ways, but the mind needs to be stable to make use of such *maji*."

Nyx cranes his head around mine to get a better look at his friend. "How are you doing?" His voice is all gravel and rocks.

Ivar licks his lips and is lost in space for a moment. "I don't know. I guess I'm alive, so that's something."

Humming, I fix the top of his bandage that's peeling away from his battered skin. "It's everything," I say. "It shouldn't take much longer with the pace the healers are going. And with Eira's help, it'll be no time before you're fully functioning again."

"How do you know?" Ivar asks, uncertainty hiding behind his eyes.

"Because I know my best friend," I scoff. "She's growing fiercer by the day and doesn't back down from a challenging client. Eira believes everyone can be saved and won't take no for an answer. Not even the Devil themself could dissuade her, I'm sure of it."

Nyx nods and gives a knowing smirk. I suppose he would know after the past month with her.

Gods, has it already been a month for them? Their souls are incredibly intertwined already, but that shouldn't be a surprise. If they're that close of soul mates and finally found one another again, their spirits fit together like missing puzzle pieces. I chance a quick glance at where Hadwin is lying nearby. His and mine are the kind from a puzzle with all black colored pieces, where it takes an exasperatingly long time to find even a few that fit together.

"What do you remember from the night of the festival?" I ask Ivar, shifting my focus back to him.

His eyes shutter at the question.

"I don't think so," Nyx tells him sternly. "You don't hide behind that wall of yours. We need answers if we're going to figure out our next steps, and you were acting sketchy that night before all that fucking shit went down."

Ivar glances over at Odin, who's now studying us with weak attention. Those cerulean eyes are similar to his sister's, but they're foggy today, as if a layer of mist now covers them. He's the image of a breathing ghost, especially with the way his inky hair falls across his pale face and the blue coverings contrast with his waxy skin.

"Doesn't he need contact with water for his water *maji*?" I ask Nyx.

He exhales harshly. "Yeah, good fucking point. I'll tell Stefanie after we're done here." Nyx turns back to Ivar. "So?"

Ivar and Odin share a silent conversation we're not privy to. Odin gives the barest of nods before closing his eyes and resting back against the cushions once again. He seems to be healing the slowest of our friends so far. I have to wonder how much it has to do with his will to live. His sister, Erika, is still missing. Losing that significant of a relationship is devastating for even the strongest of souls.

"Some of us were approached that day," Ivar begins. "I wish I knew who they were. It was right after we finished getting ready for the festival, and the *fimmes* were dressing up in their coverings. The *solliqas* cornered us against the side of the Council building, near that tree that protects Eliina's quarters. All of them were wrapped from head to toe in intricate, gold, silky coverings. Even their eyes were covered in a black material. Ulf was riled up by them from the very beginning, saying he couldn't pick up a scent. I usually can see a general color or outline of a soul's aura, you know this, but it was just blank. Everything in the air was clear surrounding them. I thought... I don't know. I don't know what I thought exactly. Maybe that I couldn't trust a *solliqa* who wouldn't show their form, whether human or creature or monster. What did they have to hide, you know?"

"You had never seen them or their coverings before?" I ask.

"Never," he grinds out. "I would have recognized a being with such emptiness to them. And those *voices*. They crackled and didn't sound quite normal to my ears."

"What did they want?" Nyx barks.

"Their words were too obscure," Ivar whispers. "Too

confusing and full of riddles. They said if we were to follow them immediately on their task to right the wrongs among us, we'd connect to our true spirits once again. We only needed to take their hands, and they'd show us the way forward." He shakes his head, his dark eyebrows furrowing. "It didn't make any sense to us. Odin asked them why they approached our group out of all *solliqas*? The one in the middle, a leader I think based on their stance, had laughed. They said we're but a speck of stardust in the universe, and there's many more where they come from. That they need the strongest souls and fighters to survive the journey ahead."

Nyx has gone still next to me. I look over at him briefly, but he doesn't move an inch. He's as still as a statue.

"So, this was earlier," I continue. "What happened at night?"

Ivar sinks further down into the cushions but doesn't break eye contact with me. He chews on his bottom lip for a few seconds and huffs out a breath, the dark strands framing his face moving out of the way. His angular jaw flexes as he clenches his teeth.

"I know this isn't what you want to hear, but I don't remember much. Just... *such* immense darkness. A tunnel of black and white sucking me into its center. There was a voice. It was soft, like a *fim*. A mixture of terror and ease filtered through me when it spoke. It said to fly free—I must release my wings. For even they can weigh my spirit down. And then everything went dark. I was... I was simply there. In space. Floating with a sense of nothingness before I was brought back into my body here and the pain became unbearable."

His lips tremble slightly, enough for a trained therapist to notice. Nyx moves out of his stupor and opens his mouth to ask another question, but I cut him off with a glare. We want information here, but I refuse to push any of our companions past the point of return when they're only speaking to us now.

Companions. Interesting. I guess I do consider them to be

friends after a mere three weeks. Time definitely has fucked with me since arriving here.

Shaking my head, I grab Nyx's hand. "Thank you for sharing what you remember with us, Ivar. Rest again while Eira's fire continues to burn the shadows away."

"Don't let her take all of them. They add quite the charm to my mysterious persona," Ivar mumbles with a faint wink. Both eyes are closed before his head hits the lush pillow.

I roll my eyes at his nonsense. A big part of me can't wait to see the souls hidden under this disease. I turn toward Nyx. "Do you think Erika, Daya, and Del went through this portal, or the strange black and purple darkness? And are trapped somewhere?"

He blows out a breath. "I really fucking hope not."

With Nyx's hand still in mine, I pull him over toward Fraya and Ulf. We pass by Fraya, since she is very much knocked out and curled into a ball under Eira's fire. My friend's fox is cuddled up next to her hip, and I'm sure this is Eira's way of sending additional healing *maji* to such a sensitive area. Fraya's hazel eyes were bloodshot before, and I can only imagine how waking up surrounded by this much pain is taking a toll on her empathic self. *Poor soul*. Glancing back at Nyx, he gives me a curt nod. A silent agreement that we'll speak with Fraya at a later time, after she's received more healing sessions. My feet pad against the stony floor, and I hesitate before lowering myself next to Ulf. He's one of the *solliqas* here who's managed to terrify me.

Grimacing at that thought, I force my back to straighten into a confident poise. He might be death incarnate, but I can't let him scare me. He hasn't met the thrashing demons that I keep on a tight leash—the hardened parts of my soul that could match his angry and depressing energy without fail. Fuck Ulf's intimidating aura. I'm here as a healer right now, and he can get fucked if he thinks he'll scare me away.

Nyx dives in front of me at the last second, before my knees can even touch the ground, and places himself firmly between Ulf and me. "He might be healing," Nyx grumbles. "But I won't take any chances. Eira would never forgive me if I knowingly placed you in danger."

There's that Prince Charming of Darkness my Eira is so enamored by.

I'm grateful that Nyx is sitting closer to Ulf. He opens his dark, swirling eyes, and I'm met with a menacing glare that I definitely don't deserve. Black coverings and brown bandages are pulled tight across his broad chest. His features are striking and pronounced in a way that reminds me of sharp glass. The stubble he keeps along his jawline matches the darkness of the veins that have spread over most of his pale skin. In a flash, he lunges at me, an iron-clad grip on my forearm. I grunt as he brings me closer to him, loose strands from my braids falling against his rugged face. I'm close enough to share the air he breathes, and instinctually push back against him. Nyx's shadows snap at Ulf's fingers, and he's forced to let me go. I sag with relief that he's no longer touching me, my *maji* squirming in discomfort from such close contact with his own. My hand quivers as it rests against my racing heart while Nyx places himself fully in between Ulf and me this time.

"The fuck am I doing here?" Ulf snarls in Nyx's face.

"Trying to heal your ungrateful ass, you piece of shit," Nyx growls right back. "Settle yourself. You're acting like a fucking animal."

Ulf snaps his jaws, his canines eerily growing larger as each second passes us. Eira's fire pushes down harder against his shadows, and I hear her whimper behind us. Worry etches across Nyx's face at the sound, and he grabs Ulf's face in a whirl of shadows.

"You want to be an ignorant prick, be my fucking guest," Nyx growls in his face. "But don't fight against my *almaove* unless you want a bigger problem on your hands. Understand me?"

Ulf glowers at Nyx before moving his gaze to mine. His jaw ticks once. Twice. "What am I doing here? What do you want from me? Why am I bound to this fucking room?"

Ah, I see now. His wolf is eager to break free, and he's quickly losing control.

"You'll be free from the healing quarters soon," I tell him, keeping my voice as level as I possibly can. "The more cooperative you are with the healers, the easier it'll be to work through the additional darkness settling into your soul from the attack. It should only be another day before you're able to leave and function without their aid."

He grunts at me in response. *Grunts*. Like a fucking caveman. *I might need to reconsider that word "companion".*

"We're here to check in on you and see what you remember from the attack. Eira and Stefanie are doing what they can to heal all of you, that is, if you can stop resisting them."

Ulf rolls his eyes at that last comment. "I was tied up in my own thing that night. My *maji* connected with a soul that was concealed from this world. I couldn't find her, but I know she could grasp the energy I was sending her way. My usual darkness shifted into something else entirely. I don't know what the fuck it was. My soul was being pulled into a vortex and there was nothing I could do to stop it. *Nothing*. Not even my wolf could break free from the invisible rope tied around us. I do remember those fucks I saw before blacking out." His jaw tightens again and his eyes flick toward Nyx. "You'd remember them. Those manipulators that served Namid on the Council. The ones he encouraged to manipulate and torture souls like the sick fuck he is. They're the *solliqas* who pulled my wolf form half out of me, forcing a partial shift, before tormenting me with their powers."

Nyx's shadows flare up above him as black flames. His only response to clearly disturbing information.

"Tell Jade," Ulf grumbles. "Find those *solliqas*. They might lead us to more answers about what the fuck that shit storm was last week."

Nyx nods his head in confirmation. Ulf faces me again and my *maji* flickers, feeling the pull to fall into his sweeping and overwhelming darkness. *No, fuck him.* He's no match for what lies within.

"Yes?" I ask while doing my best to look down my nose at him.

"Hadwin's no saint," he growls. "But he's also no sinner. Don't let his harsh exterior fool you. I saw what he did to you in the dungeon. He's too much of a lovesick fuck to push you away forever."

My eyebrows rise so high, I'm surprised they don't get stuck in my hairline. *Ulf? Ulf, the deranged wolf of darkness, is telling me this? Who laughs about death? And he's telling me this right now?*

"We're all sinning saints," I whisper. "And thanks for the advice. I'll let you know when I need more wisdom from the almighty Ulf."

Ulf scowls at me before turning on his side, effectively dismissing us. *Good.* I didn't want to talk to his twisted soul anymore.

"That was weird," Nyx mutters.

I huff out an annoyed sigh. *This whole place is weird. And my emotional shield is growing thin. I can only hide for so long around everyone here, and Eira is bound to burn out soon.*

Nyx pulls me over to Hadwin. Between Ulf's comment and my quick retreat toward Eira, he must sense what I'm avoiding. "Come on, let's see what Hadwin has to say," Nyx murmurs. "I'll take the lead with this. I want to know what he remembers about this portal everyone is mentioning."

I swallow, wanting to do literally anything but talk to Hadwin. The *solliqa* I simultaneously want to stab and kiss. Nyx gives me a small push, making me realize my feet were firmly planted and my body has no desire to move toward him. *Ugh.* I'm given a look that tells me there's no point in arguing. We both kneel next to Hadwin, who's swathed in slate-colored coverings and thick beige bandages around his chest. Nyx leans down to touch a swirling snake pendant hanging on a chain around Hadwin's neck. Its golden and green colors, each in a geometric design, stand out against the dark colors of his coverings, and it shines as brightly as his eyes.

"What's that?" I find myself asking. *So much for not being interested.*

Nyx doesn't respond right away. He twirls the pendant in his fingers for a moment. His broody silence is almost insufferable, and I go to open my mouth when he finally responds.

"He received this when he was very young," Nyx rasps. Hadwin's arms shift slightly. "It's symbolic of where he comes from and meant to guide him on his journey here in Majikaero."

I hum. "I didn't see that on him before."

"You wouldn't," Nyx sighs. "He usually keeps it hidden from others."

"Why?"

"You'll just have to ask Hadwin one of these days," Nyx murmurs. "It's his symbol and journey, not mine."

These males are *annoying*.

I remain as far away as I possibly can from Hadwin while Nyx stays on his knees and leans against the wall. He drops the pendant and goes to ask a question, but Hadwin stares straight at me.

Those golden eyes meet mine and I gasp.

One second, I'm in this room next to Nyx and our friends. Eira is close to simmering out behind us.

Next, I'm thrown into Hadwin's golden orbs until we're both sinking through a sliver of time and space.

My body is physically in Majikaero. But our souls have spirited somewhere far away from this moment.

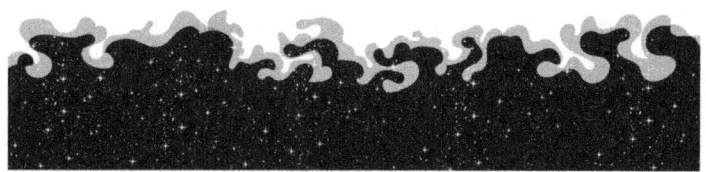

FIVE
Hadwin

The plague isn't seen only in the physical clues.
It's also seen in the ease with which souls push others away.
-Correspondence from Hauke Zionan, Master of Healing

Moments. That must be all that passes by us. But it feels like a fucking eternity.

The sensation of being pulled from my physical form, when it's barely that since we're all just souls here on Majikaero, should be unsettling. I should be horrified that my soul is leaving a carcass behind—one weighed down with heavy robes and taut bandages—while I go on this journey, but this isn't my first time.

I felt the pull to leave this world starting after Eira's healing flames kissed my skin, and I instinctively rebelled against it. This isn't how it normally is for me, where my earth *maji* shoots my soul down through the soil and allows me a glimpse of our neighboring world, Earth. I don't know what the fuck *this* is, but it's similar to how I felt near that swirling black and purple sphere that throbbed with magic. I could sense even then that it was too unnatural to be from this world, too much of an unknown to allow myself to enter it.

Yet my soul didn't seem to care. It was eager to follow through that mysterious substance into a new reality. I could *taste* its excitement at the possibilities. That was when horror sluiced through me, and if it weren't for Athena, I'd have leaped right through to a new place.

Athena.

That's right, I'm not alone. My hand is intertwined with hers as we travel through a tunnel of time. The air whips past both of us, her braids coming undone in beautiful waves. We're both essentially naked, but a thin coating of our magic envelopes our bodies in a hardened second skin. She's staring at me with a wariness I almost regret. *Almost.* Her soul, a healer gifted with earth *maji*, is too pure to be connected to what I am. She's too fucking smart, too gorgeous, too gentle and kind and everything wonderful in our world. Even now, she's not crying out in fear. Bravery radiates from her core, as if this is simply another strange occurrence and can't scare her.

But she should be absolutely petrified, considering she's left alone with *me*.

I remember the moment our powers flared for one another. A memory burned in my mind forever, one I secretly savor. The shades of green that surrounded her, her *maji* coming to life when we entered Eliina's quarters, matched those big eyes. It surprised me that her powers matched the color of mine, that they felt like home. An impossibility. There's no chance in Cudhellen I'd be gifted an *almaove*. I can barely believe I have Nyx's friendship or any of our other companions. It didn't matter how much I pushed them away, how many vile words I spat at them after I was infected with the plague. They all held on tightly, even Ulf, that grim fucker.

It's a damn miracle I'm now connected to Eira, a healing and beautiful soul. When your inner demons have woven their way through your entire heart, you stop believing you deserve to be loved. To be healed. To be saved.

So, I fight against the disease as much as I can, not wanting to turn into a *canielor* and eventually be scattered as stardust. There's a tiny piece of my soul, buried deep enough that I can't find it, that wants to live. It *craves* life just the way it desires Athena. She might think our *maji* are similar to one another. And maybe that's true at their core. But she's a doe made of sunlight that filters through the forest and I'm a fucking python waiting in the leaves, ready to sink my fangs into her delicate soul.

Sometimes it's best to cut our losses before any serious damage is done. And that's exactly what I'd do to her—damage that precious soul sent here like an angel.

The angel herself moves her hands—those long fingers I want nothing more than to take into my mouth—to grip my biceps. Her green-colored nails cut into my skin, as sharp as little claws, and a shiver moves through me. *No, Hadwin. Not the time. It'll never be the time.* Athena's face morphs into something fierce, and she bares her teeth at me. No, not at me. Past me. I whip my head to see what's caught her attention, and an invisible force scoops us out of the vacuum of time and space we were caught in.

Down, down, down we travel, Athena finally screaming as we tumble through a black substance similar to the one I saw the night of the festival. My mind swerves uncontrollably, and it takes me a second to realize we're diving straight into Earth. *The fuck?* Watching the atmosphere whoosh straight past us, my body goes into survivor and protector mode. *Think, Hadwin, you dumb fuck. Think!* Athena's grip on my arms loosens, and I throw my arms around her body, trapping her against my chest. Her mouth is open in a silent scream as we continue falling, tears racing upward toward the sky as they well up in her pretty eyes. I cradle her as close as I can to me and will myself to shift into anything that can save us. As I try this, a number of things happen at once.

Our bodies become translucent, a sparkling green that meshes with the air around us.

My body can still shift, and I transition into a large python with scales of steel, praying to the gods who've never listened to keep Athena safe. My body, my soul, and my spirit can certainly break. They've watched that happen a number of times without stepping in to help me. The Council, family, friends, all of them breaking me down—or worse, seeing me fall from the plague and not offering to help me up.

Gold light seeps out of my snake form and wraps us both in a silky shield.

The ground rushes up to meet us and instead of the crash I'm expecting, the verdant land swallows us whole before spitting us back up, dumping our bodies in an unceremonious heap next to a thick tree. The bark is a dark brown, so different from our realm of magic. The leaves are a simple green, not the multi-color spectrum I'm used to. Yet the plainer colors are oddly reassuring in their simplicity. Grounding, even. We're surrounded by many of these dull trees, and as I look onward, I can see more of them are clustered together as part of a forest.

"Gods, what the fuck," Athena groans next to me. I'm still in my python form and my tail is wrapped around her waist. Even though our bodies are translucent, we can still make physical contact with one another. I instinctively curl her closer to me before I realize what I'm doing and hastily unravel myself until she rolls the other way and lands with an *oomph* on her face.

"You're such a fucking dick," Athena mutters under her breath. Her glower is enough to scare any soul away, but I find I enjoy that spark of fury.

She pushes herself to her hands and knees with an angry huff. The green glow of her body shimmers against the grass. As she sits back on her heels with her long hair cascading down her back, she's a damn ethereal goddess. My soul urges me to stay in this python form as an added level of protection, but with the glare Athena shoots my way, I don't think I have much of a choice to coil around her in silence. Especially not after traveling through time together into Earth. My body shrinks down in a green and golden light until my humanoid form stretches out on the ground. The grass pushes against my back before I roll up to sit on my own knees next to Athena.

"Care to explain what just happened?" she asks me.

I scoff. "As if I know."

"Oh, save the snark for someone else," Athena grumbles. "How did we get here? Have you done that before?"

My mouth folds down in a frown. "Not quite like that," I say. "I have the ability to travel and communicate through the earth itself. Similar to Eliina. It's a rare gift that's been passed down my soul family line. It's similar to when your physical form or skin is left at the barrier between the worlds and your soul travels on its own through the soil. I've often been able to travel in my whole form without issues. This? What happened to us? I've never experienced that before. I can assure you, not in any of my lifetimes."

Athena chews on her lower lip, and I can't look away. It only makes me more antsy to figure out why we landed here and to get the fuck out.

"You can use your *maji* to travel back to Majikaero, right?" she asks.

"Well, yeah, of course I can," I growl. "And you can, too. You wouldn't have been able to travel here in the first place if you couldn't use your earth *maji* to travel between worlds."

Her eyes grow as big as saucers, wide with wonder and awe. "*I* can do that?" she whispers.

I can't help but chuckle. "Yeah, *zamia,* you have many abilities that I'm sure you'll continue to discover."

Her eyebrows furrow in confusion at the term I carelessly called her. I have to be careful with my words. She's too smart and observant for her own good.

We both jump at the sound of voices coming our way. Athena's eyes widen even further in fear, and I lunge toward her, flinging us both behind the tree we landed near. Fortunately, the trunk is thick enough to hide both of us behind it if I keep her glued next to me. I'm expecting her to turn around and scowl at me for keeping such a tight grip on her, but Athena is too hyper-focused on whoever is walking nearby.

"Zaya, we can't be gone for long," a *misn* chuckles.

"But you *promised* to show me," a *fim* mumbles. I can hear the pout in her voice.

"Alright, alright, but really quick, okay? The herd is not too far from here," he says.

The *fim*, Zaya, shrieks with a high-pitched giggle, and they continue to walk right past our tree.

Athena peers back at me, her voice barely above a whisper. "Zaya is Eira's cat's name."

I grunt in response, unsure why she deems that important to share right now. Athena gasps and moves back into me, almost knocking us both back on our asses.

"Keep it together," I growl in her ear. "We don't want to draw their attention. We don't even know where the fuck on Earth we are."

Athena swallows. Three times. "L-look at them, Hadwin."

I roll my eyes in annoyance but lean forward to peer around the tree trunk, keeping myself as close to the rough bark as possible. I suck in a breath, and the arm I have hooked around Athena's stomach twitches when I see the humans standing mere feet away. The *fim* is tall, tan, and has curling black hair flowing down her back. She's smiling at the *misn* next to her, who has broad shoulders and a good foot on her with the same tan skin. They both have green eyes, but where her hair is dark, his is a light blond that's shaved on the sides and pulled up into a bun on top of his head. His jaw is wide with a sly grin and pointed nose. Her features are more narrow and petite than his. She has plump lips, the edges tugging into a smile as she dances from foot to foot in front of him. They're both barefoot but have tight, thin coverings wrapped around their torsos and legs. The color matches the tree Athena and I are leaning against.

"Come *on*, Had," Zaya whines.

He full on laughs at this point and scoops her up in his arms before running down the hill with her. As I inch a few steps beyond our tree, I can see they're on their way toward a herd of animals, what might be short horses with tufts of hair sticking up along their backs.

I hesitate before turning back to Athena. I know what she's going to say. I saw it, too. I saw how fucking similar they were to her and I. Felt the strangeness of their eyes, even though his didn't match my gold, but she called him *Had*. Gods, what the *fuck*? Her name was the same as Eira's cat, who managed to follow her soul into Majikaero, even though Del only pulled Eira's into our world. Slowly, I force my body to turn in a half circle until I'm looking into Athena's eyes.

"Tell me you saw it," she breathes.

"Even if I did, I don't know what to make of it," I rasp.

Her eyes search mine, so frantic and wild at this moment. "This must be similar to what Eira experienced. That must be it! When she had dreams of her past life memories. We're watching a past life of our souls."

My hands go out in front of me, gently stopping her shoulders before she barrels right into me. "Whoa, let's stop for a second. Even if those humans are, uh, were us, this is no dream. Athena, our souls traveled through time and space to come to this moment on Earth. If what you think is true, which we don't know if it is, then we're *in* the past life memory."

Athena's eye twitches. She doesn't speak and is watching me with a crazed look in her gorgeous eyes.

"*Zamia*," I whisper. "If those are our souls, and we're currently alive in Majikaero, then we didn't only travel to another world. We traveled to the *past*."

Athena shakes her head and starts mumbling to herself. "I—none of this makes any sense. I didn't ask to come here. You didn't try to take us here. So, why are we here? What brought us to this moment in time?"

What can I tell her? My tongue slides along my top teeth and I glance around us, hoping a solution will present itself. The truth is that I'm mildly petrified, but I don't want Athena to know this. She's right. Neither of us tried to come here. Something *forced* our souls to leave our forms back on Majikaero to come to this specific moment in time and space. To witness... what? To see that our souls had a previous connection? To see that we were happy? But *why*? I'm more than capable of pushing my soul back into the earth to go home. As much as I've been avoiding Athena, I can either take her with me or show her how to follow, but that doesn't solve the problem at hand.

Athena brings her hands to my neck, and I suppress a shudder at how close we're standing to each other. "Hadwin," she breathes. "Maybe something wanted to show us how powerful our soul connection is. Just like Eira and Nyx's relationship."

For a split second, I allow giddiness to travel through me at the prospect of our souls being that close, that she's my *almaove*. But it's only for a split second. This is too complicated of a situation and honestly, *too fucking weird*, especially in light of last week's events. I place my hands on her shoulders again, and this time, I push her back a few steps. It's time to do what I do best: destroy the source of love spiraling my way.

"That's a big maybe," I growl. "Most likely improbable. Something, maybe related to what came for us on the night of the festival, forced our souls to Earth for some other purpose. Any soul connection has *nothing* to do with it. Besides, is that what you think you mean to me? You don't even know me, Athena. You're simply a new *solliqa* in Majikaero, brought over for your friend. Keep your thoughts focused and away from that silly heart of yours."

I watch the optimism drain from her eyes at my words, at how effectively I shut it down. Guilt presses into me from all sides when I see how deep the hurt goes in the swirling depths of her eyes. Athena slides a mask of numbness over her face, one I'm all too familiar with, hiding the beauty she often shines on those around her. A part of me wonders why I have to crush everything good in my life—that it's a mistake to hurl these words at her. But the other parts of me know that it's a waste of time for her to hope. For her to believe something otherworldly brought us to this moment so that we could see our love for one another. Now *that* would be a dream.

The scene around us shimmers with the gold light coming out of us in subtle waves. The voices and laughter of the two humans, those entirely too similar souls, down the hill fade into nothingness. Until a transparent curtain is lifted, a patch of a dark world is opened in the air next to us. Athena leans further into me and stares at the gaping section of air with intense concern across her face. She swallows before turning to look up at me. Those plush lips open and close without sound, as if peering into this window of Earth has rendered her speechless.

"Is... is this another world? Or another version of Earth?" Athena asks, her voice quivering.

I peer around the version of Earth we're in. Based on what we've witnessed, it's obviously not the current time or reality we're in. As my gaze follows the landscape to the patch of darkness near us, I see the colors have changed, but it matches the shape of the hills we're sitting on. It's frightening that Athena would rather this be a gateway into another world, that she's that scared of which version of Earth we'll walk into. I almost wrap an arm around her shoulders, anything to soothe her, but I don't. Instead, I harden my face into that of a warrior, not giving her a glimpse of what I'm going through.

"This must be another time on Earth," I grumble.

"No," she whispers. "No, it can't be. That looks like Hell."

"Only one way to find out," I say gruffly. "Let's go."

I grab her elbow to pull her along with me. Athena scowls and rips her arm out of my grasp, huffing in annoyance. *Good.* That's better than the numb expression on her face from before or the naive hope she had after watching our previous lives interact. I step through the opening, not giving myself time to reconsider, and hear Athena's feet land next to mine a second later. Her sharp inhale grabs my attention, and I watch as she falls to her knees, choking on a sob.

Taking in this new reality, I don't blame her. It has the general appearance of Earth, yet it's different. A totally new, disturbing version. The dark brown bark is now an ash gray. The grass has lost its lush green, and there are no flowers to be seen, no wildlife, no sounds. Just the eerie silence that echoes between abandoned buildings and homes—*a sound I'm all too familiar with*. Buildings appear burned in the distance, some as close as the bottom of the hill we're standing on. A sickening feeling slithers through me when I realize there are no people here.

"Do you recognize this place?" My voice rumbles around us, amplified by the lack of life.

Athena swallows. My gaze homes in on the movement, an image swiftly passing through my mind of my hand wrapped around her throat as she squirms underneath me. I let it fly out of my reach, willing it to travel far from us.

"This was Northern Sweazn. My home," Athena says quietly.

"Was?"

"Dammit, Hadwin. *Look* at it! A country is nothing without its people, and do you see anyone? Hear *anything*?" Athena cries.

"Just because we don't see them doesn't mean they're not still here," I bark. I need to reel in my harsh tone, but I fucking can't. My constant desire for this *fim* is a weight on my chest, and it's *infuriating* me. "Let's go check out those buildings. There might be clues to what's happened."

"No!" she shouts. "No, I'm not going. I'm not walking through the husk that was once my home. This is too much for me. I didn't ask to be here. I didn't ask to come with *you*. To be shown happiness that I know in my fucking soul was my own once upon a time, only for it to be ripped out of my arms. As if I don't deserve that kind of love. And now we're here, in what looks to be a war-torn village—of what's left of my home. With no friends. With no animals. It's—"

Athena's next words are swallowed up by her *maji*. Her translucent body is sheathed by a wild green and gold flame. Only her darkening eyes peer out at me, and her even darker hair swishes around violently. There's no breeze where we're standing, but her powers pull me next to her body like she's the eye of a hurricane. They whip around me, the noise deafening, making my soul powerless next to hers. Athena doesn't speak, at least from what I can see, but her voice filters through my mind.

"I've seen enough. I don't know which fucked up force sent me here with you or how, but it was a mistake. *I'll speak with the others to figure out how to find our friends in this world—without you or those past-life memories."*

Her fire licks at my skin, the burning sensation brutal and fierce and deliciously dark. I'm wrapped up in it, in how her *maji* feeds off her emotions and teaches her how to connect to the earth. Wrapped in her powers, hurtling us through the soil to the earth in Majikaero with such desperation, similar to my own magic. And I'm hit with the realization that our souls might align more than I thought.

SIX

Astira

*You'll lose your own soul in an attempt to force peace,
yet that might be the price you pay when at war.
-Dabria, Goddess of War*

"Thought you could escape me?"

His stupid voice grinds against my ears. I fight the urge to tell him *Duh, obviously. That's why I'm far away from where you left me.*

Muscular arms wind themselves tighter around my torso until their grip forces the rest of the air out of my lungs. Wheezing and sputtering uncontrollably, I use what's left of my energy to thrash against my captor. I refuse to go down without a fight, even if it kills me in the process.

A memory of Ruse showing me what to do if one of my client's gang members tried to kidnap me flashes behind my eyes. I've always toed the line with danger, and this current situation is no different. Memories of him tend to find their way to me when I'm having near-death experiences. He was the friend I had a crush on for longer than I can count, but I settled for Tryg in the end. My heart can't help loving a man in authority, and with Ruse's physique, grim humor, and dark complexion, I was a goner. I thought Tryg would curb my craving, with his angst and love for control. While he wasn't the worst I've been with, sadly, he definitely wasn't the best. It's in moments like these, where I might be dragged to my grave, that I wish I would have been more honest with both of my friends, and really, with myself.

I let my shoulders and head sag in defeat and go limp, imagining myself lifeless and nothing but dead weight. Oily laughter spills down my back, and I grind my teeth to keep from flinching at the sound of his voice.

"You're nothing but a weakling, *Astira*," he huffs. "But you're lucky I enjoy our game of cat and mouse." He brings his lips to the shell of my ear and licks the curve of my earlobe. "And the reward for chasing you is *so* sweet."

Unable to take much more of his coarse voice, I drop my head further before rearing it back toward his scruffy face. With a loud *crack*, the back of my skull collides with his already bent nose. The action causes him to loosen his grip enough for me to slither out of his reach. My adrenaline spikes, and in a flash, I spin around to knee him in the balls—*if he has any*—my tangled red hair whipping me in the face. He lets out a startled yelp, and I can't fight the content smile that tugs at my lips when I see all the blood gushing out of his nose. *Gotcha, fucker.*

I don't give him a chance to recover before I'm sprinting down the dark tunnel made from mud. The only light surrounding me is from the flickers of candlelight in tiny alcoves along the walls. It reminds me of the dreams I've been having—always running through the woods or a tunnel or on a mountain, with a shadowed wolf hot on my heels. It hasn't caught me yet, and I'm hoping I'll have the same luck with the psycho behind me. There's barely enough light for me to see the ground in front of me. At least I don't run into any stones along the path or twist an ankle in one of the many holes scattered throughout the dirt ground. I unfortunately learned the hard way what happens if I stay to gloat in front of Damon.

Damon. Even thinking his name sends icy shivers down my spine. Fair-skinned with greasy brown hair and a perpetually broken nose, he couldn't even woo a pudgy swine. With each step, each lunge of my battered feet, I swear I can feel his dark gaze on my pale, freckled skin. As my hair flows behind me, I stifle a whimper. Too many memories fly around me as I run. All of them are reminders of how much Damon loves to weave his grimy hands in my hair. He's done it to drag me across the filthy room I've been trapped in, to yank my head back when he's rutting into me like some savage beast. He even plays with my hair and enjoys weaving thick braids after he's thoroughly abused my now-fragile body. Because he's a sick fucking freak.

But never again. *I won't let him.* A snarl involuntarily leaves my mouth as I near the end of the tunnel. The few candles I pass seem to shudder at the intensity of my emotions—at the explosive sensations wrapping around me as my anger surges to the surface from what I've been forced to endure. We're all a good one hundred feet underground and back to how life apparently was after the First Nuclear Wars: communities built under the earth through burrows, tunnels, and various segments of the layers of earth with indistinct boundaries. And I've been imprisoned in this particular shithole for the last two years. Some areas are further developed with electricity powered through solar panels and generators. My "home" has been one long tunnel of stony dungeons caked with clay-like mud, food cooked over fires, and resources created from nature itself. This underground community of any survivors of the war was dug out with the sole purpose of acting as a prison.

How did I end up in prison? I *didn't*. None of the poor souls stuck in this area did anything wrong. It's every person for themselves down here. If some fucked psycho decides they want to dig a section out of the earth for people they capture, whether as a reward or to own or simply to kidnap, then they can do it. I don't know how it's working with the other underground cities, but here? *No one* wants to start another war. Even after it ended a few years ago, or I assume it ended since we *all* had to go into hiding, very few people wanted to step forward to lead. It's the same now. Small communities are carved out down here, each group peering over their shoulder and focusing on protecting their own. Which means those of us stuck at the bottom of the food chain in the worst of the tunnels are buried too deeply to be found.

And there hasn't been a single fucking thing I could do about it. Until today.

It breaks my heart, as beaten up as it is, whenever my feet land on one of the metal bars camouflaged on the ground. My only warning that I'm close to one is when another voice cries out in agony, their wail winding its way up to me and tightening in a chokehold. I don't want to leave anyone else behind, yet if I don't leave today, there's no way I'm going to survive another hour—not with someone as cruel as Damon. He'd used a whip on me last night just for the hell of it, as if my body isn't already painted in puffy scars from the abuse over the years. A sadistic smile took over his face, pulling his mouth wider and wider with each crack of the whip until a woman came in to speak with him. Her lithe body was cloaked in a heavy mauve material, which kept her face hidden from view. The pain racked through my torso as my muscles finally relaxed when Damon put the whip back on its spot against the wall. Even so, I couldn't stop gaping at this mysterious visitor. Someone fully clothed when those kinds of materials are such a rarity nowadays.

I wasn't able to hear what the woman said to him, but the second Damon glanced my way with a vile smile, I forced myself to perk up enough to hear him. *Nothing* good ever comes from that look on his face.

"I'll have her ready to go for your inspection tomorrow,"

Damon had said to the woman. *"But I get to have one more hour with her before you arrive, with every tool at my disposal this time."*

Alarm bells blared in my mind. I knew it didn't matter what my current physical state was—I had to get the hell out of here, or I was going to die.

My lungs are on fire, scorching me from the inside out. Now that I've passed the last part of the tunnel, I force myself to count some of the last of the prison cells. *Number 409. Number 410. Number 411. Number 412. I made it.*

I hastily skid to my knees next to the tarnished cell door. Some of them are mere metal bars. Others have prisoners that are locked down under the worst restrictions. I knew the day I'd leave here, I couldn't escape without one of my closest friends.

Liv.

She managed to get captured too, and we'd only seen each other in passing. That doesn't mean we didn't figure out a way to communicate, though. We've memorized each other's schedules, when each of us is allowed to bathe or receive our meals or be forced to exercise—our captors detest us looking *too* much like skeletons. Last night, with the blood still dripping from where Damon whipped me, I forced myself to leave for my evening meal. I marched down the long darkening tunnel, surrounded by intimidating guards with enough muscle for three guys. Only twice a day would Liv and I pass one another. With the heavy exhaustion already settling over my body, I wasn't optimistic that I'd be up in time for the morning meal shift.

It was challenging to focus on both walking and searching for my friend. I almost stumbled, and one of the guards hit my shins with a sharp stick, growling at me to watch where I was going if I wanted to eat. *Yeah, beat up the girl who was already whipped and has lost a lot of blood as a way to motivate her—that totally makes sense.* Right as I hobbled my way forward again,

Liv and I made eye contact. Hazel eyes searched my own for the briefest of seconds before she stared forward again. When I was a step away from her, I hissed at one of the guards, "*What's the meal tonight anyway? Is it worth my time?*"

He started to growl something at me, but that didn't matter. I didn't, and will never, giving a flying fuck about the meals down here. The same mashed roots with no salt or spices and a small portion of mysterious meat gets old really fast. What I paid attention to was Liv's eyes flaring wide for a second. I needed to make sure she heard the code loud and clear: Is it worth my time —aka get ready because we're busting out of this horror show.

I now tap frantically on Liv's cell door. Damon screams out in frustration, and I slam my hand down even harder, the motion sending a group of insects scuttling away. He's somewhere behind me, far enough away that I have a few minutes, but he's definitely coming. *Come on, Liv.* We've talked through this. Sort of. We've found ways to leave messages for each other. I took some shitty punishments in turn for other prisoners switching out their schedules with me or passing along a coded message to my friend. It's each person for themselves, but we're not complete monsters. *Yet.*

My breathing hitches as the seconds tick, tick, tick. *Fuck.* I can only wait another minute before I've got to *move*. Red hair falls in knotted layers around me, covering me from the rest of the tunnel while I wait. Hornets swarm in my stomach as my nerves kick into overdrive, and I'm convinced my organs are twisting around themselves. Beads of sweat drip down my neck, and I swear if she doesn't open this fucking door, I'm going to vomit over this whole area. My heartbeat thunders in between my ribs, and I'm about ready to scream her name when the door finally lifts open.

"Gods, what the *fuck*, Liv!" I whisper. "We don't have much time!"

She winces at my tone, but she waves her hand around, indicating she needs help getting pulled up. *Great, as if I'm in good enough shape to sprint for my life* and *do this.*

"Hurry," she croaks. "He'll only be sedated for so long."

That's another thing I won't miss from this crumbling, dusty version of Hell. Each night, the guards sedate us to keep us from yelling to one another or trying to plot a way to escape. The joke's on them, though. Liv and I are utilizing this to our advantage. Her guard has been pining after her for the past year, but no one is allowed to touch us except for our captors. Or, as I've personally experienced, if our captors decide they want to share. When he climbed down into her cell to sedate her tonight, our plan was for Liv to seduce him until she had access to the syringe. I didn't originally approve of this plan, since I know better than most how soul crushing it is to have your body used. Liv insisted that it's for a greater purpose, and she'd do *anything* at this point if it meant she could escape.

Liv's captor isn't as demonic as mine, but no human that takes another person as a personal prisoner can be considered good. Owning anyone as a slave marks you as evil in my book and gives you a one-way ticket straight to Hell. Between our horrid living conditions, living with barely enough resources, and being *owned*, Liv is just as eager as I am to be free of this shithole.

My friend is barely able to reach the cell door opening. She's standing on her toes while she balances precariously on the wooden bench we're given as a bed. I grasp her bruised hand, and she flinches back a fraction before baring her teeth and gripping my hand tighter. It takes a few tries, but I manage to yank her up until she lands on her forearms and can push herself the rest of the way out. We're both panting hard by the time she's fully wiggled her way up next to me. The deep cuts on my back decide now is the time to make their pain known. I shudder and lean my weight against Liv's side as we mold into one another.

Two friends who are hopefully defying all the odds stacked against us.

Leaning my head on Liv's shoulder, I peek up at her face. She's as exhausted as I am, with fresh bruises peppering her neck and traveling down her arms. There are so many of them, they almost cover up the black tattoo that she has from her fingertips to right below her earlobe of the different countries in our world. I remember when she wore her hair cropped short with white and silver streaks woven through her black hair. Now, it's pulled back in a loose braid that ends around her mid-back. Her hair is as dark as the look clouding her usually bold hazel eyes. Liv and her sister have always had petite frames, but my friend is at risk of disappearing into thin air—even with the exercises they make us do to maintain muscle. The makeshift dress made of animal hide will swallow her whole if she doesn't eat more soon.

Gazing at the outline of my own body, I'm not doing much better right now, especially with the blood still dripping down my back after I reopened the lashings. *It'll be just another scar to add to my collection.* The tattered rags of old deer skin leave little to the imagination and show each welt and bruise along my freckled skin. Damon always wants my hair down, and the sick fuck prefers if it gets all tangled up. It gives him a reason to groom me. I don't see what he likes about it at this point. The usual golden and ruby red waves have dulled, and the ends are annoyingly frayed beyond repair. It doesn't matter which part of me Damon admires—there's no physical piece of me that I love anymore. The only good part is the star necklace I was allowed to keep on me. Although, that's slowly turning into a heavy reminder of my captor. Damon loves when I wear it while he ties me down. He says it brings out the angry spark that glimmers in my amber eyes.

He's such a piece of shit. Little does he know that the only reason I care about it is because it's the one item I have left from my family. An heirloom passed down from woman to woman on my mother's side. It's meant to symbolize the power of the name that's been given to each woman—*Astira. A beautiful, shining star.* It's a shame it doesn't also mean vengeful. My family and my relationships have always been on again, off again. They've sometimes been strained at best, but we always come back to one another in the end.

Not this time. No, I'm sure they're long gone. Dead to this world. Maybe their ashes are in the very walls surrounding us.

The sounds of multiple men barking orders bounce off the stone walls. Swallowing, I glance quickly at Liv and see she's already nodding. We're still breathing pretty hard, but the crack of a whip behind us has us both scrambling to our feet in a hurry.

"*Shit*, we have to go. *Now!*" I breathe.

SEVEN
Ceira

Creatures of the light aren't immune to darkness.
They adapt to it in lethal ways
and accept there's darkness in us all.
-Council Member Elio, Grand Commander of Sunlight

"Breathe deeper," Stefanie murmurs.

I inhale a jagged breath and do my best to push the air out as smoothly as I can. Between using the blue flames and what I've learned is sunlight *maji*, my insides are burning to a crisp. After I felt Athena and Hadwin's souls depart from this realm and was nearly pulled with them, my powers banked to embers and smoke. I collapsed on the polished floor and now blink up at the fuzzy outlines of Stefanie, Nyx, and Zaya—each hovering around me in concern. Zaya is meowing, the noise blaring as loud as a siren. My heart squeezes in gratitude for my feisty pet. I swear if she doesn't turn the volume down on her screaming, though, we're going to have a serious problem—*and maybe a fried kitty.*

The polished stone walls are coming back into focus around me with each inhale I force myself to take. A shimmering glow casts the walls and low ceiling in shades of blue and gray, most likely remnants of my fire *maji*. Each colored shadow falls over my friends. I won't know for certain until I get a closer look, but I think they're breathing slightly easier and are safely nestled against their abundance of cushions. Pushing myself to focus on my own body, I notice that the faded bear marking from Tryg is itching. That can't be a good sign. Smoke still smothers my lungs and wraps around my throat with curling, wispy fingers. I cough loudly while Nyx pulls me into a sitting position. He bats Zaya away as she bites his fingers and gathers me into his arms, draping what might be a blanket made of shadows over my shivering body.

"Is this normal?" he barks at Stefanie.

She doesn't wince even a fraction at his tone. One of the many gifts of being a healer—we're relatively unfazed by a soul's outburst, understanding it comes from a place of pain.

"To be transparent with you, nothing about Eira is exactly *normal*," Stefanie counters. She places a hand on my back and sends soothing tendrils of *maji* to the blisters that formed on my skin and down into my charred lungs. "Considering she threw her healing *maji* into all of her friends' souls at once, and even extended some of it out toward Athena, then yes, I would say this is normal."

Nyx growls in frustration. "If this was a possibility, then why did you let her do it?"

Stefanie snorts. "Okay, first of all, I don't *let* our queen do anything. She decides for herself what she wants to try and which areas she can push through. Second of all, none of us knew healing multiple souls at once would result in her body literally smoking. When we discussed possible risks of burning out or losing energy at a quicker rate, Eira insisted that she wanted to at least try it to see what happens. She said this would be an opportunity to not only heal her friends but also to test the boundaries of her *maji*."

I don't have to see Nyx's face to know the menacing glare he's giving Stefanie. Coughing more smoke out, I wiggle myself up until I'm peering into his heated eyes. *I better nip this before he and his demon spiral completely.* I force myself to smile softly and reach out with trembling hands to cup his face.

"I'm fine. I'm safe," I whisper.

Nyx directs the full brunt of his bubbling irritation on me. *Good. Give me your darkness, you wicked prince.*

"You're coughing up fucking smoke, firefly," he snaps. "How could you possibly be fine or safe in this condition?"

"Because it's *my* body and soul, so I get to decide how I feel about this," I say. "I wasn't sure what would happen, but I'm glad that I gave this a go. My powers were previously described in the *Healers of the Light* book as fierce and unmatched. There were detailed examples of times I healed more than one *solliqa* at once. Now I know how many I can heal that have been damaged by the plague before my energy starts to sputter out." I jab a finger into his firm chest. "And you nor anyone else gets to determine how I figure this out."

Nyx huffs in annoyance. *Yeah, you and me both, darling.* I chance a look at our companions, and some of the strain around my heart eases. They're all remarkably more relaxed. My eyes linger on Daru and the swathed wound around his neck. As if sensing me watching him, he subtly shifts his head, his eyes peeling open into slivers. A foreign sensation bounces between my lungs, giving me pause.

Zaya doesn't care about what I'm mentally processing. She swishes her tail wildly and jumps into my lap with a loud meow, nearly knocking me onto my back with how hefty she has become. Her green and blue eyes fade into a bright gold again, and she growls low in her throat while her ears fall flat against her head. Nyx's attention flips like a light switch to her agitated demeanor. Stefanie immediately jumps up in front of us as she frantically scans back and forth across the room. Nausea rolls through me in staggering waves. Still, I try to push out of Nyx's embrace in an attempt to stand up, but he swiftly swoops me up in his arms. At the same time, Zaya leaps out of my arms and transitions into an even larger form. Her size is akin to Daglo's huge mountain lion—one of the kindest *solliqas* I met in Eliina's group of healers, whom I've been fortunate to work with.

My whole body shudders when a pulsating energetic force swirls out from Athena and Hadwin's catatonic bodies and flows around us. A muffled cry leaves me, but it's not out of simple fear. The energy is horribly different from the *maji* I've experienced in Majikaero. It's dense and foreign and pushes against my skull in the most uncomfortable way. And that *smell*. It's sickly sweet and causes another wave of nausea to crash into me. Something about the way it clings to my skin like thin plastic is familiar. *The scent reminds me of those rare moments I'd watch my mother hum happily in front of her mirror, her skin dewy while she'd plait her long dark blond hair. The overbearing sweetness floated out from her bathroom, an area of the house I was forbidden from entering. My siblings never paid her room much attention, content with their own spaces and personal objects. Not me, though. I've never been fond of being kept in the dark and vowed to learn what she coveted so dearly that not even her children could know.*

Yet when I ran through the house searching for my missing family, there wasn't a bathroom attached to her bedroom at all. There was... nothing.

A shockwave of pain strikes through me, but it's not intolerable. In the blink of an eye, the force and overpowering smell materializes into a thick substance that both oozes and drifts out of Athena's and Hadwin's catatonic forms. I still can't believe Athena transported out of this realm with Hadwin, and in an unexplainable way, I was kind of ticked off when it happened. My *maji* was tied to every single soul in this healing room. The second my best friend was sent hurtling out of Majikaero, my heart strings might as well have been ripped from my chest. How *dare he* snatch my Athena in a whirlwind of golden magic and remove her from my healing embrace?

Yet now I'm confused if it was actually Hadwin who transported them. There wasn't only his golden aura and her beautiful green *maji*. Both of them were consumed by a pulsating dark power that pressed against my soul with the same suffocating pressure the purple substance has now.

I shriek in horror when Nyx is brought to his knees by the now throbbing purple and black matter. My body tumbles out of his arms back onto the floor, yet he still manages to tuck me under his shoulders, and I let him. I *need* him to keep a hold on me. There's a fragment inside my body, small enough I can barely sense it, that's urging me to not be afraid. To reach out to this substance and say hello, as if I'm greeting an old friend. It's unclear if I'm uncomfortable from the overwhelming scent and the way it squeezes my body with an invisible force... or if I'm uncomfortable that this substance is calling out to me.

No, it doesn't matter how I'm feeling. That shouldn't be my focus, not before and certainly not now. I need to look out for my friends, for *Nyx*. I'm convinced whatever the fuck this is will cut right through my friends—they're all gasping for air and waiting for the sword to come swinging down on our souls. Everyone except for Zaya and my fox. Zaya's now the size of a tall horse and is crouching low in front of us, ready to attack with her honed claws extending from her paws like knives. My fox is standing guard over Fraya's limp body, and the substance jerks in static movements away from her.

Athena lets out a startled yelp as a churning green fire flares around her and overtakes the dark matter. She falls against Hadwin's stilled form, and he gasps loudly as life flows through his body. There's no fire or smoke when he comes to—only a silky and shadowed darkness that slithers its way back into his pores. Both he and Athena blink with wide eyes at the purple matter still seeping from their bodies and watch with weary expressions as it hovers near all of us. Zaya lashes out at the substance, but as soon as her paw swipes through it, she rears back with a whimper and falls over unconscious. I'm about to push past the intensifying ache in my head to ask what the hell this is. How am I not as affected? Why is it connected to our friends? The matter throbs once more before snapping out of existence. As if it was never here. The only proof any of us saw it is the disgusting smell that still floats way too close to my nose.

All exhaustion bleeds out of me as the five of us erupt into chaos.

Nyx starts barking questions at Hadwin and throws a whirl of shadows at the nearest wall in an outburst of agitation. *Here comes Mr. Temper Tantrum.* I might have only been with him for a month here in Majikaero, but I can tell he's reaching his limits and will snap at any moment.

Athena stumbles her way toward me, but I'm throwing myself at Zaya and examining her massive paws. I swallow back the sinking feeling that's churning inside of me and try to keep a steady head as I check each little—now quite large—bean in her paws. Zaya hasn't shrunk down to her usual size yet, and I'm disturbed by the sticky liquid that's dripping off one of her claws.

Stefanie appears torn between checking on our tormented friends and lunging toward me. She ultimately must think our companions are okay because she takes one look at my distraught face and kneels down next to me. Frightened Stefanie is gone, and the focused healer is back in her place while she whips out a small jar from inside her robe. She carefully places Zaya's claw over the top of it and takes enough of the opaque liquid dripping off them before securing the lid on tightly.

Stefanie mutters a spell under her breath and waves a hand over the jar. It's pocketed back in her robe before I can blink, and then Stefanie the *solliqa,* my trembling friend, is back. She heaves a sigh and buries her head in her hands, a sob breaking through that cracks at my heart. I curl into Zaya's side, her warm fur brushing against my cheek, while Athena settles behind her head and strokes one of her ears. We don't say anything for a few minutes and give Stefanie the gift of silence—even Nyx and Hadwin's blustering has simmered down to a low hum. I allow myself to be comforted by Zaya's even breathing, an indication she's still alive, and tell myself over and over that my pet will be okay.

Stefanie rolls her head up and fluffs out the waves in her hair. Red splotches paint her pale face and make her seem more drained than she already is.

"I don't know how to fix this," she hiccups and rubs her puffy eyes. "I want to say Zaya is fine, but I've never seen that substance before or witnessed whatever in Cudhellen that purple matter was. Is this from the plague? Is this related to the scattered Council members or what happened at the festival? Is it something else?"

Swallowing, I press my head further into my unconscious pet. Fatigue wraps itself around me and tries to pull me down to a world of sleep. I'm bruised and still semi-charred, and each movement reminds me there's unhealed blisters decorating my skin. Even though I've gone through a few healing sessions for my own soul at this point, there's still deep-rooted pain that manages to slither up and around me at the worst possible moments. Such as right now. It's not just the fatigue—it's the way my stomach has been whipped up, all frothy and starting to curdle. My thoughts are spinning too fast for me to fully keep up with them. I feel stuck in my skin when I've never had this problem before and don't quite know how I'm supposed to break free of all these physical symptoms.

Oh gods, and I don't know how to answer any of Stefanie's questions. I'm certainly not in the right headspace to handle Athena's explanation of where she went with Hadwin. *Alright, get a fucking grip. Pull from any leftover* maji *and at least try to leave this room gracefully. Then, I can release my sorrow in peace.*

I'm dejected, but I won't give in to this wariness and doubt. "Stefanie, I don't—"

"I've worked with those who've caught the plague for so damn long." Stefanie's voice reaches a higher pitch. The sharp tone causes more shadows to drift out from Nyx, and there's a relentless pounding beat in my head. "But this is a whole other level. I don't know where to even start, and *that* terrifies me. We need to find Eliina and get more answers."

I force myself to speak. "Maybe we should—"

"But *how* can we get those answers if she's nowhere to be found?" Stefanie is sitting up straighter, and her fist keeps curling and unfurling in a rapid pattern. My *almaove* is definitely a smoking beast, Athena's leg is bouncing continuously, and I'm going to scream from the restless energy in this room suffocating me. "Have I learned to rely on her too much? Yet I *know* she'll have more answers about that purple matter. Eliina will be able to connect what happened to Athena and Hadwin of all *solliqas*. I mean, they obviously traveled through the earth with their spirits—their bodies physically remaining here while they were transported is just like the examples in my old book, *Souls and Traveling Realms*. I didn't think Athena was at the same level as Hadwin yet, but our whole realm is full of fucking surprises lately."

"Alright, hold up," Hadwin growls. He and Nyx have inched closer to our little group, so they're practically breathing down our necks. Hadwin is hunched over on his knees with labored breathing. I forgot for a moment that he's also injured, and he places one of his calloused hands over his chest wound. His tone is rough enough that Stefanie's mumbling instantly ceases. I don't even want to look at Nyx and the waves of dread coming off him. "Whatever we did is not how I usually travel between Majikaero and Earth. My earth *maji* allows me to move through the soil between our two worlds, and my body doesn't have to stay in this realm while I go."

My eyebrows furrow in confusion. "Your whole body moves in between worlds? Like Del did?"

"Not just any worlds," Hadwin grunts. "Only some of us with strong enough earth *maji* can move between Majikaero and Earth. From what I understand, Del learned from other world-traveling *solliqas* how to shift in between our two worlds and went in the form of a bird. He quite literally pierced the air between the two realms to travel to where you lived. He wasn't able to stay very long after he found you and didn't risk going to Earth again after deciding to bring your soul over here. I have the power to move freely through the soil, the grass, the trees, and other elements of the earth. Athena and I did *not* travel that way. I believe our souls were teleported against our will to another point in the future of Earth and—"

"Teleported?" Stefanie whispers. The last flicker of light in her gaze is snuffed out. I'm close to breaking all together in the same way as fragile stained glass, the colors scattering into hundreds of pieces.

"Yes, and if something foreign is manipulating where our souls go, then we must take action. Urgently." Nyx runs a clawed hand through his locks of hair. His shadows quiver under the orbs of light, some of them transforming into black feathers. Those dark eyes that I love so much flash to a more opaque color every other second. *That can't be good.*

"It might be useful to check out the library again," Stefanie murmurs to herself more than us. "Large portions of the city have been destroyed, but there were enough protection spells placed around the library of Rioa to ensure it lasts eternities. If our friends are almost better, we can head over right now and see if we can still access it without Eliina."

"We certainly could," comes a smooth voice from the open

doorway. "But that might be hard to do with a scorched Queen of Light, exhausted crew, and half-asleep friends."

That flicker in Stefanie's eyes lights up again, and a sliver of bright green shines through the dull haze.

"Hauke!"

He waltzes into the healing chamber with skin-tight, gauzy pants and a short-sleeved copper vest that dips low enough to show off his built chest. Hauke has longer waves of purple hair than I remember from when he greeted Daya, Del, Daru, and me during our journey to the healers. He's even more of a towering form of chiseled muscle and bronze skin. His smirk, with those orange and yellow eyes of pure fire, give him the appearance of a demon. *A charming, insanely handsome demon that I didn't realize would be visiting us anytime soon.*

Athena and I openly ogle his gorgeous physique, and I swear I catch Hadwin and Nyx giving him an appreciative once-over, but Hauke is focused solely on Stefanie.

"You're here," she exhales.

"Of course I am," he mutters and comes to stand right behind her. She gazes up at him with a mixture of longing and confusion. "You know better than anyone that we might play with others, but there's no other soul that has my heart the way you do, little *luxriel*. I came as soon as I could once the other regions caught wind of what happened here in Rioa."

Stefanie's blush crawls up her neck, but she looks far from embarrassed. An ease washes over her that I haven't seen since the festival. *Oh, my little ginger healer has some spicy secrets to spill.* Hauke glances up at me for a second and winks before pulling Stefanie into his arms in one quick movement, her bright green coverings bunching up around her. Nyx catches him winking at me and visibly bristles. *Gods.*

"This is most definitely an urgent matter, Prince," he says to Nyx. "But with anything this delicate, we must proceed carefully." Hauke mumbles the last part while pushing a few pieces of hair behind Stefanie's ear and gazing down at her adoringly. He snaps his attention back up to Nyx. "Let's take tonight to rejuvenate any lost energy and *maji*—your girlfriend *absolutely* needs to do this. Get some sleep. Get the others lying down back there cleaned up and changed. It'll be much easier to approach the situation with a refreshed and clearer mind."

"Fuck that," Nyx barks out. "We can't fucking rest when a purple haze just came out of our friends. You don't get to order a prince and his companions around. And she's not my girlfriend. She's my *almaove*, the soul I adore."

Hauke's eyes flash a bright white before the color mixes with his orange and yellow tones. "Let me rephrase that, then. As Master Healer next in line to replace Eliina's spot on the Council and Official Alliance Former, I'll be making my own decisions about our next steps. *We'll* be resting and clearing our heads for tomorrow morning, as well as making sure the rest of the group here is feeling better after our queen's healing. You, a *former* prince, can go fuck a tree for all I care. And Eira might be tied to your soul, but have you professed your *love*? Have you taken any steps to take your connection to the next level?"

Dark purple and black wings swing out from behind Hauke's shoulders, and his feet shift enough to give the appearance of golden talons. "Lick your wounds without rest or, maybe, tend to the queen you adore so much, *Prince*. Have you forgotten she might have a say in this, too?"

Nyx lunges toward Hauke, but Hadwin wraps an arm around his waist, forcing him to pause. We watch as Hauke swiftly carries Stefanie through a side door, and they're gone. My *almaove's* shadows swish wildly around him, and the black veins crawling up his arms start to pulsate. He roughly grabs my arm and pulls me up into his chest, knocking the remaining air out of my smoking lungs.

"You're the reason I can't stop to rest," he growls in a low tone. "I don't know what's going on, and I can't have these foreign creatures manipulate your soul, too."

My face softens as I peer up into my love's predatory face. I don't have a chance to answer because in the next moment, a few healers enter the chamber's doorway.

"Eira?" One of them turns to face me. It's Daglo. His jarring eyes peer out at me under the hood of his black and gold silk robes. "Stefanie gave me her jar with the opaque liquid in it that's on your feline's claws. I'll be studying it carefully today, and we'll keep your pet under close watch as we complete the healing process. I'd offer for you to join us, but I think it'd be best if you go take care of yourself. Your friends and pet will be under the highest quality care this afternoon and evening, and we can touch base tomorrow morning. Does that sound okay with you?"

Nyx is glancing from the healers to Hadwin and Athena to our friends to Zaya with such quick movements, it's making me dizzy. He appears overwhelmed by a question not even directed at him.

"Yes, that's fine with me," I tell Daglo. "Thank you for coming and helping all of them. Especially Zaya. She's incredibly precious to me, more than most other souls."

Another healer I haven't met before steps forward from behind him. Her purple and pink hair is braided down her back and out of her tired face—her dark eyes and patterned blue skin illuminated by the soft glow of the orbs. She gives me a small smile and nods her head. Daglo grasps my hand momentarily and then abruptly motions the other healers to follow him, and I take that as our cue to leave. Athena comes from behind me and delicately loops her arm with my own, pulling at just the right angle to rip me out of Nyx's unyielding hold.

"I have so much to tell you," Athena whispers and stifles a yawn. "But not right now. I'm fucking beat. I don't even know how *you're* still standing."

I snort in response and a plume of smoke comes out of my nose. Both our eyes widen, and we break out into a fit of giggles. Hadwin gives us a look that tells us *exactly* what he thinks of our random laughter during a time as distressing as this.

"Shall we leave to find food?" she asks me with a hesitant smile. Seeing this makes my heart skip a beat—she's been a shell of a soul for the past week, and even this small slip of her usual laughter makes me cautiously hopeful.

Athena thinks that I haven't noticed the ripples of self-desolation coming off her. I can tell by the tightness of her smile and the washed-out color in her eyes. I always have and always will, but I've never brought it up to her. I've learned from my own wounds that when a melancholic entity buries itself deep in someone's heart, grievously hidden below the light, you can't simply reach inside to pull it out. That's a quick way to get yourself burned. The one carrying the burden has to be willing to admit the weight is too heavy. They have to be ready to put down the light they've previously used as a shield and wield it as a newly forged weapon to strike the pain down. It's a form of bravery not spoken of enough. I can't be sure when Athena will find the courage to acknowledge her healing light might be a hindrance when it comes to herself.

It doesn't matter, though. I love my best friend, whether she conceals the true nature of her personality or not. We all wear masks in one way or another. It'd be shameful of me to expect Athena to remove hers when I can't bring myself to remove mine.

I turn back to ask Nyx what he thinks about eating, but he's still fuming with a flurry of emotions. I blow out a quick breath and, maintaining eye contact with Nyx, I mutter quietly to my friend, "Absolutely. We'll meet you at the UFS in a little bit, okay? I think I need to have a chat with a frazzled prince first."

Athena smiles faintly at the nickname we've given the rooms we're staying in. Most of the Council building is nothing more than dilapidated stone and broken Council members' furniture, except for the library, a spacious dome room typically used for meetings, the stables, and a handful of spare bedrooms and living areas. When Nyx said the Council building's formal name translates roughly to *The Magnificent and Formidable Izadiah*, I couldn't contain my laughter. Why on earth would anyone officially call a building magnificent and formidable? Has the Council been preparing to suppress the *solliqas* of their world and needed to design a structure to hide behind? A few of us came up with a new "formal" name: *The Uninspiring and Feeble Shithole,* or *The UFS* for short.

It's the little things, sometimes, that help us cope with all-consuming anger and misery.

"Good luck with that," Athena mumbles to herself. "I'm going to go see where I can scavenge some *veina* for us and maybe check on the *alklen*." Hadwin forces himself into a contorted standing position. He tries to stalk up next to us and gives her a disapproving glare, his gold eyes acting as luminous candles in the dimming room. The floating orbs above us flicker until they're muted, giving me the sudden urge to curl up and sleep. *Huh, a healer must have these timed to make healing* solliqas *sleep in set intervals. Smart. I've totally got to get some of these for myself.* Athena huffs loudly, pulling me out of my sleepy thoughts. She scowls at Hadwin and stomps off, not realizing that he's limping after her out the doorway and can't take his eyes off her. Hadwin has a predacious glint in his eyes, even while still injured. I don't think he fully grasps how the *solliqa* he's following is just as easily able to capture her prey.

"Come," I tell Nyx. Taking his hand draped in shadows and intertwining my slender fingers with his now taloned ones with clawed nails, I lead us out the same doorway our friends hurried through. It's difficult to decide where we'll go to calm Nyx's demon, but it won't do us any good to stay in the same space. All too often, we find ourselves stuck and unable to move even an inch, too consumed by antagonizing emotions. That's why we have to move in another direction—a foot, a room, a whole building away—and force those feelings to release their jaws from around our chests. We need to find space to *breathe* so that we can think. And I'm so depleted from trying to heal my new friends, my poor, hurt kitty, and the gravity of our situation; I'd need to cross an entire mountain range to fully take a breath at this point.

We make it a whole two minutes when my body is jerked to the side. Nyx winds his other hand around my neck and pulls me into a smaller healing chamber tucked away along the narrow hallway. I stumble into his chest and need to reorient myself—there's only one floating orb in here and the space is full of darkness, Nyx's shadows, and an unsettling silence. Nyx pushes me back into the wall behind us, his hand never leaving my throat, and uses his hips to lock me in place. A low rumble starts in his chest, and as my eyes finally adjust, I'm at a loss for words as his layers of sinfulness thrash violently around me.

My eyes were on Hadwin and Athena as they left us alone with our healing friends. Perhaps I should have been focused on the one *solliqa* I've physically bonded with here. He is still struggling with the weight of the plague on his soul, and he has the power to bring me into his insanity.

He might already have.

EIGHT
Tryq

To welcome in demons is to welcome your own death.
-Cajsa, Goddess of Spirit

Have the shadows always clung to the dungeon wall like this?

I can't be sure. I also don't know if that's my own cynical thought or musings from the monsters I've been consumed by. The voices go around and around in my head, and the pressure of them is painfully thick—I'm surprised my skull hasn't cracked yet. A shiver rolls its way down my spine until my entire back is littered with goosebumps. They could be from the unsettling freezing temperature in this dungeon, or I could be having another reaction to the conniving whispers that won't. Fucking. Stop.

"Shut up!" I roar at the wall facing me. Spit flies from my mouth, painting the stony surface with bloody specs. My mouth —well, my entire body—is still healing from the last visit with the protectors and manipulators. Each claimed to be loyal to the Council, but I have yet to see an actual Council member make an appearance.

Do they exist? Is the idea of them some fabricated joke?

The Council's mighty protectors who've come use blunt force and vicious physical torture in an attempt to get me to talk. I don't mind this too much. Pain, in any form, brings me back to the current reality around me and reminds me that I'm alive. The manipulators slink into my mind and body, forcing a different form of physical torment I didn't know could exist. They're able to contort my blood and deep tissue, slicing through the different layers with each inadequate response. My mind becomes hazy as they slither around inside of it, searching for answers that I don't have.

The recent manipulators who've come don't only service the Council—they dedicate their basically immortal lives to torturing any lost souls in these dungeons. When they came by earlier today, they didn't receive the answers they hoped for. That only led to carving me up from the inside out and leaving me in a puddle until they return later. As if storing me away in this sliver of a room isn't punishment enough for sins I didn't intend to commit.

I crave compassion from one of the healers—any of them at this point—instead of the Council's protectors and manipulators. I'm not sure when they'll be back. Some of the healers came to rescue Nyx's friends and the other poor fucks trapped behind these walls. Me, though? Will the healers deem me worthy of redemption?

I don't remember the night of the Moons Cycle Festival. Fuck, what I wouldn't give to know what I fucking did. Maybe they'd all put me out of my misery then. The only part that is clear in my memory, as fresh as the blood they drain from my bruised body, is when Eira engulfed herself and Nyx in angry blue flames. Her *eyes*, gods, her fucking eyes. Those terrifying burgundy-red eyes set their intentions on me, and the moment another part of me laughed at her words, she lashed out. A cord of fire almost whipped straight through me, and the Eira I knew was no longer there. A queen of horrors and flame stared me down and left me there in the dungeon cell to bleed out and burn into nothingness.

Terror swirled through me, yet all I could do was lie there while she and Nyx barked orders to protectors and healers. My flesh curled in on itself at the way she easily disposed of me, as if it's too late for me and the monsters inside of me have festered too deeply. Eira didn't see the unshed tears begging to fall down my cheeks or the agony that I wanted to cry out. She *couldn't* see that this is what my demons wanted—to feed her the truth about our friends on Earth in such an ugly and brutal way while watching her cave into her anger. It's felt like years of the demons taking their turns burrowing inside of me, but I know it's only been weeks, maybe a few months. I've been losing my fucking mind and everything I thought I was and stood for. I didn't realize all of my struggling was for nothing.

I'm all alone and trapped beneath the surface of the creatures that have sunk their claws deep into my soul. Just a shell of who I used to be, with no ability to communicate with the other *solliqas* here. The only moment I had some form of control over myself was when the monsters learned what's been happening on Earth from other foreign beings. I knew I had to get this information to Eira and the others. Even fucking Nyx. I didn't think these fucked-up creatures would throw violent scene after scene into Eira's mind without a care of how it would impact her. No gentleness. No empathy. No love.

But why am I surprised? I can't give any of this to my own self, so how would I possibly be able to give it to Eira?

A loud sound clambers down the gritty hallway and reverberates under my feet. I'm barely touching the dirty floor. My arms are shackled to the frigid wall behind me, along with my neck, waist, and knees. Wounds continue to form where the metal chains of starlight touch my thinning skin. Healers come here in random rotations to heal them slowly, not allowing me to pass out. The room itself is a small rectangle and large enough to hold my hanging body. The opposite wall extends a few feet in front of me, giving the necessary space for one or two *solliqas* to enter and warp my body and soul further. There's no window or light or even a remote sense of time in here. Unlike the other dungeon with open bars acting as a gate, I'm suffocatingly isolated behind a thick, heavy door.

A high-pitched cackle escapes me. I shouldn't laugh, but it's hard not to. These fuckers think physical harm and cornering me into an unbearably tiny and dank space is enough to break me. To unleash plans that are even kept secret from me. Little do they know that there's nothing to break, not when my demons use their monstrous ways to alter and distort me, to do their worst. As if I've summoned them, I'm overtaken by a cacophony of brittle sounds and choppy voices. I have the urge to smash my hands against my ears, but without the use of my arms, I'm left with guttural screams that are endless. Others might be impacted by the plague of darkness differently, but I'm not consumed by one mere demon—I'm suffocating under the pressure of multiple monsters, each with their own merciless personality.

I close my eyes tight and bang my head back against the wall, hoping it knocks me out. I'm not that lucky, *of course*, and my least favorite of the diseased creatures slithers around the inside of my head. The image of it ripping out chunks of my brain makes me want to hurl, and its presence overwhelms me. I can't discern the rest of its body, but I can see its seething black eyes staring back at me. There's no nose, only a wide, sharp smile that takes up most of its putrid face. The shape of its head is nonexistent and warps from one form to the next with its eyes staying fixated on me. A sickly sweet smell hovers in the air, and I can't stop the near invisible vapor from messing with my senses. I find myself thinking this demon is trying to torment me, wanting to play with its prey as it pushes and pulls me in and out of consciousness. But no sooner have I thought this than an image floats behind my eyelids, and I have to swallow back bile.

It doesn't want to only agonize me—it wants to taunt me, to smash my heart into a million pieces while I'm already knocked down.

The image forced upon me is one of Eira. She's backed up against a dark wall with smooth stones and vines hanging down from the ceiling. A shadowed figure has a hand wrapped around her throat, and her hips are locked in place. She glows a bright blue, her flames dancing with the shadows smothering her pretty skin, until the creature in front of her lets go. As the fire around her flares brighter and higher, she slowly hooks a leg around the creature's calf and in a swift motion, forces them to change places. Now *she's* the one with a hand against his throat, and impossibly slowly, the shadows take the form of a man. No, a *solliqa*, and it's Nyx. He murmurs something to her, but all she does is throw her other hand out and blinding white shackles appear around his wrists.

My Eira has a man chained down before her? I can't help the reaction I have, even if I am watching her with *Nyx*. I shift uncomfortably against the wall, since I can't use a hand to relieve the building ache of my growing erection. I growl as this image shows Eira sinking to her knees and ripping—*with fucking blue claws*—his pants off in a few fluid motions. Her eyes glow a dark red as she wraps one of her delicate hands around the top of his cock and lazily strokes him. Nyx arches his back with a groan and tries to pull his hands out of the shackles, but he can't budge them an inch. Growling, Nyx mutters something else to Eira, and she smirks up at him before swirling her tongue along the tip of his cock. He lets out a snarl, but I don't get to watch what comes next. I'm pulled from the image, and the demon's seething eyes are now glittering with anticipation.

One heartbeat. Another demon with dark purple and silver eyes bounces along under my skin. Two heartbeats. A third demon with light blue and opal eyes twists and turns up the sides of my body. I'm afraid to take another breath knowing a fourth demon could emerge at any second. They all open their slimy mouths and voices of various timbres rattle against my ears. *Fuck.* I *hate* when they all talk at the same time. They do this when I least expect it and have even more power to morph my personality each time that they do.

I'm absolutely going insane, and there's nothing left on Earth, Majikaero, or any other universe that can save me from myself.

I don't know how much longer I can hold on. It's a miracle that a piece of me even still exists in this *solliqa* body. It might not even belong to me anymore. I'm just another soul trying to survive in it, and it's becoming too much to handle. It'd be easier to let go than to endure the power of these demons pushing down on me from different directions with greedy intentions. I'm being strangled and at this point, want to wither away in peace. I'd be better off dead than being another form of destruction against those I care for in Majikaero.

And besides, even if I could fight back and survive this, who would want me? I'm irredeemable and as much of a monster as the rest of these hideous creatures. I have no purpose in any realm, and the longer I exist, the more fuel I give to the demons who've infected me.

Or did I infect myself?

Muffled yelling spirals down the hall, and I'm momentarily distracted from my thoughts. I blink furiously, willing myself to stay focused on the sound of those voices and not cave into the restless half-sleep I've been stuck in. Heaving a sigh, I let my chin fall toward my chest. It doesn't matter how sharp or blurry my attention is—those torturous thoughts will be back eventually. And when they are, I'll need to come up with a plan before I'm lost completely to the battling demons who are effectively taking over my soul as their new home.

"Did I ask for your permission?" a female voice rings out.

Her tone slashes through the tangled walls my demons have fortified around my senses. "I'm announcing myself as a courtesy, but I most certainly don't need *you* or the others to approve of me coming here."

A metal door slams against a wall in the distance, the movement so aggressive the hinges squeak in protest. I manage to peel one eye open in the chance this mystery *solliqa* is on her way to see me. But I can't assume that. There could be a hundred other prisoners in here, yet with the walls thickly piled up with dusty stones, there's no way I'd know. I can hear shuffling and hushed voices, and after several minutes pass by, I let my eye snap closed again. *I knew no one was here to see me. Who would want to?*

I must have dozed off. Not even the mumbling of my demons could have kept me up. Blinking away the daze of fractured sleep, a loud thud jolts me fully awake in a flash. My door creaks open, and a petite form draped in gold silky robes tiptoes inside. *Huh. Why are they being so quiet?* I don't have to wait long for an answer, though. Huge eyes and a smirk greet me from under their hood, and I'm left gaping at a *solliqa* I didn't think I'd see again any time soon.

NINE
Nyx & Eira

Our spirits long for soul-level connections.
We're not always prepared for what this includes, which often
leads to pushing away the positive connections in order to
avoid anything negative.
-Dr. Antonio Piernt,
Founder of Seeds of the Lotus

Nyx

Soon I'm lost in the scent and mesmerizing way Eira has my body shackled to the coarse wall behind me. I didn't realize how quickly I'd morph back into my demon. Not when Eira spent so much of her energy healing a layer of my pain only a few weeks ago in the healing pools. Yet the darkness drank me like the thirsty bitch it is, and those puckered scars Eira opened up to heal are already scabbing over.

All it took was the image of my *almaove's* body collapsing—drained to her last drop of energy—and watching that purple substance weave its way in her direction.

I was already rattled by what Ivar shared with Athena and

me. The foreign being had told him we're but a speck of stardust in the universe and there's many more where they come from, and that we'd connect to our true spirits once again. Words from my parents that I had heard throughout my childhood, and I can't make sense of why they're coming up again now. Trauma and pain have been my foundation, and fear is now my undoing. Zaya was foolishly brave to swipe at the substance with her lethal claws. None of us can confirm what the fuck it is, and the last thing anyone should be doing is touching it. I can't blame her, though. Not when she matched my same feral energy and would stop at nothing to protect our Eira.

"You must need more pain if your thoughts are drifting this easily," Eira murmurs against one of my pecs.

She has no idea. I adore her light, yet I *crave* the pain only she can give me. It's a craving I didn't realize I had until our moment during training this morning. If she loves pain with her pleasure, then gods, I pray she relishes in giving it as much as she enjoys receiving it.

My hand jerks as Eira bites down on my nipple—*hard*—and I have the urge to snake my hand around her head. To cradle her tighter against my writhing body. She's right, my thoughts are drifting in every direction. When my monstrous demon overtakes me, I lose all sense of control and understanding of where I am, of what I'm thinking, of which step to take next. I was only vaguely aware of Eira's presence when she wrapped shaking fingers around my darkened wrist in the other healing room. She dragged me behind her, forcing me to follow the blue flames still trickling down her waves of white hair. It wasn't until I managed to inhale the very air she was breathing that I came to my senses and tried to pull her into another room to calm down. I didn't want to be paraded around the healing quarters while being fucking exposed.

The demon within me had other ideas. As soon as I had her all alone, I noticed her bear marking glowing again. All sensible thoughts left me at the idea of her still being tied to Tryg, and primal urges leached out and forced her against the nearest wall. What my monster and I didn't anticipate was the way Eira would counteract us, and sweet gods, how much we would *love* it.

As soon as Eira flipped me against the wall, she used her *maji* to burn some of my coverings to soot. *The rest of them were clawed apart with blue fucking claws.* Now she sends a burst of blue fire into the chains of white flame licking around my skin. The chains are wrapped around my wrists, shoulders, hips, knees, and ankles. They further tighten until the burn is just hot enough to bleed with pleasure, and my breathing comes out in bursts of shadows. My *almaove* fucking smirks as the darkness washes over her in waves. Her pouty lips stretch into a full smile against where my heart should be, a soft coolness against the heat simmering along me. The more I've been consumed by this aching sadness and rage, the less I feel there was ever a heart to begin with inside me. Eira nips a path down my torso until she reaches my hip bones, where she bites down hard enough to make me bleed. *Shit. All thoughts of that bear marking are officially gone.*

"I thought... I thought your *maji* was—*fuck*—used up," I pant.

Eira takes her time licking her way around my cock, purposely leaving the one area I want her at untouched. When she peers back up at me, her eyes are full of pure red fire.

"You pulled us into another room of the healing quarters. I thought you needed another healing session," Eira whispers, her voice as smooth as silk.

Not breaking eye contact, her tongue snakes out and licks up the drops of pre-cum budding at the head of my cock.

"Is this your idea of healing?" I rasp.

"If you keep interrupting me, you might not find out," she snarks.

Eira swirls her tongue around the head once more before slowly taking me inside of her. Only half of my dick fits inside her mouth without forcing myself deeper. I'm about to ask if she can take it when she lets me go with a loud *pop*.

She snakes her way up my strained body and latches that pretty mouth at the bottom of my neck. I groan and twist in agitation, loving anywhere her mouth travels on me and the way she tastes my blood but desperately needing her to finish what she started. Eira giggles and loops her arms around my neck while pushing her chest flush against mine. The delicate fabric of her thin covering brushes against each sensitive bite mark, and I shiver in anticipation of her next move.

Eira laughs again, and her fox of blue and white crystals drifts out of her upper back and leaps onto the gray plush rug underneath our feet. She peers up at me with the same predacious look that Eira has with gold and red flames in her eyes. I'm watching an extension of my *almaove*, except if I dare to touch her, my skin will turn so cold it'll burn. I can tell she's searching inside me for something, yet I can't be sure what she's expecting I'll give her. How can I when all my attention is on the fiery queen now kissing down my neck?

Her fox dashes in between us, and much to my amazement, nuzzles into my legs. *She's showing me affection? Not ripping another layer of trauma from inside me?*

A whisper swirls around my mind and speaks faintly; I barely hear it at first. The words are jumbled and gritty, but the warning behind them is as clear as the fucking moons at night: *danger.*

"What's getting into you?" I huff. It pains me to stop her, especially as Eira winds her hand around my hip and abruptly squeezes my pulsating cock. I jerk and grow more disheveled. But there's that voice again.

Danger. Predator. Terror.

Yet, is that voice talking about me or my queen?

Eira grips my length a bit harder, forcing a grunt out of me. She smiles in such a coy way, I'd swear she was another *solliqa* full of shadows, a soul who belongs in my group of companions. "A part of me is starting to wake up, my dark princeling, and it wants to come out to play."

Dark princeling? That might fit. *But are those the words of my firefly? Especially after being so drained?*

"Firefly, why don't—"

"Shh. Let's see if I can make your fire dance with mine."

She takes gentle steps backward until she's staring at me from the other end of the room. Her fox prances next to her, almost as if in anticipation. Tiny sparks crackle along Eira's skin until a low buzzing fills my senses. Her light illuminates the compact size of this room and casts long shadows on the single bed. A wooden table sits next to it, full of jars that glitter with different potions. Images of our world's gods and goddesses are engraved into the ceiling, peering down at us from behind the many vines trailing the tops of the walls.

I can feel their silent judgment of what I've become. This is a quiet and therapeutic space that my darkness *had* to tamper with. I make eye contact with the god of healing, his face the very image of serenity. *Fuck him. Eira's face is what should be up there. At least she knows healing isn't all about tranquility.*

Eira's body shines even brighter and nearly blinds me. I can only see the outline of her form, and that's when I see *them*. Hundreds of fireflies circulate around Eira's glowing form, each pulsing with a frozen blue, soft purple, or scathing red. They stand out against her skin-tight black coverings with subtle threads of dark green woven throughout them. The green sparkles in the light of each firefly and the glimmer of fire coming off Eira. Each one of them has wings the color of my queen's hair and is a living flame that flies in swift movements between us.

All I can do is stare as they twist and turn around the parts of me not chained down. *Oh, my sweet firefly.* She herself resembles this term of endearment, but all the fucking gods hear me when I say *these* fireflies are terrifying. I'm seconds from asking Eira to send those insects of fire toward another soul—preferably Daru—when they stop flying and barely hover above me. *The fuck?*

My eyes widen in horror as my blood presses against my skin, whirling and boiling like lava. It percolates under the surface until thick bursts of smoke and ruby red flames flicker along my arms and fingers.

A choking sound escapes me. It's been so damn long since I've last felt the heat of my own fire smother the dark parts inside my soul. Blinking slowly and forcing my mouth closed, I shift my gaze toward Eira. Her *eyes*. They're a combination of her usual crystalized blue with red flames for pupils, and thin tendrils of smoke curve from the inside of her eyelid to the outer corners. I know I should take *this* as a warning, but I can't fight how drawn I am to this side of her and the way it tenderly washes over both of us. It's akin to the cozy warmth of a home fire, a glowing light of safety that I refuse to turn away from.

I allow the muscles in my jaw, neck, and shoulders to loosen their strangling grip on me, each one feathering slightly as I breathe out. With each exhale, my skin stretches and grows taut. The sensation is almost as unbearable as the way the fireflies pull my blood out of my veins into larger flames. I want to rip my entire body apart, but I'm scared of what that would reveal about what I am at my core. The stark hollowness.

A few of the fireflies swarm near the center of my fracturing body. The dark red fox full of shadows I turned into at the festival comes sailing out of me. A slice of my soul physically goes with him as he dances around Eira's fox. They circle one another in playful movements until my fox is on top of Eira's and they're tumbling around toward the other wall. I can't place where the fear is building from, but *something* is trying to warn me to call my fox back.

"Sweetheart, *why* are you doing this?" My voice carries around us in a whoosh of air.

Eira's light blossoms into a mixture of blue, purple, red, black, and green. Her manifested fireflies crackle and sting my skin with minuscule bolts of energy before disintegrating into smoke.

"If you're going to smother your healing progress at every opportunity, then I'll need to make the cut even deeper," Eira declares. "And I thought you missed your fire?"

"I-I—yes, of course, I miss it," I sputter. Her light surges forward and wraps around the red flames oscillating in my vision. I grind my teeth in an attempt to stifle the scream of agony, but a piercing cry leaves me anyway. "But *what* are you doing to my fire?"

"Nyx, darling," Eira purrs. "You are your fire, and your fire is you. One cannot truly separate from their destined energy and power."

Her coverings break down into fluttering ash. She tiptoes her way back toward me, a mighty creature taking graceful, feline movements. Colorful flames still lick up and down her naked body, and she falls to her knees once again before me. I go to move toward her, but the chains of light are still cutting into me. Straining against them, the scarlet fire swarms us in my aggravation.

"*Why* are you doing this!" I yell at my firefly. The rage I keep on a tight leash finally aiming right at my *almaove*. "How the *fuck* is this healing me?"

Eira's eyes flutter as she looks up at me. She places a hand on each of my thighs, unaffected by the hostile fire lunging at her. "My dark prince, my fireling, my sleek and angry panther. Your fear blinded you in the form of darkness. Sometimes, we can't only heal each little wound on our way to the true issue. Sometimes, we have to dive the dagger right at the heart of it all. You are your fire, and your fire is you. Break out of these chains or don't. You're the one with the power to do so."

My fear? I, myself, am the fire?

"You just bury all that power beneath your darkness," Eira whispers.

"My darkness *is* power," I growl at her. As if to show their agreement, a surge of dark shadows and smoke whirls around my fire and now demented-looking skeletal form.

"Is it? Or is it a lesser version trying to mask what you're capable of?"

Eira shines even brighter as my shadows fill every crevice of the small room. She doesn't cringe or budge an inch. My queen takes matters into her own hands and grips my cock, making it grow hard again. *Who am I kidding—I'm always hard around Eira.* She gives me a wicked smirk and moves close enough that her lips are touching the head again.

"Show me that true power of yours, Nyx," Eira rasps against the head. "Remain chained and fill me with your darkness or break free and consume me with your fire."

She dives forward and takes my dick all the way to the back of her throat in one swift movement. I choke on my next breath, startled that she can even do this. Eira doesn't strike me as a soul with a lot of sexual experience, at least based on our brief conversations and how she responded in the crystal cave. But as she sends sparks of her light up my legs and through my torso, I don't give another thought to what I believe she can or can't do. My queen will do whatever the fuck she wants, at least in this world, and that's how I want her to stay.

Pulsating darkness warps my vision of Eira. She's the very visual of perfection, sucking and slurping her way up and down my dick before taking it all the way back into her throat again. She gags slightly but tightens her grip on my thighs and rocks herself forward. My fingers are pure fire at this point, desperately craving to grab her hair and release my fury and the pain of this healing into her. The top of my skeletal form breaks with loud cracks, each shard making my fire breathe and crave more destruction. Out of the corner of my eye, I watch as Eira's fox bites down onto my fox's neck, and he yelps in panic.

Eira is burning a layer of my pain away, and she's using her fox to strike directly into my soul. *Again.*

"Fuuuuck!" I scream, an animalistic sound racketing in echoes around the room. One of the chains on my right wrist burns and sizzles; the smell of burning flesh overwhelms me, even though I'm shadows and fire itself at this point. The chain cracks, the sound thunderous, and instead of relief, I experience a flash of lightning flowing from me to the door frame. My hand is consumed by the fire now overtaking my shadows, but I don't have time to focus on this new blistering heat. Every single shackle sputters into my fire, and electrical currents surge straight through the darkness into my heart.

Wait, my heart? That part of me was one of the first pieces to cave into the heavy emotions I've carried for too long. My heart was warped into a knotted mass of black veins, tangled intrusive feelings, and shards of memories best forgotten. I didn't realize it still had a pulse until Eira first graced my dreams. Now it's enduring convulsing waves of lightning? Fragments of light have pierced through to it?

My eyes widen as I watch my queen in horror. Eira has the capability of healing love and compassion, yet without a doubt, *she* is the reason pain is sluicing through my soul in unbearable embodiments of light. When I'm convinced she was sent to me as an angel of death, the fragments of embers expanding in the new spaces of my heart sweep in a wall of flames over me. Until all I am is a passionate spirit of fire and smoke and everything dark in the world.

I shudder. I'm untethered except for the vines of inky shadows that weigh my heart and mind down. I force hands of flames to appear where I imagine my sides would be and test out each finger and wrist. An eternity must pass by as I imagine each of my usual body parts appearing, as I push the flames and shadows into a skin I'm used to wearing. Locking eyes with Eira, I notice she hasn't moved from her position on the ground—she's sitting back on her heels and gazing up at me with adoration in her eyes. Perhaps I should take a moment to bathe in her affection, in the scent of her neediness to finish what she started. But what started as an erotic healing session has turned into another, deeper layer being unleashed through agony.

And I'm fucking *pissed*.

I'm furious. At the gods. At myself for giving into my demon again. At Eira for using a new gut-wrenching way to heal me and that she even has to when she's surely close to burning out. At my own *maji* for not working the way it should. At the Council. At the *solliqas* who've abandoned me. At whoever attacked us at the festival. At our friends for fucking still being hurt or missing. At the fact that something feels *off* about my queen right now. At Tryg. At fucking Daru. At the plague. At the entire universe and that purple substance and everything and anything that has remotely deigned to leave its negative presence on me.

And I know the perfect way to relieve these whirling, nonstop thoughts.

I reach forward, still smoldering as a humanoid flame, and grip Eira's throat. The only indication she's surprised is the slight flare of her nostrils and the parting of her lips. I yank her until she's flush against my legs and her mouth is lined up with my cock again.

"You'll take *both* my fire and darkness," I growl. "And you'll swallow every drop of heat until I tell you to stop."

The fury rattles inside me, but I don't break eye contact with her stunning eyes.

Eira gives a deep nod, the answer to a question I didn't ask but should have. As her head raises up again, her tongue licks up my hardened length, not even phased that we're two beings with barely contained feverish heat. Hers is the kind that heals, and mine is the kind that destroys. But she's going to wrap those lips around a cock of ruinous fire and fucking *enjoy* it.

"That's a good prince," she winks, causing me to blink back in surprise. "Now use me. Let me be the soothing balm to such a devastating night."

And then I'm losing myself in her mouth, in her touch, in the way we scorch one another. The blaring alarm of *danger* continues to rattle my senses and urges me to pay attention, but I blissfully ignore it while my hips collide angrily with Eira's head. I'm starving for my queen's touch—a deep, unfilled need since the moment I laid eyes on her—and I'll take what I can get at this moment. Her eyes fill up with tears as I continue to gag her, yet there's no indication of fear or regret or resignation. She eagerly holds onto my legs, and by the scent drifting up to me, she's wet and ready for me to return the favor.

I pump into Eira's mouth one, two, three more times until I'm shooting my cum down her slender throat. Without me saying anything, she licks up and down my length to clean up any last drops. Her whole body is shaking with anticipation for what's next. *As she should be.* I groan when Eira sits back, arching her back enough to give me the perfect view of what's mine. *Yes, Eira is mine, and I don't plan on sharing her any time soon.* Licking my lips, I lower myself to my knees and lazily memorize each inch of light on Eira's skin—each brilliant color, flame, and heady scent that I get to explore.

Each coil of darkness that thinks it can hide from me.

Whether Eira realizes it or not, I'll soon expose this new corruption that's stained my *almaove's* soul and heart. And she's not going to see it coming.

Eira

The orange and blue sunlight filters through the gauzy blue curtains next to our bed. Nyx is still sleeping, the usual tension around his eyes smoothed out as he rests deeply. We arrived back at the small room we're sleeping in at the Council building late into the night. My cheeks flush when I recall how I burned all our coverings, and instead of making new ones, Nyx carried me back to this room in his arms. He wasn't at all phased by our nudity, which was both thrilling and potentially humiliating.

I'm not sure if anyone saw us. Nyx kept me tucked into his chest, his skin still as hot as coals after turning into what looked like a god of *fire*. My eyes had drooped, Nyx's walking sending me into a lulled state of sleepiness. I was too worn out from healing our friends, the purple substance nightmare, my poor Zaya baby getting hurt, and the way Nyx and I absolutely ravished each other in the healing quarters. A brief memory flickers to life of Nyx pulling back the lush blue and white covers —each blanket as soft as clouds with splatters of colorful designs— and curling me into him on the inviting bed.

Now, I have to pray I have enough stamina for another long, overly eventful day. I already know it's going to be mind-boggling when our group gathers to talk. We'll be discussing our next steps and what Jade has learned about our contemptuous Council members and the city that is at the center of it all.

"Does your mind ever stop to rest?"

Scrunching up my nose, I give him my best withering glare, but all he does is laugh. The sound is low and smoky, curling around my senses and drawing me closer to him.

"It's hard to rest when the darkness rarely stops," I mumble into his chest while tracing one of his thicker black veins.

"But if you don't rest, how will you have enough *maji* to take that darkness on?" Nyx murmurs. He curls a white strand of hair around his pinkie finger.

I scoff. "You clearly haven't spent enough time with healers if you think that's how any of our power works. It doesn't matter if we're on Earth, Majikaero, or any other world. Those of us who are destined to heal the wounds and violence souls can't help but spread to one another, we're not meant to fully rest."

"What happens when all of that fire burns you out?" Nyx's tone is soft enough to mitigate the severity of his question, but I sense the fear behind his words. It's a thought I've wondered for years.

I don't respond right away, not wanting to utter such bleak musings first thing in the morning. Rolling out of Nyx's warm embrace, his scent of smoke and rich darkness reaches out to me. I place the bottoms of my feet flat against the multicolored rug next to the bed. He grunts as he rolls up to a sitting position, and I can see his hand wave in a swirling pattern out of my peripheral. New coverings lay at the end of the bed, mine a dainty silver dress, and fresh *einral* is poured into two clay mugs.

There's no way my mind or *maji* can produce coverings, no matter how simple they are. It's not even a craft that I want to attempt to learn. If I'm ever in the position of needing new coverings while being stranded alone... then I guess everyone will get a naked Eira.

Now conjuring *einral*, a rich, creamy beverage that's close to the taste of coffee from back home, *that's* a skill I need to learn. As in *yesterday*. What have I been doing focusing on my healing fire *maji* when I could be serving myself caffeine and chocolate?

One of the gray mugs floats over to my hands on a tendril of smoke, courtesy of my *almaove*. I stare down into my steaming cup and the way it floats up around my face. My breasts feel heavy from last night, and the rest of my body has a dull ache pressing down onto my tendons. There's a delicious soreness that still throbs in my core, but *that's* a type of pain I'm more than willing to accept.

"Firefly?" Nyx asks.

"Yes, my shadow prince?"

The steam drifts right into my eyes as I bring the mug to my lips and take a drink, savoring the way the warm liquid splashes down my throat.

"You didn't answer my question," Nyx rasps. He grabs his own mug of *einral* and pads over to stand in front of me. He reaches his other hand down to grasp my chin and tilts my face to peer up into his crackling eyes. "What will happen when you burn out?"

I let my eyes act as a mirror into my soul as he stares down at me, waiting for my answer.

"Then I'll be set free, my flesh disintegrating into ashes and absorbing back into the earth. We'll all end up there again anyway."

TEN

Astira

If you stare at your reflection long enough, you'll finally see which pieces have been influenced. The parts you meant to control will pull the chains until you accept reality.
-Wrathiala, Goddess of Manipulation

Coming at me from all angles, heart-racing adrenaline puts me both on edge and keeps my head spinning as Liv and I struggle down the dim, stony tunnel.

"Yeah," Liv pants. She takes in a deep breath, thirsty for clean air. "We have to get to the last cell. The trapdoor is hidden in the wall across from it."

"There they are!" Damon bellows. My heart hammers in my chest, the panic I usually push away whirling dangerously around me.

I grab Liv's elbow roughly and force us into another sprint. We're near the last cells already, and I can see the end of the tunnel up ahead. It's taking impossibly long to reach the cell, yet when I'm in a panic, that's always the case with time. I either don't have enough of it, or it's moving too slowly. *We have to make it. I can't do this again. Number 421. Number 422. Number—*

"I see it!" Liv shrieks next to me, right as we hear a garbled yell behind us.

I chance a look back and see Damon's lower leg at an odd angle. He must have fallen over Liv's open cell door, which would be relieving if there weren't more captors clambering their way toward us in the distance. As we skid to a halt next to the last cell, my senses are going haywire. The man in the cell below us makes a tragic hiccuping sound and calls out for help. Damon is still yelling a good fifty feet away, and the shadows of the other captors are growing larger as they round the curve in the tunnel. Liv mutters to herself as she feels along the wall for the trapdoor. It's supposed to lead to another tunnel that's no longer in use, which means we can travel through it to another community surviving underground. *Or, with my luck, another captor.* One of the previous prisoners gave me a heads up about it when they realized they were going to die. They wanted *someone* to know it existed, and I happened to be in the right place at the right time to learn about it. I hope they were telling the fucking truth, or we're about to meet them in the afterworld ourselves.

"Liv, they're getting closer," I rasp.

"I'm doing the best I can," she snaps. "It does no good for you to be on the lookout right now. Come help me find the opening."

I growl, abruptly incapable of coherent speech. Liv continues to search the side of the wall while I take the middle part. We push and prod for what must be an eternity, but in reality, it's only been a minute. I'm close to throwing in the towel and preparing myself to fight the captors off. I will *never* go down without a fight.

"Found it!" Liv clamors.

We throw what's remaining of our body weight against the sliver of an opening. We're suctioned into a secret passageway, but as soon as the door closes again, we're able to stand with more space. It's pitch black, and it takes me a minute to feel along the wall and Liv's body to reorient myself to the dark.

"Where do we go now?" Liv breathes.

The captors are screaming on the other side of the wall like maniacs. I'm tempted to scream with them from all of this fucking stress, yet I don't want to draw attention to where we are hiding. I can't be certain if Damon was in too much pain to process where we went, or if the other captors saw us before we found the door. My fingers inch along the doorway again and as I get closer to where the opening was, I touch the outline of a metal bolt. *Bingo*. I flip it to the opposite side, hoping this means we're locked in here and the captors can't get in.

"I think I locked the door," I whisper. "We can't go back out there, so there's only one way for us to go."

Liv hums. "Okay. Let's keep one hand on the walls and the other laced together."

"Good thinking," I agree. It's hard not to let myself sway. There's been too much blood loss, and the adrenaline rush is fading after its punch of stamina. "We can't let go. No matter what."

"I won't."

We shuffle next to one another until the screaming captors are a rumble in the distance. *Thank fuck*. Who knows which direction this passageway is taking us? I'm grateful to all the gods that we're walking *away* from those vile beings. Left foot, right foot, stop to breathe. Push past spiderwebs that try to cling to us. Liv leads for a second, and then I do it. We're walking corpses at this point, and I'd kill for some water, but we can't stop.

The sooner we get out of here, the sooner we can figure out our next steps. We can wash the blood off and clean our wounds —physical, of course. I don't want to know how long it'll take to heal the emotional ones. There should be food and water and maybe actual clothes. *Anything* will be better than what we've gone through. And I don't care how long it takes us, if we have to crawl until there are new scabs on our boney knees. We're getting the fuck out of here and finding our other friends.

They must still be alive. They *have* to be. We've already had Eira, Athena, and Tryg taken from us. That was an unexpected bloodbath.

Liv, Lyk, Ruse, Jace, and I had been on edge when Athena and Tryg didn't leave Shira's home four years ago. We had taken turns, each of us shivering in the fucking cold, to keep watch on our friends. Shira insisted that Eira needed more time to rest, and she wouldn't even let us take Zaya home. Something felt inexplicably off, and being a mixture of therapists and investigators, we sure as hell weren't leaving until we had answers.

The last straw for me was when I saw a translucent green and gold serpent peeking out behind one of the pine trees. Captivating gold eyes stared right into me, and I nearly jumped right into Jace's arms as I scrambled to move behind him and Ruse. No one else had seen it, but I was as pale as a ghost. This was enough to convince the others to sneak back inside Shira's home to grab our friends and get the fuck out of there.

Ruse crouched low and managed to make his way into Eira's room. His rich brown skin looked sickly under the dim lights of Shira's home, his eyes darting around the hallway in frantic movements. He had signaled for her to stay quiet and gently grasped her hand to lead her back into the hallway toward the rest of us. Zaya weaved in and out of our feet and leaned against Eira's legs. As we tiptoed our way toward where Athena went to find Tryg, my stomach had slowly dropped into a pit of dread. We all had felt it —that nauseating sensation that creeps its way in when something is off.

As soon as we entered the room, it felt like we ventured into a bizarre crime scene. There were broken shards of wood scattered everywhere, and strange, bubbling liquids dripping out of overturned jars. The curtains were nothing more than flimsy, shredded pieces of cloth on the floor. And the beds? Broken and lying at sharp angles with Athena and Tryg split in half in each one. We could recognize both of their faces, but the rest of their bodies were jaggedly sawed in half and were covered in charred holes. Lyk immediately vomited while Liv sobbed into her back. I must have been trembling because Jace threw his arms around me and tugged me into his chest, horror etched in his normally serene face. Ruse had fallen to his knees and was muttering a prayer under his breath before Tryg's body, or at least the pieces of it that still remained.

I should have known at that moment that Eira was no longer the friend we knew. She had barely reacted to seeing her closest friends dead. We thought she went into a state of shock, as any normal person would, but we were so far from the truth. Eira moved stiffly from the room, almost as if she was still getting used to the very action of walking. It was peculiar, but it wasn't something I could give my attention and energy to while processing the stench of death consuming me. None of us knew where Shira was or if she was hurt, too. We could barely speak, let alone form coherent words and critically think about what had happened.

The hours blurred into days, into weeks. Eira distanced herself entirely, and my only contact with her was through Jace. He continuously hounded both her and Morgan—their lead therapist at Heart and Mind Care and essentially, Eira's second mother—to figure out answers to what happened. Eira wouldn't talk about her feelings and immersed herself with work and clients. Morgan was everywhere, doing a million jobs while searching for Shira and organizing a memorial service for Athena and Tryg. We all knew in our hearts that Shira wasn't who she made herself out to be, and even without proof, it was determined she was guilty in all of this. We were all going through the motions of existing, of meeting the bare minimum of being a human, until Eira shook us to our cores.

One minute, I was walking on muddy cobblestones on my way to the memorial service, my boots splashing in puddles from the freezing rain. Next, Liv and Lyk nearly tackled me from either side and yanked me into an alleyway next to the building Morgan picked out for the service. The sisters were dressed in matching plum and coal-black dresses, the only difference being their shoes and hair: Lyk with her bright colors and Liv with her subdued gray and black. Flowers they had brought with them laid in trampled petals at their feet. I expected to see looks of mourning on their gaunt faces. One glance told me they were unsettlingly alarmed.

"What?" I had asked them. "What's going on? Aren't we going inside?"

"No," Lyk whispered. "It's not safe."

My eyebrows furrowed in confusion. Both sisters had a knack for sensing harm and picking up on people's true intentions, but this didn't make sense. What wasn't safe about a memorial service for our best friends?

"Let's talk about this inside," I told them.

Liv had grabbed my elbow and pulled me closer to them. "No, we can't go in there. We both had dreams last night that something horrific was going to happen today. Please trust us. Jace and Ruse should be here any minute, and we'll figure out a new game plan."

I wanted to protest, but I didn't have the chance. Jace came flying around the corner, Ruse hot on his heels. Both slammed into the side of the building with such strength, I was surprised the wood didn't splinter.

"Run!" Ruse screamed. His eyes were so wide, so unnerved, the whites swallowed up his brown irises. "Fucking go!"

Me being me, I peered around the corner of the building, wanting to see what freaked them out this much. I still really wish I hadn't—perhaps I'd be plagued with one less nightmare. I saw Eira—not her real self, considering what she was doing—stalking in our direction. Zaya strutted next to her with blood-soaked fur and spine-chilling black eyes. This version of Eira had the creepiest smile I'd ever seen, something out of a horror film, with a dark *liquid dripping down her chin. Her eyes were a deep black and purple with streaks of red, and with each second her chest heaved another breath of air, that smile stretched impossibly wider. My eyes finally washed down the rest of her body, and I stumbled backward with a shriek.*

Eira. Our friend, Eira. This fucking impostor. This couldn't be our friend. Not as she trailed a path of blood with Morgan's severed head in one of her hands. Morgan's eyes were still open wide with fear, the deep blue matching the frozen chill working its way up my body. I couldn't move and might have been next on Fake Eira's list when Ruse scooped me up in his arms. He sprinted until we caught up with our other friends, occasionally staggering into a building or overflowing dumpster when he checked to see if anyone was behind us.

Jace was up ahead of all of us and motioning for us to follow him into an abandoned building. Ruse never let me go and took us deeper and deeper into the basement. I never once asked where we were or why or what happened. Because what would I have asked? What would my friends have told me? Little did I know that in that moment, such chaos would erupt around the world. It would only be the start of too many questions with zero answers.

"Astira!" Liv cries my name, shaking me out of my spiraling memories.

"Yeah?" I ask more harshly than I mean to. My mood is dampening by the second. I hate being stuck in tight spaces, being trapped like a caged animal.

"Where did you go? I've been calling your name for the past minute with no response. I thought you passed out!"

Swallowing down the surge of guilt that bubbles up, I reach next to me for Liv's hand. I didn't even realize we stopped shuffling in this dark, sooty space and are now slouched against the grimy wall behind us. "I'm sorry," I croak. "I must have spaced out while walking. I was thinking back to the day of Athena and Tryg's memorial."

Liv imperceptibly stiffens at the mention of that day but still laces her fingers with mine. A spider crawls over our hands, and I let it sit there in our misery.

"I think about that day all the time," she whispers.

I rub one of my boney fingers against hers. One of the few unmarked parts of my body that's managed to form calluses and blisters while underground. A reminder I'm not meant to heal. "That was one of the last moments we were all together in the same place."

Liv doesn't answer. She doesn't have to. I know her thoughts are already coiling tightly around her. The day the two of us were captured and she was separated from her sister still haunts her every dream.

"We'll find them," I breathe. "They have to still be out there."

Liv sniffs. Our energy has bottomed out, and I'm surprised she even acknowledges what I'm saying.

"Ruse, Jace, and your sister have to be alive," I urge. "I won't accept any other answer right now."

Lyk, Ruse, and Jace have been the flame on our candles of hope. Neither of us will stop until we've fully escaped, and we find our friends—whether they're whole or not. Liv especially won't stop until she finds her sister. There's a feral energy that crackles around her when anyone has brought the subject up. I know deep within my soft friend is a monster that will be unleashed if anyone has harmed Lyk.

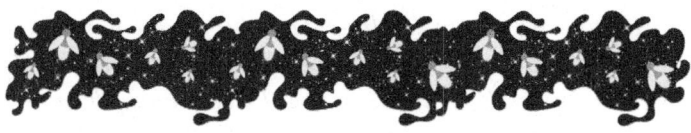

Footsteps surround me. Liv and I are tied to one another with thin, coarse hair. The smell of decay bathes me in its scent, and I

welcome it. I gorge myself on it with the hope it kills me faster, and my spirit can finally be set free. More footsteps shuffle around us. Low murmurs cloud my mind and make me restless. The tone sounds familiar. Too familiar. My skeleton is lifted from the dirty ground and caked mud drifts off each bone like ash. I want to open my eyes to see who is holding my body together, but there are no eyelids to open and close. I don't know where Liv is, if they left her behind. That idea pains me, but maybe it means Liv has already gone to a better place. Wherever the fuck that is.

"Are we too late?" a voice asks.

"No, they're barely holding on, but we can save them. Their spirits are strong," another person responds.

The person holding me runs a large hand through my unwashed hair, getting stuck on some of the knots. I'm not sure how much time passes, only that I'm carried along a bumpy path. There are still no eyelids, but I'm able to see; the sensation is abrupt and jarring. A robed figure is breathing heavily over me, still keeping their arms locked around my body. Each crunch of their steps has me glancing at what we're walking on, and I would vomit if I could. Tiny skulls of children lay in waves under us with various bodies still decomposing in the distance. Am I in Hell? These poor babies. Children don't go to Hell, so then where am I?

We come to a stop, and another robed figure peers down over me. I recognize this person. It's the same robed individual who spoke with Damon. Oh, fuck. No, no, no. Is he here? Who is this woman?

"I'll find you eventually, little star," this new woman coos at me. Long, delicate fingers with flashing jewels and rings slowly move up to the hood. They lower it, and I suck in a deep breath. A person I once trusted peers down at me, her eyes boring into my soul. Her face is decomposing with squirming maggots working their way through a hole in her right cheek. Thick, black liquid oozes down her neck.

"You and your friends can't hide forever," Shira growls, her exposed teeth grinding down into a dark smile.

I let out a bloodcurdling scream.

"Astira!" Someone shakes me. "Astira, it's okay! Don't panic!"

I'm still screaming and struggling to get out of a man's arms wrapped way too tightly around me. He grunts, and I want to show him how good of a fighter I am, but my muscles are now too damn weak.

"P-please, miss," he grumbles. "We were searching the tunnels for any new survivors and came across your bodies. We mean no harm."

"He's okay, Astira," Liv rasps. She's being cradled in another guy's arms. Black, wavy hair falls down to his shoulders, and he has a square jaw with scruff. He's dressed in a long-sleeved shirt and dark pants, and these aren't the mere rags or animal skins that I've been used to seeing. Cloth has been sewn into an actual shirt and loose pants, although not loose enough. I can see every muscle moving as he shifts on his feet and faces Liv a little closer to me, allowing us to see one another.

"It's a good thing we found you," the man holding Liv mumbles. "Another few hours even and you'd be gone. We gave you what water and soft food we had with us, but we really need to get back to our home. You can fully heal there and get checked out by our doctor."

"Doctor?" I whisper. My throat is dry to the point that I can barely swallow.

"Of course, miss," he says. "I don't know which colony you ladies were in, but we've heard horror stories of cults breaking out. We're going to keep walking now, okay? Our leader will be overjoyed to see you."

I huff out a breath. "Leader?"

"Yes. Jace has been searching everywhere for his family and friends. We've finally found two of you."

ELEVEN

Ceira

A soul believes it knows Evil when it barely knows its own self.
-Page 1, Healers of the Light, Volume 1

You don't realize you've dissociated from your current reality until all your senses wake up at the same time. It's akin to floating in the middle of the ocean, and all of a sudden, your body is uncontrollably rushing toward the surface. Invisible hands press against your skull from the inside out, and that first inhale *slams* into you.

Blinking, I take in my surroundings. Nyx, dressed in his usual all dark colors, with a splash of blue today, is speaking to an incredibly huge crow with pale green eyes. Athena makes a growling sound at a still-bandaged Hadwin and throws her hands up in the air. She might have asked me a question. No, it wasn't a question. She was explaining their brief time on Earth.

She's radiant in the dark gray and pink coverings that hug each curve and dip up her hips and torso. Hadwin is puckering his face like he just ate something sour, clearly annoyed. Stefanie and Hauke are looking cozy. He has one arm curled around her waist while she receives updates and reports from a group of healers. One of them is talking animatedly, and judging by the vicious hand motions, I suspect they're imitating Zaya clawing at a *solliqa*. A hurricane of sensations swarms through me as my skin soaks up the heat of the two suns above us. Three separate conversations swirl in too many directions around my ears, and I'm hit with the dreadful odor of a *canielor*.

Ugh, not the best time to come back to reality. We haven't spotted many *canielors* or other gruesome creatures over the past few days. The only ones with even remotely similar destructive *maji* are the poor *solliqas* with the plague of darkness. They're currently tucked away in the healing quarters. It didn't fully click in my deranged brain that we were even near one of these creatures until a swarm of birds collectively dropped an injured one they'd caught nearby in front of us. This one is apparently called a *skelter* and typically wanders in the depths of forests. Pus-filled eyes peer up at me from the ground. It has pointed, leathery ears, a gaping mouth set in a permanent scream, and a humanoid skeletal form, except for its withered tail and whetted claws. Black discharge oozes out of the many punctured holes littering its loose skin. As it opens its mouth slightly wider, dozens of pointed teeth come into view along with a long, slimy black tongue. I fight the urge to tremble and try to remember it used to be a *solliqa*. Nyx said this type of *canielor* was a soul who was trapped in some way, such as a hostage, or never allowed outside. Now, it prefers to roam the different forests in this realm in search of other souls to devour, specifically those who live freely and haven't suffered their specific pain.

Jade swoops down to a lower branch in front of Nyx. At first, I didn't realize Jade was a bird, yet should I be surprised? My first interactions in Majikaero were with featherbrained, moronic *solliqas*. It makes sense that more birds are in my present and likely in my future. My heart pinches briefly and some of the sorrow I've been keeping at bay creeps back in. Daru is at least almost healed, and I'll get to give him and the others a proper hug today. We still have no idea where Daya and Del are, if they're safe or together or have banded with Erika. If a foreign creature has taken them, I don't even know what I'll do. In such a short amount of time, I've started to bond with all of them. I'm *so* wary, and each of these circumstances is becoming more and more cumbersome on my soul. Instinctively, I reach to scoop Zaya up in my arms, yet I'm met with empty air. My heart sinks. One *solliqa* can only take so much, especially one without her pet there for comfort.

And it's been a whole day since that purple substance made an appearance, and I disturbingly took control of Nyx. *One day*. It feels like months have passed, yet, *again*, I can't say I'm shocked at this point. Our unconventional group of *solliqas* has commandeered some of the abandoned Council rooms, meaning we're still in Rioa. Time can get warped here more than in the other regions. With the recent attacks and what are probably portals—of all fucking things, let's throw in magical transportation to an already chaotic world—Nyx thinks the veil between multiple other worlds is even thinner and more distorted. *Fantastic. Excuse me while I manically scream into these said portals.*

"Firefly, you ready to go back to the rooms with Jade?" Nyx asks. He tilts his head to the side, a loose strand of brown hair falling over one of his eyes. One of his hands reaches out to play with the fringed ends of my silver coverings billowing around my thighs, an unnecessarily short dress. It's formfitting and long-sleeved, yet the material is cut in so many places, my body is very much exposed. I mentally make a note to ask Stefanie for more practical coverings.

Nyx doesn't seem to mind, not as his gaze peruses my body like I'm his next meal. I can barely look at him without shame sluicing its way through me. The role of a healer isn't an easy one, but through all of its challenges, it's a responsibility I take seriously. It was unsettling the way another slice of my soul unraveled as I chained Nyx up to the wall. The sensation almost felt forbidden and dangerous and risky, as if the moment I accepted this new part of myself, I wouldn't be able to turn back. The rest of me, especially my fox, battled with it until there was a compromise; I'd still overall heal some of Nyx's core fears, and only a sliver of my darker thoughts would weave themselves in my *maji*. At least this is what I'm telling myself.

Deep down, I think I know the truth of what happened: I'm in denial of a hidden part of me, one that easily took over and is rather explosive and untamable. It's clawing at my skin, desperate to get out. I don't have a name for what it is yet—it's my soul... just *altered*.

A cold sweat trickles down my back. I'm scared to accept the truth. When I had chained Nyx to the wall and my fireflies bled him dry, forcing him to erupt into frames, I *savored* his cries like they were a decadent piece of chocolate melting on my tongue.

When it comes to healing, I know tough love is sometimes necessary, and anything sexual can be quite powerful and help a soul release emotions that otherwise might not budge. I mostly don't understand where the dark thoughts of wanting to chain someone I care for came from. Nyx asked me *why* I chose chains this morning, and I told him I'd been wanting to try something different since he took me to the room of crystals. I said that he needed to burn some of his darkness away to be more present and aware. These weren't exactly lies. How do I put into words the truth when it's nothing but the form of a shadow inside me? It's petrifying to be out of control, and there isn't a word to describe the brutal fear that's churning within me. *What if this fear pushes me further into a cycle of anxiety or stress or debilitating fatigue?* I refuse for this to happen. I need to keep a clear head for whatever Jade will share with us today.

And it certainly doesn't help that a nightmare I first experienced a week ago while I fell into a fitful sleep after rescuing Zaya, has crept into my dreams each night. With the experience of different realms and timelines, I can't be sure if it's a memory from a past life or a premonition. Or is it something in between?

It's always the same. My eyes flash open with a jolt of alarm. I'm lying on my back in a bed of damp leaves, the moisture soaking through my black, lacy dress. Steam swirls in lazy circles around me until it covers my bare feet and exposed legs and arms. I shakily lift a pale hand, the fingertips an icy blue and purple, and unfurl a fist I didn't realize I had clenched against my heart. Hundreds of used matches spill out of my hand onto my dress like shards of bone. They pile up higher and higher until the terror of being buried unleashes itself, and my mouth opens in a silent scream.

A crackling sound hits me first. Then the smells of burning wood, smoking leaves, and blistering flesh overwhelm my senses. I scream out all the madness that's built a home inside my chest. The same one that's been using my ribcage as a home, as a form of shelter from a consuming darkness. My skin flares bright and transforms into thousands of butterflies. Each one has delicate wings made of smoke and flames, and I'm floating up to the tops of the towering trees with them. I'm pulled against my will—my soul is desperately clawing at the soil and scratching along the peeling bark. I don't want to face what I know I'll see: a raging forest fire.

When I'm floating above the sea of fire and smoke, a sob begs to be released. For all I see are miles of burning trees without a single soul in sight. It's not me facing what I've done. It's me being swallowed by the devastation of who I've become.

As I coast along the treetops, having surrendered to the force that wants to drag me through the forest, a voice tickles the back of my ear. I turn onto my back, and the breath catches in my throat the moment I lock eyes with her. *I'd know that charming timbre anywhere. I open my mouth, and she slams her hand around it, suffocating me with smoke. I thrash and buck to get out of her hold, and she leans her face closer to mine.*

"Run, Eira," Kota, one of my sisters on Earth who disappeared, whispers. Her face warps into anger and melts into the grim expression of my mother. "Run!"

"Sweetheart?"

I gasp and struggle to take a breath. Cracking open my eyes, the image of Nyx against the cloudless sky sways above me. *Did I fall asleep?* Nyx's eyes gaze down at me, dark orbs tinted with misery. One hand cups my cheek, and the other is on his sheathed dagger with billowing shadows pulsating down his leg.

We haven't spoken about that fancy, pointy death-stick yet, but now I'm even more curious about it. Why does he carry it around with him when he has powerful *maji*? More so, why am I drawn to it?

"Why am I on the ground?" I clear my throat, hating how raspy I sound right now.

Nyx arches an eyebrow, and Athena pops her head over my forehead.

"The *canielor* made eye contact with you, and after hissing garbled words, you immediately passed out," Nyx grumbles. His eyes keep searching mine, as if they'll find an answer there. The only truth I know is that I'm drowning in flames in one reality or the next, and nothing can stop the fire from taking over.

Athena scans my face and glances at something behind her. "Yeah, that's probably what happened. She also could have been fed up with Hadwin's complaining. And gods know he smells just as bad as one of those creatures."

An angry huff and a growling sound comes from behind Nyx. "I'm *not* complaining. Some of us are still physically healing, in case you didn't notice. And don't you dare compare me to that hideous bag of traumatized shit."

"It's not my fault you haven't bathed."

Hadwin's arm pushes past Nyx's shoulder, and if Athena wasn't so nimble, he would have grabbed her by the neck. I snort at the expression she's giving him, one full of mirth and judgment. My best friend lies right next to me on the partially razed white grass and tangles her fingers with my own. I manage to turn my head to face her, and she leans in with a glint in her dark green eyes.

"Some souls are too persnickety for their own good," she whispers. "It's best if we put him out of his misery."

A giggle bubbles past my lips, and I choke on a deeper laugh when Hadwin's eyes bulge in vexation.

"See, Nyxie?" Athena singsongs. "Our little fox is good to go. She's ready to be swept off her feet and taken to the unconquerable Council rooms." She glances back at me and lowers her voice slightly. "I hope you're okay enough to sense my heavy sarcasm. Those monsters did some serious damage, and let's be real, we're staying in one-star rooms right now."

On the outside, I'm watching the exchange of this conversation with a slight smile plastered on my overtired face. Internally, I'm screaming that my bestie gave Nyx a nickname.

"The rooms are just fine," Nyx huffs, unfazed by his new name. "Unlike Eira. You can't brush off what happened."

Athena turns those sharp green eyes on my *almaove*. "Who said I was? Maybe I know a better time and place to have this kind of conversation."

Nyx drags a hand over his face. Sighing, he glances up at the pastel-colored sky and mutters under his breath. By the way Athena narrows her eyes at him and Stefanie slinks a little closer to us, it can't be good.

"I'm *scared*, okay?" Nyx snaps. "I don't understand where Eira keeps mentally going or why she had that reaction to a restrained *canielor*. I'm terrified of who will discover my queen and her healing light. What if they can manipulate her? What if this creature already did? I can't let them steal her away and shred her soul again."

"*We* won't," Athena says, annoyance simmering under the surface. "You might be her *almaove*, but I'm the one who's grown up with her. She's the closest thing I have to a sister. None of us who love Eira will let that kind of harm come her way again. And you think you're the only one horrified, almost paralyzed with fear?" Athena scoffs. "Get a grip. And save that rage for someone who cares. Our focus should be getting back to the Council rooms, making sure Eira is relatively functioning, and hearing what Jade has come to share."

I should side with Nyx, but, well, she *is* right. Except for the part about not letting that kind of harm come my way again. New suffering might have already dug its claws into me, and maybe a sick part of me welcomed the pain.

Athena sits up on her elbows and sends a scorching glare at Nyx and Hadwin. She's totally going to take on both of them, and while the idea is delightful to imagine, I doubt it'd end well for any of us. She might just be learning how to use her *maji*, but my friend is fucking fierce. Combining that and her wild magic could mean total destruction of our little group here. I push myself up to a seated position with a low groan. Unexpected weakness wraps around my muscles and begs me to lie back down. *Not today, fatigue. I've got annoyingly protective and emotional friends to calm down. And those pesky, heightened feelings won't be soothed on their own.*

"Okay, okay, breathe for a second," I rasp. They all pause to look at me, and Stefanie peeks over Nyx's other shoulder. She falls to her knees next to me, her red hair cascading in the slight breeze like a warm blanket. Stefanie is wearing a flowy crimson top that crisscrosses along her slender back and waist. Tight glittering white pants cover her legs and blend in with the fluffy white grass. Hauke, dressed in aubergine and scarlet coverings, nods at the departing healers and stands next to Nyx. His biceps bulge as he crosses his arms, and his gaze flicks between Stefanie, Athena, and me on the grass. Jade swoops in to sit on Hauke's shoulder, pinning me with her celadon stare.

Athena bumps my shoulder with her own. "Sorry, foxy

dear," she mumbles. "I suppose we all respond in our own ways when frightened."

Hadwin scowls at her. "You didn't have to bring my cleanliness into it."

"You best get used to that, Had," Stefanie chirps. She scoots closer and wraps an arm around my shoulders, her scent reminding me of a warm drink and cinnamon on a cold day. "You won't be able to tame this one. I'd accept it, or you can check your body odor a little more. How well we take care of ourselves says a lot about our headspace, you know." Stefanie turns her focus on Athena. "Maybe this is his call for help."

"Or it could be part of his mating ritual," Hauke chimes in with a smirk, his orange and yellow eyes dancing with mischief. His purple hair flows freely around his face with the wind. With the relaxed posture he takes, one would never expect he's on his way to discuss the attack on Rioa.

My smile grows wider as Nyx barks out a laugh and Hadwin's entire body tenses in agitation.

Stefanie howls with laughter, loudly enough that the other crows by the *canielor* ruffle their dark feathers, each tinted with a different color that glimmers under the suns. "That's the secret to his heart, Athena. You simply need to entice him with some soap and a bathtub."

Athena rolls her eyes, but she can't hide her smile from me. "He's got a lot of work to do if he wants me to touch *his* body."

Hauke's smile turns devilish. "He might be into that. He's secretly waiting for you to take control and order him to beg and crawl."

"Enough!" Hadwin roars. The usual smirk or mask of indifference he has plastered to his tawny face is long gone by now, and it won't be returning anytime soon. He stiffly turns to Jade, and I don't miss the way her bird form shakes with a chortle. "You brought this *canielor* here and wanted to meet with us. We're walking the rest of the way to the Council rooms. *Now.*"

Jade fluffs out her feathers, the tips tinged with gold, before soaring into the sky. The other crows, each with a different set of colorful eyes that sparkle under the suns, gingerly lift the now unconscious *canielor*. They follow behind Hadwin as he stomps his way along the gravel path leading from the healing quarters up to the Council building. The cobblestones originally on the path have been demolished and lie in scattered, tiny stones now. *At least we don't have far to walk.* Hauke leans down to help Stefanie stand up, and Athena leaps to a standing position. Both she and Nyx pull me up to stand in between them, and we begin our short walk up the hill toward the entrance of Eliina's quarters.

Chunks of the golden multistory building are missing or destroyed from the unidentifiable monsters at the festival. Some of the different living quarters are still standing with minimal damage, or a few windows are smashed in. I don't know which section belongs to which Council member, and I'm positive whoever lives here won't be too happy to find their rooms and belongings gone. Even some of the trees that normally stand as tall as the building itself have been tragically crushed into splinters of bark. I can hear their uneven breathing, the way their souls are barely holding onto this realm. It makes me sick with the realization that *every single thing* in Majikaero has a soul that can be shattered.

"Do you think we'll get to explore the rest of Rioa?" Athena whispers to me.

I frown. It's relieving to hear my best friend speaking again, but some of the questions she's asking me have my mood spiraling downward. "If it's anything similar to this Council building, then I'm afraid there's nothing left to see. I was hoping to explore the city. It's more of an empty shell, a carcass that's been feasted on."

As if to accentuate my point, a group of *solliqas* trudges out from the entrance of the Council building. Nyx helped organize where souls could stay after their homes were ruined, especially those who haven't found their soul families or don't have *solliqas* in other regions they can go to. A few of them are now leading a few of the *alklen* we rode in on to a nearby pasture. They wanted to help in some way this past week and not knowing what else to do. The *drekstri* certainly wouldn't let the hordes of grieving *solliqas* near them, especially Ambra, with her knack for biting at those she doesn't know. All of them are wan or ashen in some way or another, with lackluster features and dull coverings. Any *maji* that overflowed the cobbled streets of the market and twirled with the living nature of the forest has been washed out by fear from being violently attacked in your own home. So, while the healers, Nyx, and I have done what we could to assuage the panic and suffering of others this past week, that doesn't mean the majority of *solliqas* who live in Rioa have been assured. There are physical and emotional reminders of the attack everywhere they turn, and for all of us, this is only the beginning.

"I'm sure we could find something to breathe life into," Athena says while nudging my side.

I smile at her, grateful she thinks we can find more life in this city we're still stuck in yet haven't been able to check out. We've been between the Council building, the healing quarters, and some of the forest on the night of the festival. Only I've been fortunate to visit the Crystal Trance, which very well could have been destroyed in the chaos.

Another heartstring is pulled. *Who was at the Crystal Trance the night of the festival? What happened to Xylia and the other tree-shifters?*

Our small group approaches an archway that now, thanks to one of those gruesome monsters slamming the ceiling to pieces, opens up to the vast sky. The heat of the two suns engulfs us as they warm the chilled stony pillars and walls. Jade flaps her black wings, traveling through the exposed ceiling into another room. I follow the direction she flies and try to make sense of where we're going. My understanding of time breaks down more each hour that I'm here. It's as if I've been here for years, yet it's been mere weeks.

"You're doing it again," Nyx murmurs.

"Doing what?" I scrunch my nose.

"Trying to use logic to understand time and this realm. You need to let yourself exist. Relax."

My eyes narrow at being told to relax, and I fight the urge to push him down the slanted stairway to our left.

"I know how to clear your mind," Athena whispers. The playfulness in her tone almost convinces me she's feeling better. *Almost.*

She loops her arm with mine and drags me away from Nyx and back a few steps toward Stefanie. Hauke gives us a questioning look, but Athena leaves no time for answers. She loops her other arm with Stefanie's and pushes us in the opposite direction of the crows and *misns*. Giggling softly, Stefanie tucks a lock of red hair behind an ear, and I notice she's wearing white studs that glimmer under the sunlight.

"Alright, spill the goods," Athena orders.

"Yeah, where'd you get *these* beauties?" I ask while touching one of the sparkling studs. My focus homes in on the shiny metal holding the white stones. *I adore shiny, pretty things.*

Stefanie laughs. "Eira, your face! You're like a thrilled little raccoon."

"What? They're lovely!" I say, still mesmerized by her earrings.

Athena snorts. "And Eira's brain gets a little distracted by glittering objects, among other things."

My brain tends to work differently. It hasn't stopped me from reaching my goals, though. I might take a slightly different route to get there. A shinier, prettier one.

"You can ask Hauke where he got them," Stefanie giggles.

"He was just in Sunnadyn, so I'm guessing he gave some *maji* for them at one of the many markets along the coastline."

Athena grins like a cat and dives in at the opportunity. "Hauke, eh? Tell us more."

Stefanie blushes so red it almost matches her hair.

"Oh, leave her be," I mutter and swat at Athena's arm. "They're together in some way. It's not really any of our business."

"It could be," Athena quips. "We're still new to this realm, little fox. I want to make *everything* my business. If Majikaero is going to keep us on our toes, then we better prepare ourselves as best we can, and that includes understanding the relationships here."

Muttering under my breath, I roll my eyes. "Yeah, yeah, alright."

Athena faces Stefanie. "So?"

"Okay, fine, he's one of my soul mates," she gushes. Stefanie looks incredibly carefree in this moment—she's absolutely stunning. "We realized we were *almaoves* years ago. Some *solliqas* have one main bond, but most of us have many souls we're connected to. The bonds are just stronger or weaker, depending on the relationship. Hauke and I... we'll always be each other's first, strongest connection. But it doesn't mean we're not open to finding our other soul mates in this world."

"See?" Athena jabs a slender finger at me. "Now we know how they're connected and that they might have other soul connections. Which means you and I have other bonds, too."

"We'll address those bonds as they come," Nyx grumbles behind her. Athena jumps slightly before flicking her long, braided hair in his face.

"My friend can be with whomever she wants, Nyx," Athena snaps at him.

It's now Stefanie's turn to loop an arm with Athena and pull her away before she starts more trouble. Good thing, too, because the mixture of Nyx and Athena is energy drenched in gasoline, waiting to explode around me.

"I just don't want to share," Nyx murmurs, shame lacing through his words.

He throws an arm around my shoulders, and as I lean into him, that wandering hand travels down my back until it's cupping part of my ass. Each day with him, he gets a little more handsy, claiming any part of me that he can when we're near others.

"You worried a *solliqa* will steal me away?" I ask.

Nyx flutters his fingers in front of us, little smoking flames dancing up and around us.

"With the way our connection inches closer and closer to detonation? No. I don't think any other soul can match your flames the way I can."

He pauses for a few seconds, staring down at me seriously. "But that doesn't mean you won't have another *almaove* out there for you. And I'd never deny you that—you'd have us all bowing down to you, firefly. Right now, I don't know how I'll ever bring myself to share you with anyone else."

I lean up on my tiptoes and peck his lips. His hand shoots up to hold my chin, deepening the kiss. When he breaks away, giving me a chance to catch my breath, he smirks. I can see the uncertainty in his eyes, though.

"If that happens," I say in between another kiss. "We'll just have to learn how to play nice with others, won't we?"

Nyx chews on the inside of his cheek. A devilish glint lights up his dark eyes.

"I can think of a few ways to *play* with you, sweetheart," he murmurs. "As long as you remember who that sweet pussy belonged to first, yeah?"

My eyes widen at his dirty words. I smack his arm, and he chuckles, pulling me with him as we follow the rest of the group.

We've managed to wind our way through the twists and

turns of the Council building and have reached one of the untouched living room areas. Black stones with gold streaks cover the walls, and multicolored woven rugs decorate the polished floor. Plush blue and white chairs and floor cushions are placed in a circular shape in the middle of the room, along with two large sofas. Two oval windows face what looks to be a courtyard and garden, and a large marble fireplace is on the opposite wall. There are a few shelves of dusty books. I don't think the room has been touched in quite a long time. It leaves me wondering what the other parts of this building store that are deemed important enough to destroy.

Nyx folds me into his arms. The crows carrying the *skelter* unceremoniously dump its body onto the ground by the hearth. One of the birds with golden eyes stares at me for a moment before flying up and out of the room. Nyx squeezes tighter when I flinch at the way the creature's head cracks against the hard floor. Jade swoops into the room and perches on top of the nearest couch. She blinks at us and says, "Some of the rooms are barely recognizable. Nova is going to be furious when she returns."

"Then let it be a warning to the Council that they're not as untouchable as they think they are," Nyx snarls. He turns his attention back to me. "Do you remember the different Council members?"

I can tell he feels guilty for not giving me all the information earlier, but honestly, I wouldn't have been able to comprehend everything at once. Still, it's endearing how often he's quizzing me now.

"I think so," I murmur while scrunching up my nose in concentration. "There's Eliina for the healers. Namid for the soul readers. Nova for realm travel and space. There are the Council members for the elemental magic, right? Haliean for water, Enya for fire, Rakiana for air, Weke for earth, and Lesak for spirit. I can't remember the names of those representing moon and sun *maji*. Um... there's also Waneta for the shifters. I'm forgetting who represents the manipulators."

"So smart," Nyx affectionately taps my nose. "That's okay. We'll review the last few later and where everyone descends from."

"That's the main reason I'm here," Jade chimes in. "I need to inform you where each of the Council members have fled to and why. And we've made a rather unfortunate discovery about the *canielors*, which is why we brought this one with us." She sweeps her gaze around the room at each of us for a minute with that eerie stare. "Except Eliina. I couldn't find her."

"Speaking of her," Hauke interrupts. "We should check on the few traitors that have been connected to Eliina, whom we locked up in the dungeons. They're almost directly below this room, and it won't take long. I want to ask a few questions before we settle in for everything you have to share, Jade. Respectfully."

She bows her head in agreement and shifts her focus to Nyx. "I'm with Hauke on this one," Nyx says. "Jade, you and your crows can stay here with the *skelter*. Hauke, Stefanie, Hadwin, Athena, Eira, and I can take a look at the *solliqas* in the dungeons and will be back soon."

"Actually, I'll stay up here with Jade and the others," Stefanie says with a shudder. "Or I might go check on Ambra and the other *drekstri*, since they haven't received nearly enough attention this past week. I've been in those dungeons too much recently. I need to monitor how much energy is going toward such a vile place if I want to keep healing more souls."

Hauke kisses her cheek and nods his head toward the doorway for the rest of us to follow his lead. Watching him take control and act as a leader is jarring for me. It clashes with his initially sinful smile and flirtatious behaviors when I first met him with the healers. Except, he still very much acts this way toward Stefanie, so maybe he was hiding the authoritative side of himself underneath all that muscle. Nyx grabs my hand and sends a burst of shadow fireflies dancing along my wrist, immediately erasing any thoughts of Hauke. Hadwin and Athena follow closely behind us.

"If I suggested we visit the dungeons first, you'd be attacking me for it," Hadwin mutters.

"Well, Hauke isn't a condescending asshole," Athena whispers back.

"What the fuck did I do?" Hadwin grinds his teeth loud enough that even I can hear it.

"It's hard to say. It's more about everything you *don't* do. Like refusing to take off that detached mask of yours." I can tell by Athena's breathing that she's close to losing it. *Yeah, definitely not feeling better yet.*

"All the spirits in Cudhellen! You don't know what the fuck you're talking about. You're fucking nuts."

"If you think this is crazy, just wait until I finally snap that mask off myself," Athena snarls.

"Ooookay, we have arrived," Hauke says a little too loudly. Hadwin breathes out a loud sigh, and Athena shoulders her way in between Nyx and me, effectively sending the shadow fireflies sputtering everywhere. Shivering, I lean closer to my best friend and take in the warmth of her rage. My usual flames are nowhere to be found, not since I woke up outside this building from another nightmare.

"Alright," Hauke starts. "Eira and Athena, I'm not sure you know what I do. I work with Eliina's main team of healers, which is a neutral group of *solliqas*, wishing to serve every soul in this realm. Not only the ones the Council has deemed 'safe.' I also work as an envoy between this group and other healers in the different regions, such as Sunnadyn and Wyndera, and support in forming alliances between each region."

"Not all of them are healers, though," Nyx adds.

Hauke nods his head thoughtfully. "True. Some are *solliqas* in royalty who wish to defy the Council's distorted rules. But for right now, what's important to know is that I caught a few new suspicious *solliqas* along the outskirts of Rioa."

"What makes them so suspicious?" Athena asks.

Shrugging, Hauke flicks his head in the direction of a few locked cells. "You'll see. Half their forms are floating shadows and darkness. You don't see that often, not unless they're close to turning into a *canielor*."

I hum in understanding and try to put on my bravest face. A flicker of blue flame twirls in my chest, and my fox stretches her crystalized paws deep within me.

"I want to see Tryg first," I say, startling even myself.

Nyx looks at me incredulously. "Are you positive, firefly? He nearly killed you a week ago."

Swallowing, I force myself to nod. "I know," I whisper. "But he's locked up now, right?"

Hauke stares at me before confirming this is true, and the four of them go still around me. Last week was the first time my flames twisted into a red so brutally angry, it took over my mind. Seeing Tryg makes all of us uncomfortable in one way or another. I can't bring myself to turn my back on a friend, though, even if he's a lost and faraway one right now.

Sensing my resolve, Athena squeezes my hand. "Let's do it," she murmurs. "It won't take long, and maybe he'll have a different reaction after spending some time alone with his thoughts. He could have needed time to calm down and let the shadows dissolve."

Hadwin and Nyx glance at each other and snicker. "His shadows won't simply *dissolve*," Hadwin grunts. "They're a part of him as much as he's a part of them. But let's get this shit over with."

The sound of all our feet is thunderous against the uncanny silence of the dungeons. There's a dripping sound in the distance, and I can't decipher if it's water or blood. Other manipulators and soul readers have been down here over the week to torture any questionable *solliqas* and Tryg. I thought I'd hear moans of pain, perhaps of regret, but all we hear are our echoing steps and the insufferable silence.

"You're not alone," Athena murmurs to me. "We can both be scared of what Tryg has become. Together. We'll be stronger together."

I release a sharp breath and glance at my best friend. "Stronger together."

We finally approach his cell, and I exhale roughly in anticipation of seeing my darkened friend once again.

"Shit," Hauke murmurs. He spreads his arms before us in such a swift motion, it reminds me of his massive wings. "His door is slightly open," he whispers.

"No fucking way," Nyx growls. He pushes past Hauke's outstretched arm and thrusts the door open. I suck in a jagged breath. I hadn't seen how they locked Tryg up before, but *this* I wasn't expecting. There are at least a hundred chains against the wall, and the room itself is much smaller than the other cells down here. *Oh, gods, have mercy on him. This would have driven him to madness.* Sure enough, Tryg is not in this claustrophobic space. I nearly scream when I see who has one arm chained to the wall, though.

"Is this some kind of sick joke?" Hauke seethes before laughing at the soul locked up. "Then you chose the wrong *solliqa* to chase. There's no way you could have beat her, not when you know what she is behind that facade."

Hadwin chuckles darkly. "The day is getting more and more interesting."

"Eliina?!" Athena gasps.

My brain empties out as I stare into Eliina's swirling green and black eyes. One of her hands is chained to the wall Tryg was pinned to, and the expression on her wearied face relaxes into one of relief. She sags slightly against the wall, her stained robes and matted hair sticking along the stones, and lets out a weak laugh.

"You've finally come," she croaks. Her voice is sandpaper against my ears. "I have much to share with you, and now I finally can. Please take me to the library. It's the only safe space to speak of such horrors."

TWELVE

Athena

*When you rip your own roots out of the ground,
you might be surprised where you decide to go.
-Abarrane, God of Earth*

Horror after horror is piling up on top of each other, and if it wasn't for having Eira next to me, I'd walk out of this cell without another thought. Hadwin's sour attitude has been buzzing around me like an annoying bug I can't seem to kill. He then vacillates between ignoring me and literally being one step behind me at any given moment. After he followed me out of the healing quarters yesterday—which was idiotic considering he's still recovering—he felt the need to rudely comment on anything and everything. The topics included the length of my hair, my lack of shoes, the amount of exposed skin, and of all things, the specific foods I was scavenging up to eat.

If I point out his harsh switch in moods and that I don't appreciate being talked down to, he plays it off as if *I'm* the one acting crazy and it's all in my head. I'm close to shoving one of his sheathed daggers into his brain and showing him what'll be inside *his* head if he doesn't make up his fucking mind. Leave me alone or don't. I don't care anymore. At least that's what I tell myself, but he needs to stop being an infuriating prick.

And maybe Hadwin wouldn't be so insufferable if he'd *go back to the healing quarters*. He's more stubborn than I am, and that's saying something. Some of his wrappings have shifted down his chest. I keep catching glimpses of the stab wound in his chest, the scar tissue as puffy and irritated as I am.

Now I'm stuck in these grimy dungeons with him. I *hate* it down here. The scent of damp soil calls to my magic, but I'm unable to reach it. I'm trapped in a box made of rough stones, metal doors, blood-stained torture devices, and the energy of *solliqas* who've given in to their darkness. There are no windows —which is enough to drive me insane—and the few orbs of light floating near the low rocky ceilings are muted. The temperature is cold enough to bite at my skin, sending shivers and goosebumps down my arms and legs. My sparkling charcoal and rose-colored covering wraps around my shoulders, torso, and thighs in a pattern that leaves most of my chest, back, arms, and legs free to move as I please.

Down here, though, I'm *freezing*. It's exactly how I remember it from a week ago. With how much shit has happened, the one week has drawn on forever, as if an entire year has gone by.

I only came because I knew Tryg was down here, and there's no way I could leave Eira alone to see him. Nope. Not in a million years is she being left alone with him again. He might be afraid and encased in his suffering, but I've worked with enough clients to know the difference between battling one's pain and succumbing to it. Tryg made his decision, and until he has the courage to walk the path back to his light, he won't be receiving any trust from me. He has to earn that shit.

It's ridiculous. I worked myself up to go down here with Eira, but the bastard I called my friend isn't even here. We're all blindsided by seeing Eliina chained in his cell. Hauke hasn't even talked to the other *solliqas* he came down here for in the first place. *I'm over all of these freaks.* Hauke can deal with Eliina. Nyx can deal with Hadwin and convince him to travel back to Earth—*alone*. *I'll take Eira and find one of those spooky portals. Okay, Stefanie can come with us... and Zaya... so maybe a lot of souls can travel with us away from this fucked up realm. Just not Hadwin.* And *definitely* not Eliina after disappearing on us and ending up in Tryg's cell, of all places. *Too suspicious, Eliina. I don't care if you're a healer—I learned long ago that the ones we're supposed to trust the most are the ones with the power to scar you beyond repair.*

"Is no one going to release me?" Eliina whispers. I want to find an ounce of compassion, but it turns out Hadwin has the power to vacuum any empathy out of my soul. *Such a nuisance.*

Eira places a shaky hand on Nyx's arm after nervously weaving her long hair into a braid over her shoulder. I'm waiting for her fire to make an appearance. I think we all are. Yet the past few days have taken too much of a toll on her mind, body, and soul. Nyx growls, the sound low and menacing in the back of his throat. He takes half a step and places his body partly in front of Eira. The action is more symbolic of his willingness to protect her than anything. I'm stunned when Hadwin does the same thing with me while he tucks that mysterious serpent pendant back under his gray covering. *Who does he think he is? And who said I need protection?*

"You must understand how this might look," Hauke grinds out. "You know how much I admire you and yearn to follow in your footsteps, but the Grand Healer I normally emulate is nowhere to be seen right now. Stefanie shared that you told everyone you'd be somewhere different on the day of the festival. Then, you vanish without a trace for the past week while chaos reigned in Rioa, especially with the Council members disappearing to the other regions and abandoning those living here.

You left the healers to take care of the poor souls who were attacked that night. Tryg was one of our prime suspects, and now he's *gone*, with you standing here in his place. And you expect us to immediately release you?"

Eliina's frown deepens more and more as Hauke speaks. She appears to be utterly defeated, but honestly, what does she expect? She's smarter than this. She knows what she's doing, and I refuse to subject Eira, myself, or anyone else to more bullshit than necessary right now. Heaving a sigh, I push myself around Hadwin's massive tattooed arm and step right next to Nyx. He looks surprised. *Give me a break.* Females, or *fims* here, are just as strong as these assholes, and I can't wait to prove I'm right. Starting now.

"We don't have time for this," I snap at Hauke. Turning to face Eliina, I focus on leveling out my breath and inhaling the sweet smell of the earth. It's hiding under this dungeon, but with each exhale, its energy quivers at my fingertips. I imagine some of the healers, like Alyosha and Ebele, standing next to me and directing how to allow the earth *maji* into my skin and muscles and bones. An uncertain amount of time passes, and that's fine with me. I don't care right now. My focus is on breathing, in and out, out and in. I do this until the magic curls around my very soul, and when I look Eliina in the eyes, she inhales sharply. Wonder crosses her face, and I know there's a green light coating the outline of my body. I breathe in and reach a hand out toward Eliina's chains. With a flick of my wrist, I exhale and verdant vines slip out of my fingers, slowly winding around her wrist and locked chains.

"Here's the deal," I breathe out. "We don't have time to question you or stay trapped in this dungeon together. We need to get upstairs to Jade and the others. Jade holds vital information, and I'm not missing it because of you. I'm going to snap these chains off you, but you're going to be kept close to our group."

"But she has the same earth *maji* as you," Eira whispers to me.

"We might both have magic of the earth, but that doesn't mean our powers are the same," I murmur back. With an acute slash of my hand, the vines break through the chains holding Eliina down. Resentment swells inside me at the fact that even Eira thinks Eliina could be stronger than me. I refuse to accept that. I clench my hand into a tight fist, and the vines dig into Eliina's skin without warning. She cries out, not realizing I have another plan up my sleeve.

"Eira, can you lend me some of your fire?" I ask quietly. I don't want anyone to hear the subtle tone of vulnerability at what I'm about to do.

I expect some hesitation. Eira has been through so much—*too much*—and her skin is even starting to appear more transparent and worn out. Instead, she places that same shaky hand on my upper arm and gives a little squeeze. *Best friends, soul sisters, a soul bond through and through.* Spurts of blue flames travel down my arm and swirl around the vines still flowing out of my fingertips. The combination of her fire *maji* with my earth *maji* sears into Eliina and forms a chain of black flowers and golden-green vines lit up in blue flames. As the fire burns the petals, new colors appear in a dazzling light. They attach to both Eira and me, making it even harder for Eliina to escape.

"Fucking gods, your arms!" Hauke whispers.

The image of our newly formed, intricate chains wraps around both Eira's upper left arm and my upper right arm. A spark of pain ignites before the chain melts into our skins, replacing some of the dark tattoos I kept from while on Earth. I peek over at Eira, and despite our current circumstances, her face is lit up with a beautiful smile. We'd learned about this, how when the soul mate bond snaps fully in place, each *solliqa* receives a matching symbol or tattoo to represent their connection. Our design is *perfect* for us. There's the lush green of nature with the darkness and beauty of despair, but with our light, we can burn the true petal colors brighter.

I smirk at Eliina's surprised expression and the way the *misns* are gaping at Eira and I. *Don't underestimate either of us, you fools. I'm a fast learner and won't take no for an answer.* I also can't wait around too much longer before figuring out what the hell is happening on Earth right now. Eliina will *not* get in the way of us saving our friends from home. Mine and Eira's soul bond solidifying only urges me onward, and I loop an arm with my friend's.

"Look at our soul bond markings!" Eira laughs.

We both stare at each other, and I can physically feel the love and gratitude pouring from her soul into mine. Fear briefly grips me when I realize she might see through my mask. If Eira does, she gives no indication that she's seen anything. She only sends gentle flames through our connection, the warmth of them similar to the contentment of *home*. I grin and give her a quick side hug before turning to face the others. Not even Hadwin looks grumpy for once, and Nyx's face is a mixture of awe and worry.

"Don't fret, Nyxie," I coo. "You'll get your soul bond marking soon. Just don't underestimate the power of soul sisters next time." I wink and hook my arm with Eira's. "Now let's drag this dubious *solliqa* back to the others. We've got a meeting with Jade, and if we're bringing Eliina along for the ride, then I think we should gather the rest of our group. Hauke, think they can join us?"

I'm amazed to see him give a deep nod of respect. "The healers told Stefanie and me this morning that the rest of our group is rested enough to leave the healing quarters. I'll go get them, if they aren't in the Council rooms already, and we can begin."

The pungent smell of the *canielor*, or I guess *skelter*, harasses my senses as the six of us step back into the living area. It's a mixture of disease, decay, and a sour, moldy smell that none of us should be subjected to. *Hm... except Hadwin.* Maybe it'll disgust him enough to break through that tough mask he has in place. He brusquely knocks into my shoulder on his way toward the healers and the rest of our group that's arrived. *Jerk.* I'm relieved to see the others are here, though, even Ulf. In my short time in Majikaero, we've all quickly developed an unlikely union.

All of us have been brought together by Eira in one way or another. She's the blazing sun, and the rest of us are planets and moons orbiting around her. Each soul is pulled into the safety of her healing gravity, which almost makes me laugh. I wonder who'll be the first one to get burned by my friend's flames. *Will she spare any of the* solliqas *with the plague?*

As I watch Eira bound toward one of the lavish couches and floor pillows where everyone is settled, my eyes catch on different items across the room. There's an entrancing piece of artwork hanging above the fireplace, and consequently, tied up *canielor*. It's beautiful enough to distract me from the vile monster, and it's oddly familiar. A woman with swirling purple eyes and smooth antlers growing out of her head is lying in a field of different colored grasses. The longer I stare at it, the more her eyes pulsate and call out to me.

I manage to drag my gaze to our companions. Ivar and Odin are lounging on a few of the floor cushions, each still wearing bandages around their wounds and dark, loose coverings. They're conversing in low voices with Nyx, who's crouched down in front of them and is firing question after question at the poor souls.

A few feet away, Fraya is sitting alone on one of the couches in beige coverings that wrap along her whole body. Her brown hair has lost its shine and is cut in a shorter bob. She's playing with a few loose threads on one of the pillows, not paying attention to anyone. Past her, Ulf is leaning against the far wall while talking to Hadwin, their tones harsh yet quiet. Ulf is wearing all black, as usual, and the patches of burned fur along his body are now bulging scars. I'm still irritated that Hadwin didn't stay with him and the others to get more healing services, but if he wants to act like a lunatic, fine by me.

I suppress the urge to walk toward them. I'm not trying to damage more brain cells by speaking with either of them, but I'd like to admire the impressive garden outside the window they're standing in front of. I'm drawn to the entangled plants and flowers and the way the orange and blue light from the suns trickles over them, as if they're pouring fresh *maji* into the ground to help them grow. It's a miracle that these plants were deemed crucial enough to protect under Eliina's spell. My magic tingles in my chest, and against my better judgment, I start to walk in that direction.

Except my attention snags on Eira and Daru, a few of the chairs to my right. He doesn't have the same vacant, empty stare as everyone else. Daru's green eyes glimmer with joy while Eira points to the different wounds still physically healing along his neck. It almost makes me gag just thinking about how close he was to losing his head. Eira is sitting across from him and sending spurts of blue flames into the different lesions, and he doesn't even flinch. Instead, Daru is smiling and leans slightly into Eira's hands. Squinting my eyes, I pivot and march my glorious butt over toward them, ready to pounce on this interaction.

"You're looking comfortable," I chirp. My arms instinctively cross in front of me, and my hip cocks out to the side. I'm in full accusatory stance and ready to dish the sass. I keep a critical scowl on my face, even though I'm full of wicked delight knowing I'm about to make my best friend flustered. And I can't wait to see if I ruffle Daru's feathers while I'm at it.

Eira's cheeks flush a deep pink, and she shoots Daru a questioning look. Her eyes ping back to me, now glowing a bright white, blue, and silver before flashing to the gold eyes of her fox. She squirms at the insinuation she's doing something offensive, and I can taste her panic through our tattoo. *Interesting. I wonder what she will feel from me.*

"I am, obviously," Daru remarks. His blond hair has been cut, with the sides shaved again and a few longer strands hanging in front of his face. He's quite at peace sitting next to Eira—there's not a hint of ruffled feathers. *Disappointing.* "I have my stunning queen sending extra healing surges into my neck." He grasps one of Eira's wrists that still has blue flames lapping against her skin and places it gently across his lips. Daru's near-death experience has certainly made him more plucky. I won't be so easily discouraged and *can't wait* to find out what provokes him and all the others. "Who wouldn't be this comfortable with such tender care?"

"Certainly not me," Nyx barks from across the room. I'm surprised that he hasn't physically moved in front of Eira or instigated a fight. It's as if I'm observing a beast on edge yet tamed enough to think before lashing out. *Eira must have done a number on him last night if she helped him get better control of his feelings.* Still, Nyx's eyes mirror the dark stone in this room with a hint of flickering red flames, and a few of his shadows convulse on his skin. He's taking deep breaths and is ready to break at any second. A high-pitched scream of laughter is stuck in my chest, and I'm absolutely loving how Eira's looking right now. Our group of friends on Earth would always mess with one another, and with all the heaviness and grief and a new magical world... I really need to laugh. It's one of the only things that keeps the melancholy at bay and reminds me there are slivers of joy in life.

Eira fidgets with the chair cushion and appears ready to split out of this entire building. My eyes are watering from trying to control my laughter.

"Quite the intriguing group we have here," Hauke's voice booms from the doorway.

A mixture of a hysteric laugh and scream peels out of me at the sound of his loud voice. Eira narrows her golden eyes at me, finally picking up on my true intentions of messing with her, and much to my surprise, Ulf and Hadwin chuckle.

"I appreciate her feistiness," Ulf grunts. "And her ability to throw her friend under the bridge for the sake of a laugh." Hadwin doesn't respond. He stares at me thoughtfully for a moment. I swear I can see another transparent crack through his mask—right next to his mouth, where the corner of his lip twitches upward.

Stefanie saunters into the room next to Hauke. He's now silent, standing vigilantly by her side as if a guard. Jade is perched on her shoulder and is locked in a staring contest with Eliina, who's leaning near the fireplace. Eira's and my chains are still locked tightly around her wrists and ankles. They're long enough to give much needed space in between us but powerful enough to keep her shackled to our souls. "I guess we should begin this meeting," Stefanie chirps. "There's quite a lot to cover." Her eyes land on me, and her mouth blooms into a brilliant smile. "Starting with *you*. How marvelous that you and Eira have your soul bond markings. It'll bind your souls together for eternity."

My mouth drops open. "That only just happened! How did you know?"

Stefanie giggles and nudges Hauke with her hip. He smiles softly down at her, the appearance of a tamed bad boy, and laces his pinkie with hers. My vision homes in on a subtle design on their fingers, one I haven't noticed before—swirling feathers in white and gold. *That must be their soul bond marking.* "One of the perks of being a healer is having the ability to sense both pain *and* happiness in a *solliqa*. We can't exclusively work with trauma, or how else would we help a soul peel back their layers to find moments of joy? Even if I couldn't do this, the very air between you and Eira right now is abundant with magic. The most emotionally dense of us can even sense it." At this, she narrows her eyes at Ulf.

Most of us laugh, especially as Ulf grumbles like a crotchety old man. Stefanie beams at me again and pecks me on the cheek before moving to Eira to give her a quick hug. It warms my heart in a dangerous way to have established such trust with souls such as her already. *What if she warps the faith I have? What if her friendship is snatched from my hands?*

I slide into another chair next to Eira, any thoughts about our soul bond or previous comments about her and Daru disappearing into the recesses of my mind. Eira shifts anxiously on her cushion. I notice she's been doing that a lot more recently. Her hands either keep touching at an area along her lower abdomen, or she's wringing her hands while bouncing with nervous energy. *Is it her chronic illness?* But would she still have most of that while in a new world? It might be something else, and I'm going to figure it out—especially with our new soul bond markings. There *must* be a way we can use them to check in on one another.

Ulf and Hadwin plop their hulking forms on some of the floor cushions. Everyone shifts uncomfortably as Hauke and Stefanie gather a few cushions to sit near Eliina in front of us. Jade flies off Stefanie's shoulder and lands in front of them, fixing that piercing green stare on us all. I'm eager to learn what Jade has to share, and more so, what the hell Eliina was doing in Tryg's cell. I'd be lying if I said I wasn't a nervous mess. I needed to laugh so badly because it's been nonstop action since Eira's nightmares took a dangerous turn back on Earth. I want to avoid what's to come, but I know I can't. None of us can.

Jade takes us all by surprise, or I'm assuming this is the case based on the collective gasp. In a plume of black feathers, gold dust, and swirling bursts of *maji,* Jade shifts from her crow form to a humanoid figure. Silky tresses of jet-black hair hang down her petite back, and she's wearing matching dark, skin-tight leathery coverings. They're nothing fancy, at least not compared to what I saw Daya and Stefanie create. The coverings fit Jade's slender body perfectly, and the darkness makes her pale green eyes pop even more, especially with how big they look compared to her small nose and mouth. All her features are set in a stern line; she's focused and ready to continue her work as Nyx's spy.

"I haven't seen you in this form since I was banished," Nyx murmurs. He pulls himself up and walks in large strides toward Eira. She watches him with her big blue eyes, and I stare in amazement as both she and Nyx have silver and gold crackling through their eyes at the same time. He arches an eyebrow at her and extends a hand, sending a few small crows made from his shadows into her face. She chuckles and places her hand in his before standing up to face him. With a mischievous smirk, Nyx spins her in a half circle and promptly sits down where she was before. He pulls Eira down into his lap, pulling her long white and blue braid over her shoulder and places a kiss on her neck. Daru is staring daggers at him, and a muscle is twitching repeatedly in his jaw. *Ah, I see now. He doesn't care what any of us say to him. He cares if he's made to feel Eira will never be his.*

Clearing his throat, Nyx directs his attention to Jade again. "Why the change in form after so long?" His voice is as smooth as dark chocolate, not even remotely fazed that Daru is bristling with different colored feathers sprouting in and out of his tawny skin.

Jade throws her head back and lets out a throaty laugh.

"You're such a troublemaker! No wonder one of your animal forms is a fox." She shakes her head, her hair swishing back and forth like soft waves. "I shifted because we have a lot to get through, and I'll need to use my hands."

"We've missed you, Jade," Ivar says. Inky dark hair falls across his forehead and he gives her a small grin. It's the kind of smile one shows while still healing, the type that can't be full because there's too much pain. But it's a smile from a moment of joy, nonetheless. A gauzy deep blue covering stretches across his chest and arms, and his black pants are loose and relaxed. Ivar is one of the *solliqas* I'm most curious about in our group. When we first arrived in Rioa, some of the healers told me about Nyx's banished group of friends. Their names were Takisha and Rahim. *I hope they're doing okay in the healing quarters with the increase of harmed souls.* They had mentioned Ivar being from Wyndera, and he not only knows his way around a bow, but he can also shift into various flying creatures. The idea of being in the air terrifies me, and that makes me all the more curious to learn everything I can about Ivar.

Ivar nudges Odin next to him, and my heart squeezes. Glancing up at Eira, I can tell she's thinking the same thing: *Odin is grieving over the fact that we still don't know where his sister, Erika, is, let alone Del and Daya.* He has that hollowed expression on his face and keeps staring off into the distance. I know that habit all too well—sometimes it's better to disconnect from yourself than face the grief hovering right in front of you.

"She might know something about Erika," Ivar murmurs to Odin.

"I don't," Jade shares. Her eyes soften marginally when Odin slowly lifts his gaze toward hers. "I know someone who might, though. And I've missed you all, too, but don't get used to seeing me here. I must not stay in one place for too long or risk having my identity known."

"Let's get on with it then," Ulf barks.

Nyx gives him a *don't-be-an-asshole* look.

"What?" Ulf snaps. "She keeps saying we need to talk about everything and can't stay for long. So, someone better fucking talk, or this is a waste of time."

"So courteous," I mutter.

"There are a lot of updates to get through. We don't have time for pleasantries." Ulf stands up and starts pacing near the windows.

"And we don't have time for your rudeness," Eira speaks up. "This is tense for all of us."

"Don't," Nyx orders Ulf when he opens his mouth to respond. "Just give it a rest. Jade, continue."

"Honestly," she sighs. "I wasn't expecting Eliina to be a part of this. We'll start with what the healers have learned about Zaya and what the manipulators have to say about the newest soul to cross over, Mayra."

Emotions jolt through me like electricity. My head whips to Eira, and we both have the same expression: bewilderment from Mayra having shown up in the dungeons last week.

"Don't worry, we've all been blindsided by *this* soul showing up here," Jade says cooly. "We'll then move on to what I've learned about each Council member who fled before and during the festival, as well as what we've learned from this *skelter*. Trust me, you'll all want to physically see what we have to share. Nyx, you'll report what you and Athena learned from your friends, and, Eira, we need to include what's been happening with your bear marking."

Eira peers down at her forearm with such sadness, my own heart aches with her. She seems... disappointed? As if she wanted to keep the return of this bear marking a secret? Nyx had shared with me this morning that he noticed it glowing yesterday but wasn't in a position to talk to Eira about it. I'm sure they were in quite a few positions if some of the bite marks on his neck are anything to go by, but I didn't bring that up.

"I'm reluctant to spend more time than necessary here, as I've said, but then Eliina will explain whatever in Cudhellen happened to her," Jade continues. Those pale green eyes shift to the windows. I had wondered where the other crows—or I guess her team—flew to, and they're hidden under dark leaves on the multicolored trees. "Then we split into different teams."

"I'm sorry, what?" I blurt. Looking around at everyone, only Eira is as confused as I am. The rest of them are laser-focused on Jade. Even Eliina is watching her with a look of acceptance. Fraya is the only one sitting with a vacant expression. She's wearing the thickest coverings I've seen here so far, as if she'll be sent to a land of snow and frigid temperatures. I swallow. I can see part of her bandages around her pelvis. *Her poor, tortured soul. I don't want to know what kind of trauma she faced the night of the festival.*

"We'll need to divide and conquer," Jade tells Eira and me. "Nyx and I have debated on what to do for the past week before conversing with everyone here. Some of it depended on who survived the attacks a week ago and if anyone remained missing. When he shared what Tryg showed you, Eira, it became evident that mass destruction is happening on your home planet. With portals and foreign beings involved, there's no way we can tackle everything without splitting up."

"But why do *we* need to take care of everything?" Eira asks. "Athena and I are new here and have been doing our best to experiment with our *maji*, but we're not trained anywhere near where we should be. And isn't there a Council of experts to organize how to handle world issues?"

"Did the leaders from your time on Earth adequately handle world issues?" Jade throws back at her.

Eira bites her lip. She doesn't say anything, but she doesn't need to. Our leaders tend to make things even *worse* back home.

"Don't make the mistake of thinking because you're in a new magical realm with souls who've witnessed every horrific decision on Earth will respond any differently," Jade continues. "Those elected for positions of power aren't always the solution. Nyx and I decided that we can't sit back and wait for the Council to make the first move, not after how they've handled those touched by the plague of darkness. Sometimes, the rest of the souls in the world need to find the courage to strike the enemy down first, or at least find the right information. My loyalty is to Nyx and what he was trained to be as a leader in Drageyra. But we won't commit to any plan without all the information being shared with the rest of you, and we'll then decide as a team how to proceed."

Team? I raise my eyebrows at everyone, one face at a time, and my breath hitches when my eyes meet Hadwin's. He's not staring at me with a mask this time. He's... lost. Vulnerable. Unsure of which step to take next. Jade's right. We're all a team, and who am I kidding? I'll go wherever Eira goes, and there's no way she won't launch herself into action if it means she can save more *solliqas* here.

I blow out a shaky breath. "Okay, we'll go over everything here?"

Jade shakes her head. Hard. "Absolutely not. As much as I'm finding it difficult to trust Eliina, she's right about one thing: We *must* hold our meeting in the library. It still has the protection spell that Eliina put on it long ago, and we won't risk anyone hearing us."

"Shouldn't we've gone there in the first place, then?" I ask.

"Would you have blindly followed me and the others into the library with a *canielor* and Eliina in chains?"

Obviously not. I'd much prefer to be here, close to the garden and an easy escape out the windows.

"Let's head down," Jade says, her tone sharp enough to cut any one of us, and inclines her head toward the hallway. The movement is as rhythmic as in her crow form. It takes me a moment to focus again. "Stefanie and Hauke, you both get the healers and manipulators we'll need. And let's hope that we can find the strength to all work together during one of the most perilous times in Majikaero."

THIRTEEN
Hauke

Sometimes you must fly with caution
or risk falling to your death from the heavens.
-Aapeli, Goddess of Air

"There are many unexpected changes," Stefanie murmurs as we walk side by side down the twisting corridors of the crumbling Council building.

Our fingers are interlaced, her anxiety pulsating down her pale arm and into my hand—a living extension of herself. My little *luxriel* is typically the calm oasis in an endless desert. She's so full of golden light, and her emotional intelligence is unmatched—except for maybe Eira and Athena now. All three of them together are a storm of healing rain that will drench you until your inner demons are drowning. That's the way of my Stefanie. She's as sweet as a luscious bite of fruit. When she's in her healing mode, though, she'll turn that sweetness into a thick poison your darkness won't be able to survive.

I still remember the night I met her. It wasn't my best moment in Majikaero, but to be fair, I wasn't here for very long at that point. I had been told about *almaoves* and the intensity of finding one of your soul connections. That doesn't mean I believed it, though. Why would I? Finding the missing pieces to my soul felt like too much of a dream to take seriously.

My motto was the three F's: fly, fuck, and fight. If I wasn't spreading my wings up in the sky, I was spreading a *fim's* legs open or punching a *solliqa* hard enough, their wounds would split open and an infection would spread throughout their broken body.

I was spreading chaos in some way, shape, or form, and I didn't give a fuck what that said about me. It wasn't my fucking problem, at least not until Stefanie made it *hers*. For some reason I'll never understand, Eliina had seen a speck of light in my devious eyes. During one of my nights out in Rioa, she found me and insisted that I join her healers at a bonfire of sorts. She stated that it was an evening meant to celebrate the success of one of their prized healer novices. I had rolled my eyes, but even I wasn't stupid enough to turn down a Council member's request. It was that night when my life as I knew it was flipped upside down. All it took was a few healers pointing out Stefanie's mesmerizing dancing form and staring into her emerald-green eyes for my world to flip on its axis. It was her, and her alone, who was able to coax out the better pieces of myself I didn't even know existed.

Her sweet poison was the ailment for my ruined soul, and I wouldn't be the healer or envoy I am today without her. Stefanie isn't only my *almaove*—one of what might be a few—she's my saving grace, the one who rescued me from my own personal Cudhellen.

Any time I think back on those days, I have to wonder if that was the beginning of the plague of darkness, or did even the evil in this universe not want anything to do with me?

"Hauke?" Stefanie asks.

I blink away the memories and the painful bite of how Eliina is no longer that *solliqa* who finds the light in others. She's her own special kind of monster, and it brings me sick joy to know these other *solliqas* will get to see the real her.

"Yes, my love?" I grin down at my *almaove* and place a kiss on her forehead.

"You're not here right now, are you?" she murmurs.

Sighing, I stab a hand into my locks of purple hair. "I don't think any of us are, truly."

Stefanie hums and turns into my side, silently asking for a hug. We stay locked in an embrace for a few moments, lost to our own spiraling thoughts, before she blows out a breath and steps out of my arms. No matter how many times we're together, I never want her too far from where she belongs: right next to my side. She tucks her gorgeous red hair behind her ears and gives me a grim smile.

"I'm going to get the manipulators and healers. And Zaya, of course. Meet you down in the library?"

I toss her a wink. "It's a date."

Stefanie giggles and waves before twirling around and striding down the hill toward the healing quarters. I normally would go with her, craving any amount of time we get to spend together, but I told her earlier I have some envoy business to finish.

I really fucking hate lying to my girl.

Sweeping my gaze around the ruined patches of white grass and rather desolate surroundings, I walk casually to a small grouping of trees that managed to survive the attacks on Rioa last week. My raptor senses kick into overdrive. There are no sudden movements anywhere I can see, and I don't get the prickling sensation I usually do when a soul is watching me. Flicking my eyes to the healing quarters one last time, I settle deep into my *maji*. In a flash of purple and white swirling power, I shift into my massive raptor form. I ruffle out some of my feathers before shrinking down to a slightly smaller version, hoping to remain as inconspicuous as possible.

It won't take Stefanie long to gather the *solliqas* she needs, and I don't want to be more suspicious than I already am. I flutter up to one of the higher branches, the pink and blue bark peeling under my ribbed talons. Guilt rushes through me as I wait up here. It's for the best, though, and I have to keep telling myself that.

If Stefanie or anyone else were to know what I'm actually up to, she'd be in immediate danger. And I *refuse* to put her in that situation. Let her be angry with me if she ever finds out. It's better than seeing her dead.

A few of the bright-colored leaves crinkle against one another as the branch above me sways slightly. I don't have to look to know who's occupying that space.

"We must be quick," I mutter.

"Agreed," Del chirps. He's in a tiny bird form, the kind that's known for its melodious sounds. His azul and yellow feathers fluff up in the warm breeze. "They don't know I'm here?"

"Of course not," I huff.

"I know you hate being in this position, but it's for the best until we know who exactly is behind the portals. You know they're coming for us next."

I grunt in response.

"Tryg has been taken and Eliina was put in his place," I grumble.

"Good," Del says. "Very good."

"It's destroying me that I can't tell Stefanie who I think took him," I push out. I shift my weight from talon to talon, agitation rolling through me. You don't hide these kinds of secrets from your *almaove*. You just don't. But I don't want to say this to Del. That'd be rubbing salt in old wounds for him—he's met one of his *almaoves*, and they hid enough from him that it crushed his vulnerable heart.

"I know," Del replies, his tone soft. "You know how smart she is, Hauke. She'll dive right into her tomes and scrolls, not stopping until she figures out how we're all connected to one another. The truth will be easier to explain when we *all* can tell her, backing you up."

"I hope you're right."

"There's more than one world at stake here," Del continues. "When the moment is right, the others will learn the truth of the full war happening here. It's coming for us all. The more energy we feed the incoming darkness, the easier it will spread to those we love."

I know he's right, but *damn*. I fucking hope I'll get to tell Stefanie before that war hits us, and it isn't during a moment of life or death where my charred soul is turned into something worse than stardust.

"Any news about Daya or Erika? Eira and some of the others are desperate to know," I grumble.

"You know I can't tell you that."

"I told you I'm not going to share any of that with Stefanie. I want to be able to genuinely reassure her and everyone."

Del just stares at me in disbelief.

I snort. "You must enjoy this, huh? Being in a position of power over a soul like me?"

Del cocks his head to the side, remaining silent.

"Fine. Any updates on where the Council members have scattered off to?"

"No real news yet," Del says curtly. "We're also still trying to figure out if they're all to blame for the portals or if only some of them were involved. I'm most suspicious of Namid."

"Yeah, who isn't," I mutter. That *solliqa* is a slimy fuck. "Jade is going to tell us what information she's gathered. I was hoping to be able to confirm what she says is true against what you know."

"I can say with certainty that Nova aided in opening those portals, and we both know Eliina's role in the situation."

I nod. This whole attack was so fucked.

"We also know the plague of darkness is connected to the portals being opened," Del continues. "The creatures who traveled through those portals are supposed to be escalating all the pain and trauma that's already here."

"Great." I force a laugh. "Just splendid. Trauma is already all-consuming. If more portals appear here, there's no way Majikaero will remain safe."

"No planet will be," Del sighs.

Edginess works its way along my muscles, and I know I need to get back to the Council library.

"Till next time," I mutter. As I spread my wings, Del stops me with a single question.

"Are you still having those dreams?"

I pause, not knowing how to respond. I forgot that he was there when I disclosed them.

"What's it matter to you?"

"I care, Hauke," he says. "It can't be that hard to believe other *solliqas* other than Stefanie care about you."

I suppress a cruel laugh. It's not just hard to believe—it's impossible. Stefanie turned my life around, but that doesn't mean I think other souls view me differently.

"I'm still having them," I breathe. "I haven't told others about them yet."

Del tilts his head to the other side.

"They're confusing," I grumble. "I know there are two sisters in them—one dark, one colorful—and their faces are never super clear. My gut tells me they could be my other *almaoves* calling out to me, but I don't know how to find them. It doesn't matter, Del. I can't force fate, you know that, and I need to focus on where the Council members have scattered to. Such fucking cowards."

"Just remember the power of dreams," Del warns. "They might not appear significant right now, but they started happening right before the attacks on this city."

"I'm more than aware, thank you," I growl at him, causing him to flinch back. I can't fully keep my bristling anger on a leash—only Stefanie has that power. "But I won't be focusing on that right now. I have a strong feeling that as an envoy, I'll be the one paying these Council members a visit. Keep me updated on what you find out."

Del nods. "I will."

"Without us knowing who's behind these portals here on Majikaero, the safety of everyone we know and care for is at risk. Remember that when you decide to hold back information from me next time."

With a flap of my purple and black wings, I'm gone in the blink of an eye. I soar toward the entrance of the Council building, spotting Stefanie chatting to a scratched-up healer carrying a squirming Zaya. Her emerald eyes meet mine mid-flight, and while she makes my heart feel lighter than air, the secrets I'm holding weigh me down more each second.

FOURTEEN

Tryg

Aren't we all monsters, in some way or another?
-Page 259, Dark Maji of the Realms, Volume II

Majikaero is an enchanting world that is slowly smothering who I thought I was. At least, this is what I'm thinking about as I lie across what's apparently a colossal *drekstri*. It has the head, mane, and hooves of a horse, except there are vicious-looking teeth, black claws that extend out of the hooves, and the body is covered in scales. Oh, and there's fucking huge-ass wings.

I traveled on an *alklen* on our way to Rioa, and I saw the others ride smaller *drekstri* that were similar to an enormous version of a horse and small dragon combined together. This, though? There's no mistaking this breed of *drekstri* is more monster than anything. And I'm strapped down to its back with a million jagged, shimmering scales, each an iridescent navy and purple color, piercing through my body.

Fuck.

My stomach lurches as this gigantic creature dips lower before surging higher, up above the clouds. We pass through their lavender mist, and I force myself to breathe in the thinner air as deeply as I can. As fucked as it is that I was captured by another *solliqa*, I'll admit this is better than being trapped in the dungeon. The truth gnaws away at me, though. Whether I'm bound to a wall or to a *drekstri* makes no difference—I'll be isolated until insanity kills me if another soul doesn't wreck me first. I've accepted this is how my story will end.

It's what I deserve.

What I don't understand is how I'm no longer forced to listen to the multiple, frenzied demons inside my head. I'm not even seeing their black, silver-purple, and blue-opal eyes. It's as if they were never here, but I *know* that's bullshit. They didn't simply brush up against my soul and leave. I know they're hiding and waiting to lash out when I least expect it, when I can't afford to fuck up. I can't let myself forget that they've been inside of me for the past week or so. I'm the only proof I have of them—although, what good is my word now? How much worth does it hold anymore?

Nothing. I'm worth nothing.

"Have you always been this bleak?"

I jump, the cords binding me to the *drekstri* tightening at the movement. It's been silent the past few hours, and I was so lost in my thoughts, I forgot another soul was near me.

"You know nothing about me," I grind out.

"Hm... you give away more than you realize, Tryg. Not to worry, though. You'll receive no judgment from me."

My body twitches as I struggle to turn my head. I *hate* being forced to stare at the sky. It might be open space compared to the dungeon, but I'm still limited in what I can see, what I can feel.

"Why are you doing that? I'd rather not have to stare at your unpalatable face."

"*Unpalatable?*" I growl. "What's wrong with my face?"

"Nothing some powerful *maji* can't fix."

I stop moving and focus my attention on relaxing each

muscle in my body. There's no escaping this reality, and if this asshole doesn't want to converse face-to-face, then fuck them. I haven't been near a mirror in ages, but I know my face can't look much different from on Earth. *Right?*

They sigh. A few minutes pass by, and then they sigh even louder.

"Argh, fine!" they mutter. "If you're going to shut down on me and lie there like a slab of meat, then I'll fix the cords."

I don't respond. I am a slab of *spoiled* meat, left out with the purpose of poisoning those who consume me.

Slender fingers settle on top of my head. "Now, don't move, okay? Or you can, if you want, but that'll really mess things up for both of us. I've set a spell that will set you on fire if you move even an inch. Only I can move your body. Now sit still."

"An inch?!" This *solliqa* is fucking crazy.

They, or rather *she*, waves off my comment as if it's nothing. The taut cords loosen until a few are removed completely, finally letting the blood move in my veins again. She pulls me up, so I'm sitting on one of the sharp scales. I stay quiet, not wanting to interrupt her and change her mind about readjusting the cords. A few are reattached to my legs, and she fucking floats with the cords down under the *drekstri* while it's flying. Just floats there, like she's a summoned ghost or a fucking bird.

"There we go!" she chirps happily. "Now you still can't leave, and we can face one another. That was bothering you quite a bit."

I huff out a laugh. "And where exactly would I go?"

Daya pins me with a weighty stare. "Please. I've trained as a healer and have other magical abilities. You can't hide your suicidal ideation from me."

The hood of her gold patterned robe falls to her shoulders. Each vibrant design of gold threads makes her red hair stand out like flames blowing in the breeze. Hazel eyes shine with the reflection of the orange and blue suns, and as she slowly smiles and exposes sharp canines, I'm convinced I've been captured by a fairy. A dark, troublesome fairy that plays with fire and can shift into enormous multicolored birds.

That's how she snuck me out of the dungeons. After partially shifting into a bird of prey and using her talons to break the chains, another robed *solliqa* came running in after her. I couldn't see who it was, but they must have been important because Daya gave them her full attention and urgently gestured to where I was sprawled on the ground. My limbs were useless after hanging for nearly seven days, and when I tried to stand up, I ended up crashing into the wall next to me.

Daya's bird form had given me an irritated look, shifted back into her usual humanoid form, and *punched* me right in the face. I was knocked out, and the next thing I knew, I was hanging like an injured mouse from her talons as she flew us to this monstrous *drekstri*.

The more I think about the lunacy of this situation, the more I want to get knocked out again.

"That still doesn't mean you know me," I mutter.

Daya arches an auburn eyebrow. "I know enough."

"How did you break me out of those chains?" I ask.

"Magical abilities," she says with a shrug.

"Are you always this difficult to talk to?" I push.

"Are you always this much of an oaf? I'd think the answer would be obvious."

I growl and make the mistake of rocking back too far. One of the pointed scales pushes up into a hole I'd rather no one ever explored.

"Fuck!" I shout. I lean forward, hoping the ache will ease soon enough. "Why can't you tell me how you got me free? What do you want with me? I thought you were coming to rescue me."

"I mean, I *did*," Daya mutters while examining a red nail.

"The souls keeping you chained up weren't the good kind and are working for the wrong side."

This *solliqa* is a fucking brat. And I hate to admit how turned on I'd be if she wasn't so infuriating, we weren't gods know how many feet high in the air, and she didn't have my legs tied down to this beast.

"Honestly, you've got some powerful *maji* inside you," she continues. "I'm surprised you can't sense it, even though you're well on your way to becoming a *canielor*. If you really knew your strength, you probably could have broken those chains yourself."

I shake my head, laughing. "Yeah, there's no way I have magical powers."

"*Every* soul in Majikaero has some kind of magical ability," Daya huffs. "You just have to be open to finding it. The worse the plague symptoms, the harder it is to connect to your *maji*. I don't envy you, Trygster."

Scowling, I say, "Don't call me that."

"Why not?"

"Because I'm not a five-year-old!"

"Did people call you that when you were a child?"

"Oh, gods! I want to chuck you off this monster."

"Just another good reason to have you tied up," Daya says with a wink. "That'd be rather silly of you, though. I can fly, remember?"

Fucking duh.

"Fine, keep your magical abilities to yourself. Who gives a fuck."

"You do, apparently."

"I regret having you untie me. Are you this frustrating with Eira?"

Daya's eyes shutter. I'm astonished that they're tearing up.

"It won't make any sense to your kind of soul. You're so attached to what you think is right and wrong, to which world you belong in, to who you think you're supposed to be. There's too much rigidity holding you down to understand this concept. But Eira and I have strong soul bonds, I *know* it. I felt it the second she entered Majikaero. We just needed more time for the connection to snap together." Daya sniffs and glances away, still blinking back her tears.

"You mean a soul mate? Or whatever you call it here?" I ask.

"An *almaove*," she mumbles. "Souls can have more than one strong soul bond. It doesn't have to be sexual or romantic. It could be that way with *her*, though. Love is *powerful* and can withstand any distance, any change in realms or time." She sighs. "You wouldn't understand."

"Why? Because you think I'm stupid?"

"No, because I *know* you're stupid, and you've caved too much to the demons clawing through your soul as we speak."

I cough, not expecting such an abrupt change in subject. "What?"

"See? You can't even hear right."

"You fucking... just tell me. Please?" I grumble.

The sadness in Daya's eyes vanishes briefly, replaced by some sick joy at me begging her.

"I *love* it when you beg," she purrs. Daya pushes forward onto her knees and pokes me in the fucking nose. "You're kind of cute. I can see why a soul would be into you."

I let my glare speak for itself, and she cackles. "Alright, I'll let you in on one of my magical abilities. If you tell anyone, I'll slit your throat from the inside out." She smiles.

The fuck?

"Yeah, yeah, who am I going to tell? Say it."

"Those in Eliina's group are all a bit... hmmm... different? We're special. We have multiple magical abilities that vary in degrees of power. My *maji* connects to the air, winged-creatures, fire, the ability to heal, and a few other capabilities. One of those being I can sense the darkness in another *solliqa* and how far along they are with the plague. For some souls, I need to physically touch them to use this ability. For others, they're so close to caving into the sickness, the mere proximity is enough for me."

"Huh," I mutter. "So, you can sense what's going on in my head? As in, visually see it?"

"Sort of!" she says, way too damn cheerfully. "Each *solliqa* is very different. You're practically screaming your pain, though. I'm able to hear some of your words and get a visual on those demons slithering around inside. It's quite draining, but I can definitely feel your pain."

I sag, slightly relieved. "Those demons are real, then."

Daya surprises me. She leans forward, but this time, she places a hand on my taut arm. A look of compassion shines in her hazel eyes. It makes me uncomfortable to have anyone this close to me and showing even a shred of kindness—*unless they're Eira.*

"Of course they're real, Tryg," Daya continues. "You've made them real. They're able to crush you in a heartbeat, but make no mistake, they're very much cowards. The moment your demons felt my fire trickle into your body, they scurried off into the furthest corners of your soul. They've attached themselves deeply within you, which is why you can't understand what I'm talking about with soul bonds. You yourself are already turning into a demon and might be too detached from the warmth of love to understand."

"Demons can't feel love?"

Her mouth quirks to the side and she hums. "Not often. It's easier to cave to hatred than to rise to love. You'd have to start with self-love, which could have been possible, but you attacked one of the most powerful healers we have in this realm. I'm not sure you're ready for such healing."

It's my turn to blink away tears. "I didn't mean to attack Eira. I-I needed her to *see.*"

Daya cocks her head to the side. "See what?"

"Those demons have been showing me everything that's been happening on Earth. There's chaos and destruction everywhere, and the people I love are fighting for their lives. I don't even think it's the same timeline anymore. My friends are somewhere in the future, if they're even alive. I needed to send all that information to Eira, so she can hopefully do something to fix it. If all I did was hurt her, though, then what a fucking mistake." I rub a hand down my face and sigh up at another cloud. The *drekstri* swerves to the side for a second, and now I'm grateful I've been tied down to it.

Daya nods at the cords. "There's a number of reasons to tie you down, huh?"

"What do you want, a sweet *thank you*?"

She grins widely and sharp canines appear again. "Maybe."

"You have nothing to say about what I showed Eira?"

Daya sits back and gazes out into the sky. She lazily strokes the scales next to her, and it's truly terrifying to hear a beast this size purr. "We don't know if the demons were trying to manipulate you or not. They could have shown you those images to strike more fear into your heart, which would further intensify any symptoms of the plague. You're already in pain, have tried to harm Eira in the past, and have experienced multitudes of trauma through various lifetimes. That being said, the demons also could have *wanted* to show you the truth and make you believe there's nothing you can do about it. Another way to strike fear into your heart." She pauses. "If you were able to send this information to Eira, perhaps there's still a chance you can connect to your *maji*."

"What do you mean? That doesn't make any sense."

Daya scoots closer and knocks her fist against the side of my head. I go to swat her hand away, and she laughs. "I was just checking to see if your skull is empty or not."

I smile despite myself. Daya hums again. "You might have

the ability to manipulate thoughts and can communicate telepathically. That'd make sense if you were a manipulator."

Staring blankly at her, I wait for clarification.

"That would have been an easy way to harm Eira in a past life in this world. I can't ever imagine you physically harming her, at least not intentionally. I can *definitely* see you manipulating her thoughts to make her love you back or to do something against her will. That's more your style, Tryggy."

"Blech, that name's even worse!"

Daya shrugs. "One of them will stick. Oh well, too bad we won't get to find out about your *maji*. I'm awfully curious now if you can be saved or not."

"Gods, help me. What do you mean we won't find out? Where are you taking us?"

She jumps up and, balancing on the tips of her toes, she swivels around and prances to the head of the *drekstri*. Straddling an area by its neck, she peers into the distance up ahead—probably using some magical bird vision and hearing that I'm better off not knowing about. Still, though. Daya can't just up and leave after delivering that kind of comment. *Is she honestly that cruel?*

"Sometimes, I can be!" Daya yells over her shoulder.

"Argh! Stop reading my thoughts!" I yell.

Daya throws me a sassy glance. "Why don't you come over here and make me?"

"E-excuse me?" I sputter.

"Don't flatter yourself. I'm not into *you* in that way," she calls. "If you want more answers, figure out how to free yourself from those cords. Shadows or not, your *maji* should be strong enough to break your new chains."

I look down at the twisted cords winding up and down my legs in a crisscross pattern. Bending a little closer, I notice electrical sparks encase thousands of tightly woven threads that appear to be writhing. *Is this magic? Something alive?*

"Did you use a living creature to bind me to this *drekstri*?" I yell.

Without turning back, Daya responds, "Aren't you supposed to be an investigator or something? For someone so smart, you're asking me a lot of questions."

I scowl at the back of her head, and my frown deepens as this beast drops a good six feet before gliding diagonally toward the right. A tiny turquoise spec glitters far below, surrounded by layers upon layers of colorful trees. My brain keeps telling me that these colors are all wrong, but my eyes eat up every vibrant color I'm exposed to. Shaking my head, I turn back to the cords. *Keep it together. Even if this is a breathing creature, you don't know what the hell it is. It might be nothing and a magical illusion. Daya seems like the type to play tricks on her prisoners, or whatever the fuck I am.*

"You said I might be able to manipulate minds or whatever. Talking through the mind isn't going to help me break through these."

"It couldn't?" Daya goads.

My face officially has a permanent scowl from this conversation alone. "No, of course not."

"Oh." Daya shrugs. "If you say so, Tryg-Bear."

Clenching my hands into fists, I release an annoyed growl at the new nickname. I barely fucking know Daya, but she's proving to be a hassle. I'm mocking her under my breath when it hits me: *bear*.

"My soul is associated with bears, right?" I yell. The wind is becoming more turbulent. I swear to every god out there, if Daya is the reason we're entering a storm, I'm going to pluck every last feather out of her. She doesn't respond.

"Come on!" I scream. "Come back here for a moment."

"You know," Daya yells back. "I'm trying to focus here." Her body is gliding back and forth with the *drekstri's*, and she manages to hold on as it speeds faster in circular motions. I, on the other hand, am grateful I was barely fed in the dungeon. My stomach is churning fast enough to turn my insides into butter. "We're going to have to jump!"

Like fuck am I going to jump off this beast.

"How do you expect me to do that?"

"You have to break through the cords to join me—I don't have time to cut you free!" Daya screams as the *drekstri* does a nosedive, and my stomach flies to my throat. We level out finally, but the winds are blowing hard at us. It's as if someone is physically pushing up against me.

"We don't have time to go through your strengths and all that. Follow your breath and think about connecting with your bear," Daya calls. "Our magic always starts with the breath. You have to be calm."

"Are you fucking nuts?! You want me to do this in these winds?"

"There's never an opportune time to find yourself!" Daya screams again as we drop another few feet. She lets go of the *drekstri's* neck, and I feel more than hear its deafening roar. Part of me is petrified that we're inside a raging tornado, and another part of me is doing everything it can to shut down the oncoming panic. I watch as Daya is blown sideways. There's now a third part of me that's reconciling with the gods, even to tell them I don't actually want to die.

I'm not ready. Not yet.

I can't become the monster everyone thinks I am. The demons sewing themselves into my soul, born from my own pain and sorrow, can't vanquish what I still might become.

FIFTEEN
Hadwin

We fear less the portal,
and more the mystery of where it takes us.
-Correspondence from Council Member Nova, Grand
Commander of Travel and Space

Becoming a widely known banished *solliqa* across all the regions of Majikaero hasn't done me any favors. There are a number of souls who understand I didn't purposely infect myself with the plague of darkness. Unfortunately, the *solliqas* in power believe otherwise. Being consumed by the plague was a trap, I'm positive. There wasn't a specific incident where I was full of sick brutality or rage. I might have a darker sense of humor and lean more toward the cynical side. How could I not when I've witnessed the fucking atrocities on Earth with my *maji* over the years? That doesn't mean I should have caught the plague.

If anything, I'm one of the *solliqas* born into a royal family that's not aligned with souls like Nyx. I couldn't stand with what the Council was starting to do. The constant withholding of information from the souls in this world. The manipulation of rare *maji* abilities. The push to observe people on Earth. The cruel reactiveness to anyone who disagreed with their decisions... the list can go on and on. My family was okay with it, though. They'll forever support those who give them more power in return. Perhaps that's why I was one of the *solliqas* to catch the plague; I was too resistant to atrocities.

When I learned that Nyx was seized by the Council members after his *maji* turned a loved one into stardust, I knew I couldn't sit back in Eikenbien and do nothing. Nyx wouldn't have left me, and there was no way in Cudhellen I would do the same to him. We're brothers, he and I, even closer than the apparent soul families we were born into in Majikaero. I'm amazed that we don't have our own soul bond markings between us or with the others in our small group of misfits. When I mentioned it in passing to Ivar, he said he didn't think it'd be possible to form that kind of pure bond when our souls are drenched in the plague. I had pushed back, unsatisfied with his response. I insisted that Nyx and I had known one another for many years before either of us caught the plague.

Ivar was, and still is, such a perceptive friend. He simply stated that receiving the gift of an *almaove* starts with building trust, devotion, and acceptance within ourselves.

I never brought the topic up again with any of my companions. Ivar nailed the problem for me. I was born with immense power rooted to my core and have always been resistant to accepting the different parts of me. I don't know who that carefree male was on Earth that I saw, or at which point in time my soul shriveled in on itself, full of self-disgust and the feeling of being a letdown. That's who I am now, and I have to wonder if it's best to start embracing everything I detest about myself. *Would I finally be free?*

After deciding I'd make my way toward Nyx, I traveled in different woodland forms to where the Council's cruel protectors kept him in the dungeons in Rioa. My goal was to keep myself hidden, but *someone* knew I was coming. To this day, I still don't know who planned the trap for me. The only thing that was clear was that an ambush was waiting in the trees outside the Council building. *Solliqas* were ready to pierce through my *alklen* and wildflowers form with chaotic *maji*. I was dragged against my will into the dungeons for a crime that didn't exist.

I have to give the Council credit. It was rather clever of them. If you confine miserable souls all together, there's no way the misery won't spread like wildfire.

I try not to think about my banishment too often. It does me no fucking good to consider how others still view me. Really, the thoughts I struggle to push away are the ones from my soul family. I can still hear what they all said now.

The sardonic Prince of Eikenbien, The Land of Woods, has finally bitten his own tail.

Hadwin, the endearing asshole of the forest, has rightfully lost his god-given earth maji.

He didn't deserve such magical powers. What did he do to earn them? Be born?

His python bit the many hands that fed him. May his own poison rid us of his existence.

It doesn't matter how often my created family, the one I have with Nyx and the others, has assured me that my siblings' and parents' rapid change in behaviors had nothing to do with me. My friends have stated time after time that those awful souls spoke out of spite and jealousy. The churlish thoughts spin around in my head until my *maji* surges up in one of my favorite forms: a neutral mask only I'm able to see.

"Why are you here if you aren't going to listen?"

My attention rapidly shifts to the green-eyed beauty scowling in front of me. Athena's hair is plaited back out of her face, a style I notice she wears when she's trying to work or focus. She went to change into different coverings when Jade said we'd be moving down into the library. Thick orange and pink robes hang loosely from her body, and I bite back the urge to tell her she needs to eat even more. *Ridiculous of me. What a sappy fuck.*

"Hellllooo?" Athena waves her brown hand back and forth in front of me, causing her sleeve to fall back. I can see the black floral tattoos she chose to keep on her physical form in this realm, a choice I'm longing to ask her about. She'll eventually have more control over which shape her skin takes—*will she stay attached to these tattoos? Why or why not?* One of the designs is a ripped flower with black blood flowing down to her hand. That same hand taps a massive map of Majikaero that Jade rolled out for all of us. *Ah, yes, we're preparing to talk about the Council members. That's why I was thinking of my banishment.*

"I'm listening just fine," I grunt.

Athena narrows her eyes at me and steps forward. I battle with the need to pull her into my arms and the discomfort of having her scent surround me. She lifts a slender finger, and much to my dismay, taps the area right outside my left eye. My inner python uncoils itself at her touch, causing my pendant to flash with warmth against my chest.

"These say otherwise," she mutters. "If you were listening, you wouldn't have been looking away from the map."

Impossible. I have the mask firmly in place. I've perfected it over the years to give the impression I'm still present with others. Not even Nyx can see through it. That's how much control I have over this. There's no way she could see past it.

"I'm not sure what you're talking about," I hiss. "And if *you're* paying attention, then you wouldn't be looking at my face, would you?"

Athena sighs and rolls her eyes. Eira whips her head around to where Athena, Ivar, and I have been standing next to a wooden table.

Our haggard group managed to shuffle its way down the narrow, chilled hallways to the library. It's miraculous that this part of the building remained untouched, and I have to wonder what exactly Eliina did with her *maji* to wield such a powerful spell. What did she sacrifice of her soul to ensure this room full of thousands and thousands of years of knowledge forever remains safe?

All of us silently walked through the giant wooden doors, as sturdy as the ancient trees that usually guard the Council building, and searched for a place to situate ourselves. Nyx originally kept an arm around Eira, her built form also draped in thicker robes like Athena's. They maneuvered their way around the curved tables and woven baskets full of tomes, scrolls, and random articles. Eira was startled as she peered down one of the looming bookshelves, and I recalled her last time down in this library was disturbing. A little over a week ago, Eliina had shown her one of the *canielors* who loiters in the darkened back areas of the library. Today, Eira immediately grabbed Nyx's hand and pulled him in the direction of the enormous windows that expand all the way up along the ceiling. It was decided we'd pull chairs and tables in that direction. With the suns starting to set and full moons rising, we'd need little light from the orbs to see what Jade wanted to share with us.

"Would it kill you to be decent to her?" Ivar mutters next to me.

His inky-blue eyes are fixated on Jade, and he shifts to his other foot, subtly shaking out the knotted tension still stuck in his muscles. The healers have done a phenomenal job working on all of us, but even their *maji* can only go so far. They can only meet us where we're at and mend any physical injuries the best they can. I suspect Ivar is still spiraling in his head about the madness that happened at the festival. Until he is ready to release some of that tension, it'll keep a tight grip on him.

I'm not one to talk, though. Truly, I'm the last soul to make any comments on how the others are healing. That is their journey to take, as the path I've chosen is mine. So, I keep my mouth shut.

"It might," I mumble.

Athena's back stiffens slightly—I bet she's listening. My pendant flickers again, and my python glares at me internally. *Nosy fuck.* Eira narrows her eyes on Athena, more in tune now that their soul bond solidified through their marking, and makes her way over to us while Jade gathers other materials. Not that we're standing far away, but Eira has been sitting right under Jade's nose to get a good view of each scroll.

It's still unsettling to see Jade in her humanoid form. She reminds me of a bloodthirsty assassin of the night, with that bright white skin and astonishing dark features. Nyx is right next to Eira, dressed in his signature gauzy black coverings, and the others are scattered in seats behind them. I do a double take of Nyx, and I notice he's added tinges of blue, the color of Eira's fire, to his coverings. *Nyx, you sappy fuck.*

Eliina is curled up on a floor cushion near the end of the row of chairs. Her chains of fire and vines reflect off the floating orbs and sunset, with hues of navy blue and flames of yellow and orange above us. She's a far image from her usual polished form, with her shredded multicolored robes and gaunt physique, and I'm anxious to hear what the fuck happened to her. Her coverings are splattered with blood stains, and from what I can sense, they're days old now. We're in no way close, oh no. But she's one of the most talented *solliqas* with earth *maji* here, and for that reason alone, we're intrinsically connected.

Eira strides toward us, her hair plaited in multiple thick braids around her head and her robes swishing around her feet, never taking her eyes off me. She looks down her nose, a striking reminder that she's called a queen. Even if it's in name only, I wouldn't be surprised if she ended up ruling as an actual queen —especially if Nyx ever decides to reclaim his title as prince, and eventually as King of Drageyra. Eira hooks her arm with

Athena's and murmurs something in her ear, making her burst out in laughter. *I'd bet my soul that they're talking about me. I can't stand the jealousy I have of their easy relationship.*

The two of them waltz over to the front where Jade is standing with more scrolls of different regions. Athena leans her head on Eira's left shoulder, and Nyx places a hand on his *almaove's* right knee. From this perspective, I can see Daru shift uncomfortably right behind them, and if I wasn't in such a shit mood, I'd laugh. Ever since Nyx whisked Eira off to go dancing, Daru has been a restless fuck. He's *insisting* that Eira is one of his *almaoves*, and if it'll get him to shut up about it, I'm hoping Eira hears him out eventually—for all of our sakes. At Eira's and Nyx's feet, Zaya is back to her usual size and curled up in a ball of fluff. Her body is limp, and she's fast asleep, very much at peace now that she's been fully healed.

Jade had started with what the healers learned about Zaya. Stefanie explained that the healers worked tirelessly yesterday with our companions and the feisty cat. I couldn't help chuckling when she said Zaya was the most challenging little soul the healers have ever encountered. A few of the *solliqas* working on her were clawed up like fresh meat, and fortunately for them, the paw with the purple substance on it was already wrapped up. Even though Hauke had taken Stefanie away from the healing quarters to get some rest, the healers frantically called for her support. She was able to identify that Zaya's paw still had some of the purple substance on it, and while that was the case, she would respond in lethal and feral ways with anyone and everyone. It took five healers—and Hauke, the poor bastard—to hold the cat down, and Stefanie was able to use some of her *maji* to remove the last of the purple substance. Zaya had immediately relaxed and let out a small whine.

They're still studying the mysterious material, and Stefanie said that is going to be one of her primary tasks for the foreseeable future.

If that purple substance, which disturbingly fucking came out of Athena and me while our souls were on Earth, spreads onto *solliqas* here, the plague of darkness will be the least of our worries. Athena and I didn't respond the way Zaya did, so Stefanie is assuming we didn't make contact with it. She believes the purple substance traveled through whichever small portal we went through to come back to Majikaero, which leads us all to think it's coming *from* Earth.

But the question still remains: What the fuck even is it, and why is it traveling to our world?

And I'm not convinced that Athena and I didn't make physical or even *spiritual* contact with it. There's no way we didn't. I'm not surprised that my soul didn't have a reaction, considering it's too far gone to be saved at this point. But Athena? I chance a look at her and those thick braids. She doesn't show any signs of the plague of darkness, yet she also wasn't impacted by what happened to us in the healing quarters or by the portal. Is there something she's hiding from us?

Then a couple manipulators, Esen and Riker, reported what they've learned about the newest red-haired *solliqa* to this world, Mayra. Esen is in one of her half-shifted forms, where the upper part of her appears human with short brown hair, and the lower part is a floating mass of flames. Riker is in his humanoid form, but he's as creepy as ever. Dark hair frames a stoic face, and his white coverings make his large black eyes even more intense. I managed to pay attention to what they both said, though, even with their ghoulish appearances.

Every single one of us is baffled that Mayra is even here and ended up in the dungeons of all places. Eira was visibly the most distraught, considering this is one of her clients from Earth. Riker explained that they needed to work with a couple healers, Nomusa and Rahim, first before they could enter the girl's mind. Mayra would thrash around violently, and then she would enter almost a comatose state. The healers were able to use their *maji* to both mend and communicate with Mayra's tormented soul, but it left them too worn out to continue working with other *solliqas*. She didn't take well to Esen and Riker, which is understandable considering how creepy they look, and wasn't able to recall how she even entered Majikaero. Her first thought was that she died and ended up in a part of Hell, or what we call Cudhellen here.

When Mayra had managed to calm down, Esen and Riker dove into her mind to investigate how and why she crossed over to our realm. It's a relatively painless process and only becomes agonizing for the *solliqa* when they fight back. With our luck, Mayra was like a bucking *alklen* and resisted each step along the way. Esen explained that after hours of working on her, they discovered three troubling facts. Mayra's soul somehow already had the plague of darkness. She had blocked a recent memory of being transported through a purple and black portal. Even more troubling, tiny drops of the purple substance were soaked into her skin. She's continuing to rest in one of the rooms of the healing quarters, not yet wanting to come face-to-face with Eira.

Riker declared that they would assist Stefanie with scouring the library for any information related to portals and the substance that has now been identified on two souls in Majikaero. Manipulators are typically only used to probing a soul's current thoughts and memories. Their *maji* slips into the mind like a slithery snake. Riker and Esen are a bit different, though. They grew up with Stefanie and some of the other healers, and when they vowed to serve Rioa, they meant their loyalty was to this world, Majikaero. *Not* to the Council members. So they'll perform certain duties, but if someone such as Stefanie tells them our world is at risk of being harmed, they'll push those aside to help the healers instead.

The rest of our group launched into a heated discussion of where else this purple substance could be. Something was obviously trying to get to Eira if this happened to one of her high-need clients and her beloved cat. I had stopped listening, though. As soon as Jade's crows, other *solliqas* determined to fight against the Council's preposterous decisions, flew overhead, and Jade quickly mentioned that she needs to tell us about the Council members... my mind emptied out. Nyx has a thirst for vengeance at all moments of the day, and he is constantly thinking about these sick, twisted *solliqas*. Me, though? I have tumultuous enough emotions going to war behind my hardened mask about my family; I try not to think about these Council members more than I need to.

Yet here I am, about to face more of my demons head-on. Bring on the painful memories, fuckers.

"Alright, everyone," Jade snaps, her voice coiling around us as fast as a whip. "My team just shared that we're being followed, and we must be out of Rioa tonight."

"By whom?" Nyx asks, his voice loud in the hushed silence.

"What? Don't you mean, *how* did her crows communicate with her?" Eira huffs. She snags a handful of crispy, teal roots, the color fascinating enough that Eira and Athena had spent multiple minutes gaping at the snack Nyx whipped up from his shadows. She has no problem eating what she claims are "strange and abnormal french fries" now.

Nyx does a double take at her, with the blue crumbs around her pout, and a few of us break out into laughter at Eira's puzzled expression. Her face is *so* exasperated, *so* fucking tired of learning something new every day about our world.

"No, firefly," he murmurs while wiping away the crumbs with his thumb. "As shifters, and considering they've lived together for years now, they all have ways to talk to one another. Some of them speak through the mind and others through the direction they fly in. We can talk more about it later."

Eira frowns and looks at Athena, who shakes her head in disbelief. I forget how new all this still is for the both of them. Athena and I might have seen versions of ourselves from a previous life on Earth, but I have no recollection of my time there. It's been quite a few years in Majikaero, and *maji* is all I've known. I can't imagine a lifetime without magical abilities. When I take in Athena and Eira, though, and how they're able to take everything they're learning in stride, I wonder if they've always had magical powers. Perhaps those abilities, such as mastering how to stay calm or throwing themselves into someone else's trauma, look different on Earth.

Yet I also think of Tryg and how quickly he succumbed to his pain, to his savage demons. Not everyone has *maji* or the capacity to connect with it. *Rather abysmal, Tryg.*

Jade ignores Nyx's question and flitters between a few different scrolls before landing on a different version of a map of Majikaero. This one details the current Council members and which regions or *maji* they're representing. She smacks it onto one of the tables rather hastily and motions for Stefanie and Hauke to place sparkling gemstones on the corners to keep the map down.

"Gather around this table," Jade demands. Eira, Athena, and Nyx squeeze in between her and Stefanie. Daru walks to Stefanie's other side while keeping his eyes on Eira, and Hauke slides in next to him. I can feel my eyes dancing in amusement as Athena sends one swift glare at Eliina. That's all it takes for a *fucking Grand Healer*, one of the Council members herself, to scramble off her floor cushion and toward our table. Eliina's eyes remain downcast, and she has a nervous edge to her that's alarming. I don't hide my entertained expression fast enough, and Nyx smirks and raises an eyebrow after making eye contact with me. *Asshole. He better not say a word right now. This stupid mask is slipping all over the place.*

I can't be too concerned about what my friend will or will not say, though. Seeing Eliina uncharacteristically skittish is putting me right back in the dungeons. Athena's *maji* had flared with an exhilarating intensity. *Will she become even stronger than*

Eliina? Why is Athena making a solliqa *so powerful this frightened?* Ivar shakes the thought from my mind as he bumps into my shoulder, and then Odin, Fraya, and Ulf follow suit on my other side. It's oddly comforting being surrounded on all sides by my banished friends, even if we're all barely holding onto our magic, onto our souls.

The manipulators, Esen and Riker, are nowhere to be seen, as they're still searching for relevant tomes about portals in the shadows of the bookshelves.

Jade places a slim finger at the top of the map where it lists the Council members. I notice the tip of her fingers are a mixture of gold and black and partially shifted into talons. *Interesting.* She's anticipating the need to bolt out of here at any moment, yet she values sharing this information more than saving her soul.

"As most of us know, these are the main Council members. There are, of course, other influential and, hm, rather formidable *solliqas* that have rammed their way into power. You'll all notice, though, that *their* names are not listed. We won't be discussing them. The Council members of importance are the main ones listed here."

Jade traces along each of the names, giving us a moment to read them silently.

Eliina

Grand Healer
Eikenbien, Land of Woods

Elio

Grand Commander of Sunlight
Sunnadyn, Land of Sunlight

Enya
Grand Commander of Fire
Drageyra, Land of Fire

Haliean
Grand Commander of Water
Lagunit, Land of Many Waters

Lesak
Grand Spirit Reader
Viorfelle, Land of Mountains

Mohi
Grand Manipulator
Reykashin, Land of Smoke

Namid
Grand Soul Reader
Myrellden, Land of Darkness

Neoma
Grand Commander of Moonlight
Skugvaytir, Land of the Shadows

Nova
Grand Commander of Travel and Space
Rioa, Land of Natural Cities, The Capital

Rakiana
Grand Commander of Wind
Wyndera, Land of Wind

Waneta
Grand Shifter
Shymeira, Land of Tropics

Weke

Grand Commander of Earth
Sayfters, Land of Clay and Buildings

"Eira and Athena," Jade continues. "I'm not sure how much has been explained to you. What's important to know is that the Council must have at least one *solliqa* from each region in Majikaero. While they can have more, the Council has never officially listed more than one name per region. The ones selected are decided through a mixture of voting and recommendations from any previous Council members, and the goal is to encompass as many different *maji* abilities as possible. While the process has worked for centuries, it should be obvious that even a just and fair system can spiral into a biased and inequitable group. I believe you should both be more than familiar with how this works on Earth."

They both nod, their faces grim.

"My crows and I noticed something peculiar about their actions during the day of the Moons Cycle Festival, as well as the days immediately following it. Each of them, except for Namid and Nova, traveled back to their home regions, one after the other. As in, Elio left a week before the festival, then Neoma left the next day, then Waneta left the day after, and so on. We even had tracked Eliina's whereabouts to Eikenbien," Jade says and cuts Eliina a scathing look. "However, she disappeared right after we spotted her. Namid left for Myrellden the day after the festival, when you'd think he would have stayed to help with the disastrous aftermath. Nova is technically in Rioa, since this is her homeland, but she's managed to evade every single meeting requested by the healers, protectors, and all the others."

She gives us a moment to digest this pattern. "We believe each of the Council members had a set task to complete related to the events at the festival, and what's worse, they *knew* what was coming. I'm most suspicious of Eliina, since Rioa might not be her original home, but she's the Grand Healer. Even if she didn't know what horrors were to come that night, she should have been here the past week supporting all the *solliqas* working tirelessly to help others."

"I wanted to be," Eliina croaks.

"No one cares what you wanted to do," Fraya rasps. It's the first time I've heard her speak in days. "It only ever matters what a soul commits to. Your wants are mere wishes. Your commitments are actions."

"But you don't understand, I—"

"We don't need to understand," Athena snarls. "You obviously knew something was going to happen, and the least you could have done was warn us."

Eliina's eyes are lined with silver, the tears on the cusp of falling.

"You claimed I'm the Queen of Light," Eira says quietly. "You said you needed to find me before the rest of the Council members, that you needed to find Nyx's group. Yet they're the ones who've been harmed the most out of all of us."

"Sweetheart, you'll find some souls can't be fully trusted here," Nyx grumbles.

Eira scoffs while Athena forces a laugh. "That fact doesn't change no matter which world we're in," Athena mutters.

"You have to give me a chance!" Eliina cries. Her skin is sickly, and it seems more and more life drains from her by the second. "Please let me explain."

"Quiet," Jade growls. Her black hair swishes around her, those long waves becoming straighter, like sharpened blades. "Nyx, some of what you've shared with me lines up with our theory about the Council members. Of them knowing what would happen the night of the festival. Daru had thought he'd seen everyone bloodied and tied up, yet when he approached his friends, he was surrounded by a dark purple and black sweet substance. Athena saw Hadwin almost get pulled through a similar substance with the same sickly sweetness. Ivar claims to have seen a black and white tunnel, and he, Ulf, and Odin were approached by hooded figures. They were wearing intricate silky coverings, had covered their eyes and faces, there was no scent or color in their aura, and their voices crackled. These figures approached them because they needed strong *solliqas*, yet they also claimed they were specks of stardust." Jade is breathing hard. "And *you*, Ulf, felt as if you were being pulled into a vortex and then saw the manipulators that serve Namid."

Jade is looking at all of us fiercely. There's a glint of mania in those typically composed eyes. "Don't you all see?"

No one responds right away. Her words are whirling around us, funneling us into a storm of uncertainty.

"Most of us saw the same kind of black and purple... substance," I mutter.

"Portals," Jade clarifies. "These were all clearly portals. Even the black and white tunnel that Ivar mentioned."

"Ha!" Athena grins. "I knew it."

"But we haven't been taught about this," Ivar interrupts.

"Of course you haven't," Eliina speaks up. "These portals can go *anywhere* and are highly dangerous. It was supposed to remain between the Council members unless absolutely necessary."

"You didn't think the combination of portals and a big moons festival meant '*absolutely necessary*,'" Eira throws at her.

"Is that where Erika went?" Odin murmurs.

We all shut up. He's been even more reserved than Fraya and barely functioning, a ghost of his soul.

"It could be," Jade says gently. "But we don't know that yet."

"Then what *do* you know?" Fraya asks. She's definitely overloaded and swamped under everyone's emotions, yet her eyes are full of hope. *A rarity among us.*

"I know there were multiple portals on the night of the Moons Cycle Festival, and they all had similar colors and scents. This leads me to believe the portals all went to the same place. I know there's a connection between the portals and the Council members, especially Namid and Nova. I know there were peculiar creatures who approached some of this group the day of the festival, and their voices and inability to be read indicate they weren't from here. I'm convinced this was Nova's doing, especially with them using the term 'stardust,' one that's in her jewelry and very soul. I know the scent of these portals is similar to the purple substance seen on both Mayra and Zaya. It came out of Hadwin and Athena when they were traveling between worlds against their will. Based on what we've now identified about the portals, I think it's clear that Hadwin and Athena were portaled to Earth by something."

"Fuck," Nyx hisses. "Someone is clearly targeting our group. But *why*?"

"Why, indeed," Jade muses. She shifts her focus to Eliina. "And you did state that the Council members were needing Nyx's group of banished *solliqas*. We learned this from you long before the festival."

Eliina swallows. "They're all quite powerful souls."

"*What?*" I bark. "So, what were we needed for? For these fucking portals? Some sort of sick sacrifice from the Council to who in Cudhellen knows what?"

"That's not all," Jade adds. "Eira, what did you notice about your bear marking this week?"

"It's—It's gotten darker and more uncomfortable," Eira mumbles. "I thought it had to do with something related to Tryg."

"While Eliina shared with you that Tryg has a family connection to bear *maji*, what she didn't tell you is that others do, too,"

Jade responds. She rolls her tongue over the top of her teeth. "Do you know which *solliqa* does specifically? Council Member Waneta."

"What the fuck?" Ivar mutters. "You're suggesting a Council member, who we've never interacted with, is behind the bear marking on Eira?"

"I'm saying that there could be more than one *solliqa* harming her right now," Jade says. "We don't know everything. These are the facts of what's happened. And to make matters more confounding, watch what this *skelter* can do."

Gods, I managed to forget there was an injured skelter *down here. It reeks bad enough. I should be constantly aware of it. I won't admit this to Athena, but maybe I do need a bath.*

We all turn wide-eyed faces to the *skelter*. It's lying on the ground, and it looks semi-alert to its surroundings, or I suppose, however alert this kind of creature can get. Jade marches right up to it and gets in its pus-filled face. "Show them what you showed me, you piece of shit," she growls. Her agitation is palpable and feathers start to sprout along the backs of her arms.

I stare at this monster. This poor soul, consumed by its trauma, its pain, its misery. It has a gaping mouth and sunken sockets where eyes were moments ago. The body is morphing quickly, and it's currently made up of writhing shadows and strings of tendons. Nothing happens. We don't make a sound, trusting that Jade wouldn't have brought this up and physically transferred the monster to the Council building unless it was important. Jade narrows her eyes and huffs. She turns on a heel and walks toward Eliina. Without a word, Jade grabs Eliina's arm and shoves her in front of the *skelter*.

"Show them!" Jade cries.

The *skelter's* lanky neck twitches, and its abnormal head flicks from side to side, taking Eliina's face in. Eliina's eyes are glued to the raveled rug below them. A few seconds go by, and right when I'm convinced Jade is going to shift into her crow form, the *skelter* squirms into motion. It's still tied down with Jade's *maji*, but its body alters and changes until humanoid arms and legs and a normal-looking head appear where its decaying form just was. Blond hair sweeps over the *skelter's* shoulders and striking black and green eyes pop into where the sunken sockets used to be. Eliina slowly raises her head from the floor and stares into the mirror image of her own face.

Gods help us. Everyone collectively gasps and either cries out, shrieks, or screams. I'm speechless as I watch Eliina gaze... at *Eliina*. The monster changed into an identical form of the Grand Healer. They could be twins. This creature that's been taken over by the plague, the disease that everyone wants the Queen of Light to fight against, has camouflaged itself as a regular *solliqa*. No, not regular. A really fucking powerful *solliqa*. *Does this mean the* skelter *has Eliina's same powers?*

A sinister silence wraps itself around us, raising the hairs on my skin. No one says a word, and then chaos erupts. It's a detonation of fury.

I instinctively transform into a python, and my tail is already wrapped around Eliina's ankles.

Eira explodes into blue flames, and Nyx's shadows form into lethal daggers, each one pointed at Eliina's quivering body. Zaya shimmies in between them, her fur sticking straight out while a low growl builds in her tiny throat. Those gold eyes shine as brightly as Eira's light.

Athena snarls and yanks on the chains already around Eliina, causing her to shift forward and closer to Nyx's shadows.

Daru shifts into a large bird of prey, green and black feathered wings sweeping out to his sides. He snaps his beak at Ellina's back, keeping her trapped between him and Nyx.

Ivar summons a gust of wind that funnels around Eliina and the *skelter*.

Odin—Odin is seething and overwhelmed by worry for his

sister. Rain starts to pour against the windows, pounding in full force, begging to be let in.

Fraya is watching with bared teeth, but her body is shaking.

Hauke has Stefanie in a tight hold, and they're watching. Waiting with bated breath.

Ulf is crouched low in front of us, his wolf's shadows growing larger with Eira's light shining on them.

Jade steps forward and gradually closes the distance between her and Eliina. She has a blade in one hand and deadly talons on the other. None of us have much use for blades anymore, not with how powerful each of our *maji* has become. It's one of the reasons I admire Jade—she keeps a blade close to her at all times, always relishing in the way it feels to slice open the skin of a panic-stricken foe.

"Go ahead," Jade spits. "Share your secrets—while you can."

SIXTEEN

Astira

Humans will adapt if we allow ourselves to,
but we have to believe that it's possible.
More so, we have to believe that it's worth the pain.
-Rike Tonish, Commander of Sweazn Investigative Forces

Can a human die from the weight of their own emotions? Possibly, but the question spins around me until it flows up into smoky shadows, rising from my body as if my flesh is crackling with fire. The smoke circulates and swirls into the form of a hostile wolf. It snaps its jaws at my neck, each tooth as sharp as a whetted knife. Yet I don't wince or protect myself in any way. I relax my body further into the fresh hole in the ground, my shoulder blades burrowing deeper into the bed of soil. It's a bed I've made for myself. I'm no longer resisting the way it calls to me—in my sleep, in the waking hours, in the nightmares that blur the two states of consciousness together.

I've been here before, I'm sure of it. Lying in this specific grave, alone and unafraid.

I can't stop thinking about how I got here. Did someone kill me? No, no, that's not right. I made this bed. I knew what I was *doing. I allowed my own emotions to get the better of me and crush my soul into a million pieces. Grief swallowed me whole, and I threw myself into its greedy mouth.*

Is that what this wolf is? It's familiar, too. I know that I've seen it before, somewhere, perhaps so long ago, that it's barely a memory. This predator opens its jaw wide and tries to clamp down around my frail body over and over and over again. Doesn't it see that its attempts are useless?

Smoke and shadows can't move me. I'm already dead.

The wolf starts to whine, and a low growl saturated with fear rips through the air above me. It starts to dig out the dirt, which is odd. This wolf can touch and move the dirt, but it can't make contact with me. I sink into the ground even farther until I've become a part of the earth itself in the worst ways imaginable. I have the urge to cough up the dirt that's piled into my throat and is now caked along my withered bones.

Something is clawing at me from the inside. It's trying to break free, but I don't know where it thinks it'll go. I'm so far beneath the surface, much deeper than six feet under. It's okay, though. Whatever is trying to escape doesn't need to fight this hard. I've been here before, and I'll travel to this grave once again in another lifetime. It's the cycle I'm chained to, since I can't remember what to do differently. At this moment, I know my life doesn't need to end this way. My soul could finally be done with all these vicious life lessons, if only I could learn from them. Yet I don't. I wallow in my emotions and all common sense and instincts are lost.

What is trying to get out of me? It's starting to scratch the surface, but I can't say that I'm upset. The pain is incredible, as if I'm full of life once again. Is that what this is? A new life? Another chance to learn the lesson given to my soul? I want to start again, so that I can finally show I understand. I need to get a better handle on my feelings. I can do it. I know I can. A pressure builds at the center of my body of bones, and then a release as sweet as thick honey cascades over me. When I peer up, I expect to see more dirt or perhaps a tiny opening, allowing me to see the sky. I don't see any of this. I see that smoky and shadowy wolf again.

It's staring at me with eyes as dark as the absence of light underground. When I look into them, I'm met with the same sensation I just had, where I'm buried in a grave. Waves of darkness lap against me, and I'm surprised I can feel them. They're not wet. It's a warm caress letting me know that it's going to be okay. This predator above me becomes more frantic, and there's that low whine again. Possessiveness ripples toward me mixed with a fresh coat of fear.

This wolf is scared and trying to protect me? From what? Can't it see that I'm unable to move?

"Astira," the wolf growls in my ear. "You must wake up."

"I don't want to," I mumble. It's shifting into another form, yet I can't make out what it is. It's no longer smoke and shadows. There's a glimmer of starlight woven throughout it—especially in its eyes. It's staring into my soul, and I'm gazing back into the galaxy.

"You need to," the wolf insists. "There's no more time. You won't get to learn the lesson. You'll have to master it in a new world. I won't let your soul die a permanent death."

Confusion overtakes me. None of this makes any sense. I always take a final rest in this grave before entering my next lifetime. There's always more time to learn and grow. Always.

"Please," it whines. "Please, you need to let go. You're holding onto Earth too strongly for me to take you with me."

"Why would I go with you?" I ask. I can't look away from the solar system deep in his eyes.

"Because," it growls. "You've hidden from me for centuries, denying yourself the love you deserve. I won't let you do it again. You belong to me."

The wolf's head changes forms into hundreds of faces. So many flash by, some men, some women, some humans somewhere in between. My mind can't keep up with each image, yet one thing stays the same: those ruinous eyes, somehow full of the brightness only found in stars. They peer right through me, and I'm hit with a sudden longing to touch this creature. Hands I didn't realize existed reach up toward the wolf. It latches onto my arm and tugs me upward. My back starts to arch off the dirt floor I've made my home. I'm being lifted and—

"Astira," someone hisses.

My eyes fly open, and I let out a breath I didn't know I was holding. Gasping, I roll to my side, coughing up any dirt still lodged in my throat. Yet... nothing comes up. The immediate sensation I felt upon waking up was suffocation and something I can't quite explain. It's similar to the ache in one's chest when they hear the person they love is going away for a long time, and they'll have limited contact. That specific moment where grief slashes its way through you, until you're consumed by rage and a deep, numbing ache in your heart.

None of this makes any sense, and the environment around me is even more confusing. I'm disoriented, and even with the soft, buttery glow of the lights in this room, I can't make sense of where I'm at. *We were just in the tunnel. Liv and I wiggled our way out of their clutches.* I glance wildly around the room, and my gaze snags on my forearm. *Is that a bite mark? Was I not dreaming? Where is the wolf now?*

"Astira." The voice is a bit louder now, though still muted. I think I recognize it. "Hey, it's me! You're okay."

Blinking the last of my dream away, the outline of Liv comes into view before me. She crouches down next to the small bed I'm lying on. *Wait, a bed? With actual sheets and a pillow?* I hesitantly place a hand against the blue cotton sheets, its softness startling me. My gaze moves back to my friend. Liv's wearing a normal white T-shirt with baggy black leggings and some kind of leather shoes. Her straight black hair has been cut shorter into an asymmetrical bob. There are no white or gray streaks in it, but even a simple haircut makes Liv look more like her usual self. Hazel eyes find mine, and I gnaw at my bottom lip as I take in the dark circles under her eyes and the wary expression on her face.

"You're okay," Liv repeats. I know she's saying it for my sake, but I can't shake the feeling that it's also a question. *Am I okay?*

I open my mouth to speak, but my throat is too dry to utter more than a raspy sound. Liv jumps up, and in her haste, nearly knocks over a jug of water on the bedside table. She manages to fill a glass of it despite the tremble in her fingers, and she gets on her knees next to me. It's annoying to not be able to do this myself. With the clear worry on Liv's face, I let her bring the glass to my lips and lean my head back, so she can more easily pour the water down my throat. I swallow and glance at the walls behind her. They are tan with brown and blue swirling designs painted on them. Thin tubes glow with a faint light along the tops of the walls. There are no picture frames or artwork hanging around us. I can see a small statue sitting on the floor near the open door, a wooden carving of blooming flowers in a vase.

Liv notices where I'm staring. "We don't have much artwork anymore," she murmurs. "Some of us have had to get creative to bring life to our new home."

New home? "Where are we?" I croak. Liv helps me take another drink before answering.

"Hm, there's a lot to catch you up on," Liv mutters. She strokes the side of my head and tucks some of my hair behind my ear. Twice. "I'm just glad you're awake."

"How long have I been sleeping? Days?" I clear my throat and swallow more water, soaking in the way it flows down into my body.

Liv frowns and plays with the ends of my fiery hair. Even without looking at it, I can tell it's seen better days. At least it still spills down my back—a protective blanket.

"What do you last remember?" she asks.

I search as far back as I can in my memories. It's difficult to think about anything when I'm still partially consumed by my dream. I want to tell her that I remember being buried in my grave and how a wolf tried to rescue me, but I doubt that's what she wants to hear right now. I push myself to go deeper into my mind and check every corner, even the ones with cobwebs. My body jumps as a memory hits me.

"We were in the tunnel," I whisper. "You were being carried by a man with black hair. He was wearing clothes similar to what you're wearing now. And he mentioned *Jace*. He knows Jace!"

Liv's eyes light up. "He does. You then passed out. I mean, we both did, but I woke up soon after arriving. You've been asleep for a frightening amount of time."

My eyebrows furrow. "How long have I been out for? And where were we taken?"

Liv makes a popping sound with her lips and looks away. The way her muscles are ticking in her jaw tells me she's stressed about whatever she's going to share with me. Fatigue rushes over me—I'd kill for some more sleep.

Groaning, I stretch out my ankles and toes until they crack in relief, and the rest of my muscles extend in a domino effect. I move onto my back again and let my eyelids droop. "You can tell me later," I mumble around another yawn. "Time for bed."

"No!" Liv says a little too harshly.

She yells out and footsteps bound toward the doorway. My eyelids are heavy, and this bed is too comfortable for me to care. Crackling, white noise starts at a low hum inside my head, and I nestle back into the cozy bed. I haven't been on an actual mattress in at least a few years. *Liv and anyone else will have to drag me off this thing.* The sound gets louder and fizzles in my ear drums. As I breathe in, a saccharine smell slithers up my nostrils, and I become unnerved and restless. *Perhaps I'll end up in that grave again.*

Firm, calloused hands grab my shoulders, and I'm being shaken before I can process another thought. I narrow my eyes and scowl at whoever is moving me. "Don't touch me," I snarl. Even I can hear how halfhearted it is. "Just let me sleep."

"I'm afraid I can't let you do that," a deep, yet honeyed voice says.

I open my eyes wider and nearly choke. "*Jace?*"

His wavy blond hair is pulled up in a messy bun on top of his head. Cautious gray eyes search mine, and I don't miss the exhaustion that radiates off him. He still offers me a crooked smile, and that's all it takes for a sob to break free.

"Jace," I cry. He swoops me up in his cozy arms, even bulkier than I remember, and burrows his face in my neck. I don't know how long he holds me, but it must be at least an hour. I'm still hiccuping as he cradles me in his arms, now rocking me gently back and forth on the bed.

"Jace," I whisper. My voice is hoarse. He pushes back the heaps of hair that keep falling in front of my face. Because he's him, he uses the back of his sleeve to wipe under my snotty nose.

"Ugh," I grumble. "Gross."

My friend chuckles and gives me another hug. It's tight—the kind you give someone when you're afraid they'll disappear again.

"I'm so glad you're here and awake," Jace mumbles into the side of my head.

I sit up straighter and wipe more tears from my eyes. "That's what Liv said," I choke. "I'm starting to think I've been knocked out for months. And you—I can't even believe you're here with me!"

"We have *a lot* to share with you, my friend," Jace says. "I need to make sure that you're okay to move around, though. Once the doctor checks you out and gives the green light, we'll get some food in you and can talk about what's been happening."

I hiccup. *Embarrassing.* "Can you at least tell me how long I've been asleep? And where are we? I'm in an actual bed!" I glance down at my body and squeal. "And I'm wearing normal clothes!"

Jace cringes. "Yeah, it's disgusting what some groups of people have done over the past few years. Not to worry, though. You won't be going back *there* anytime soon." He shakes his head and looks me dead in the eyes. "You've been in a coma for four months. And while you and Liv were snatched up by a fucking cult that believes in torturing women, I've been climbing the ranks here into a role of leadership. I realized early on that only those in power would have even a chance at survival, and I wasn't going down without a fight. We've been separated by tunnels and ruthless psychos with terrifying weapons for almost two years now. I've been searching for our friends nonstop, but there are too many different pathways out of this city. I just—at least you're here *now*." He drags a hand down his face and heaves a tired sigh.

"Where is here?" I ask.

"We're in Nedrazon. The subterranean city that was built beneath the country of Sweazn."

My eyes are as wide as dinner plates. "Our whole country is underground?"

Jace's eyes darken to the color of a stormy sea. "No. Only a certain number of people could fit down here, given the amount of space and limited resources at the time. One city was constructed beneath each country, at least for the ones still existing after the beginning of the nuclear war. That's all they had time to build. These only exist because of the first nuclear wars and our governments knowing that if it happened once, it could always happen again. This place, Nedrazon, wasn't built with the goal of moving all of humanity underground. It was the government's half-assed safety net that they knew could only catch a handful of citizens. The rest of them died in the nuclear fallout, their bodies burned from the inside out from radioactivity."

The room spins. I force myself to take deep breaths. "Yet we survived?" I whisper, hoping he hears the question I'm too afraid to ask.

"I only know that you, Liv, and I are alive from our group of friends. I—I have suspicions about Ruse and Lyk. Please. Please let Dr. Acklin check on you first, and then we can talk more, okay?"

As if on cue, a thin woman wearing all black strides into the room. She has thick brown hair that sticks out in all sorts of directions around her narrow face. She's not wearing a typical doctor jacket, yet what do I expect? Jace did say we're living in a subterranean city. I imagine wearing a white jacket is the farthest thing from their minds. This Dr. Acklin has a bright crimson band wrapped around her arm, which I'm assuming alerts others of her position. *How interesting. Wearing the color of blood to represent what you do for a living.* Warm eyes greet Jace and then settle their attention on me. I can feel her assessment from here: *a woman consisting of tangled hair, thin skin, and brittle bones— a living ghost.*

This doctor might read too much about me, which I'm not fucking about to let happen, so I focus my attention on my friend, the warmhearted goofball of our group. Well, whatever is left of our friends. He stands up to greet the doctor and gives her a quick hug. *Our Jace, that affectionate soul, has always shown his love through touch.* I can get a better view of him now, and he's still relatively lithe. There's some more muscle packed into his arms and chest. A bright blue band is wrapped around his arm, and I wonder if that's to indicate his leadership status. *What kind of leader is he?*

It's challenging to imagine him in any form of leadership. Jace has always been smart and hardworking, but his attitude toward our world leaders? Absolute shit. He's the one who chose the path of therapy, so that he could help people heal at the ground level, and he couldn't stand politics or the government. He and Tryg used to get into it all the time, and Jace was insistent that he was meant to be in a more gentle and compassionate field. Yet *he* is a leader here? After fumbling around for gods know how long and knowing most of humanity has died? *Fuck, the world has turned upside down.*

A few days pass before I'm fully cleared to explore Nedrazon. Dr. Acklin hasn't been too bad, but she's spent more time poking and prodding me than I'd prefer. She's mostly reserved and immerses herself in each task. She carries around what I think is a tablet, and when I asked how it functions this far underground, I was told electricity in a subterranean city isn't impossible. It's still sparse around the world and limited to the major cities. Tap, tap, tap go her dark fingers as she makes notes about my progress. The moments Dr. Acklin places her entire focus on how I'm feeling, though, or asks if there are any prior injuries I'd like for her to check out, genuine empathy hits me at full force. Both she and Liv were the ones to help me bathe after I first woke up, insisting that it's okay to wash myself, that I deserve to be clean.

An emotional wreck doesn't come close to how I was the first day interacting with everyone. The never-ending kindness from each person I met, from the way Dr. Acklin held me as I cried when Liv had to cut a few inches off my hair to being given a choice—*a simple fucking choice*—of which colors I wanted to wear, has nearly broken me. I caught myself tearing up at first because it reminded me of Eira and Athena. They were meant to be therapists, and I hope wherever their spirits went, they're getting a well-deserved rest.

Liv holds my hand as we walk down a paved pathway to where Jace lives. She claims it's because she's missed me, but by the stiffness of her grip, I know she needs to physically touch me because she's afraid to let go. I get that. While I can be a moody prick, so similar to how Tryg was during his worst moments, my heart isn't made of stone. I've always relished the love from my friends and their ability to see the best in me, even when I haven't. I'm also scared to let go of her and, now, Jace. There are too many demons still out there, and knowing my luck, they're hiding in plain sight. Damon, Shira, and the others flash behind my eyes, and I can't deny that the nightmares I've been having might be more than just dreams.

What if I'm heading down the same road as Eira, Athena, and Tryg? Where... where did they go?

The clattering sound of metal brings me back to the moment. A few people in matching black and blue clothes drop a few steel sheets across the large pathway we're walking on. It's wide enough to accommodate a few cars—the models that were finally built again less than a decade ago—but there are none of those machines down here. I don't even see the motorbikes that Eira was fond of or hear the roar of a train.

Much about technology has been lost over time. I still can't be sure why our government allowed certain devices to be distributed, like the phones or robotic teachers in schools or insisting we had to scan our faces in order to enter a work building. *Fuck, I hope that isn't down here.* I snort thinking about the times this came up in our friend group, and Jace was adamant the government was trying to control us. He had said it's the only thing that makes sense for them to have the power to create more effective transportation yet only allow citizens to engage with robots or screened devices.

Jace thought, and I bet still thinks, the government wanted a way to keep an eye on each individual while limiting our ability to easily flee the country. I think it's a mixture of that and people being paralyzed by fear. The less technological advances given freely to the world, the less of a chance we'd have at repeating history's greatest mistakes. *Yet the ones in charge made sure to keep missiles ready for another war, so they couldn't have been that afraid. Maybe they were more afraid of their people than anything.*

I pull Liv to a brief stop and stoop to touch the paved concrete we're walking on, desperate to physically touch anything and everything in this new city. *So few of our country have survived to walk this same pathway as me.* It occurs to me that whoever designed this city wasn't thinking realistically about which items or inventions would be the priority in the case of nuclear attacks. These steel and concrete buildings were built on the foundation of hope. So that means the pathways are big enough to fit a vehicle or two. Some of the buildings are in the shape of traditional homes when that size of a house is a luxury *no one* can afford down here.

Jace had explained the apartment he's in is small enough to drive someone crazy, but being able to live in one signifies that you're safe, that you survived the attacks above.

Nedrazon reminds me of a smaller version of the cities in southern Sweazn, except the buildings are only made of metal here. And while they're tall, they don't reach as high as some of the skyscrapers I used to walk past on my way to work. Some of the structures are made of clay, contrasting with the coldness of the metal. I soak up every detail of this place that I can. Varying sizes of tubes run along the different buildings. They flicker with the light from the solar panels. The mixture of lights on metal is disorienting, as if we're wandering in a futuristic world on our own planet.

Everywhere I look, I see people working in some way. Half a

dozen workers—each with a dusty gold band on their arms—are constructing a new building down the road. There are no tubes on this structure yet, a shadow in this city of fabricated light. Small groupings of young adults hover close together across the street. They're not laboring away as much as socializing and throwing insults at a different group that struts by them, slandering one another to pass the time. A woman and her two children scurry around them, each with a satchel of crops from a nearby field. Even the children have marked arm bands, a bright purple. There are fields designated for growing food in patches of soil. They're sprinkled in between groupings of buildings, and they each have bigger solar panels placed high above them. For some reason, it's more jarring to witness a functioning society underground than the primitive environment Liv and I were stuck in.

"I can't believe we can grow food down here," I murmur.

Liv shifts her gaze to where I'm looking. "I know," she agrees. "It's incredible. That's an area I've been helping in and can show you the ropes tomorrow, if you're interested. The workers have also been able to grow cotton and other supplies. And to think we were stuck in a cult that starved us of these resources. It's nauseating how they treated us and so many others."

"Ain't that the fucking truth," I mutter. "They couldn't get power in a respectable way, so they forcibly took what they could get."

Liv shoots me a look. "I don't imagine those living in this city are any more respectable. Knowing what Jace had to do to survive, both the cults and Nedrazon are neck and neck with one another. The leaders here don't keep people in cages, though. That's a plus."

"Hm," I hum. "What exactly did Jace have to do?"

Her eyes shutter. "He made himself a villain, so dangerous and feared, to ensure those who can't protect themselves are safe.

But that's our friend's story to tell, Astira. You should ask him about it."

The idea of Jace being *dangerous* is laughable, but so is the idea that we're all living underground. Who knows what's possible? Liv has been awake longer than me, and it makes sense that she'd have a better understanding of how our friend is doing and what he's been up to. Even though it's been a few months, I don't think it's hit Liv that we're no longer prisoners. She has busied herself with helping Jace find others still imprisoned in the tunnels by violent leaders. Our situation was pretty fucked, and at least for me, it'll take years beyond my death to fully process what I went through with Damon. Liv might be cut from a different fabric than me. She lets her tears fall freely while she's working or planning, while I lock everything in a vault—not even I can get to it.

My friend is relentless with her work. She's convinced that her sister, Lyk, is being held in a different tunnel. We've discussed how we can't know how Lyk will be and what kind of state she'll even be in if we find her. The only response Liv has given Jace and me these past few days is that regardless of her sister's physical or mental shape, there are certain bonds that you can't break. She said that she's positive there's love for her out there somewhere, but as long as she has her sister, she doesn't need anyone else. Liv believes her twin sister is a type of soul mate for her. It won't matter what's been done to her; they'll be able to heal one another in time.

Liv nudges her head toward another group of people to our right. I follow where she's pointing, and near what could be an area for communal bathing are large basins full of soapy water. Small clusters of adults, ranging in ages, huddle around each of them while scrubbing dirty clothes. I instinctively touch the edges of my shirt, the cotton so light compared to the animal skins we were forced to wear. It's been a good two years since I last wore anything even remotely normal, and it's unsettling. Dressed in a new shirt and pants, covering most of my body, makes me feel almost human. It's an idea that was kicked, shoved, hit, and whipped out of me back in the tunnels.

Damon made sure when he picked me out of the captured women that I'd roam from my cell to the dining hall with only his dirty animal skins on me. He had said it's important to mark his territory, and to emphasize his point, he'd forced me to my knees and whipped out his dick. I thought I'd go through another round of being coerced to give someone head, yet he proceeded to take a piss all over my shaking body. I still can't decide which is worse—being covered in his urine or believing I deserved it.

I ball the soft material of my shirt in my fists. *Fuck him. Fuck him for everything he did to me and for shaming me, as if I don't deserve to wear normal clothing. Fuck him for making me feel unworthy, for making me feel inhuman.*

Liv touches one of my hands and laces her fingers with mine. "I know," she whispers. Her eyes are glassy. "I couldn't even leave the makeshift hospital for a week after I woke up. Going from being treated the same as the filth under their feet to seeing people act so *normal* was surreal. It'll take some time. The fact that you're out here walking around with me after only a few days shows just how strong you are, Astira."

I let her unfurl my fists, but I don't respond. I don't want to be told how strong I am. I want to be told that I don't need to be.

I'm not cruel enough to laugh at the idea of me being strong or throw back in her face what she just said to me. Both the tunnels, or apparently fucking cults, and this city are neck and neck with one another. That thought should terrify me, really, but I learned at a young age that fear won't save me. Only *I* can save me, and I do it best when I unfasten the hold I have on my rage. That wolf I met in my last nightmare comes to mind. A beast of shadows and smoke and beautiful, snarling energy. *That's exactly what I am.*

I don't know who the Damon is of Nedrazon, but gods help me, he won't know what the fuck hit him when he meets my wrath.

SEVENTEEN
Tryg

*You have to foster the relationship
between you and the creature you shift into.
It might be one or two or hundreds.
Every single one of them is directly tied to your soul.*
-Nixie, Goddess of Shapeshifting

Wrath that these could be my final moments coats itself along me like black ice. The demons tremble in anticipation, finally surging to the surface again at the sound of my temper flaring. *Fuck, I don't want them here, but they feed on any negative energy that swells beneath the surface of my soul.*

A flash of burgundy and ruby feathers swarm in front of my vision. My jaw drops as I stare up into the eyes of what must be a mighty phoenix. A labyrinth of gold designs weave in and out of the feathers and form a crystalized mask around its eyes. Those incredible eyes. They're purple and green and brown and black. Streaks of red flow through them, the same color as the feathers. *Am I meeting a god before my soul leaves this new realm?* That must be it. I'm still stuck to the back of this *drekstri*, and the wind has pushed me flat on my back while my hips and legs are forced in a sitting position. There's nothing I can do, and I'm left with an aching sensation of regret.

How did I let my demons take over? Why did I let them win? All the wrath in the world couldn't fix the situation I'm in.

"You're a bleak one through and through," the phoenix booms.

Eyes wide and mouth open, I can't do more than gape at this magnificent creature flapping its long wings in front of me.

"I am rather magnificent, aren't I?" The phoenix chuckles in a deep voice this time.

It lands in front of me, its head towering above me before it brings its large beak in front of my face in a swift, swooping motion. "Tryg, you need to wake up. You know who I am."

My brain stops functioning as I take in the different tones of red and the hazel eyes. *Fucking Daya.* I look around, my movements becoming more feral by the second. "This *was* you, wasn't it?" I scream up at her. The *drekstri* is back to its peaceful, casual flying, and there's barely a breeze. "What the *fuck*?"

She chuckles again in that profound voice, wildly at odds with the short humanoid form she usually takes. "I needed to know if you were able to be saved before we arrive."

"So you turned into a fucking phoenix?"

Daya fluffs out her feathers and opens that huge beak. She cries out, the sound blaring as loud as an alarm. The first image that comes to mind is of a warrior in battle calling for help. *But who is she calling for? And why?*

"I needed to see how you'd react if you thought you were going to die," she says and snaps her beak. "Even with those desolate thoughts, you didn't give up when this form flew in front of you. The main emotion I could taste from your aura was *regret*."

My face screws up in a scowl. "You can taste my emotions?"

"This form can!" Daya shouts and lifts her head up again,

screeching. "Eira isn't the only *solliqa* with the powers of a goddess."

"You—you're a goddess?" I ask with wide eyes.

Daya doesn't respond. She snaps her beak at my face again and shifts into a smaller scarlet bird that soars in a circle around me.

"I'm sorry you thought you were going to die," she calls out. "That kind of stress is fuel for your demons, but I *needed* to know for sure that you weren't going to give up. Some souls experience peace upon giving up their spirits and knowing they'll be turned into stardust. Others face confusion or sadness. Feeling remorseful that you caved into your pain is key, and the only way you'd know this was to face the actual possibility of dying." She lands right in front of me, and it's remarkable how so much power exists in such a tiny creature.

"You've accepted that you'd regret dying," she continues. "So, don't let it come to that. Free yourself from your chains."

"Why do you care this much about what happens to *my* soul?"

"Each of our souls holds a key in this universe. Some keys are rarer than others. I care about you as a healer. I need you to survive for other reasons. We all do."

"Who the fuck is *we*? What are you keeping from me?"

Daya stares me down. A hundred words are expressed in one look, and I can't keep up with them. "That kind of information is earned, not simply given. You'll learn more when you've proven you'll do what it takes to survive."

"But I'm a *monster*," I whisper while forcing myself up into a sitting position again. "Even if I could get these cords off, why take that kind of risk?"

Daya cocks her head to the side, and both hazel eyes penetrate through what I am. As she stares at me, the demons shiver and move back to darker corners. *They know she can destroy them.*

"Even monsters deserve a chance at redemption," Daya says. "Until you're a *canielor*, there's always a chance to heal yourself if you're willing to try. Eliina's method didn't work for you, for more than one reason. She wanted to keep Eira and everyone else safe. While I understand why she did it, all it did was isolate you and didn't really push you to make a decision about your life. Do you have what it takes, Tryg? Or have you already labeled the situation as 'too late' and aren't able to put the work in?"

"Look at me!" I scream. One of the demons senses the dread that's creeping its way back in, that hopelessness that I won't be able to free myself. It pushes out of my neck, a slippery, dark substance, just enough to make an appearance, and wraps itself tightly along my shoulders. The black markings that appear under it are like lashes—a reminder that my soul has been tainted.

"I am," Daya says calmly. "But are you?"

I stare at her as she shifts back into her humanoid form. That auburn hair whips wildly around her narrow face, and those hazel eyes have turned a deep red.

"Look at the cords holding you down," she commands. I do as she says, but I don't understand what she's getting at.

"Thanks for the reminder," I mutter.

Daya leaps toward me and smacks me on the side of my head. Twice.

"Wake up!" she barks. "Look at the cords and compare them to the markings around your shoulders. What do you notice?"

My eyes dart back and forth multiple times until both images combine as one.

"They're the same," I whisper. My head raises to face Daya. "How are they the same?"

"It was quite easy," she whispers back. "I wanted something to hold you down that'd be next to impossible to break through, yet once you did, a piece of you would heal and realize what you're capable of. I manipulated the demons' shadows with my own healing powers and formed them into these cords. You were so busy focusing on your own internal battle, you didn't even realize what was going on around you in the present moment."

Did Daya trick me into a healing session?

She smirks. "Pretty clever of me to do so, huh?"

"Argh!" I yell. "Stop listening to my thoughts."

"Break out of these cords, and I will."

"How?" I mumble.

"Remember, focus on your breath," Daya says. There's an edge of seriousness to her tone now. "Only *you* can connect with your own *maji*. No other soul can do this for you. You have to be the one to decide you want to live and be free of these demons and this sickening plague. Consider your strengths, your connection to bears, *anything*. Inhale and find that strength. Exhale and let your breath connect to your powers."

The cords tighten enough to cut into my skin. Blood trickles down my legs, and I watch it drip onto the flying beast underneath me. My breath can stay at a steady rhythm, but any sources of power or abilities eddy from my mind. *What can I do? What makes me so fucking special?*

"Why am I connected to bears?" I ask.

Daya shrugs. "Who knows? My soul didn't ask to be connected to birds. I don't imagine Eira asked to be tied to blue fire and creatures of light. None of us ask to be born into our soul families. Some of us luck out, and our connections are stronger than ever. Others, such as some of our companions, find their families only appeared real on the surface, and they need to search for their actual *almaoves*. It doesn't matter where your soul comes from. It matters what you do with the power connected to it."

We sit in silence as I let that thought settle over me. *It doesn't matter where my soul comes from. It matters what I do with the power connected to it.*

"If I was a bear," I finally rasp. "I'd want its courage and ferocity. If I believed I also had magical powers in this world, I'd choose to transform into a bear and use its strength to help others. My bear form would help me dominate the hold these demons have on my soul. I suspect they've been with me for lifetimes. *My* bear would be able to mangle them, to crush them with my paws."

I place my hands on the cords around my waist, knowing full well that I'll get shocked in the process. Electrical waves spasm their way up my arms and into my chest, but I don't let go. I keep my focus on my breath and watch as the sparks bound from joint to joint. On my next exhale, I send every thought and feeling possible toward my hands, practically begging them to transform into a bear.

Daya's face is millimeters from my own. "And what will you give your bear if you can use your *maji*?"

An unexpected sob escapes me, and I lower my head, hoping Daya doesn't notice how many tears are streaming out. "Respect," I cry. "I'll give my bear gratitude and respect. Anything it wants. I don't want my soul to be overtaken by these demons. I want a chance to be better. *Please.*"

Tears fall onto my wrists, and I instinctively cringe away from them. *Why am I crying? I don't cry. It's weak. Why am I crying on top of a* drekstri? *Why won't the tears blow away in the wind?*

I don't have time to consider my questions or why this is happening to me now of all times. My hands glow a bright white and tan and brown, and inch by inch, they shift into ginormous gold paws. Long, lethal claws grow out of them, my own personal form of defense. I can't speak as the claws glimmer with splashes of orange and yellow—all words get caught in my throat. I don't know what the rest of my bear form will appear as, but based on the paws, I'll blaze as hot as a sun. My head moves between my new paws and Daya, hoping that she'll provide some kind of explanation and what I should do next.

Fragments of thoughts splinter through me, each of them in a state of shock that *I have fucking paws*. I can turn into an animal. *Shit*.

Much to my dismay, Daya throws her head back and laughs hysterically. *Fucking. Psycho.*

"Tryggy," she coos. "You *are* an animal. Now use what those paws are here for!"

I hesitantly raise my right paw and prepare to swipe at the cords on my legs. Swallowing, I pause. "What if I slice into my legs? And what's the catch? I don't trust that you're actually helping me for the sake of doing the right thing. I don't fully trust you."

Daya giggles. *One of her other forms must be a hyena.* "Good. That's a good first rule in this world. Trust yourself first, before anyone. Except for your soul bonds. But hopefully you'll give us a chance." She winks and pulls herself up. "When we heal ourselves, we'll often get hurt in the process. We must kill those parts that don't serve us if we're to ever free ourselves. Go ahead and swipe into your leg, Tryg, and watch as some of the demons' holds on you loosens."

I blink at her and raise my hand higher. "Does this mean I shouldn't trust you? Are you taking me somewhere... bad? And who is *us*?"

She smirks again at me and walks back to the head of the *drekstri*. The beast roars into the setting suns, and some of the clouds surrounding us clear away. My heart stutters as I take in what's flying next to us. Hundreds of cloaked figures with delicate gold designs—the same ones I saw on Daya's phoenix form—on their robes are riding smaller versions of *drekstri*. Some are soaring high on creatures I haven't seen yet in Majikaero. They have long snouts with slanted, colorful eyes full of crystals. *So similar to Eira's.*

Graceful feathered wings glide in the now pleasant breeze, and their riders are holding on to thick ridges on their crystalized backs. One of their lengthy tails swings past my head, and I can hear one of the robed figures cackle with delight. I don't think my eyes are playing tricks on me. I sure hope not as I see slightly smaller, fluffier creatures swoop in around us, coming to life in the sky. They're vicious felines with both fur and crystals lining their agile bodies. One of them twirls their way toward a robed figure and lands behind it. The catlike creature stares right at me and shifts into a different form—and now I *definitely* think my eyes are messing with me. It transforms into one of Eliina's healers. I couldn't forget this one, not with her brown and white skin, those red eyes, and how she could shift into that huge as fuck deer.

Daya turns to face me.

"You'll just have to break through what's tying you down and find out."

EIGHTEEN

Athena & Nyx

Strength and power are not often in alignment,
at least not when it counts.
-Written musings from Athena Lilar, Novice Healer

Athena

Out of sight, out of mind is the old saying, isn't it? By the expression on Eliina's face, her secrets are no longer out of sight—quite literally. She doesn't react even remotely stunned by the identical *solliqa* facing her right now. If anything, she looks like she was caught red-handed moving a dead body, which only sparks my anger. Green *maji* thrashes down the chains of leaves and flames toward where Eliina is standing. Her body trembles and jerks even closer to Nyx's blades of shadow. I savor the rush of overpowering such a strong and entitled soul. It's doubtful that I'll always be able to do this, especially to a *solliqa* who's on the Council. Something must have injured Eliina if she was able to be chained to Tryg's dungeon cell.

Part of me doesn't want to know what kind of creature has

that power, not when we're learning about portals and other worlds. A bigger part of me is enraptured and wouldn't mind catching a glimpse of whatever can overpower the strongest souls in Majikaero.

I'm a vicious bitch when the situation calls for it, and *damn*, does it call for it right now. I don't respond well to being manipulated or lied to. No, that's not something I have patience for anymore. Memories of my parents exploiting me as a young girl for their own needs, any way they could use me to get back at one another. Family separations are tragic enough as it is, let alone when your mother paints your skin in fresh bruises and blames it on your father, or when your father force-feeds you false stories about your mother's affairs. The second anyone lies to me now or uses me in any way, I'm *done*. If they do it to my friends, I don't need Eira's fire to burn them to ash. I'll do anything for my friends. The thought of Eira has my magic nearly blistering my skin as I feel her flames blend with my earth *maji*.

Yes, there it is. We'll burn the world to ash as sisters.

Just the thought of Eliina putting all our lives at risk makes me want to slice right through her skin and shred whatever pit of soul hides there. No mercy will be given. I think of Eira and Stefanie selflessly giving themselves this past week to healing various *solliqas* and our friends. Tryg's broken spirit comes to mind. I have to wonder if Eliina was the one who did this to him, if it was her isolating him from us that strangled the last of his goodness. My eyes glance from Hadwin to Daru to Nyx to Ivar to Odin to Fraya to Ulf. There's a glint of renewed betrayal in each of their eyes and the obvious new scars makes me want to scream. And Zaya.

That poor, ferocious baby.

Seeing all these worn out souls in one room, all thanks to Eliina, sends my green *maji* shooting toward the ceiling in bursts of fireworks. The others appear distressed but have their magic restrained and focused on where Eliina is standing.

Not me.

None of them know that my magic is uncontrollable when my temper bubbles over its threshold, and more so, *I don't care.* I've had to keep a tight lid on my darker emotions my whole life, not wanting others to see the vast fury and misery that drowns me. To be able to unleash these pent-up sensations at someone else, especially a soul that deserves it? It's a maddening rush I never want to end.

I lunge toward Eliina, drunk on the surge of my powers, and I nearly stumble into Eira when I see Hadwin briefly spasm in front of us. I'm surprised to see him unwind his thick tail from around her feet. *No, wait, there's something still wrapped around them.* Hadwin's python tail shreds a scaly, silvery layer of skin—as delicate as lace, I find myself wanting to touch it—that sheathes itself around Eliina's legs.

As he slithers out from the glossy material, he glides in my direction. *So, I guess that skin is more robust than it appears.* Hadwin's blond hair has fallen out of its bun and is billowing in soft waves around his ears. The upper half of his body is still humanoid, with sweat dripping down each curve of his muscles on his sculpted chest and abdomen. His chest is moving fast, and instead of that hardened mask or infuriating amused expression he constantly wears, there's a frenzied look plastered across his face. The bottom half of his body shifts back into two legs, and it takes a second to register that he's *running* at me with no intention of stopping.

Hadwin runs straight through the *maji* whipping around me and wraps those burly arms around my waist, forcing us both back onto an empty table. I bounce with a loud *oomph*, my back colliding with the wooden surface. In this moment, everything pauses. My head ricochets and my hair falls out of the twisting braids that were woven on top of my head like a crown. Waves of my dark hair splay out around me. Hadwin holds me tighter as he braces for us to land, forcing my back to arch up into his bare pecs. The swirling pendant falls in between us, its heat reaching out to me even with these robes on. Our eyes lock, and our lips are an inch away from one another. All it takes is that one inhale, of breathing in each other's scents, and I'm a goner. A voice in the back of my head tells me to enjoy this while it lasts because he'll go right back to hiding his emotions and denying our connection. Hadwin's hand reaches up behind my head to cradle it as we finally land with a grunt. His hair swishes on either side of my face, hiding us from the others.

Hadwin's eyes are liquid gold, pouring unspoken feelings into my own. Desire. Shame. Fear. Rage. Concern. So many conflicting, raw emotions flow into my green eyes, and I eagerly soak in *anything* he's willing to give me.

"Hadwin," I whisper. My lips brush against his, and my entire body becomes a live wire.

All the *maji* dangerously shooting out of me funnels back into my soul and seeps into Hadwin's heaving chest. His eyes grow wide as the first of my *maji* reaches for him, needing an outlet for the twisted energy hurdling everywhere inside of me. Hadwin's invisible shield, the one he has up at all times, is a tangible thing as it cracks underneath my power. Relief swells in my heart when his body relaxes marginally against my own, and his mouth slides along my lower lip.

As quickly as it happened, it's gone. Alarm flashes in his eyes, and all those glorious muscles coil back up again. He rears back a few inches, but he doesn't break our staring contest.

"You need to be more careful," Hadwin whispers. His breath still mingles with mine, and I lick my lips, attempting to taste it. To taste *him*. His eyes follow the movement, and a shiver winds down his entire body. "All that power could get a soul killed."

"Would that be such a bad thing?" I ask, savoring the fact that his hair is still hiding our faces.

"That depends." Hadwin's tongue glides over his top teeth.

"On what?"

"On if the soul being harmed is yours."

I suck in a breath. "I'm stronger than that. I could take Eliina down with me."

"But why do you have to go down at all?"

"Maybe... maybe then I can be free," I breathe.

Hadwin shakes his head, his hair moving into my face. It's pure silk that I want to run my hands through.

"No," he murmurs. "You wouldn't be free, *zamia*. You'd be sacrificing yourself to take down a little darkness. There's nothing freeing about that. It'd only be damning."

My eyebrows scrunch up in confusion. "What is that word —*zamia*? And how do you know I'll be damned?"

He raises to his elbows, leaving me wanting to grasp out for more. *No, don't leave yet.*

"Because I felt your *maji*," he mutters. Those golden eyes bore into me. "I felt what you've buried beneath all your healing light. Perhaps you can fool yourself, but you can't fool me. The second you think you're stronger than your magic is the second you're no longer aligned with it. I *know* you're smart enough to understand that, which means you were caving into your powers willingly. Secretly hoping that you might be destroyed in the process of taking out your anger on Eliina. And—and I couldn't stand to watch another soul give up so easily."

Tears blur my vision. I can hear our friends shouting at one another and Jade yelling at Eliina, but I can't bring myself to listen. "Another?"

"Yeah." Hadwin's jaw locks. "Mine."

All the restless fury inside me blows out like a snuffed-out candle. My heart cracks at the realization that Hadwin *saw* me. He saw me for who I am through my *maji*, and he didn't turn away. Hadwin ran straight at it and threw himself at me, hoping he could douse the growing green flames before it was too late. Hardened gold eyes look down at me now, that mask patched up and back in place.

"Let's not distract the others from what's important here," Hadwin grunts.

I gasp at the whiplash of his responses. One of my hands pushes me up from the table, and the other touches the side of my face. The mixture of his glare and words feels like he physically slapped me, but when my fingers push against my cheek, there's nothing there.

"Athena's *maji* has simmered down. She was just being an explosive brat," Hadwin barks to the others. He's stomping over to them, all business again. *Did I imagine that conversation? Was it a dream when he touched my lips?* Hadwin prowls up by Nyx and Eira. "All of us threatening Eliina and whatever the fuck this *canielor* is won't do us any good. Jade, thoughts?"

I watch as Jade turns her glower from Eliina to Hadwin, and then her shoulders drop slightly. Ulf is still in his wolf form and is now settled in between Fraya and Odin. Perhaps he can sense that they're too paralyzed by their feelings to go on the offense. Hauke has moved to place a hand on Ivar's arm, causing his funneling winds to die down to a brisk breeze. Stefanie is holding hands with Eira while her blue flames still travel back and forth between her hand and Eliina's body on the chains we made. Nyx hasn't moved his daggers even an inch while a small Zaya bristles and hisses from on top of his shoulders. And Daru is still in his bird form, but I'm too distressed to acknowledge how gorgeous he looks—all those deep green and black feathers that are nearly glowing with *maji*.

Jade lets out a sharp exhale. "You're right, Hadwin. We need to check ourselves. Nyx, move those daggers to the *skelter*, and Ivar, shift your winds along to this monster, too. Maybe Hadwin can shed more skin to bind it up. Let's keep it contained and in sight. I don't think it's a normal *skelter*. Eira, those flames should keep Eliina locked down." Jade glances back at me. I haven't been able to move from the table, glancing between my friends and the space Hadwin was just occupying. "Athena, keep those powers in line. I know you're still adjusting and learning about them, but giving in completely is reckless. Something we don't talk about enough is how easy it is to overdo a good thing, to let it overpower us until we're lost to it. Our souls don't become stardust from death alone. Sometimes, we destroy our own souls by using our virtuous powers for the wrong reasons."

She tucks away the blade she had drawn on Eliina and pulls over another chair to place right in front of her. Jade takes a seat and leans forward, her forearms on her knees. The others shift to be either next to Jade or in front of the *skelter* to keep a watchful eye on its behaviors. Daru doesn't shift back into his humanoid form, and instead, he flutters to Jade's side and snaps his beak a few times at Eliina's trembling body. Stefanie is the only one who makes her way toward me, her crimson and white coverings glimmering from the flow of all our *maji*, and takes my hand in hers. She smiles faintly and pulls me up, steering us toward where Jade is sitting in front of Eliina. We're under the expansive ceiling windows, but when I peer up at the sky, it's now dark; the suns have finally set. A star-filled sky shines down on us, the maroon and silver moons peeking out in the distance. The outline of Jade's team of crows shifts restlessly on some of the branches. Their colored eyes shine brightly under the reflective light of the rising moons. Stefanie keeps pulling me until we're standing next to Eira, and I'm grateful all their focus is on Eliina right now.

They don't need to see how much I was hoping to lose myself to my powers, or how much I yearn to be *free*. And this was the perfect excuse.

"Hey," Eira murmurs next to me.

We've all taken a few moments to collect ourselves after the *canielor's* reveal and my inability to contain my deeper emotions. I'm in the furthest corner away from everyone else, staring mindlessly out at the night sky. The stars flicker in and out of view, their light sparking a pang of longing. I'm not sure where that comes from and why it's settling at the bottom of my heart. It's there, though, and I have an inkling it won't be leaving me until I follow one of those stars to a place that feels like home.

Eira's fingers tangle with my own. "I felt all of that, too."

Blinking, I lower my head until I'm facing my best friend.

"You can feel *all* of it?" I ask.

Eira smiles at me, the action soft and as warm as my favorite cup of coffee from on Earth. Wisps of her white and blue hair have fallen out of her long braid, and they sway around her face as she moves closer to me.

"*All* of it," she whispers.

We stare at one another. Crystalized blue meets the deep and haunted green of a forest.

"It doesn't scare me. None of it, Athena. We're soul sisters. That hidden darkness that's building within you likely mirrors my own."

I don't realize I'm crying until Eira swipes her thumb along my cheek, brushing a tear away.

"Sometimes," I rasp. "I wonder how I'm still hanging on after all these years of masked pain. I-I don't know how to keep going. What I can do to align with my new power. If I have the courage to embrace my deepest fears and flawed perspective."

Eira grabs my hand tighter. "Your power isn't new, and your

courage isn't missing. We're all holding on by a single thread right now. When your thread snaps, I want you to remember that I'm right here. If you fall, I'll fall with you until our love for one another catches us in its safe arms."

"You promise?" I breathe.

"I swear it on our soul sister marking. When those emotions you've buried come surging to the surface and you cave into despair, I'm going to free-fall with you."

I huff out a broken laugh. "That sounds like a curse."

Eira smiles. "It sounds to me like a *blessing*. To love someone enough that the moment they start to sink, you know without a doubt that you'll dive right in next to them. To have the peace and reassurance that you won't be swimming out of the deep waters alone. Our souls have each other's backs."

Zaya curls around my ankles and meows up at me, almost as if in confirmation of what her momma said.

"And Zaya?" I sniffle.

"You better believe she'll be plunging into the water, too, if it means she'll be near us," Eira sighs. "Wet kitty or not, Zaya won't abandon her people. *Ever.*"

Eira wraps an arm around my shoulders, turning us to face where the others are chomping at the bit to break Eliina.

"Come, my friend," Eira chirps. "Let's go investigate this creepy *skelter* situation. What's one more step into the dance of insanity?"

I laugh, leaning my head against her shoulder. I don't know how I got so lucky to have this kind of best friend, but I send a quick thanks up to any gods or goddesses who are listening.

"But I warn you, don't let me near Hadwin right now," Eira whispers lowly in my ear. "He dared call you an explosive brat? He has *no idea* what's coming."

As if on cue, Zaya growls in the back of her throat as she trots next to us.

"There's no hiding," Jade snaps at Eliina. It's been a handful of hours of questioning her, and I'm starting to think Nyx is right: We should interrogate her the violent way. "Why won't you tell us what you know?"

Eliina lets out a sob. I'd think it's genuinely heartbreaking, except I'm numb from the incident earlier this evening. Frankly, I don't give a shit what Eliina is going through now. I just want to sleep, and for once in my life, I want to be far away from a library.

"I told you," Eliina cries. "I *can't* tell you about it. They won't let me."

"Maybe some healing fire will change your mind," Eira says in a devious tone. "We can burn away all that apprehension until you realize you *can* tell us. You are simply choosing not to."

Nyx smirks at her. "While I'd love to hold her down with my shadows for you," he purrs, one of his shadows slinking its way around Eira's ankle and caressing her. "Surely there's another way."

Daru makes a clicking sound at Nyx and jumps forward near Eira. She looks down at him. Between the savage glint in his big eyes and the way he curls his talons around some of Eliina's chains, I get the impression he's in full agreement with Eira's idea. The juxtaposition of Daru and Nyx's reactions makes my head spin. *Nyx* is the one telling Eira to wait? She really did a number on him with her fire if he's acting so level-headed.

"I really disagree," Stefanie sighs while rubbing a hand down her face. "I'm sorry, Eira. I want answers as much as you do, but I don't think torturing her will be the right decision. We're *healers*. We don't travel down the dark path unless it's truly necessary. There has to be another way to get her to talk."

Eira hums. "A little darkness doesn't hurt sometimes. Not when her answers could help us keep other souls safe."

Biting my lower lip, I shuffle from foot to foot. My best friend's willingness to dive into the darkness *should* make me slightly uncomfortable, but it doesn't. She's right—we both have darkness building within us. Even if we go with her idea, I don't like this situation. Something isn't adding up. The more I'm numb, the easier it is for me to detach and see what's going on clearly. "Hold on," I say. All their eyes land on me, but I ignore them. "This doesn't make sense. Eliina isn't saying that she doesn't want to tell us. She's saying that she *can't*." I turn to face Eliina and narrow my eyes. "Are you physically unable to tell us what you know?"

Eliina's eyes fill with tears, and she gives a curt nod. As she does this, she cries out in pain and cut marks slash up and down her pale arms and neck.

"It's a curse," Jade growls. "*Fuck*."

The seconds tick by while Eira and Stefanie debate which healing magic can see who has harmed Eliina. Stefanie calls down to the manipulators concealed in the stacks of books behind us to add curses to their list, yet I don't know what that'll do for us right now.

Zaya is sending a rather terrifying glare at the *skelter*. My mind can't comprehend the way she is responding, as if her feline soul is seeing something we're not. Daru, Ulf, Ivar, and Nyx are all standing in intimidating stances between Eliina and the *skelter*, not convinced that Eliina is telling the truth. Fraya and Odin are now sitting, and Hauke is between them with his massive purple wings around both of them. The only one looking at me is Hadwin. *Of fucking course. What does he want now?*

I decide to blink back at him with a vacant stare, letting him know that I'm too detached to care. Hadwin stands up straighter, his eyebrows furrowing at my response to him. *Yeah, asshole, how does it feel to want a reaction and only get a mask?* Green sparks of his *maji* crackle up and down his arms, and then an idea hits me square in the chest.

"Let's use earth *maji* to communicate with Eliina," I blurt.

"What?" Jade asks.

"Remember in that tent, Eira?"

Eira's eyes brighten with understanding as she remembers. "Ah, yes, that's right! Eliina shared all sorts of information about Majikaero with you through your similar earth *maji*. You both can communicate through the soil."

I regretfully look at Hadwin again. Sighing, I ask, "Can you do this, too?"

He nods once. *Fine, go back to not talking to me.*

"Why don't Hadwin and I use our *maji* to connect with Eliina? We can then relay to everyone else what we learn."

"Will that be safe?" Fraya asks. She's terribly tired, the kind I'm all too familiar with. If she's able to sense what we're all going through, then gods, that's a heavy burden. No wonder she keeps getting close to becoming a *canielor*. I can barely deal with my own trauma, let alone being able to sense everyone else's. I mean, I'm aware enough of those around me as a healer, but that's different from being able to feel *all* the tangled, dark emotions of each soul passing by you.

"It'll have to be," Jade barks. "We've been at this for hours. I'm willing to try this, and then my crows and I are leaving." She turns to Nyx and her voice softens. "You understand, I hope."

"Of course," he murmurs. "We can't lose you. If this doesn't work, then we'll keep trying and report back to you the next time you're in Rioa."

"I think this also makes sense considering the way you and Hadwin already connected," Stefanie adds, bringing the focus back to me. My cheeks heat in embarrassment from the way we were physically close earlier, his body fitting against mine flawlessly.

"H-how so?" I ask, desperately hoping this doesn't turn into an ambush against Hadwin and me, everyone pointing out the obvious attraction and frenetic energy that's building between us.

"You were the only ones to travel to Earth while Eira was healing everyone yesterday," Stefanie replies slowly, as if this should be crystal clear and she's afraid the words won't properly stick in my brain. "It happened naturally for the two of you, and while neither one of you were harmed by the purple substance, you still came into contact with it."

"And it's probable Eliina is linked to the portals and attacks on Rioa, which could have been how your spirits transported to Earth," Hauke chimes in. He's sending a death glare at Eliina's trembling form.

My stomach churns when I watch her stare up at him without denying anything.

"Then it's settled," Stefanie claps her hands.

"But what about splitting up and making a plan?" Eira asks. She's moving from foot to foot, which tells me she's just as agitated that this is taking so long. There's a flicker of warped emotions through our soul bond marking, and I'm also hit with her overwhelming fear that it's *me* who has to deal with Eliina.

"There'll be no plan if the Council members catch us," Jade responds. "My team is the reason we're all able to connect. If we go out, you'll be on your own."

Nyx steps forward and places an arm around Eira. "We'll still figure out our next steps, regardless of what happens after this," he murmurs into her ear.

Eira frowns at Jade as she leans further into Nyx. I swear I can see a shadow mix in with her blue flames as she processes the idea of us being on our own. *There's no time to worry about that.* All my friends here are either preparing to use darkness, zapped of all energy, or stuck somewhere in between. I can help, and regardless of how detached I'm becoming, I know I want to do this. I don't care how dangerous it might be, or the possibility that Eliina isn't who she says she is. I'm going in.

"Alright, if there's no time, then let's do this," I mutter. The best part about numbing out is I don't have the capacity to feel afraid about what Hadwin and I are going to do. I step forward quickly and plop myself on the patterned rug right in front of Eliina, taking note of the detailed carvings on the bottom of the table legs right behind her. They're different faces, ones that might be gods or goddesses, surrounded by swirling, intricate symbols. Hadwin is next to me in a flash, knocking me out of my reverie, and he pulls Eliina down to sit on the floor with us.

"She can keep these chains on," he says to Eira. "But our earth *maji* will work best if we're all on the same level together. It'll be easier to connect with the soil and get on the same wavelength."

Eira nods in confirmation and plants her feet, almost as if she's bracing for our earth *maji* to combust all together. Jade makes some kind of symbol with her hands up to her crows way above us and then kneels near us. She's laser-focused now, in the way one needs to be if they have to flee at any second.

I block out what the others are doing. Zaya's fluffy tail swishes in the corner of my eye, which tells me she's still glowering at the *skelter*. *Again, I can't worry about that now.* My focus needs to be on the task before me. The magic flowing through me was unleashed hours ago. As I breathe in and connect to it, I will it to extend out to both Hadwin and Eliina instead of exploding above me. My *maji* pulsates, reminding me it's a living force inside my soul, and Hadwin's words come back to me. *I have to be aligned with it, or this isn't going to work.* I can't let myself think about my desire to be free of my pain or how it felt to untether the magic before. We need answers, and fuck, I can at least do this. I close my eyes and continue to follow my breath.

With each exhale, my *maji* flares brighter and brighter, until the three of us are anchored to the same patch of soil under this library.

Nyx

My firefly and Zaya are both twitchy as they watch Athena close her eyes, and she sinks deeper and deeper into wherever her earth *maji* is taking her. Eira's nervous energy is loud enough that it crackles along my ears. It can't be easy for her to stand back and watch as her soul sister plunges deeper into her powers with Hadwin—who's been a walking asshole on a stick—and Eliina.

There's a fleeting moment where I'm apprehensive about what Hadwin is doing, but it's gone as quickly as it came. We need answers, and he's a strong motherfucker. More so, he's stubborn and prickly with a dark sense of humor. There's a fierce protective side to him that I've often seen in our banished group of freaks, and I can already tell that Athena has him wrapped around her finger. Hadwin hasn't come to terms with it yet, but when he does, it'll be a rough time for anyone who even looks the wrong way at his girl.

Both of them will be just fine with Eliina.

My heart squeezes at the sight of my firefly so anxious. She was all for going the darker route and torturing Eliina, not an ounce of fear coming out of her. But the second her best friend is getting involved? She's a nervous wreck.

With a snap of my fingers, my shadow daggers slither out of my fingertips and cut themselves off from my body. I weave them in such a way that the *skelter* is surrounded by them, each within an inch of its oozing body. I make eye contact with Hauke, who's shifting his stance to be closer to Stefanie. We share a silent agreement that our *almaoves* need more support than ever before, especially with how sensitive they are as healers. He blinks, turning his focus back on his girl, who's prattling off to Riker and Esen about which other tomes to search for and bring back to her.

An idea suddenly swarms in my mind, and I can't fight the devilish smile that overtakes me. I know *just* what my firefly needs to take her mind off Athena, and we'll technically be helping Stefanie while we're at it.

"Stefanie?" I murmur.

She raises an eyebrow at me in response. The way those green eyes stare into me, followed by a slow smirk, I can tell she knows where my mind's going.

"Any tomes Eira and I can help you find?"

Eira snaps her head in my direction, her eyes wide. She has to crane her neck as I prowl up and tower over her.

"Nyx, I need to stay by—"

"I most certainly do," Stefanie chirps with a wink. "I need a few volumes that outline where our gods and goddesses are supposed to be residing, as well as other worlds' powers. Riker and Esen can't do *everything*. I believe you'll find what I'm searching for all the way at the end and take a right down the last row of bookshelves."

"Why do we need to read about the gods and goddesses?" Eira asks her.

"I'm confident that they're aware of *everything* that's been going on in Majikaero," Stefanie mutters to herself as she rummages through a stack of scrolls to her right side. Her eyes light up like glittering gemstones when she finds the correct one.

Stefanie flattens out the wrinkled piece of parchment on the colorful woven rug in front of her. Her hand snakes around to grab a few of the smaller tomes to place on each corner of the scroll, keeping it flat while she points to a drawing.

"See this?" she asks Eira. My firefly scoots closer, her eyes scanning each and every detail of the intricate sketch. I take another step closer to peer down at what they're looking at, antsy to get Eira alone but also intrigued by what Stefanie has found. She's a clever *solliqa*, and if she strongly believes an image or chapter can help us, she's usually right.

Eira traces her fingertips along the outline of one of the known goddesses. It's Nicola, Goddess of the Soul, and she's standing tall with her arms out to her sides. Long chocolate waves cascade down her back, and her large brown eyes pull us in, even though this is only a drawing. Nicola's lips are tilted up in a soft smile, their color a rose pink, and she's wearing a long, sheer purple dress with a plunging neckline. Around her bronze neck lies a necklace with a large pendant—a combination of amethyst and labradorite. At least that's what the description says next to her face.

Below her standing form is where Stefanie is adamantly pointing and whispering to Eira about. Nicola is standing above a planet that has pink and coral waters and colorful landscapes. Even without the obvious moons orbiting around it, I can tell it's Majikaero. A sparkling, white power is flowing out of one of Nicola's hands and into the world. Below this, there's elegant handwriting describing the scene and what it's meant to represent.

"These paragraphs explain the ways the Goddess Nicola has crafted the world of Majikaero and her strong connection to each of the *solliqas*. On these other scrolls," Stefanie says while grabbing a few of the other rolled parchments. "You can read examples of when *solliqas* over the years claim to have made contact with Nicola. There are tomes describing which gods and goddesses are connected to the other worlds, at least the ones we know of, and where they exist in relation to Majikaero. Legends are not simply a story in this world, my friend. They're part of our history."

My firefly looks through the other few scrolls before glancing back at Stefanie.

"But how will this help us?"

Stefanie smiles like a cat. "I plan to figure out *just how* these other *solliqas* contacted a goddess. I have questions, Eira, and I won't rest until they're answered. We're going to find out how much of a role these gods play in the plague of darkness and the portals."

Eira licks her lips before murmuring something to Stefanie again, and that's all it takes for my patience to run dry.

"Then we better get you these other tomes, hmm?" I *try* to sound composed, but I know Stefanie sees right through me when she openly laughs.

"You better," she giggles. "I'll be here organizing the scrolls and tomes I already have, so I can better determine if what you find is helpful or not."

I smile down at Eira, baring my teeth. She blinks up at me with those big blue orbs. With a roll of her eyes, she lets me take her hand, and I pull her behind me as I steer us toward the last row of bookshelves.

There's a hunger I can't keep ignoring, and I'm about to devour the beautiful feast right next to me.

NINETEEN
Eira & Nyx

*As much as we want to deny it, human beings
prosper in the dark just as much as in the light.
-Lyk Tyonela, Lead Therapist at Arms of Healing Love*

Eira

"N yyxxx," I whine. He's practically dragging me with how quickly he's rushing us to the back area of the library. "You know I don't like it back here. I don't want to see another *canielor* lurking around."

I shiver, remembering how not even a month ago, Eliina had spoken to me in a different part of the library. It was still hidden and tucked away in a back area, too far away for me to have called for help. She had acted surprised when we came face-to-face with a *canielor*, and I was pulled into their traumatizing memory of sexual assault. The more I think about it, though, there's no way it was a chance occurrence, making me even more resentful toward her.

I *hate* being kept in the dark, and I hope Athena uses her formidable earth *maji* to lure out Eliina's secrets.

Nyx pulls us down the last row of bookshelves, my body jerking from the abrupt movement. He takes at least a dozen steps—each one equivalent to one of my *lunges*—until he spins around to face me and pulls me flush against his chest.

"But sweetheart," he purrs. "We can't let Stefanie do all the research on her own, now can we?"

Swallowing, I lock eyes with his dark, crackling irises and force myself not to blink. He trails a clawed finger up from my wrist all the way to my neck, pressing down just enough for me to feel the sharp edge of his nail through my billowing robes. "Where do you think we should start?"

Thick, pulsating shadows dance across Nyx's shoulders until they're swelling out around both of us, creating a barrier between us and any potential danger. Or wandering eyes...

Nyx already has me against his chest. I'm close enough that his beating heart is going to jump into my own rib cage, but he manages to draw me even closer as he pushes us back against one of the bookshelves. He leans forward, forcing me to break eye contact, and brings the bridge of his nose down to the base of my neck. The way he inhales and releases a low groan has me squirming—just him breathing in my scent has blue embers crackling down in my core.

"Hmm, firefly?" he murmurs against my neck. He places a slow kiss on my neck, his lips melting into my heated skin. "Which tome should we find for her first?"

It's hard to focus when he moves his lips over my collarbone and uses his teeth to snap some of the threads holding the top of the robe together. When Nyx glances up at me, his eyes are a mixture of that deep, crackling brown, opaque white, and inky black.

"Nyx darling," I whisper. "I-is that y-your beast?"

He growls in response and bites through a few more strands of shimmering fabric. My *maji* glows blue and white along my exposed skin, and the lower Nyx's mouth and tongue travel down in between my chest, the brighter my flames flash. He leans his head under my left breast and stops to peer up at me, those gorgeous eyes flashing between the three colors.

"Where do you want to start, sweetheart?" Nyx rasps.

I think of the chaos and tragedy that's been smothering all of us. Stefanie needs us to find tomes about the gods and goddesses, as well as other worlds' powers. These are important, I imagine, especially if there are portals involved. It's imperative that we hurry because we don't know how much time will be gifted to us or when Athena and Hadwin will come back to this library. But as I gaze down into my *almaove's* eyes—my dark prince, my soulmate—none of that matters. Not as worry after worry has been slamming into me, knocking my tower of sanity to the ground, destroying my false sense of confidence that everything is going to be okay in Majikaero. In any of the worlds.

There's been so much going on. *Too much* happening all at once. And when all the pieces of who I am get knocked over, there are few souls I can count on to help me pick up the damaged parts and put them back together. One of them is out in the main area, using her earth *maji* to find out what Eliina has been hiding from us. The other is gazing up at me with such lust, such *heavy* emotions, I know exactly where we need to start.

"With you," I gasp. "I need to share with you what I've been learning about myself."

My chest is heaving as he moves up a few inches and bites down on my nipple through the coverings. The cord connecting us has been pulled tighter and tighter this past month, my inability to fully open up to him weighing me down. I swear I can hear an audible crack when it completely snaps free, no longer tethering us to one another with a mere cord. As his dark shadows and fire swarms in to meet my own power, I realize that cord wasn't a connection—it was holding us back, keeping us tied down.

"I want to see it," Nyx growls against my chest as his black nails start to rip my coverings to shreds. My body is burning up for him in such an intense way, these same shreds turn to ash before they can even hit the floor. "I *need* to see the darkness you've been hiding from me. From yourself."

Nyx's hands curl tightly around my hips as my head leans back against one of the books with a loud gasp. There are going to be bruises there, and I can't wait for him to soothe the pain away with that tongue of his. He keeps one arm latched around me, and the other goes up above my head. He taps one of the thicker tomes behind me.

"I have ideas of how we could use this," he whispers. "But I don't want a *canielor* or anyone else to ruin our fun when they sense I've damaged some special property." He leans down and inhales deeply again. "Next time, sweetheart. For now, we'll have to just stick with our *maji*."

"Just our *maji*?" I ask, arching an eyebrow.

Nyx smirks. His eyes fully transform into the opaque white and oozing black liquid travels down his cheek. I don't overthink anything at this moment, focusing all my energy on staying in the here and now with my *almaove*. Pushing up onto my tiptoes, I lean my head forward and lick up some of the darkness pouring out of Nyx's eyes. The black veins along his arms and chest throb, dancing to the same rhythm as my aching clit.

"How does my darkness taste?" he murmurs.

"Like it's only the beginning, and I want so much *more*."

We become a frantic clash of mouths and teeth and me clawing at his thin coverings. Our mouths sink into each other, little moans escaping me when his tongue tangles with my own. Flickers of blue flames come out of my fingertips, setting his shirt and pants on fire. As soon as they fall off of him, his shadows slink in to put out any remaining flames. He doesn't care if there are burns all over him—if anything, he *wants* them. Nyx holds me close with his arm and plunges one of his hands into my long braid. He pulls slightly, causing a burning and delicious wave of pleasure to coarse through my nerve endings. Smoke rolls around us, starting at our ankles and weaving up through our legs and hips.

His soul has set mine on fire, and *gods*, I'm ready to burn down anything he wants if it means we can stay in this moment forever.

"Show me all of you," I breathe.

He pulls back for a second, the energy still whipping between us, catching us in a chaotic storm. My pulse has gone into overdrive, and if he doesn't answer me right this fucking second, I'm going to rip out of my own damn skin.

"A darkness for a darkness?" he asks.

"I'll show you mine if you show me yours," I pant.

Nyx leans forward, his lips brushing past my own. "This is a dangerous game, firefly. Once we show one another what we're masking, there's no going back."

My breathing hitches. If I urge my *maji* to show him *everything* about who I am, will he still want me? If he shows me the beast within, will I still stand here, fearless, before him?

"You first," I whisper before kissing those plump lips.

He groans and pulls me closer, kissing the fucking hell out of me. We break away, the space within his shadows spinning for a second before I break out of the daze he put me in. Smirking, Nyx looks down at me, ever the cocky shadow prince. It's not until he brings a trembling hand up and pushes back the hair that's fallen out of my braid that I see how afraid he is.

I reach up and tangle my fingers with his.

"I'll walk with you through the darkness each time as you remember your light," I encourage, pushing all the love in my heart into those words.

Nyx's eyes soften slightly at the reminder of what he told me. "As I'll walk through yours, my firefly."

With that, he takes a step back, both of his arms falling to his sides. It's a struggle to keep my eyes focused on his face when his hardened cock is *right there*. Licking my lips, I remember how he tasted in the healing quarters days earlier.

"Eyes up here, sweetheart," Nyx says with a smirk, amusement dancing again in those milky eyes.

"New rules," I purr, surprising myself. *Now's not the time to get stuck in your head.* "For each darkness revealed, we get to reward one another."

His eyes flare wider. "Well, *that* was quite the dark thought," he murmurs. "For you, at least. I think that already earns you a treat."

Nyx winks and lunges forward, pulling one of my bare nipples into his mouth in one smooth motion. He swirls that damn tongue around the tip, and I'm moaning like I'm in heat, already pulling him impossibly closer to me and not letting him stop. He releases me with a loud *pop* and chuckles against my skin.

"Now it's my turn."

Standing to his full height, I watch as dark as night feathers and even darker fur sprout along his neck, arms, chest, back, and legs. I suck in a breath at the sight of him. This isn't even his whole beast, but it doesn't matter—I think he's beautiful in *all* his forms.

"I'm terrified," Nyx rasps. "For you to see this side of me. For you to run away at the sight of my beast form. For all of who I am to still not be enough to protect you."

I take careful steps forward and stop in front of his towering form. My fingers reach out and caress the mixture of textures on his bulky muscles and across his shoulders, down onto his broad chest.

"To protect me from what?" I ask.

He swallows. "From the plague of darkness and what's behind those portals. How can I when *I'm* part of the darkness?"

My fingers continue to move through his fur and feathers. His body quivers from the slow, intentional strokes.

"Sometimes we need to become what we fear the most in order to survive," I murmur. My gaze flicks up to his. "And that's okay."

I sink down to my knees and take his still aching cock into my hands. Without hesitation, I push the tip of his dick into my mouth, swirling my mouth around and around as he moans and digs those sharpened claws into my now loose hair. I take my time pulling more of him into me, and just to see how he reacts, I reach up to grab onto his balls. Nyx jerks in my mouth. *Good*.

Pleased with myself, I release him and push myself back up to a standing position. I realize that it's now my turn to show him a piece of my growing darkness. I hesitate, unsure of how to expose this side of me.

Nyx grabs my chin with his large hand and forces me to look up at him again. He leans down, nipping along my neck until he pecks me on the mouth.

"I'll walk with you through the darkness," he prompts.

I sigh, relaxing into him. "As I remember my light."

"Good girl."

Heat flares to life in my body at the praise. I'm not sure which is more unsettling—that I'm *definitely* into his monster form or that I have a praise kink.

Taking a deep breath, I stand up as tall as possible, mustering up all the courage that I can. I close my eyes and focus on my breathing. It's a loving caress as I travel into my center and connect with my *maji*. All that beautiful healing light and fire. I keep searching, though, for that shard of darkness that's starting to embed itself inside my soul.

The darkness caught inside of me is a deep purple, as dazzling as an amethyst, but as dark as sweet poison.

With my next exhale, I open my eyes and coax out that darkness. The purple flares bright as waves of lavender fire replace my white and blue hair traveling down my back. My nails grow out into longer black claws tinted with purple and blue edges, and my body glows a swirling and vibrant light purple and white. I know there's more inside of me. But this is enough for right now. It has to be. I didn't know it even existed before now, and I don't think my heart can take how much is still left inside.

"This is my darkness," I breathe. "I'm afraid of where this has come from. Is it from Tryg? Has it always been with me? Is it the plague?"

I shift my gaze to Nyx, and he's staring at me in awe. He pads forward, keeping the fur and feathers along his skin, and bows down on his knees before me. My breathing stutters at the sight of such a lethal creature bowing down to *me*. He raises his head and locks his eyes on mine.

"You're a queen of fire," he whispers. "And I'm here to serve what you want, what you absolutely *need*."

Nyx grabs my thighs and pulls me closer. He wastes no time and suctions his lips against my clit, causing my knees to buckle at the way he knows how to work me up. Not even a moment passes by—not entirely enough time at all—and he loosens his hold. I think he's going to pull away, but he surprises me by licking straight up my pussy and, without warning, sliding two thick digits inside of me.

Pumping a few times, he lets out another groan. It's louder this time.

"Tell me, sweetheart, are you ready for my cock?"

Goosebumps travel up and down my back at his question. *Am I ready?*

He doesn't give me time to answer. Instead, Nyx jumps back to his feet, but he stays a mere foot in front of me. Webbed, leathery wings shoot out from his back, making him look very much like a demon sent out to hunt me. My eyes flicker back and forth between the outline of his large wings and his delicious mouth—my juices are still covering his lips, and *gods*, I don't know if I'm going to survive this wicked game.

"I'm full of so much fear," Nyx shares with me. "I already know where we'll need to go after leaving Rioa. I must take you back to my homeland, Drageyra. There's a number of resources there that'll help with figuring out your special powers of healing light, the darkness plaguing our world, and a library full of coveted knowledge. But I'm terrified, I"—his voice cracks. My heart splinters with him—"I'm terrified to see what's left of my family, if any of the *solliqas* who pledged their loyalty to *me* specifically are even still alive. If my father... if he can even stand to look me in the eye. I don't have a lot of hope or trust in anyone from that land, not really. Anyone who stayed behind while I was banished either sided with me and was thrown into the dungeons, or they chose not to follow me. *Those corrupted souls* are not friends or family to me anymore. The only ones who might be worth saving—if they haven't been destroyed already—would be some of my extended family on the northern part of the island."

I can't believe the emotion tearing its way through me at his confession of fear. Tears stream down my face, and Nyx reaches out to touch them with his shaking fingers. They're not ordinary tears. The liquid is a dark purple, sending fresh alarm through me. I don't want the focus to be on me, though. I peer back up to him and cover one of his trembling hands with my own.

"If you feel it's best to go to Drageyra," I tell him gently. "Then that is where we'll go. But we'll be there together. You won't be alone on your journey. And Nyx? We can change our minds at any time. This is our timeline."

Nyx kisses my forehead. "It's not, though, firefly. That's the thing about being a prince. I was raised to think like a king. I can't shut off the part of me that knows without the available resources in my homeland and going straight there to get them, so many *solliqas* might suffer the consequences. Majikaero is already swarming with the plague of darkness. Souls are being turned into husks of themselves. They don't need to suffer more because of my selfish fear."

"It's your homeland, though," I whisper, thinking of Sweazn. "But it's truly not your home?"

His opaque eyes close briefly. When he opens them again, there's such determination piercing into me.

"No, it's not," he confirms. "It's a place. That's not what I consider a home."

"Then what is?" I ask. My heart aches for my beast prince in front of me.

Nyx bends down slightly so that he's at eye level.

"You."

I allow myself a whole minute to kiss him senseless, to show him my gratitude and love through my mouth. Abruptly, I tear myself away from him, now having the courage to show him the next layer of darkness inside of me.

My purple hair of fire still floats around my face, and those dark claws are very much a part of my fingers now. I breathe in deeply, and as I push myself down, down, down to the lowest part of my soul, I ask that darkest part to show itself. To reveal itself to Nyx and me. I tell it that we won't judge it, won't admonish it, but rather we'll give it the love it rarely receives.

A startling, loud gasp escapes me as patches of my skin decay into white and blue bones. This continues up and down my arms, torso, and legs in random designs. Boiling fire swirls around my hips and lower abdomen, causing the skin to pucker in abnormally large scars. A black, skeletal hummingbird swooshes out of my chest, its wings dripping in what could be gooey oil. She flutters in front of my face, those tiny eyes a bright lavender that peer straight into the center of who I am. My mouth moves to speak to her, but no words form on my leaden tongue. In a flash, she flies in circles around my body until she crashes back into the center of my chest and melts into the partially decayed flesh.

A tragic, bewitching mark that's tattooed near my heart. One I immediately know the symbolism of without needing to speak to her.

As I turn to tell Nyx what I've learned about this darkness, a sharp, twisting pain slices through my shoulder blades. Screaming, I fall to my knees. Nyx mirrors my movements like a magnet, sitting right there with me as I sob. I hear him inhale a sharp breath as he grabs onto my arms, half of which are bones I'm petrified will crumble in his textured hands.

"Firefly," he whispers. "Sweetheart, Eira, you need to see your beast."

Tremors rack my entire body, but with a few gentle nudges from Nyx, I manage to scramble to a standing position once again. He mutters something I can't hear to his shadows, and in a heartbeat, a smoky mirror materializes before me.

I... I'm a fucking *monster*.

More dark purple tears well up in my eyes at the image before me. Purple fire hair. Decaying flesh. Wrinkled scars marring my normally smooth skin. Thick, black liquid oozing from parts I can't fully see. The black hummingbird tattooed on my chest. I'm at a loss for words. Then, my eyes catch on the dark, sparkling feathered wings coming out of my back. They're fluttering as fast as a hummingbird's wings, with sparks of purple embers drifting off them.

I look at Nyx's face through the mirror, too frightened to turn around and face him myself. Licking my lips, I do everything I can to keep my focus on him. I can't stand the way my eyes are full of purple and red flames or how patches of decayed flesh slide down my jaw and onto my bony shoulders.

"I know what this is," I breathe, barely able to give life to the words *begging* to be released from my heart. I clear my throat, watching the way I can see each muscle move beneath the thin layer of skin. "I didn't realize I could turn into a monster or that I even was one. This wasn't from Tryg. There's no way. Everything you see is representative of the chronic illness that's still leeching off my soul in this world. The fatigue pushes and pulls against my flesh and muscles until they disintegrate into ash. The scars surround the core of my body that have *ruined* me—for men, for women, for my fucking *self*. These scars are *nothing* compared to the way my heart and mind have shattered from not having control of this pain."

Those traitorous purple tears are coming down one thick line after another on my cheeks.

"And the hummingbird?" Nyx pushes, his eyes lined with their own black tears.

"She's been with me for my entire life. Always working twice the speed, going harder than the rest, if it means I can serve all those around me. Giving them endless supplies of my love, of my energy, of my time until I'm drained of it all. Going and going and going... I'm just always *going*, Nyx, and I"—my voice catches on a sob—"I'm fucking beside myself that this is the purpose of my soul. I'm heartbroken that I'll forever be the healer and never the healed."

Nyx roughly grabs my chin again and forces me to turn around to look at him. I shake my head, unable to stand whatever I'll see in those eyes, but he won't take no for an answer. Not this time. He bares his teeth, long fangs sinking into his lower lip.

"You know what?" Nyx grinds his teeth. "You're fucking perfect, firefly. All of this that you're showing me. It's *everything*. You're my fucking everything, and I *adore* how you've suffered and embraced it as a part of your soul. I love that you *understand* what it means to actually suffer, and you know why?"

I'm crying so hard, his face comes and goes in a blur of color and smoke.

"Because I've been going out of my fucking mind that our

soul connection would be nothing compared to what you have with Athena. That we wouldn't understand one another on a deeper level, that we wouldn't be able to climb out of this fucked trench as a team."

His eyes sear straight through me, and I gasp as I lean further into him.

"We're more than the suffering we've been forced to choke on. You and I, firefly, we're meant to take the darkness inside of us and show the world how damn beautiful it's made our love."

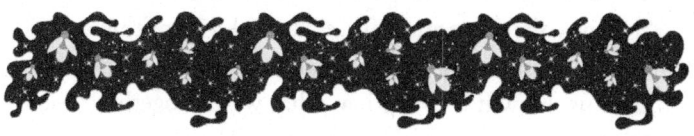

Nyx

Both Eira and I are shaking to our fucking cores, and I know there are tears, but I've never been this fucking turned on in my life. Watching my firefly bare her darkness to me—darkness I could see through those layers of light, and she wasn't even aware of it—has me releasing a booming roar of rage. It's one of agony, of indescribable joy that she and I are in this all *together*. I call out to my shadows, the ones I've resented but have become my friends, and ask them to thicken the border between us and the rest of the library.

We'll need to go back to the others, but not yet. I'd know if Hadwin came back. And I refuse to let my Queen of Light succumb to her tears in this way. It's time to *show her* what she means to me.

"Look at me," I growl in her face, my beast fully coming to the surface. Her demonic form stares at me with wide eyes, but I can smell her arousal at the command. "If you're going to cry, then it's going to be from how hard I make you cum with pleasure. Do you understand?"

Eira's bottom lip trembles, but she nods her head in understanding.

"You've given me your darkness," I rasp. "Now give me your words."

She swallows. Her emotions are going haywire, that purple hair blazing around her like a wildfire.

"I-I understand."

"Tell me what you want, and I'll tell you what I need."

Silence stretches between us, thick and tangible.

"I want," she starts and pauses. "I think I savor this new side to me, and I don't know what to make of it yet, but I love how it connects us. How it'll strengthen what we are together. There's something I've been wanting—*no*—I've been desperate for. I want your cock to fill me up until I forget that I thought my darkness was anything but strength."

A strangled sound releases from my lips. "You filthy, beautiful girl," I murmur. "When we fully connect, I want to worship you slowly, away from everyone."

"This isn't about what *you* want." Those burning eyes are scorching me to the spot, a renewed confidence taking over. "You asked what I want. I desperately want you to fuck me in this magical library because there are going to be a lot of firsts for us, and fuck, *please*, Nyx."

I chuckle darkly, ever the beast full of shadows and sin. "If you're going to beg so pretty like that, then it'd be a crime not to give my queen what she's wanting."

"And what do you *need*, Nyx?"

Making sure to slide my tongue along my fangs, I smile.

"I *need* your cum gushing down my tongue, sweetheart."

I reach forward, grabbing the backs of her thighs for the second time, and fall back onto the library's chilled floor. Eira is heating us enough that it doesn't matter how cold the room gets.

She's still in this monstrous form, a macabre goddess wrapped in fire and healing light. There's something about the way those purple tears are staining her porcelain-white cheeks that has me working up an appetite.

Without warning, I move my hands to her scarred hips and crash her sweet pussy down onto my face. A few of my shadows reach out to hold her wrists and upper body so she can focus all of her attention on finding her release. She cries out beautifully, and I lap up her arousal as if it's my saving grace. My tongue swirls around her sensitive bud, knowing now how much she enjoys it when I edge her just close enough to an orgasm before pulling back completely. We've been playing our sick game of foreplay, so I can already feel her muscles tensing up around my mouth. I hum, causing a shiver to roll through her, and hardening my tongue, I plunge straight into her core.

"Oh, Nyx!" Eira screams, no longer caring who or what could be hearing us. My shadows can block out most of what we're doing, but certainly not *every* sound. Her wings flare out wide behind her, casting her in an enchanting glimmer. She rides my face as I continue to fuck her with my tongue until a last gasp has her sweetness bursting onto my waiting tastebuds. It takes a few minutes for her body to relax against me, but I don't let her go until I've wrung every last sigh out of her.

As I lay here, that warning voice slithers around my mind again.

Danger. Predator. Terror.

But as I look up at my queen, I push those words out of my mind. Her monster isn't dangerous. She's not terror. Eira is only learning what needs to be healed and how that can manifest around her soul. I refuse to hold any of that against her when she's shown me time after time that she won't give up on *me*.

I push us both up, licking up any remaining drops of her cum from around my mouth. Eira is settled in between my legs, her body fucking glowing after her release. She has a satiated smile on her face and isn't even noticing the rotting patches of skin or thick scars that wind around her waist and hips. *She's so fucking perfect for me.*

"You're up for me to sink my cock into you?" A low rumble starts in my chest. I'm barely restraining myself from pouncing on her.

The look Eira shoots me is very much *her*, but there's a glint of sinful delight that I *adore*.

"Do your worst, Prince of Shadows."

Growling, I lurch forward onto my knees before winding my hands around her tight ass. I lift us both up and immediately push her into the bookshelf, being careful to push her wings out to the sides, so they don't get crushed. The sudden movement causes a few of the books to fall off the higher shelf, my shadows catching any lingering dust. Eira wraps her legs around my waist and hooks her arms behind my neck.

"As monsters or in our usual forms?" I ask.

I didn't realize how important her answer was to me until she says, "Fuck me in your monster's skin, Nyx, and show me that you can accept my damaged soul."

I smirk and plunge straight into her core without another delay.

Eira screams out and sinks those purple claws into my black fur. I pause, giving her time to adjust to my size. I'm not *too* large, but I also don't know the last time she had sex or how penetration even feels for her with this chronic illness. I can tell she's in pain from the way her muscles form a tight vise around my cock, and *fuck*, it's hard not to keep moving.

"You can tell me to stop at any point," I tell her.

She breathes slowly through her nose. Those red eyes bleed into my white and black ones, and she smiles devilishly.

"Nyx darling, I believe I requested you to *fuck* me. Not stuff me with your cock and watch what I do."

I huff out a laugh. "Impatient, are we?"

"You're not?" she shoots back.

"Good point." I rock into her hard and fast, causing more books to tumble off the shelves. Eira's moans have me lost in the way her pussy is clamping tight on me. I wave one of my hands, and a few shadows come to my side, eagerly ready to assist in giving our *almaove* pleasure. All it takes is a simple thought before they're scurrying up her arms and down her chest, circling around her nipples.

"Nyx," Eira breathes my name. "You're so—"

I grab her by the throat with a clawed hand, cutting off enough air supply to drag her even closer to the edge. She loves pain with her pleasure, so I lean my head down to her neck and bite at the soft spot near her collarbone with my fangs.

"Yes!" Eira gasps. "Yes, that!"

I lick up the base of her neck to help soothe the bite mark, and then I'm sending another shadow to circle her clit. Not once do I stop slamming into her, enamored by every breath, every sigh, every time she claws at my fur and feathers. I'm fucking obsessed with the way our monsters are bonding, and the image is almost too much for me. I'm going to blow my load into her soon.

My shadows pinch her nipples hard enough to make her cry out, and as they travel down and around her lower back, they dip *just enough* into her back hole. Eira's eyes roll to the back of her head, overstimulated with the way my *maji* is devouring her body.

"Nyx, please," she mewls. "Make me—"

Eira screams when I apply all the shadows' pressure to her clit, cumming all over my dick like we do this every day. *We will be... soon.*

Her walls squeeze around me tightly enough that I can't hold off my orgasm any longer, and my cum shoots up into her. I cry out and fall against her, biting into her neck once again from the sheer rush of *maji* that flows through me.

We stand this way, breathing, falling into one another. I have no limit to how many times I could take her, but I can't ignore that we've been gone a while now and still have no tomes in hand.

Chuckling at what we've been up to the whole time, I delicately lower her to the floor. She sags into my chest, and I relish at how easily she melts into my arms. How she fits perfectly as the missing piece my soul has longed for and finally has.

I place my hands on either side of her face. Pecking her lips a few times, it takes most of my willpower to not turn her around and fuck her from behind. From the way she squirms in my arms, I think she might be having similar thoughts.

"Time to bring these tomes back to Stefanie," I murmur into her lips, all puffy and bruised.

Eira makes a whiny sound. I laugh, proud as a fucking god that she'd rather stay in the shadows with our monsters.

"Are you able to push the darkness back down inside of you?" I ask. "Unless you want to show the others?"

She licks her lips, lost in thought. "No," she murmurs. "No, not yet. I've only discovered this myself, and I need time to share it with everyone else. Except for Athena, but now isn't the time. *Soon.*"

We use our *maji* to push the darkness back inside our souls, our usual humanoid forms taking over. The oddest sensation fills me as I adjust back to my usual skin. The markings...

"Some of them are gone!" Eira squeals, pointing to a few of the dark veins that have taken over my body. I look up at her with wide eyes, afraid to embrace the excitement that's bubbling inside of me. "Do you think what we did helped with some of your plague of darkness?"

A wide smile overtakes my face. "I think it was allowing our monstrous forms to exist without judgment. It was you accepting your darkness for the first time, and it was us trusting one another with our fears and pain."

Eira giggles. "I can't believe this might work!"

"I know." I lean down and kiss her softly. "Let's get you some new coverings, and we'll bring the tomes back over to Stefanie."

Her eyes furrow in confusion. *Adorable.* She whips her head around, searching for which books I'm talking about.

I snap my fingers, and a few of the tomes that fell off the bookshelf float up into my arms.

"How did you—"

"I brought us to the general area Stefanie said these books would be in," I say with a shrug. "My shadows were happy to find a few helpful tomes if it meant I'd get more time with you."

Eira's mouth stays open in amazement. I can't help placing a finger along her bottom lip.

"Be careful with how you react, sweetheart," I murmur. "I could easily take you again."

"Is that a request?" Eira asks.

I smirk. "It's a promise, firefly."

TWENTY
Astira

*Harboring secrets within your own kind
is the first step to self-destruction.
-Correspondence from Liv Tyonela, Released Prisoner 936*

"Spirits are still low, eh?"

My hands pause on one of the seams of the pink cotton shirt I'm folding. A pile of other clean clothes sits next to me in a clay basin. The low murmur of voices floats in the background at this communal washing area, and the faint scent of mint drifts around me, a clear change from the usual citrus and lavender laundry detergent I used years ago. Then again, beggars can't be choosers, and this is better than no aroma at all. None of the soaps made in the tunnels had any kind of perfume, and Damon insisted my natural smell was his favorite anyway.

Gag me.

I place the partially folded T-shirt down on the wooden table before me, resisting the urge to smooth out the wrinkles. One of the leaders of Nedrazon has asked me a question, and I know better than to keep working. You give whoever is in command your full attention, or you face the inhumane consequences.

I take a deep breath and hold the air captive in my lungs before breathing out steadily. Wiping my sweaty palms on my pant leg, I roll my shoulders and straighten my back. My eyes travel the length of the body standing in front of me—all black attire fitting snugly against large muscles, with a blue armband stretching around the right bicep. It matches the band I saw Jace wearing, so if the authority in this man's voice didn't alert me to his position, the color of his armband certainly does. I push myself to make eye contact, to even catch a glimpse of this person's face. He has a hard jawline and face made of sharp angles that's at odds with his half-smile and twinkling light blue eyes. Chocolate-brown waves fall over his ears, grazing just past his short beard. I tuck a few strands that have fallen out of my long braid behind my ear.

My body clenches, preparing itself for a harsh reaction as I open my mouth to speak.

"Of course they are," Liv chirps. Her steps are soft as she walks toward me, balancing another basin of washed and dried clothes on her hip. Liv's dark hair is pulled half up in a bun and matches the colors of her clothes today. The tip of her black and gray tattoo peeks out around her neck. "It's only been a few days since Astira was cleared to participate in our communal work, Micha. Give her a break."

This man, apparently named Micha, scoffs. "I didn't mean anythin' bad by it. She has such a solemn look on her pretty face. I was hopin' to change that." He takes a bite out of a raw carrot he's carrying around with him and mashes it between his teeth, keeping his foul mouth open while he chomps away.

My jaw tightens. I don't need a man to dictate how my face should look, especially one chewing away like a farm animal. *Fucker.*

Liv must sense my building anger at his statement because

she hurriedly drops the basin next to mine, causing a few of the shirts to tumble out onto the table. She places a hand lightly on my lower back. A single touch, one from the wrong person that would cause me to rage. Liv isn't a wrong person, though. She never will be.

"I think Astira's face is pretty with whichever expression she chooses to wear," Liv says. "Besides, that should be the last thing on her mind right now. She's helping me fold piles of the clean clothes this morning, still an unbelievably new concept for both of us."

Micha raises his hands in surrender and takes a step back. *I'm tempted to push the basin off the table—maybe it'll land on his feet.*

"I mean no harm," he rushes out. "Just came by to check on thin's before Jace and I have a meetin' to attend to."

"Meeting?" I ask, hating how my voice catches in my throat.

"Check on things?" Liv asks sharply.

Micha flicks his gaze back and forth between us, clearly unsure who to respond to first. I sigh. *Men.*

"What would you need to check on?" Liv bulldozes ahead.

"Well, er, how everyone is gettin' along. If everythin' is bein' handled appropriately."

Liv glares at him. "That might be easier for you to know if you actually did any work down here."

Micha stands up straighter and puffs his chest out in agitation. *I'm too damn tired for this. What, is he a fucking bird?*

"I do plenty!" he barks. "Yer the only one here who keeps askin' what us leaders do together and pokin' around in places not meant for you."

My friend lifts a single eyebrow and crosses her arms. Micha's thick southern accent gets stronger the more agitated he feels, which tells me he's one of the refugees that fled up north to Sweazn during the war. It also couldn't be more obvious that he's hiding something. I curl my left hand into a fist involuntarily, recognizing this guy might be trouble. The other reaches for my star necklace, the only piece of home I still carry with me.

"I just don't understand why the rest of us aren't privy to what the *all-knowing* leaders meet about," Liv huffs. "You make it all so secretive. When we were rescued, it was made clear that Jace has been searching for his friends, but now that we're here? And Astira is also awake and healthy? Our *friend* has vanished into thin air."

"We don't like secrets," I mutter, still fiddling with the points of my star pendant. "Liv and I can't be kept in the dark. It's all we've known for two years."

Liv presses the palm of her hand into my back in silent acknowledgment.

Micha opens his tiresome mouth, but he's cut off before he can respond.

"Why am I picking up on tension here?" Jace calls over to us. He's standing across the pavement in front of one of the many steel buildings. A few men lean in to say something, and Jace waves them off. He marches across the concrete path to where the three of us have been bickering next to the communal washing area, full of basins and tables and heaps of clothing. Jace's hair is up in a knot today, and his clothing matches Micha's.

He places a large hand on Micha's rigid shoulder. "What's the problem?"

Micha heaves a sigh and shakes his head, shrugging off Jace's hand. "Nothin'. Liv's just bein' Liv."

"And what's that supposed to mean?" I ask. I felt uneasy when standing here alone with this man, but now that I see two guys—no matter if one is a friend—facing Liv, I'm finding my voice again. Grinding my teeth, I take a small step closer to Liv. A few other women washing clothes stop what they're doing to eavesdrop on our conversation. They're the same ones who seem closed off, as if they'd rather blend into the dirt walls around us and disappear. *Good. Witnesses are our friends. They keep the pricks above us accountable.*

Us women have to stick together, even if we show our support for one another in silence.

Jace's eyebrows furrow, and he grabs Micha's elbow this time. "Hey, calm down. This isn't a big deal."

"It's startin' to be," Micha growls at him. "We have this city unda' control. We don't need women like Liv gettin' into trouble."

"How is she getting into trouble by asking what you're meeting about?" I ask. "What's wrong with us wanting to know what our leaders are doing? You have to understand the position we're in."

"Exactly," Liv speaks up. "We've traded one type of leader for the next. If this city is better than the tunnels, then it shouldn't be necessary to be checking in on anyone. Let us live in peace while we work. Or better yet, get your hands dirty, too, and you won't need to worry so much about how we're all doing."

"Gods, Micha," Jace mutters.

"Why won't you tell me?" Liv asks Jace. "We're supposed to be *friends*."

Jace's gaze darts to the group of women approaching us, each wearing a look of unease.

"We've been over this, Liv," Jace mumbles. "Being friends doesn't mean we're co-leaders. Some things have to be kept quiet until the time is right."

Alarm bursts inside my chest. It's only been a week at most since I've gotten a grasp on this new life. Liv had painted it to be better than the hell we were stuck in. *No. She said this place wasn't any more respectable. Jace had to make himself a villain.*

I turn to fully face Jace, but he holds up a hand. He's close enough now that his fingers reach all the way to my lips.

Muffling a gasp, my eyes widen. Did my *friend* just silence me before I could even speak?

"If you want to know so badly, maybe we should take you both there now," Jace considers. Goosebumps crawl up my arms at Micha's wide smile.

Liv narrows her eyes on our friend. *Is he, though?* The thought swirls around my mind before I can stop it. I take a step back and shake my head, trying to release my paranoia. Liv notices my movement and breathes out a rush of air, lacing her hand with mine.

"Astira and I told the other women we'd help with grouping the new crops after lunch," Liv says, her voice staying strong. "Can you show us whatever you're doing after we assist them for a few hours and get cleaned up? It'll also give you a chance to breathe. This comes off as... heavy, what you're going to share with us."

She has the appearance of a concerned friend, and her therapeutic voice is ringing loud and clear. Our hands are still interlaced, though, and I can feel the clamminess on her palm—a betrayal of the rush of anxiety she's experiencing right now. I stand next to my friend and force myself to nod adamantly at Jace. If Liv wants to delay this situation, then I'm with her. *Always.*

Jace sighs, scrubbing a hand over his face and down his chest. He stares at Micha for a long moment. "Alright. I'll meet you back here around 3:00 p.m. UGN time." With a curt nod, I watch our friend walk stiffly through the now large group of women, Micha falling in step beside him as they head toward another building. The second their footsteps fall silent, I turn into Liv's arms. We instinctively wrap our arms around each other and hold on tightly, releasing our edgy emotions into the hug.

"UGN time?" I mumble into my friend's shoulder.

"Yeah," Liv whispers. "Underground Nedrazon Time.

Remember we learned about how time passes more slowly the stronger the gravity? Down here, time ticks by a little faster. Some of the leaders here wanted to make a distinction between time in Nedrazon and time on the surface in case we can get back up there again and maintain societies both above and below. We were taught this in school in case of further nuclear wars."

Humming, I take a step back. "What do you think he's going to show us? And who the fuck is that Micha guy?"

"Nothing good, and *ugh*, something horrible. I don't like how neurotic Jace has been acting and the fact that he's withholding something important from us. Some time to cool off might do him good."

My stomach growls upsettingly loud. "I suppose I need some time, too. Apparently, my body wants lunch."

Liv chuckles and loops her arm with mine. "We've got potatoes, eggs, and dark tea calling our names."

"Oh, goodie. *More* potatoes and eggs? At least there's some caffeine this time. They're really spicing things up for us today," I mutter.

"You're *always* spicing things up," Liv laughs. "Just leave the clothes for now. Someone else will pick up where we left off—that's the way of things down here. Let's hurry to the dining space before they run out! We'll need all the energy we can get if we're pulling vegetables and finally breaking through Jace's wall of secrets."

Yes, that's what he has. Friend or not, I'll blow that wall to pieces as if I'm the nuclear missile, bringing his secrets to light and, maybe, to death.

"Where is he?" I grumble while picking dirt out from under

my nails. Some of them were damaged last night when I woke up in a panic, thinking I was still trapped in the tunnel with Damon. I had clawed at the door frame until a few of my nails bled, and the broken nail beds are currently swelling in irritation. Yanking root vegetables out of caked soil isn't ideal for hand wounds, but I wasn't going to stay cooped up with my misery. I'd rather be with Liv and interacting with the other women and few men working the field of crops they've managed to grow down here.

I need to prove my worth. *Ah, there's my mom's voice.* I haven't heard the old bitch's sayings since I woke up from my coma. *What splendid company she keeps.*

Liv shifts her weight onto her other foot in front of me. Her clothes and exposed skin have been smeared with dirt, her tattoo barely visible under all the grime, and we're both damp with sweat. We pulled crops all afternoon and only stopped when an actual farmer—a giant, burly fellow with a bushy brown beard, calloused hands, and jaded dark eyes—called out the time. They've been using a water wheel to keep track of days and time down here. The science behind this shoots right over my head. I'm a dedicated trauma therapist turned scorned sex slave. My talents lie in mental health and, evidently, pleasuring the human body.

I'm just relieved *someone* found a way to keep track of time. Liv and I never knew which day or hour was what in the tunnels, and it drove a number of prisoners mad. Many of their bodies were eventually piled up in the back area of the tunnel, rotting away and decomposing, the spaces they previously took up now desolate. Those people chose death when faced with continuous insufficient resources and the realities of living underground. It couldn't impact me, though. They had to do better than that when I always keep one toe dipped into insanity.

"I don't think Jace is coming," Liv sighs. Her hazel eyes glow under the solar light above us. "I sort of expected that to be his response. I've been asking about what he's been up to for the past few months nonstop. The few times he's caved and said he'd bring me with to one of his meetings, he'd ditch me."

"Then why did you suggest we wait?" I ask.

"I—do you remember how Lyk and I could pick up on others' energy pretty quickly?" Liv lowers her head. "It's this tingling sensation in my gut that I can't quite explain. A warning. Nervousness bubbled up through me, and I *knew* if we went with Jace and Micha right then, it'd be a mistake for us. You probably think I'm crazy, I—"

"I don't," I tell her. "We all experience that from time to time. You and Lyk simply feel it more deeply than most."

My friend gives me a soft smile. "We do."

I search her face for a moment, and swallowing, I dip my head in the direction of the room I'm still living in. "Think we can go clean up, then? All this grime on me is a fresh reminder of how it felt to be with, um, Da—"

"You don't have to speak his name," Liv interrupts me. "We might as well call him the Devil. Any of the leaders ranked with him should be called that."

I nod. Even his name rubs against my skin like pouring salt into an open wound.

"Go wash up," Liv says. "We can grab dinner after and settle in for the night."

My eyes find the dark outlines of the soil walls, far enough away to ease any claustrophobic sensations, yet close enough to remind us that we're underground. A large insect crawls over the top of my foot while another, longer one scuttles down my hip. I swat both away and shudder, never quite growing used to the way insects, arachnids, and millipedes crawl in every crevice of the colonies underground.

"Isn't it always night down here?"

Humming, I lower my body into the small bathtub carved from the earth's soil. It's filled with scalding hot water, the kind that burns away the top layer of my skin. There are a few private tubs attached outside and near the building I'm staying in for those still healing. Each one is a tiny space with barely enough room for the bathtub itself. There's a small mirror in the corner behind it, a low shelf for your clothes and towel, and a single art piece done by one of the people living down here.

The art in this room is distinct and lures me in. It's of a woman lying down with long red hair, so similar to my own, with a crown of velvety antlers. She stares at me with dark purple irises, which draw attention to the dozens of violet and plum flowers surrounding her. A bear pelt covers her sprawled out, naked body. It's comforting to behold a piece of art this far underground, that *someone* can still find beauty down here. Not me. Not even in the confines of this tiny room where I'm alone.

I could use the communal baths if forced to—we had to bathe in front of leering eyes all the time in the tunnels. Those boorish men feasted on our bare skin, scars and all. Shivering at the thought, I run a hand across my shoulders, along my necklace, and down my chest. My torso is littered with scars—a few sunken, some discolored. All are stains of my time with Damon. My ribcage is still sticking out above my stomach, as if it's eager to break free of my warped skin.

I abhor my body.

That thought only intensifies as I stick each foot out of the soapy water, one scrawny leg at a time, and the trail of scars climb from the tops of my feet all the way up to my hips. My eyes sting with tears, and even though I know I'm all alone, I can't bring myself to cry. I reject that release of emotions and prefer to keep them all bottled up inside. At least then I can feel *something*. One of my shaky hands reaches for the scrap of washcloth draped over the side of the tub. My hands are damaged in their own ways, but there are no scars on them, no constant reminders of what I was coerced to do for years.

I dip the washcloth in the heated water and squeeze out the soapy mixture down my left arm. My mind tells me to place the cloth on my arm and scrub the dirt off me, but my body is frozen in place. *What's the point? Why bother cleaning when we're still stuck underground within walls of dirt?* The picture of this city is painted in an almost convincing way. I *am* grateful for some more variety of foods and fresh clothes and the chance to be treated as a human. No amount of colors can hide the fact that I'm still under leaders who'll watch my every move, though. Nothing can erase the marks on my skin that deface me. There's no chance I can change my new reality, no arguing my way through to the air above us. *Do I want to continue living in a brighter version of Hell?*

I'm not sure that I do.

I watch as my hand lowers back into the water. My body sits with its back against the inside of the tub and my feet rest on the rim of it for what must be an hour. Enough time passes for the water to cool to the point of pebbling my pale, freckled skin. Leaning my head back behind me, I sigh and close my eyes, urging myself to get up and dry off. I can't move, though. The rest of me prefers to stay in this tub, hardly large enough to hold an adult's body comfortably, and let my head sink under the surface. I just... I just crave to be held in death's arms and carried to a place where I can finally rest.

Is it so wrong to wish for more than a respite?

With my eyelids closed, I lower my head closer to the water. I don't get further than an inch before my body seizes, my back arching and my head falling back against the tub's rim with a loud *bang*.

My eyes flash open, yet there's nothing holding me in its grip. I can't move my body and start to thrash around, kicking my feet against the bathtub. All this does is cause the soapy water to splash the walls in this narrow room, and my muscles strain with the effort to fight whatever has me in its clutches. My breathing is erratic, and I swear my heart will thump its way right out of my chest at the rate it's going. Licking my lips, I open my mouth to call for help. I'd rather risk the embarrassment of someone seeing me this way and relieving me of this tension than to stay here in a contorted position, paralyzed.

"I wouldn't do that, if I were you," a low voice grumbles near me.

My eyes grow impossibly wider, and I'm terrified enough, no scream can escape me. I move my gaze around the bathtub and see nothing, and there's no movement on the low netted material that acts as a makeshift ceiling or clay walls surrounding me. *What the actual fuck?* Black dots cloud my vision as panic sits like a heavy weight on my chest. I gasp for any amount of breath I can keep down, but each choking pant only amplifies the resounding silence encasing me.

"I'm right here," that deep voice says.

The unyielding grip around my body eases its hold, and I'm gently lowered back into the tub. The water is now as cold as death's touch. I tremble from the bitter temperature until my teeth are actively chattering.

"Hm," the voice ponders. "Now that I've found you, I think I'd like to keep you. I'd rather you didn't die on me."

A few minutes pass by in silence. I soon feel a low boiling around my hips and torso until scalding bubbles are surrounding my neck, shoulders, and knees on the surface. The frigid cold melts into an unbearable heat, and I don't have it in me to yell out for assistance. Bewilderment ensconces itself in my mind, making itself right at home next to the coiled-up fear and never-ending thoughts of self-loathing. *What's one more upsetting emotion?*

Shadows collect above me where the clay wall meets the corner of the makeshift ceiling. I push myself to follow where those shadows go, and against my better judgment, I watch as they gather in a bundle right behind my head. Tilting my head to the side, I can see that they're stemming from the small mirror to my right that's leaning against the bathtub and corner of the room. I yelp and nearly drown myself when, instead of my reflection, I see two onyx eyes peering out at me from the oval mirror. In frantic movements, I manage to get to the other side of the bathtub and sink low enough in the now steaming water for only my eyes to peek out.

Is this a ghost? Am I dreaming? Fuck, am I hallucinating now? No, no, no, I can't be. My grandmother went through this and was ostracized from the family. My sister, the one I was never allowed to talk about, also had—

"Gods, your thoughts are as swift and chaotic as a brewing storm," the voice growls. My right eye twitches as I gape at the dark eyes still staring at me from the mirror. Shadows continue to slither up and down the wall and now, unfortunately, are traveling along the rim of the bathtub right toward me. *Joy.*

As if I didn't feel unhinged enough, those eyes grow smaller until a man's face appears amid the shadows and darkness. He blinks slowly at me and looks around the room, as if adjusting to a new location and wearing a full face.

"W-what are y-y—"

"What would you like me to be?" he asks.

His tone is dripping in sin. My own voice gets stuck in my throat at the way he already physically affects me.

He smiles, the movement lazy, yet there's a menacing glint in those smoldering pits. I've seen them a thousand times now in my dreams. Too many times.

"Oh, starling. Many call me death incarnate," the man growls. His voice is deep and gravely, as sharp as the blades Damon had used to cut me.

"D-does this mean y-you're here to kill me-e?" I stutter. I wanted death so badly, to be free of the pain stored inside of me. Now that he's here, though, I'm stuck between the wish for freedom and the curse of damnation.

The man tilts his head to the side. Those black orbs are calculating in a way that both unnerves and thrills me.

He makes a low sound in his throat, and I reach for my necklace, urging myself to stay calm. His eyes track the movement and stay fixated on the silver star pendant. "No. That's not the plan for today," he grumbles. "Your soul has called to me for many days now, and I tugged on the line connecting us until I found you. I didn't imagine I'd do this in my sleep. Then again, Azrael has been rather persistent. Tireless, the fucker. I can agree that it was worth the search now."

My eyes dart back and forth between his and the way his mouth tugs into a smirk. "Azrael?"

That smirk deepens. "My wolf."

I'm stuck on a pendulum, and at any moment, my body is going to drop mid-swing. He has a wolf? *No, Astira, fucking focus. You're worried about him having a wolf when you're talking to someone through a mirror.*

"Th-this must be an illusion," I mutter. "Just overworking myself. Too much, too soon after waking up."

"I assure you that it's not," the man says. His eyebrows furrow in confusion. "You were practically screaming out for my soul and were begging to be killed. I can't imagine why such a beautiful creature would want to be done with life, even if it's spent on Earth."

I have no reason to do this. In no way does it make sense. But I glare at this man who plays tricks on my mind and thinks to call me beautiful. My long mane of hair is piled high up on my head in thick braids. I couldn't bear to wear it down with how thin it's become on the ends. My skin is ashen, my face is gaunt, and I'm still a walking skeleton with a smattering of bruises and a whole gown of scars.

Forcing myself to stand up, I brace my hands on the rim of the tub and stand on shaky legs. Rivulets of water flow down my naked body, and my skin is either wrinkled from soaking or covered in goosebumps from head to toe. My nipples harden from the change in temperature of the air, sending a shiver down my back as unexpected arousal hits me.

"This is only another dream," I rasp, not breaking eye contact with this mysterious man. "You refuse to leave me alone. You're just a man. A strange one, but still a man, blinded by beauty." I glance down at the way my scars appear to puff up more after bathing in the hot water, giving them an even more disfigured pattern. Looking back up at the man, I ask, "Still think I'm beautiful?"

He licks his lips and those onyx eyes drink in each inch of me, starting at my feet and working their way up in a slow perusal. Each patch of skin they touch becomes heated, as if he's using warm fingertips to glide along my body.

"No," he growls.

For reasons I can't understand, my heart and spirit plunge in despair at that simple word from a man I don't even know and doesn't exist.

"I think you're exquisite," he continues. Wings of darkness flutter up through my insides. "You've bewitched me already, a feat uncommon for my soul. I vow now to taste each of your scars until I know them so well, I've made them my own."

Those tendrils of shadows slink further along the rim of the tub until they're gliding across the surface of the water. One spiral of satiny shadow at a time curls around my ankles and calves, gently caressing each scar and squeezing enough to warn me I'm in this man's clutches. His stare intensifies, consuming me whole, and his face appears to press against the mirror in an attempt to break through to me—as if he's a world away, enclosed by an unseen barrier he can't pass through.

Swallowing, I lick my now parched lips. My heartbeat doubles and is loud enough to block out any thoughts of common sense. This man tracks the path of my tongue, and as if he can sense the tempo of my heart, his eyes flutter to my chest and the way it rises in abrupt movements.

"Tell me, starling," he rasps. Those shadows wind their way up to my hips, pulsating against each disfigured blemish. They thrum with the same energy of his ruinous, beautiful eyes. "Have you ever been touched by darkness? Have you ever been *commanded* to play with yourself by death incarnate?"

An inky tendril curves under my right hip bone and slides in slow, languid strokes until it brushes against the apex of my thighs. It teases the bundle of nerves, causing me to sigh in unexpected pleasure before my eyes widen, realizing this man is *touching* me. Dream or not, our relationship has turned from stalking my nightmares to physically caving into an impulsive hunger I didn't realize I had for him.

I stagger backward, but the shadows don't let me fall. More of them coil around my fingers and up my quivering arms until they're wrapped firmly around each shoulder.

"Perhaps I can persuade you." His voice grinds against my senses in a delicious way.

One of the shadows curls tighter around my left hand and fingers. Within seconds, my left elbow bends enough for my hand to rise to my bare chest. My gaze flickers back and forth between this man's eyes and the way he's pinching my fingers together around one of my nipples. Between the cool, silky sensation of the shadows, his penetrating stare, and the way my body is being touched in front of a stranger has my blood humming. I can't help it. I throw my head back and release a low moan. I'm already addicted to the way this man can control my body and use his shadows to bend me to his will.

A loud knock on the door jolts me awake.

"Astira?" Liv yells through the door. "You okay? I thought we were meeting for dinner. It's been a few hours, and the doctors said you've been out here the whole time."

I gingerly lift my head off the tub and look down at the lukewarm water. In my dream, I was standing and allowing that mysterious man—the one who keeps following me from nightmare to nightmare—to play with my body. His gravelly voice reached all the way to my core, a sensation I'm missing already. All thoughts of him dissipate as my neck screams to be stretched after lying at an awkward angle for too long. I scan each corner of the room and stare into the mirror, finding myself hoping for those dark eyes to appear. They don't, though. No eyes, no shadows, no desire. Blinking a few times, I clear my throat and turn toward the door.

"Yeah, coming!"

What a strange dream. It felt so real.

Liv pushes the door open and comes in with a few more gray towels. She gingerly helps me up out of the water and wraps a towel around my torso and then places one around my neck. I watch as she takes leather shoes and new clothes out from her cloth bag and holds out a hand to help me out of the bathtub. As I quickly change into the blue shirt and black pants, I almost forget the urge to be free of this world.

Almost. I wonder what death in *his* arms would bring me?

As I pick up a black feather from the corner of the bathtub, something tells me it'd bring more than just the peace I'm yearning for.

TWENTY-ONE
Eira & Athena

Memories might be gifts or weapons,
depending on who receives them.
-Council Member Lesak, Grand Spirit Reader

Eira

"I think I could get used to you wearing this," Nyx murmurs next to me.

I scoff. "I'm surprised you're okay with me walking around wearing a tight leather bodysuit with these sheer cutouts."

He raises an eyebrow as he snakes an arm around my waist, forcing us to come to a stop outside of the last row of bookshelves. Nyx is wearing equally tight leather coverings that have me all hot and bothered. It's not *fair* how no matter what he wears, the fabric stretches with each muscle movement.

After he manifested new coverings for both of us—since the ones we were wearing had been conveniently burned or shredded—we fixed our tousled sex hair. Mine is back in a long braid, while his is pulled half up behind him. There are no purple flames or black fur and wings to be seen from either of us. I'm not even sure when I'll allow that deepest part of myself to show itself to the others. Then again, if baring my soul in such a vulnerable way will help heal Nyx of the plague of darkness, then I'll walk around as a fucking corpse all day long.

"They can all admire my queen's stunning body. Why wouldn't they?"

Laughing softly, I brush a few strands of hair out of his now brown and crackling eyes. "So, you won't mind if Daru makes a few comments?"

Nyx scowls at me before placing one of the new tomes in my arms. "He can say what he must, as long as he doesn't touch you. Besides, it's my scent that's mixing with yours, not his."

I grin widely and knock him with my hip. "Just don't get *too* jealous, my shadow prince."

He glares at me and opens up the tome *Gods & Goddesses, Hiding in Plain Sight*. Nyx flips through the back index and scans down the thin parchment. His eyes widen when he finds what he's looking for, and then he's opening the tome up at a chapter halfway through the book.

"Before we join the others," he murmurs. "I think it's important that you keep this chapter with you."

Confused, I glance at the chapter he's referring to:

Goddess of Light and Flame: Healing, Destruction, and the Blinding Truth

Lifetimes of Survival and Past Lives

I gasp as I take in the chapter title and the intricate artwork painted along the borders of these pages. There's bright blue fire weaving with white, glowing light and red flames. A few pages into the chapter, the artwork shifts to a deeper blue and purple fire. There are a handful of images with creatures draped in thick coverings, each catching fire from black flames.

"How did you know this would be here?" I ask him, taken aback that there's an entire *chapter* about what could be my powers.

"I recognized the cover," he clears his throat. "It's similar, but a different volume, to a tome my aunt kept in her personal library. I used to run wild at their castle whenever we'd visit them up in the northern part of the island. Considering what Stefanie has been asking Esen and Riker to gather for her to research, I thought it wouldn't hurt to see if there was anything related to your healing powers."

I continue to stare down at the letters on the page. Each of them forms words that could be the key to fully understanding who I am and what I was before, not just examples of my healing light. But none of them are making sense in my brain right now.

"Why not let Stefanie have this, though? Surely she'd also be able to look for any patterns or useful information."

Nyx shrugs. "Call it a gut feeling. My shadows and smoke tug at my soul when they think there's something important for me to see or know. I also felt my fox stir in my chest after my shadows picked this tome up for us."

I hum in response and try to take the tome from him, but Nyx snatches it back. A gasp bubbles out of me when I see him *ripping the pages* from this tome.

"Umm excuse me?!" I hiss. "I don't care who or what you are. Have you no respect for this library?"

Nyx rolls his eyes. "There's plenty of respect from the group of us to go around down here. I just *know* you're going to need this, and I want to see how this compares to what's inside the tome my aunt has. If she's still alive, that is." He sighs and removes the last of the pages, carefully smoothing them out before folding them up. I'm wearing tall black boots, and he quickly shoves the chapter pages down the side of my left boot.

Frowning, I smooth over that side of my leg. It's still a crime to damage *any* book—let alone one about the gods and goddesses—but I don't want to push Nyx when he's clearly torn up about his family in Drageyra.

I take a deep breath and allow him to lead us toward where everyone is sitting under the massive windows. Athena, Hadwin, and Eliina still look to be sitting as still as death from where I can see them. Stefanie is talking with animated hands to Hauke while Riker and Esen place more tomes and scrolls down in front of her kneeling form. My gaze swings to the back area of tables and floor cushions, where Jade, Fraya, Odin, and Ivar are sitting quietly. Neither Ulf nor his shadow wolf are anywhere to be seen.

My stomach clenches when I see Daru pacing back in his human form. He's isolated himself, and I can tell from the way black and dark green *maji* flares around him that he's agitated.

Uh oh. Why do I feel guilty?

Mr. Huffy next to me should be everything to me. And truthfully, he is. He's the fierce protector that won't think twice before throwing himself in front of me if danger is on the horizon. Nyx is pure strength, both mentally and physically, and knows what it means to become one with the darkness. He joins it, so he can rise against all those who've harmed him. This *solliqa* can meet my fire while our fox spirits bond with one another. Smoke and fire, shadows and light—our souls are meant to ignite as our love grows for one another.

But Daru? I can't know where *that's* going to go. I do know that his air *maji* and ability to soar through the stormy skies are vastly different from Nyx's dark fire powers. Lighter. Able to float with ease and see multiple perspectives instead of charging in with that courageous warmth I love so much in Nyx.

I'll have to trust in the *almaove* connections I'm gifted with and learn to adapt with the ones I don't understand or think I need.

Turning toward Nyx, I stop him before we get any closer to listening ears.

"Do you really think your aunt and other family won't be in Drageyra?"

Nyx's eyes darken, his expression twisting in sadness. "I have no idea. Does it make me a coward that I don't really want to find out?"

"No." I shake my head and cup his cheek. "It makes you *human*, which is a quality a lot of souls might be missing in this realm."

He smiles and leans down to kiss me, but Stefanie's giggle makes us both freeze.

"I'm *so* glad that you were able to find those tomes I was looking for," she says with a wink. Stefanie glances behind her quickly, and then steps closer to us. "And I'm thankful that you're back now. Daru's restlessness is going to turn *me* into one of those monsters if he doesn't stop pacing soon. A soul can only keep her screams of insanity in for so long."

Emphasizing her point, my Zaya baby rushes forward away from where she was plopped down next to Athena. I bend down, letting her jump up into my arms, and hold her close against my chest. The vibrations of her purring are settling into my skin. Scratching under her fluffy chin, I throw Stefanie a saucy smile.

"Nyx and I had some things to work out," I murmur with a wink.

Stefanie raises her eyebrow. "Yes, I heard."

A blush heats my entire neck and cheeks, but Nyx simply chuckles, tucking me into his side.

"Nice touch with the matching coverings," Stefanie adds. "I bet Daru is going to just *love* it."

I stick my tongue out at her. "Any updates from Athena and Hadwin?"

She shakes her head slowly, concern creasing the edges of her emerald-green eyes.

"Not yet," she whispers. "Let's keep searching for more information, anything we can get our hands on in this library, while we wait. We don't know when they'll awaken." She turns to lead us back, but then she pauses, glancing back at Nyx. "And I *heard* you tearing those pages out. Sir, what's wrong with you? Don't you dare do that ever again, you hear me?"

Nyx starts to scowl, but I elbow him in the ribcage. Zaya hisses at him. "He won't," I assure her. I peer around my fiery friend to where Athena is sitting as still as a statue.

I really hope she's okay.

Athena

One more deep breath is all it takes to send me tilting off my axis. Colors gust in multiple directions until my spirit is traveling through the earth, and I can finally give myself over to the tunnel of rich soil surrounding me. I willingly let go of the library, the room stifling me the longer I'm forced to stay in there. Fragmented light, a mystical blend of green and white and gold, forms a layer around my spirit and nearly shatters me. Hadwin, Eliina, and I are each here, yet we're not. Our individual souls are mere flaps of a butterfly's wing, scattered to the wind as we collectively come together in the roots of this earth. Emotions flitter past me. Some could be my own, some could be those I'm bonding to.

How fascinating it is to brush alongside another soul and realize our hidden pain all tastes the same.

"Athena," Eliina cries out.

Yes, that's my name. There are three of us here, and I'm communicating through the earth for a reason.

"I'm here," I hear myself say, my voice echoing. There's no body or mouth, and I'm not sure how I transfer my thoughts.

"As am I," a lower voice grumbles. Hadwin. Hadwin is here with us. Does his spirit yearn for mine? A sudden sensation of warmth trickles over me. Perhaps that's his answer.

"Take what you can from me," Eliina pleads. Her voice is hoarse, as if she's been screaming. "Please, take it and tell the others. I don't have much time left."

"What do you mean?" I ask. Unease twists through my nonexistent form.

"They'll know the moment I share with you," she continues. "Hadwin, find a way to share these images with the others. I did what I had to, so I could protect each of you. I'm *so* sorry. Jade was right. Too much of a good thing can turn bad if used with the wrong intentions. I thought I was doing the right thing. I was wrong. Be careful who you trust here. Protect Eira, at *any* cost. Find where Daya took Tryg. She... she made the right decision from the cards dealt to us. I should have listened. Tell Nyx the blue stone is important. He must find a way to use it."

I want to ask what she's talking about, but there are no words to express my confusion. An edgy energy hooks itself into me, and I know without a doubt it's Hadwin. We're both muddling our way through the chaos of this situation.

"Eliina," I breathe, her name swirling around my spirit. "I need to know why Hadwin and I were pulled into Earth. Why us? *Please* tell me what you know."

Hadwin's energy pushes against me again, obviously irritated that this is the information I'm asking for first. I don't give a fuck in any stretch of the imagination what he thinks. Can't I be a little selfish if I'm risking my own safety to speak with Eliina right now?

"I wish I could tell you," Eliina sighs. "I don't know who or what wanted you to see the state of Earth. I do know that there's not only evil growing in all of these worlds. There's also love and light, and no matter how dark it becomes, those positive forces will persevere. It's possible someone or *something* wanted to show you both how much love exists between your souls in another past life, in another lifetime. They needed to remind you how powerful the two of you can and will be. You must allow your souls to see the light and embrace the darkness that's been holding the both of you down. I can *taste* the misery you both harbor. It's for the best that you saw the future of your homeland, Athena, and how in a different timeline on that same planet, you were capable of holding enough love and joy to light the entire sky up. Both of you need to learn the ways pain and trauma can impact a world like Earth. That's not even including all the other ones out there that are suffering…"

"Other ones? How many worlds are suffering from the darkness?" Hadwin asks sharply.

"There's some information I can't share without risking immediate death," Eliina responds, her voice quivering, being surrounded by the rich earth not doing anything to soothe her fears.

"Then what about—"

"Let me show you," Eliina whispers, cutting him off. "I wish I could share about Eira's—"

Eliina makes a choking sound, and then I'm spinning out of control. Images blur past me until a handful of them come into focus. The first slams into me so hard, the essence of my spirit rattles.

Eliina, swathed in silky robes, is trekking through a forest with a small group of solliqas. *The pink and blue trees are familiar but soon fade into the background. One of the* solliqas *is whispering, and I can't make out what they're saying. Eliina's voice is clear as a bell, though.*

"Did you confirm her whereabouts on Earth?"

"Yes, Eliina. She's in the northern part of a country called Sweazn. We can get her out as soon as tomorrow," a low voice says.

"Not yet," Eliina responds. "Only monitor her soul for right now. If you notice she's hovering between Earth and our world, then use your new maji *abilities to bring her the rest of the way. If we force her soul to come here when it's not ready, she could get lost in between realms and slip from our grasp."*

"Right," the low voice confirms.

Another solliqa *touches Eliina's arm. "What if the Council gets to her first? Ameirona gave us strict instructions to transport our Queen of Light through their portal in Rioa. It'll be—"*

"Quiet," Eliina hushes. "We can't be too careful, even out here. Any soul could be listening to us right now."

"I'm sorry." The solliqa *bows their head. "I just—I'm impatient to bring her back to our world. The sooner the Queen of Light connects with Ameirona, the easier it'll be to manipulate the Council into completely removing the* canielors *from Majikaero and putting up our idea of a border between our realm and the other infected ones. Our world won't survive without her. As the Queen of Cudhellen, only Ameirona can call such darkness away from here."*

"I know," Eliina murmurs. "She'll be here soon enough. Let's focus our efforts on corralling the Banished Ones. They'll be the key to ensuring our queen cooperates."

Shadows cloud my vision. I'm yanked out of one memory and thrown directly into another. This time, I can feel Hadwin's spirit leaning against my own. The two of us collide together in an attempt to support each other as we soak up everything Eliina has to share.

Eliina is dressed in green coverings so bright, they glow like a fire. She's arguing with a solliqa. *No, I can see who this one is. Daya?!*

"This isn't what we agreed on," Daya seethes.

"It's for the best," Eliina snips. Her tone is calm, but her body is more rigid than ever. "The Council has already made their own agreement with Ameirona, which she didn't tell me about until now. They know about the canielors evolving. Those lost souls can now be manipulated to shift into specific solliqas and are able to transform into bholei. We haven't seen those monsters in centuries, and they're deadly, Daya. They can portal in and out of too many worlds to count, can feed on a soul's pain and trauma, and further spread this plague. They're looming right under our noses and will bring devastation to our world. Sometimes, plans need to change for the greater good."

"The greater good!" Daya yells. "What a load of bullshit. You're just a coward."

"What would you have me do? My hands are tied between what the Council will likely do for the sake of power in another world and satisfying Ameirona."

"I'd have you not betray us. Think of Eira! She's faced too much already."

"I am thinking of her! When I explain to her how the odds are against us to go with the original plan, she'll understand. I know she will. It'll be worth the pain of losing a few souls if this plague can be removed by Ameirona."

"A few souls!" Daya screeches. "Y-you're talking about some of the most powerful solliqas in our world, Eliina. Eira. Nyx. His group of banished souls. How will sacrificing them mean peace on Majikaero?"

"Ameirona promised that the Sairn will use their powers to remove any and all darkness from this world. We just need to give them the handful of solliqas they've been searching for," Eliina replies with a grim expression on her face. "She provided compelling evidence that she has a strong bond with this wicked group of creatures and could persuade them to do her bidding. The Council all agreed that the loss of a few souls was better than the *destruction of an entire world. What was I to do? It was only my one vote against all of theirs."*

"We don't even know if she'll keep her word," Daya hisses.

"No, we don't," Eliina whispers. "But it's better to face the demons we know than the ones unseen."

Daya steps back as if she's been slapped. "You know me, Eliina. I'm not a demon. You know why we've needed to find Eira and what my home world is facing. We're too connected to Majikaero and Earth to not have it affect these worlds, too."

"We all have demons in us, Daya," Eliina snaps.

My heart is beating as wildly as a hundred horses galloping. There are too many images Eliina is trying to force into us at once. I don't know where to start. Hadwin somehow grabs onto me and we're diving right into another memory.

"I told you this was a mistake!" Daya screams. She's standing with Eliina and a few hooded *solliqas in a different forest. This one is eerily familiar, and it dawns on me that it's where Hadwin and I were the night of the festival. A* solliqa *lowers their hood, revealing she's one of the healers, Isa. Eyes the color of garnets glower at Eliina. Small white antlers made of velvet twist out of her head.*

"I didn't want to do it," Eliina says, her voice shaking. "Namid forced my hand."

"No, you made your choice," Isa says. "And now we need to make ours."

Another *solliqa* steps forward with a deep scowl etched on his face. I gasp. It's Hauke. He looks similar to the one in the library. This memory happened recently.

"You're despicable," he spits. "How could you assist the Sairn in opening those portals? How could you fucking go along with those irredeemable Council members, the ones who handed our world on a silver platter to such cruel creatures? You knew Tryg was redeemable and pushed him over the edge anyway. And you fucking used him so those freaks could take more of our solliqas.

Now he's chained up and under watch by the Council's henchmen. I'll have to get really fucking creative if we want to set him free."

"Leave that to me, Hauke," Daya snarls. "The Sairn have already taken too many innocent souls. I won't let them take another one."

Eliina falls to her knees, a sobbing mess. "I wanted to protect everyone from all of this fear and pain and sorrow, but souls often end up making things worse when the whole truth isn't told. The trust has been broken."

"You bet it has," Daya snarls. "It started when you chose Ameirona, and it's been officially broken as of yesterday. We know what you've been doing with those canielors *in the library.*"

"And where you've been sending these monsters," Isa adds.

"You don't understand. None of you understand!" Eliina shouts. "I kept those canielors *safe in the library. It's the only safe space in Rioa. Eira can save them. I know she can. We don't have to immediately turn them into ash and stardust. And I didn't realize where Ameirona was sending the other* canielors. *She only said she needed them for a project."*

"Are you fucking delusional?" Hauke growls. "She didn't even tell you what she was using them for, and you agreed? Because you were afraid of what the Council members would do?"

"It's too late now," Eliina mumbles. "The Council members have all fled back to their homelands. Some of them are not guilty. You have to know this. They learned what I was going to do, and they fled to warn the other regions. I had to take this risk with Ameirona and the others, even if it meant sacrificing some of the Banished Ones and innocent solliqas."

"Why?" Isa asks. "Why betray us? Why offer them up on a silver platter? Don't you realize what this'll do to Eira?"

"The Queen of Light will survive this," Eliina rasps. "By giving Ameirona the few she wanted, she'd leave Majikaero sooner and break her agreement with the Council members. I thought this would give us a fighting chance against the plague of darkness, *and even more so if those already banished were gone from this world."*

"How could you assume this?" Hauke pushes.

Eliina swallows and glances down at her hands. "Because while she didn't tell me her detailed plans, I know Ameirona. And I trusted her. I gambled with the wrong side and lost."

"Oh, shut up," Daya barks. "Your self-pity is nauseating. You know who lost? We did. Those poor children and families on Earth did, now that Ameirona can send the darkened souls of canielors into their little bodies and wreak havoc on that world. Eira will lose if you've succeeded and destroyed Nyx's companions. At least you didn't take Erika."

"You know where she's at?" Eliina gasps.

"As if I would tell you," Daya hisses. "You've betrayed us, and now we need to clean up your mess. The mess of an almighty Grand Healer. What a fucking joke."

Daya turns to the hooded solliqas. "Alert the others. We need to rescue Tryg and rendezvous back here to confirm Eira and the others are safe."

"You want us to rescue Tryg first?" Isa asks.

"Absolutely," Daya nods. "He's too dangerous in the wrong hands. I was in denial of how far Eliina would go." She throws a look drenched in sadness at Eliina. "Ameirona isn't your mother anymore. Shira isn't your sister. They've chosen your homeworld of Cudhellen over the future of the other worlds, and they followed the Sairn and their greed for power in this universe."

She takes one step toward Eliina. "And I think you've done enough harm, don't you think? If you didn't help Namid and the other Council members with sending canielors into innocent bodies on Earth, souls like Eira's true mother would still be alive."

"I can't let you take him!" Eliina shrieks. Her robes rip into shreds as her body morphs into a tree with crystalized eyes. They're glowing with ire and desperation. The tips of her branches dwindle into wisps of smoke, and she swings them around wildly at Daya.

"Then you'll just have to stop us," Daya flings over her shoulder. She bursts into a bird of red flames, and the others shift into their chosen forms. Isa grows into a smoldering alklen with white antlers. Hauke shifts in the blink of an eye into a purple and black bird of prey and carries a few of the robed solliqas with him. Another one jumps up on Isa, and they're riding off fast out of the colorful forest. Everyone has scattered, and Eliina is left to decide which soul she's going to follow. Her crystalized eyes are a mixture of white, rose, and yellow, and as soon as they find where Daya flew to, she's racing off after her. Eliina shifts from one form to the next, becoming different plants and trees and rippling under the white grass as the soil itself.

I blink, and we're standing in the dungeon cell, the same one we were in not even a day ago.

Tryg peers at Daya with a mixture of wariness and uncertainty. She squeezes his chains into shards of metal with her talons and soon after knocks him out. Another robed figure dashes through the dungeon and calls out to Daya. She throws—fucking throws—Tryg at the robed figure and they shift into a bird, their feathers a deep azul. They dive through a gold portal that opens and closes in a heartbeat. How did they do that? My mind is barely keeping up with what's happening, each image glitching as they roll into one another. I cry out when I realize what I'm watching. We're witnessing this scene from Eliina's perspective, and she pushes out of the dungeon wall—a giant wall of dirt on the stones shifts into her usual humanoid form. She's teeming with despair and throws herself at Daya. I'm amazed at the way Daya protects herself and moves as fast as liquid fire out of Eliina's reach. She forces her into one of the chains still intact in Tryg's cell.

"I don't care what family feud you're going through," Daya snarls. "I can't let you ruin our worlds while you're trying to figure it out."

A red light flares and Daya's gone. Hadwin and I are pulled out of this memory, Eliina's anguish battering at our senses.

Flashes of other memories pummel at us as we fall back into our bodies in the library.

Eira

For gods' sake, Eliina is taking her sweet time, isn't she? Maybe a little reminder with Nyx's dagger would speed things along.

Gods. I shake my head and take a drink of *lipva* from the canister near my feet, hoping I can flush out the increasingly cruel and judgmental thoughts. It isn't like me to be quick-tempered or violent. There's apparently some hidden darkness there, as Nyx and I learned a bit ago, but I'm not one to pick up a weapon because I'm getting impatient. I've taken pride in my ability to heal those suffering from trauma and being a compassionate and loving human. All of those being healthy, caring behaviors.

Except I'm not a human anymore.

The past month in Majikaero has fractured the lens through which I view my identity. And the more time I spend around Nyx and his companions, even while I'm healing, the more I savor the taste of their ruthlessness.

That's not true, a voice says in my mind. *You can blame them all you want, but they don't dictate which parts of yourself you embrace.*

I sigh, trying to ignore the building irritation that we're *still* in this library. It's been nearly twenty-four hours, and gods, I can only stare at these three bodies for so long. Athena and I are the ones who obsessively read. Honestly, I've spent the better part of my life wanting to live inside a building with thousands of books at my disposal. It's starting to get claustrophobic, though, the longer our group has to stay glued to this particular area. I've only ventured away from my best friend when Nyx stole me away to "get the tomes"—such an unbelievable excuse. What was he even thinking? None of us dare to move far in the chance Athena, Hadwin, and Eliina come back to us from wherever they've gone.

I know they're physically in front of me, but their souls are somewhere far away, communicating through their earth *maji*. It's serendipitous that all three of them can do this, and the anxiety from what they could be talking about is ready to burst out of me.

We're all exhausted. While I'm hunched over on a floor cushion with anxiety spiraling everywhere, Jade is impatiently tapping her feet next to the table with dozens of scrolls laid out. Nyx is mirroring her stance behind where I'm sitting—not leaving me alone other than when I needed to use the bathroom, claiming Daru will swoop in—and it's taking all of my self-restraint to not set that restless foot on fire. *Infuriating shadow prince.*

Between the purring and kneading of my legs, Zaya is making it easier to remain still in this cushioned chair. I scratch under her chin and take in those seemingly permanent golden eyes. I didn't want to worry the others, but it felt as if a piece of my soul was ripped from me before when Zaya was taken to the healing quarters. I'm *so* relieved she's safe. She and Athena are all I have from Sweazn. I don't even have Tryg anymore, if I ever truly had him at all in this realm. I hate to admit this to myself, but I'm starting to lose faith that I'll see our other friends from Earth again. Athena is convinced she can find them, but I'm not so sure anymore.

Will their souls want to be found?

Stefanie has been putting me at ease with her low, melodic

humming. She's sitting next to me on another cushion, hers as red as her hair, with a pile of tomes stacked next to her from the manipulators. Her eyes are fixed on Athena and Hadwin, only breaking her focus when Esen darts over in wisps of flames with a new tome or scroll for her to inspect. Riker is still shrouded by stacks upon stacks of books, his body barely seen when he moves to the bookshelves in a blur of shadows. Stefanie told me earlier in the day that they're both talented manipulators, but Riker also has the ability to manipulate components of time. She laughed at my reaction and had to help lift my jaw off the floor. *Time?*

She explained that he can slow seconds down in his immediate surroundings, allowing him to get twice as much work completed at a time. The only problem is that it'll burn him out quicker, so he only uses this part of his *maji* when he's in a rush. Stefanie insists there's no time to waste, and considering Jade's agitation and desperation to leave Rioa, we have to find whichever resources we can from the library right now. As soon as our friends awaken, we'll all be scattering to our own destinations.

My ginger friend heaves a sigh of exasperation when the next tomes are dropped into her lap, the flames from Esen's body not harming even a speck of the pages. *Foreign Materials Unseen. Medicinal Differences Across Worlds. Toxins Manifested.* Stefanie examines a few pages of the first tome and taps her chin. Some of her willowy fingers flip a handful of polished gems found on one of the tables, each with engravings of different *maji* symbols. I'm watching with rapt interest, curious to what she'll learn and if it can help our companions. Riker appears in front of her in another blur of shadows. I nearly shriek with fear, causing Stefanie to giggle before she instructs him to pack certain tomes into a large satchel he brought with them. She then turns her weary eyes on me and sends spurts of healing *maji* at my arms, tickling my skin.

An ancient scroll of a map flies past our heads. I whip my

head back to Athena and Hadwin, but then I realize it's only some of our group meddling with items they probably shouldn't be touching. Ivar was sitting on the ground near us, but his boredom apparently took over. He's shifted into a massive bird with bright blue and black feathers and is currently challenging Daru to some weird game. They're using their air *maji* to lift random objects and hurtle them back and forth between one another. Laughter spills out of me when they start messing with Ulf's shadow wolf by dropping books and scrolls next to his face as he drifts off to sleep. He snaps at them in aggravation. I wouldn't mind Ulf staying shifted because his wolf is less volatile than his humanoid form. Presently, though, he's becoming more reactive by the hour, fraying all of our nerves—especially Jade's. I'm tempted to ask if he needs to go outside to pee, but something tells me he won't respond kindly to a canine joke.

I peer around to check on the others who are huddled a few yards away by one of the wide windows. Fraya is dozing on Odin's shoulder while he talks quietly with Hauke. Their little group is sitting next to the now tied down, motionless *skelter*, waiting for it to awaken. We all are. It wasn't necessarily active yesterday, but it wasn't as still as a statue with its deranged face—*Eliina's* face—peering at us how it is now. *What a creep.* Eliina, Athena, and Hadwin are no different. Except they don't have the unhinged look in their eyes. *Yet.*

Athena sucks in a breath, and we all go still, hoping it's an indication they're done talking. I can feel our bond as a living essence, tethering me to her stilled form. It's a golden-green color and even while she's spiritually far away, our soul bond is a sweet caress. The brush of love is not something I felt with my family members on Earth. It's a firm hold on my heart, the truth reverberating along my bones that Athena and I are sisters in whichever realm we travel to.

Her upper back trembles and then slouches forward, the hood of her robe falling against the back of her head as she delves deeper into her conversation. We all groan in annoyance, and I hear Nyx use some particularly colorful words. I don't need to speak the older language, *Majian*, these *solliqas* grew up with, to know it won't take much more to push him over the edge. Much to my chagrin, Jade joins him, and now they're both feeding off each other's anger.

I jab a hand through my braid. "Should you just leave?" I ask Jade, unable to conceal my annoyance. "Or instead of arguing, can we review the plan one more time?"

"There's not much to it," Ulf's wolf grumbles from the bottom of a dusty bookshelf. "We've already discussed it a dozen times now. Either we all make it to our destinations, or we fail."

"She only wants to confirm we've got it," Nyx responds with a pointed look.

If a wolf could roll their eyes, I absolutely know that's what Ulf is doing right now.

"Maybe you've got to go easier on her in the sheets," Ulf's wolf growls. "You're ramming her so hard, she's losing her memory."

Shadows seep out of Nyx onto the floor, and the orbs above us flicker into darkness. *Great.*

My cheeks blaze with a deep blush. I take back what I thought about his shadow wolf. They're both fraught with callous harshness. The idea of Nyx going that hard inside of me again has my core clenching and both my brain and heart melting into puddles.

"Leave her alone, Ulf," Stefanie snaps. "It's not her fault that you're teamed up with Hadwin and Athena. You don't need to harass her because your ego took a hit."

"I don't need to go with *anyone*." Ulf's wolf snaps his teeth in Stefanie's direction, causing Hauke to swiftly rise to his feet. "They're going to be drained as fuck after what they're doing now. Fucking deadweight when we'll have to fly out of here."

"My best friend will *never* be deadweight," I growl. Blue

flames lick up and down my arms in a heartbeat, all embarrassment long gone from my mind. This *solliqa* has more sudden mood swings than a hormonal teenager, and frankly, I'm sick of him getting away with lashing out at the rest of us. *Good luck to his* almaove, *if he even has one.*

Nyx lowers himself to the cushion I'm sitting on and reaches his arms around me with deliberate slowness. Daru clacks his beak at Ulf's wolf with ruffled feathers, fluttering in small spurts toward where Nyx is now sitting behind me on the saffron-colored floor cushion.

Stefanie sighs again and stares up at the windows above us. The moons, in delicate crescent shapes, are right above us. "Ulf, stop being a prick. We talked about this. You're going with Hadwin and Athena to the coastline of Sayfters, where Del originally transferred Eira's soul. This should make it easier for Athena and Hadwin to use their earth *maji* to cross into and find the other souls of Eira and Athena's group of friends they've been searching for. We already decided that if they're that important to Eira, they might be a tool for what's to come in this world once they arrive here. You're going with them because you have the power to jump worlds and even across timelines. This might be necessary to use when they find the trapped souls."

"If I'm given their descriptions and general locations, I can do it myself," Ulf's wolf snaps.

"No, you can't." Stefanie gives him a no-nonsense look. "Athena will do what she can to heal the plague in your soul. You need to be with a healer, and there's no denying that, so don't bother. Hadwin will help Athena with traveling to Earth, she'll help you with healing, and you can help both of them with jumping timelines if necessary. Remember, time on Earth moves much faster than in Majikaero. One week here is about one year there."

"What if they don't approve of this plan?" Ulf's wolf asks.

"They'll trust that we came up with the best possible option," Nyx pushes back. "Athena will especially trust Eira."

Stefanie turns to face Nyx and me. Her hardened expression eases when we make eye contact, and the flames simmer down as I take in my beautiful, courageous friend. I yearn for her level of patience—I was ready to throw fireballs at Ulf's ugly head.

"Nyx and Eira, you know where you'll need to go."

Nyx groans but nods in understanding. "Once we get out of the library, I'll portal Eira and I to Drageyra."

A huge part of me is brimming with excitement to see where Nyx grew up. An equally large part of me, if not larger, is both heartbroken for him and scared shitless.

We have to leave the Council building—now in the middle of the night—in order to portal to another region in Majikaero. This library has such extensive protection spells placed on it, no *solliqa* can come and go except through the main doors. It was determined that we'd go to Nyx's homeland for a few reasons. Jade confirmed that some of his family have been trying to reach him but were held hostage on their own island by those connected to the Council. If we manage to get inside their island walls, we'll be able to see how true this is. We'll also get to talk with any trusted *solliqas*—if there are any—about any updates with the Council, discuss what happened at the festival, and explore their own wealth of knowledge.

Stefanie shared with me that Nyx's mother had been known for giving her gracious support to those resisting the Council's decisions and has used powers related to being a *seer*. It's a place in this realm where, in theory, Nyx will be most comfortable with his powers and somewhere I can continue to learn about my own *maji*. It's also possible that *solliqas* part of my soul family could be residing in Drageyra, since I've only met the healers, those in Rioa, and Daya, Del, and Daru when I first arrived.

It makes the most sense for us to be there. Hopefully, we'll meet up with our friends again with a fierce alliance, some answers about what's happened, and a better grasp on both of our *maji*.

Stefanie flicks her gaze to Hauke. A dejected look passes between them, yet one filled with acceptance. "I'll be traveling with Ivar, Odin, and Fraya," Hauke says. "We'll be hunting down the Council members between Shymeira up to Wyndera and then across to Lagunit and Eikenbien. I have sway with many of these places, and Ivar, Odin, and Fraya will each have a stronger connection to a few of the regions. Our task is to coax the Council members into one place and demand answers. We'll finally get to the bottom of what in Cudhellen they know, why they've scattered from Rioa, and what their plans are regarding this plague of darkness. They're supposed to be some of the most powerful *solliqas* of our world, and we can't address this plague and portals situation without their aid."

Hauke pauses and then clears his throat. He appears more uncomfortable than usual as he fiddles with the sleeves of his shirt. "I also have it on good authority that the Council made a grave error in trusting certain individuals who are connected to these portals." His orange and gold eyes harden as his mouth twists in disgust. "That being said, I won't know—none of us will—until we ask each Council member what truthfully happened. They must know how we went from a world of peace to a plague of darkness to fucking having portals with demonic creatures."

Ivar shifts back into his humanoid skin in a shimmer of light and shadows. "The four of us will do this, I'm sure of it. If what Jade says is true for Drageyra, I have no doubt that Wyndera is in a similar position. Some of the Council could have intentionally isolated the smaller islands. I refuse to believe that each member has turned their backs on the fate of our world. Not Council Member Rakiana. She wouldn't do that to her people."

Stefanie hums and glances back at Athena, Hadwin, and Eliina. They're still slumped over in their trance-like state.

"I'll stay here in Rioa with the other healers," she murmurs. Hauke stiffens slightly. "We'll have much to pour over to figure out the meaning of this purple substance and where these portals lead to. My purpose as a healer with power is to stay here until the rest of these souls are well enough to rebuild their city." She looks straight at Hauke. "We can communicate through our soul bond. If either of us is in trouble or needs to be elsewhere, we'll make it work."

"I still don't understand how you'll communicate with the rest of us," I interrupt. "How will we reach you?"

"You can communicate with Athena through your own soul bond," Stefanie says with a smile. "Nyx can portal you both to wherever their group goes, and he can bring you to the rest of us if needed."

"The three of us," I clarify. Zaya curls into a ball around my feet and chirps in confirmation.

"That's right," Stefanie laughs. "Yes, the three of you can go anywhere with Nyx's ability to portal. His *maji* and shadows can sense each of us. He simply needs to open a portal, think of who or where he's trying to get to, and his powers allow him to reach that intended soul or destination. It's a lot easier for him to do this since his soul has already connected with each of us, almost as if we've left an imprint on him."

I swallow, not wanting to protest too much about this. I've only portaled with Nyx a handful of times, and so far, I can say with confidence that I'm *not* a fan. I'm apprehensive about my cat going anywhere near a portal, but there's no way we're being separated again. I suppose her fluffy butt will just have to be okay with it.

"And Daru," Stefanie pivots to face him. He's still glaring at Ulf's shadow wolf. "You'll be tasked with searching for Daya and Del. You worked with them the closest, and with any luck, you'll be able to find where they've gone and any clues about Erika. You have many *solliqas* at your disposal across the regions, so you should be fine alone. Are you sure you don't want someone to go with you? It might be—"

"A few of my crows will go with him," Jade interrupts. "I'm hesitant to depart from any of them, but a few will go with *each* of your groups. I'll be with Athena, Hadwin, and Ulf to start, and then I'll communicate through my crows to find where everyone else goes."

I shiver. I don't have the greatest feeling around her crows. They give me the creeps—the few times I've seen them this past week, the only communication I've received from them has been an unnatural silence that leaves little room for discernment. Each of them has bold irises, ranging from blue to purple to bright red, and they eerily *stare* at us. Silently. I understand why Jade has to go with my best friend and her group first. Nyx explained that she has the ability to transfer memories to and from others. Hadwin will share what he can with her, and then she'll share the other information from Eliina with the rest of us as she travels across Majikaero. I had wanted to hear it all directly from my best friend before she goes *anywhere*. Nyx insisted, though, that as soon as our friends are back with us, we need to leave immediately. No questions asked.

I guess it makes sense that she'll have some of her crows meet us in Drageyra as a way to track where everyone is. That doesn't mean I'm comfortable with the idea.

And Daru will be all alone with a few of them? Better him than me, I guess. *Maybe they'll be able to speak to one another through their walnut-sized brains. Birds of a feather or flock or whatever the hell people say.*

Cudhellen. Whatever in Cudhellen. Ugh, whatever.

"Where will you start?" I ask Daru.

He turns those mossy green eyes on me, and for a moment, I forget to breathe. A thread of connection reaches between us.

It's a darker shade of green than Athena's and much thinner. The strength of it is different from what I have with Nyx. Our bond of flames and light and darkness is either a tragedy waiting to happen or the happy ending I crave more than anything. It's as wispy as smoke, though, and isn't as secure as Athena's. It's difficult to build the foundation necessary when Nyx is trapped under his layers of trauma, of the merciless plague, even if he is my *almaove*. I gaze at what lies between Daru and me, and it's tangible enough in front of me that I could reach out to touch it if I wanted to. I don't, though. The thread is too delicate, a mere strand that only Daru and I can sense.

I bring my fingers to my lips and focus on controlling my breath. I can't picture how our soul bond will be, but the way his energy washes over me is the same as the suns bathing my body while I lie in the grass. It's the feeling of trees a mile high looming above my body, their branches stretching upward and outward in a dome of protection as the breeze keeps me from overheating. Daru slowly blinks at me. A sensation presses against my heart in a warm greeting.

It's almost as if he's knocking on my ribcage and asking for permission to enter my soul, but I don't know how to let him in. Not yet, at least. *Or am I afraid of what'll happen if I do?*

"That doesn't matter right now," Jade snaps.

Nyx tenses again behind me. I slink an arm around one of his calves, applying enough pressure to bring his focus back down to me. *No*, I silently tell him, shaking my head. *Jade is lost in her own worries right now. We can't reason with someone that worked up.*

Jade's proving to be the most prickly *solliqa* I've met, right up there with Ulf and his wolf, but I suppose I can't blame her. She already snuck out of the library briefly to alert her crows about our situation, risking other souls seeing her. A handful of *solliqas* tried to enter the library doors earlier in the day, but thankfully, Eliina's *maji* must be directly connected to this vast space. The doors had remained closed, and I heard a lock shift into place. When Jade returned unscathed and with scavenged food—refreshing and plump pieces of fruit, malty bread rolls, and succulent hunks of meat—and more *lipva* from the healing quarters, her body was rigid and bursting at the seams with restlessness. After she paced the length of a bookshelf at least a hundred times, and Ulf blew up at her for making us all even more nervous, she shared why she's so strung out.

A year ago, Jade and her team had been spying on a few manipulators in Shymeira. They were hoping to gain more insight on why Waneta, the Grand Shifter and *solliqa* originally from this region, wasn't at the Council meetings. One of the manipulators could also shift and had heightened hearing abilities. All it took was one crow scratching a branch with its talon, and they were all caught. The manipulator didn't recognize them and, assuming the worst and suspecting they were spies, transformed into a deadly lion. Apparently, some of the creatures these *solliqas* shift into have poison woven into their form, and in the case of this lion, it was in his claws. Most of Jade's team escaped in a frantic whirlwind of feathers, but a few of them were captured. One was slashed through with the poison and their soul disappeared into stardust moments later. Jade forced herself to circle back and watch from a distance how the manipulators chose to torture her other team members. She didn't look away as each feather was plucked out, tearing their skin in the process. The manipulators used their *maji* to learn who the crows were before controlling their little minds—they were forced to peck at one another until each gradually died, the ground stained with their blood.

Now, Jade lives in trepidation, not for her own soul, but for what could happen to the *solliqas* who've chosen to follow her. She's also convinced the manipulator has followed her in his lion form over the past year. Jade trained her team on how to identify that specific scent and to be cautious in case word has spread about their crow forms. Fraya asked why they didn't shift to a different bird instead and let go of their crow skins. Jade simply replied that she's a crow to her core, and it's either that form or to appear human. She thinks the latter is even worse, considering she fled in her humanoid form when Nyx was banished and knows his family in Drageyra are still hunting her to this day.

I watch as the muscles in Jade's shoulders ripple with tension underneath her tight black coverings. She's standing over Eliina with a faraway look in her light green eyes. Her posture stiffens, and she crosses her arms while grinding her teeth and tapping her foot relentlessly. With the change in moons after the festival, maroon and gray moonlight seeps into the library. This mixed with the floating orbs gives Jade a haunting look. Her hair is the only soft thing about her—the rest of her consists of edges as hard as nails. Nyx implicitly trusts this soul. Everyone in this group does. I empathize with what she went through and continues to endure for the sake of this world, but something still is off to me. It's not alarming enough to share how I feel with the others, but it's enough to spark my blue flames.

If I've learned anything in this new world, it's that we're not what we think we are, and no soul is safe from the darkness.

TWENTY-TWO
Hauke

Are you still trapped if your soul is soaring free?
-Unknown

Fuck.

We have our missions set in stone, but for some reason, it only feels as if we're etching our names into a tomb.

Stefanie jams a few more papers into one of the leather satchels Esen and Riker brought with them and shoves it into Riker's ghostlike arms. As soon as she turns around, I'm already taking large steps, filling up the space in between us until I have one of my purple wings curled around her. She crashes into my chest, gasping in surprise.

"Something's not right," I murmur low enough that only she hears me.

Her emerald eyes flicker up to me. "You're upset we're separating again."

"*Of fucking course* I am," I growl down at her. "And the fact that you're gathering enough sacred texts and scrolls down here to build your own damn library. They're all important enough that Eliina cast a spell to keep this area heavily protected. Regardless of her betrayal, she had her reasons to do this and meant for all this knowledge to stay safely down here. And you're happily preparing to take valuable information about the gods and goddesses with you out into the fucking world."

"Hauke," Stefanie breathes, my name falling off her lips like a prayer. "They'll be safe in the healing quarters. You know as well as I do that we've got some brilliant minds in there who can and *should* help with investigating these resources."

My jaw ticks as I struggle to control my rising temper. I'm not one to lose control—not anymore—but Stefanie finds a way to test my patience with her courageous heart.

"I need you to trust me," she pleads. "I know the gods and goddesses have something to do with what's going on in Majikaero. There's been such a surge of power, and I don't think a plague of darkness spreads by itself as it has been. Someone... or *something* is influencing it."

"Something?" I grumble. I weave my fingers through her hair, letting the strands fall along my arm like a waterfall.

"Yes." Stefanie nods. She chews on her lower lip, a habit that's been impossible for her kick. "I have a theory that the Sairn might be tied to this, too. They're known for wreaking havoc and chaos, in general, and the attack on this city felt simultaneously planned and frenzied. As if the goal was to open as many portals as they could, plucking *solliqas* at random during the festival without any ordered reason. It reeks of the Sairn, but I don't have a way to prove it yet."

Frowning, I move my hand up through the currents of her hair until my palm is cupping her cheek.

"I just don't want to lose you," I breathe. "I *can't*."

"Worrying about the fate of our souls will only use up precious energy," she whispers back to me. "We need to stay in the present moment, darling. I don't know what's in store for me, but I *do* know that I have many healers who'd love to help and stacks of resources that might point us in the right direction."

Stefanie rises up to kiss me. It's silky smooth with enough heat to have me craving more. *Always.* I'm *always* craving more with her.

I take a deep breath and trace the shape of her lips with one of my fingers.

"Stefanie," I whisper.

"Yes?"

"Do you think we can trust Jade?"

Stefanie doesn't answer me. Instead, she intertwines a few of our fingers—the ones with our soul bond markings on them—and sends a tendril of her *maji* up into me. One of the benefits of solidifying a bond with your *almaove* is earning the ability to communicate silently through your connection. It's even easier to do when you're close to one another and can physically touch your soul markings. We haven't used this often as of late, but the fact that Stefanie is even choosing to respond this way already tells me her answer.

"We can only trust ourselves," her sweet voice flows through my mind.

"That isn't an answer," I growl back through my *maji*.

"She's connected herself to many souls," Stefanie replies, whispering even though no one else can hear us. *"The very action of becoming a spy means you learn to trade in information. Survival depends on stringing everyone into your web. We won't know if we're already caught in her gossamer lattice until fate determines it's time."*

"Fate," I snarl. *"It can go fuck itself."*

"Don't tempt fate, my darling," Stefanie whispers.

"Why not? It tempts me all the fucking time," I spit.

She leans back to stare into my eyes. More of her healing *maji* flows up through my arms until it's cradling my heart.

"We must respect what and where our souls are destined

for," she murmurs out loud this time. "Trying to persuade fate otherwise will only beg for more chaos, and our world can't take much more of that."

My purple wings curl around the two of us. I don't respond. I don't need to. Stefanie already knows my emotions and what I fear. It won't stop my *almaove* from pushing forward into the monster's jaw that's wrapped around Rioa.

I just have to pray the gods and goddesses will listen to my prayers this time around. The last time I felt such heavy tension and panic in a city was when I had to flee my homeworld, Chironant, years ago. A secret group of us had to take refuge in Majikaero—Del being one of them—all vowing to never mention our homeland until we knew it was either safe or necessary to go back. The fewer souls who know about the darkness overtaking our home, the better—misery fucking loves company. We can't take any chances that even the knowledge of it over here won't lead to it spreading.

We can't fan the flames of panic or make anyone else aware of the connection between some of these worlds. Coming to Majikaero was supposed to offer us a safe haven and give us time to figure out a way to fight back against the evil coming for all of us. But I think we might be too late, and I might as well work up the courage to share what I know with Stefanie. None of our worries of *solliqas* learning about a half-annihilated world holds any merit anymore.

Before we leave Rioa, I'll share the secrets of my homeworld with Stefanie. Maybe there will be clues in our own home's destruction that can help us figure out who's attacking all of us and why.

There's darkness taking over *so many worlds* at the same time, and the root cause might be one and the same.

Majikaero isn't the only world that's been overtaken by the plague of darkness.

And I don't think it'll be the last.

TWENTY-THREE

Astira

*Secrets wind their way around your throat,
trapping you under someone else's control.
-Council Member Mohi, Grand Manipulator*

Darkness glitters in the background. Eyes of every color glower at me from all directions, engulfing me in the feelings they can't speak. Rich chocolate brown. A kaleidoscope of purple, brown, and green. Blazing gold with specks of orange. Blue the color of the ocean. Gray as dark as a rainy day. A deep forest green. Soul-crushing black. Sockets without eyes at all, only empty pits. So many other shades that I didn't realize could exist and might not even be human. They watch me with an unnerving hunger that has me itching to back away, to cloak myself with the soil around me.

Soil. Dirt. Earth. It's caked along my arms and torso and all the way down to my feet. My fingers and toes sink into the dampness and squeeze the muddied texture. I push further until my nail beds are filled with grime. I've been here before. Hundreds of times, I've been buried in this grave meant for me and me alone. I can't remember what happens before or after, only that I'm *destined to curl up in this space dug out for me. A flickering light catches my attention, and I notice my toes are disintegrating into shimmering gold flecks. They drift straight into the soil, as if its darkness consumes the sparks of light coming from my decaying body. I should react, but I don't. I simply watch my frail bones fracture into the gold sparks, going from my feet up to my hips. All those eyes watch, too, devouring each tiny particle.*

I've been here before. I'm here so often, I have to wonder if I've ever left. Is this my reality, and everything else are simply dreams passing me by? The soil crushes my chest—is someone pressing it down on top of me? Is there another grave being carved out above where I lie?

The earth compresses my bones, and with a deafening crack, my spirit is pulled up to the surface. I push myself to look behind me, to observe the grave far below, but my body won't budge an inch. It's as stiff as a board and warm from the balmy temperature that kisses my skin. A red sun blazes up in the dark sky, at odds with the yellow and blue colors I'm used to on Earth. Then again, what would I know? I haven't seen the sky in years.

My neck cranes up to stare at the sun. It burns through my skull, but I'm not afraid of going blind. One who has truly woken up cannot unsee what's meant for them. I inhale deeply and hold my breath for a few seconds, letting it bounce between the boundaries of my lungs, and then I release it gradually. I'm breathing how I normally would as a human, yet I know that's not what I am here—not with the darkening sky and humid scent in the air. A hand grasps my arm, and I jump back in surprise. No, that's not it. I'm not startled. It's excitement that I'm experiencing. My eyes leisurely take in the creature next to me, and if I'm not mistaken, it's a male.

He towers over me in black, metallic robes that shine in dazzling colors under the sun. I can't see his hair or face, only glowing orbs from under his hood. Sharp obsidian eyes wash over me, and I'm struck by how familiar they are, by the way they manage to see straight through to the core of who I am. His gaze lingers near my chest, and I lower my head to see why he's staring at me. I'm dressed in the same glossy robes as him, except I'm also wearing a silver pendant in the shape of a bursting star. White stones decorate the center and swirl out to the ends of the star. As the sun's rays brush my covered body, the heat soaking through my thin robes, my eyes widen in wonder at the way my pendant pulsates in time with the beat of my heart.

Thump, thump, thump. Steady and measured. A peaceful rhythm.

The man clutches my hand and grows rigid. Inch by inch, his body turns to plated stone. My mouth opens to ask him what's happening, who he is, and why we're here. As soon as I go to speak, though, that same plated stone pours down my throat like cement. Eyes bulging and heart shifting abruptly to a restless pace, I let go of the man's hand and claw frantically at my throat. The stone edges its way down my body and through my bloodstream, forcing me to come to a standstill. Only my eyes can still move, and they search the man's hidden face for any clue to what's going on.

Those obsidian eyes flare into black flames. Both of our bodies shatter and fall back into the earth, going deeper and deeper until we're both nestled in my grave. His hardened eyes join the others. A look of longing and fear stares out at me, and I desperately want to soothe this man, this soul that's still peering out at me from two eyes. But I can't do anything, not when insects scuttle in and around me where flesh should be or when iridescent scales brush past my vision.

Those scales change into smoke, and it wraps around the shards of my body. A raspy voice whispers into my mind. "You can light the way for the world as bleakness suffocates their miserable lives. You're as bright as a star, but not if the others find you first. They'll dim your soul until you're nothing more than stardust scattered across the universe, abandoning those who need you the most, as you've done countless times. These eyes hold your story, the one you're too afraid to accept."

Shadows in the form of a wolf spring at me, its eyes the color of curdled milk. This isn't just any wolf—this is my *wolf. Yet it makes no difference if he belongs to me. Those massive jaws with serrated teeth still close around my decomposing head.*

"Rest in misery and choke on the power you've forgotten, Astira."

I bolt out of bed so quickly, my body tangles in the damp sheets, and I tumble to the gritty floor. My face fortunately lands on the small woven rug under the dresser, but my shoulders slam right into the rough texture. *What a rude way to wake up.* I blink my eyes open and am caught somewhere between my nightmare and the present moment. An eerie silence envelopes me. It's as if the universe is yawning for a moment—my insignificant self is simply being swallowed up in it. The stifling quiet leaves as quickly as it came, and all the blood rushes back into my contorted body. *Ow. Fucking room made of stone and mud and cement and infuriating frigid steel.* I curl in on myself and let the sheets hug me before accepting I'm too awake to fall back asleep on the floor.

The bedroom door slams open. "Astira, are you—"

Liv stops short when she sees I'm still rolled up on the floor in a pile of dark blue sheets. She's dressed in all black clothes, matching her hair and shoes. It's been a few months since I woke up from my coma, and while the underground city seems to change before my eyes, I'm grateful Liv appears exactly the same. There are dark circles under her hazel eyes from working all hours of the day, but it's nothing compared to the skeletal forms we both had right after being rescued. My friend is all sharp features and still as petite as ever, making me feel like a plump whale swaddled in seaweed on the ocean floor.

Liv laughs, the sound airy and soft against my ears. "What are you doin' down there?"

"Transforming into my true appearance—that's why I've been packing on the pounds lately," I grumble.

She chuckles and shakes her head. Her cropped, straight hair swishes back and forth. It covers her face in such a way that the signs of exhaustion are hidden, leaving only twinkling eyes and a rare smile. *If only we could all laugh this way. Who knew those nuclear missiles would detonate our spirits and steal our laughter?*

Liv gives me a small smile and saunters toward me. Jace comes sprinting into the room a second later, panting as he rests his hands on his knees. His blond hair falls forward in front of his face. Jace has kept it at shoulder length, and I don't blame him—with waves like his, he should grow it to his waist. He's tall enough to block the entire door frame when standing, or rather, the rooms in Nedrazon are compact enough that anyone above 5'8" is at risk of bumping their heads. There's only sufficient space for a bed, dresser, rug, chair, and a single lamp, which Liv annoyingly turns on now. Light powered by solar panels flashes above me, and I glare up at her as my eyes adjust. I could see perfectly fine before they came in, having gotten used to this small room, and turning the light on only exposes how bare it is in here... and the worms and other creatures that have managed to make their way into the corners of my room. Other people in this city have put woven tapestries or artwork up on their walls, anything to make it appear as an actual home.

I know better, though. If humans were stupid enough to blow up entire cities and make living above ground impossible, then there's no point in getting comfortable down here. It'll happen all over again, eventually. The less I'm attached, the quicker I can move on when those in power lose their ignorant heads.

"Ira," Jace pants. He pushes up the gray sleeves of his shirt. The soft cotton material is still something I covet. "You good?"

Ira. I haven't heard that nickname in ages. Thinking about life before Eira, Athena, and Tryg died mixed with wondering why he's asking if I'm okay is disorienting.

"Don't I look flawless?"

Jace huffs out a laugh and, standing up tall, stretches out his arms and shuffles over to where Liv is now sitting on my bed. "At least that mouth of yours isn't broken. You did scream pretty loud for someone calm enough to sass me."

Liv snorts. "That brain of yours must be empty if you think Astira is ever incapable of sassing you." She turns to face me. While gently tugging the sheets off my body, she makes a face. "*Blegh*, why are these soaked? What did you *do*?"

The nightmare I just had swarms around me as if the raspy voice never left. I could identify it as a dream while in it, yet at the same time, it felt real. *Too* real. The grave and those obsidian eyes felt oddly similar to *home*, and the longer I stare up at Liv and Jace, the more uncertain I grow whether *this* is actually the dream or not.

Jace crouches down and pulls the rest of the sheets off me. He gingerly takes my hands in his and eases me up into a sitting position before hauling me up to stand next to him. Tucking me under an arm, he steers me to the end of my bed and deposits me into Liv's awaiting arms. She instantly curls them around my arms and torso, bringing my head to rest on her shoulder. Liv's slender fingers twirl my long hair, and she smooths out the areas still disheveled from sleep.

"Did you have another nightmare?" Liv whispers.

I nod my head silently, not having the strength to hash out the details of my dream. She hums in response. She's probably thinking it's another dream of our time spent in the tunnels and, specifically, of being tortured by Damon. I'll let her think this.

Besides, it's not as if I never have them. We're both haunted by those horrors, and I know that's one of the reasons Liv has been helping Jace so much. She throws herself into any and all work, exhausting herself to the point of a dreamless sleep. Some of it has been remedial, such as when she and I give insight to the few therapists working with those also rescued from the tunnels, barely scraping by down here with their trauma. A huge part of what she does, though, is collaborate with a few others down here on a new mission. She wants to not only liberate those who've been taken as slaves and forced into cults, but to kill those psychotic enough to deem it okay to do. To find Ruse and Lyk in the process, if they're still alive. The second she looped me into this idea, I knew I'd stop at nothing until it's been seen through.

Jace has hounded us about going slow and taking as much time as we need to recover from what we went through. He doesn't understand, though. None of them do. Liv and I were tormented so thoroughly, our souls splintered like split ends until we became the hardened shells our abusers wanted us to be. There's nothing left inside of us to recover or restore—there's only armor as strong as the steel in this city that we didn't ask to wear. For two years, we suffered. The few years before that, we grieved for our friends and families and the perishing world. It'll take more than a few months of salvation to even begin to chip away at what we've built around our hearts. It might be years until we feel safe enough to admit something might be very wrong if we're now mere shells of who we could be.

So, Liv and I are doing our own version of "taking it slow." We aren't gearing up to go into battle or throwing ourselves back into the world of therapy. We're helping other civilians organize the food we've managed to grow down here and doing what we can to supply resources to each household. This city might have different living spaces centered around how each person or family can contribute, but as a whole, we're all one big community now. We have to be. One huge communal environment with those who've risen as natural leaders acting as some kind of democratic council. Each time I've asked Jace about the specifics of who's on this council and how it works, he drives the conversation in a different direction. *As if I don't notice.*

Liv and I place a lot of our attention on the mission. We're both determined to free the despondent souls from their man-created hell. Then, and only then, will we be able to drop the shields and armor and admit the ghosts of our past require saving.

"I've been having them, too," Liv mumbles. "But not the ones from our time in... before Jace's team found us."

My face scrunches up in confusion. *Alright, my interest is piqued. I suppose I might be talking about my nightmare after all.*

"What are they about?" Jace probes. I almost forgot he was next to us. Of course, I still love him and our other friends. But he didn't go through what Liv and I did, and she and I have a fucked-up, special bond now that pulls us into the same bubble. She understands my night terrors, my desperation to be near a window or open space, and the way one wrong look or touch can send me plummeting back into the purgatory I never thought I'd escape. Jace pulls over the single chair in this bedroom, one molded by clay, oblivious to the way Liv and I are on a different wavelength than him.

Liv sighs, her breath tickling my face. "Nothing that makes sense," she mutters. "They always start rather thrilling, but everything rapidly spirals into something gruesome or frightening."

"Such as...?" Jace prompts.

"I dreamed last night of a stunning man with purple hair," she says in a dreamy voice. I move to look at her face, and she's *blushing.* "I—I don't think it's possible that we've met, but I certainly wish he was real. We're either exploring a city or wooded area, or he's taking me up in the air while we soar as birds. Those are the parts that I never want to end."

Nightmare or not, I can't help wagging my eyebrows at her. "You've been keeping a boyfriend from us?" Jace snickers while

Liv scowls, playfully shoving me away from her. It's a fleeting few seconds where it's as if we're back in one of our homes four years ago, laughing at one another's expense. It comes and goes, and I struggle to keep that illusion in my hands as it slips away.

"He's *not* my boyfriend," she sighs. "But the lovely parts never last. It always turns into us falling to our deaths or him pushing me into this horrifying vacuum of air or, *gods*, other people around us are brutally killed by these hideous creatures. I don't know what they are or why my brain has fabricated them. There've recently been some figures in gold robes coming to our aid, or at least I think that's what they're doing. I can't be sure. Either way, I wake up shaking and bone-tired."

"Robes?" I breathe.

"Yeah, I know," Liv laughs. "I've been transported to one of those ridiculous fantasy stories Ruse used to read."

"Hey, don't mock that," Jace whines, jabbing a finger into her shoulder. "I know exactly which book you're talking about, and there's nothing ridiculous about such an epic tale of bravery, magical realms, and the ruination of different species. Besides, I thought you liked to read."

"I do," Liv huffs. "But with the way you guys obsessed about it, you'd think it was a real world with living characters. Sometimes a story needs to stay in the confines of the book cover, and you move on to the next book." She rolls her eyes and glances at me. "The people in my dreams are always wearing intricate, shimmering clothes or transforming into breathtaking creatures and beasts. I have yet to see most of their faces, though. It's as if my spirit is aching to travel to this fantasy dreamland and interact with these different beings, even though my body is firmly planted down here in Nedrazon. I've dreamed of them every so often over the years, but they've become much more frequent ever since we were captured in the tunnels."

Liv shakes her head. "Perhaps it's just my mind trying to cope with the reality we've been forced into. I wasn't meant to live underground. None of us are. We've been buried alive without even realizing it."

Jace hums in agreement. "We don't even have tombstones for the millions who were left above." He leans forward, tenderly squeezing each of our arms. "You both should know this from our years of therapeutic training. These nightmares are our ways of processing the trauma we've experienced. Even if some of us aren't verbally acknowledging it quite yet." Jace gives me a pointed look.

"Does that mean you've been having them, too?" I ask, ignoring his comment.

Jace shifts uncomfortably in his chair and crosses his arms. He frowns. "Yeah, I suppose I have," he mutters. "They're always the same. I'm kneeling in a garden, pulling out various crops. Some of them appear similar to what we eat here, and others have complex colors and textures that I haven't seen before. There's a swamp nearby, and the weather is absurdly humid, yet I can't recall ever visiting said swamp in real life or past dreams. The sun beats down on me—it's brutal. My clothes are lightweight and covered in dirt from the crops. It starts normal enough—I mean, exhausting, but still normal for a dream—and then the vegetables subtly shift into bones and stringy tendons. I instinctively want to drop what I'm doing, yet my hands keep pulling these body parts out of the ground. Footsteps approach me from behind, but I can never turn around to see who's there. That's when I wake up."

Liv and I are both staring at him.

"What?" he asks.

"I'd argue that's weirder than mine," Liv mumbles. "You *dig up* someone's bones? With your hands?"

Jace shrugs. "Yeah. It's logical, though. I think it's symbolic of what I've had to do here and how I'm grieving over how many people haven't survived. There's not much else to it." He stretches his arms again. "Neither of you should put too much thought into these dreams. When you're ready, we can talk about them, but don't worry. Your mind needs to process what you've been through somehow."

I don't respond. I can't. Those onyx eyes awakened something inside of me, and despite the dread I'm starting to feel before sleeping, it's also exhilarating to think I'll see him again. There aren't words to describe what's waking up within me. I only know the lines have blurred between what's real and what's not, and I don't think it's my mind processing the trauma I've stuffed deep down.

"Just because it's easy for you to act nonchalant, doesn't mean that's the case for the rest of us," Liv says. She crosses a leg over her knee and tilts her head to the side. While her face remains neutral, I know these are some of her signs that she's irritated.

"I'm not being nonchalant about it," Jace snaps. His moods are much more brittle nowadays, so at odds with the laid-back personality I'm used to. "I'm trying to offer a different perspective. Fixating on the nightmares themselves isn't going to solve anything. The sooner we can embrace why we, and I'm sure every other person down here, are having them, the better. We won't survive this new life if we're too caught up in the fabrications of our minds."

I snort. "People are surviving just fine. Humans are adaptable by nature. You're living proof of that. Who'd have thought a therapist would clamber his way up to a leadership position?"

Jace grits his teeth. Those gray eyes darken until I can see my own reflection. Silence envelopes the three of us for a few moments as we take a beat to collect our scattered thoughts and reel in our heightened emotions.

This isn't the first time we've had this argument. The nightmares have persisted enough that it was decided I should sleep in the building designated for those found in the tunnels instead of the room Jace found for me in his complex. I insisted that I'd be all right and to not go through the trouble of moving me close to the medical and therapeutic specialists that managed to survive. There are others in worse shape than me and need the room more.

Liv stated that she'd move with me, claiming that we could keep one another company at night and having quick access to a medical provider would be reassuring. Now I'm surrounded by traumatized victims who scream out in the middle of the night like their lives depend on it, and what's worse is that I frequently join them. Because in those tunnels, the right person hearing your screams could mean the difference between life and death. Whenever I see Liv and Jace, we're either talking about nightmares, new people we've rescued from other tunnels, or fuming because we're all so damn emotional and don't want to share what we've experienced. It's easier that way until one of us snaps and the rest of the conversation tumbles into an unavoidable feud.

I take a deep breath and hope for the best. "Jace, what happened to you? How'd you go from a therapist to someone with power down here?"

"And don't avoid the question this time," Liv adds with narrowed eyes. "You've shared morbid bits and pieces with me after we first arrived, but you shut down every time we ask now. You then patronize us by saying our nightmares are a logical response to agony none of us could have imagined in our wildest dreams. That's saying something, considering what Lyk and I grew up with and how Astira's family treated her as a teen. Now, spill it."

Jace's shoulders slump and he heaves a defeated sigh. I hate to pressure anyone into sharing a traumatic experience when they're not ready, but fuck, the three of us are trying to work together as if the past two years didn't happen. That's not going to cut it. I can't keep getting told that my nightmares are in my head. I'm given trivial tasks to work on each day and am left wondering what the hell is going on in my friend's head.

"I didn't want to share this with you," Jace mumbles into his hands. "We don't want the truth leaking to the rest of the city."

"You think we'd do that?" I ask, genuinely taken aback by his assumption.

"When you realize that we're no better than those who made you slaves, you'll run right to the streets to shout the truth," Jace says quietly. I've never heard him sound so bitter, not even after our friends were murdered.

That's right, Astira. They didn't just die. They were murdered. Keep that anger fresh, or you'll succumb to the grief.

"Why are you painting yourself as a villain? You're *not* the same as the ones who kept us trapped." Liv scoots to the edge of the bed, seconds away from wrapping her arms around Jace. I can sense it, too. He looks ready to bolt out the partially opened door, forever evading our questions.

"If you clip a bird's wings, does that not make you its captor?" Jace asks.

"Damon didn't just clip my pretty wings," I seethe. "He crushed me in his fist over and over until I couldn't breathe. That's not *you*."

"How would you know?" Jace suddenly shouts. The chair clatters to the floor as he jumps to his feet, emboldened by his indignation. Liv and I stay seated under the tension. *Yet another shared experience. You don't stand to meet your abuser head-on. You let them tower over you and await your deserved punishment.* "While you two were drowning in that tunnel, I was steering the ship of civilians above on the waves. And you know how? Want to guess? Hm?"

We remain silent. Panic swells in my chest at the way Jace's behavior flipped on its axis. In the corner of my vision, black spots cloud the rest of the room. I pray they're the shadows of my wolf, yet that'd be foolish. *He isn't real. He couldn't save you from your prison, and he sure as hell won't be here now.*

"I learned those first few days everyone funneled into this city that I'd have to fight to survive. Truthfully, I was alone, separated from any friends or family or coworkers or even the annoying as hell neighbors I used to have. *Alone.* You're wrong. Humans are not adaptable. Most of us freeze in fear or overreact when met with change. We become volatile or, worse, submissive to those who are violent and in control. That's how humans have been for centuries on this speck of a planet in our universe. It's infuriating, yet I'm no different. There's no use splitting hairs. I didn't lay a hand on any woman or child because of how my old man treated my momma and me growing up. The men, though?" Our friend steps closer to us and leans down, so he's right in front of our faces. Chills zip up my spine when I realize he's *growling*.

"I ripped out every one of their hearts and used their corpses as stepping stones to get to the top," he breathes. Jace's body shudders, as if trying to restrain himself from speaking the truth. His words continue to spill over. "I used every skill I learned from my fucking old man and from my work as a therapist to manipulate everyone else around me. Have you seen me building homes or shops? Have you seen me, even with my love for food, out in the fields? Have you seen me actually *do* anything since you've both arrived here?"

Liv and I are gaping at him. "You brought the doctor when I woke up from the coma. Y-you've started this mission to rescue the others still trapped in the tunnels." I curse my voice for breaking. I need to be strong.

A single tear falls down Jace's withered face. It's paler than usual, with only a hint of a rusted tan. His hands shake as he brings them to each of our faces, and oddly smooth hands trace the outlines of our jaws. *These hands haven't felt a day of physical labor.* Liv's foot taps my own, and as if soul sisters, I instinctively know that's her signal for us to *fucking move* in the next minute. There's danger in the air that we haven't scented before around our friend. Then again, predators don't only wear one skin.

"I did that—" Jace chokes. "I did that because I *needed* to, just as I must gather as many prisoners as possible from the tunnels. I swear on my momma's soul, I was relieved to have not seen either of you after we went underground. I had hoped, same with Ruse and Lyk, that you had all died and left this cursed world." His tongue darts out to lick his lips. I don't miss the way his breathing quickens. "In order to survive, I eliminated who stood in my way and guided the rest to maintain a sense of normalcy in this city. None of the children were harmed because we needed them. We still need them. They haven't fulfilled their intended purpose quite yet."

My thoughts are whirling fast enough to make me sick.

"Children?" Liv whispers.

"You remember what Tryg and Ruse were working on four years ago?" Jace asks.

I push past the fog in my mind, sprinting toward memories I haven't thought about in ages. *They were investigators. Always stressed out. Families had gone missing. Mostly children.*

"The fuck?" I mutter.

"Astira, your mind is sharper than most, but you're not going to get it. It's best that I show both of you what I'm talking about. Surely, it'll be okay if I do that. She'll allow this, and you'll understand why it's necessary."

"She?" Liv asks. We've laced our hands together, and that fight-or-flight reflex kicks in. My muscles coil as I prepare to *fight*.

"You haven't met Risha before. She's a force to be reckoned with, and you might just get along. Come. You've been persistent these last few months. Let me show you the truth of this world and all our anticipated deaths."

TWENTY-FOUR
Ceira

The taste of ashes doesn't signify you've used fire maji.
It means that you're likely dead.
-Correspondence from Council Member Enya,
Grand Commander of Fire

Death's scent looms in this library, and it takes all my power to stay focused on Jade, who's pacing in front of me. My *maji* vibrates under my skin with the need to wake Athena up and with some unknown desire to explore the rest of the bookstacks. *Where is that smell coming from?*

"Jade?" I prompt.

She blinks rapidly and casts her stony gaze on me. "I don't want to leave until I learn what Eliina has to say. This is taking too long for it not to be important."

"But you getting this worked up isn't going to help our situation," Ivar chides. His tone is gentle, and I forget how long these *solliqas* have known one another. "Go. Fly free to safety. This isn't worth you getting caught."

"And it's okay if all of you are?" Jade pulls her long black hair up into a high ponytail. She straightens out her skin-tight coverings and checks each of her sheathed blades. "The food and *lipva* I brought back before isn't nearly enough to sustain everyone. I'm aware that most of you can use your *maji* to summon food, but not at the rate our energy is draining down here from stress. If I'm leaving, then we need to figure out what to do with these three. No one should stay cooped up down here, not with the disorder of everything in Majikaero right now."

"What do you want us to do?" Ulf's wolf growls while he's stalking out of the shadows behind another towering bookshelf. The shadows of his form flicker under the orbs and appear deadly under the light of the maroon and gray moons. There's an unhinged look in his eyes, more than usual, and he's eager as hell to get out of here. The few times he dozed off earlier, I'd heard his wolf whining in his sleep. It was low enough to not bother the others, but the tone of sorrow called out to my healer heart. Something about it felt familiar, and I wanted to leap into his dream to find out what it was.

"We can't exactly travel with them unseen," Ulf continues. His gaze peruses Jade's body in a lewd and slimy way. "Unless you have some spare space hidden in those coverings of yours, which is unlikely considering how fucking tight they are, and—"

"Stop," Stefanie frowns at Ulf. "There's no need to bring her body into this. Don't take your frustration out on her."

Hauke shuffles closer to her and leans down to whisper in her ear.

"Not right now, darling," Stefanie says sharply. "We can talk more after Ulf gets a grip on his emotions. He can't just lash out at us as he pleases."

"Then maybe she shouldn't suggest dumb as fuck ideas," Ulf's wolf grunts.

The unsettled energy in this part of the library cranks up a few notches, and my *maji* can sense the second it gets too close to mayhem. That scent of death is nearly overpowering me. I naively think it's a stroke of luck when Zaya steals our attention.

Her fur is standing straight up as if she's been electrocuted. She leaps off my lap into the middle of where Eliina, Athena, and Hadwin are sitting on the rug. *So naive.* In the next few seconds, it'll become crystal clear that Ulf and Jade acting aggressive will be the least of our worries.

One second.

Zaya lets out a crazed screech and flies right back into me. She pushes into me hard, and I'd fall if it wasn't for Nyx catching my slumped body.

Five seconds.

Nyx crouches into a fighting stance next to me, keeping one arm behind me, with shadows and smoke seeping out of his skin. Daru's eyes narrow with worry at the three of us. I don't bother arguing with him when he flaps his giant green and black wings in our direction. If anything, it makes my heart flutter that two *solliqas* immediately place themselves around me as protection.

Ten seconds.

Zaya is growling, but she's not acting how she did the other day in the healing quarters. She's petrified, and I keep one hand on her trembling body while the other flares bright with blue flames. *What did that purple substance do to her?* Eliina and our friends haven't moved a muscle, but something tells me the quiet we've been resenting is about to bite us. *Hard.*

Fifteen seconds.

Hauke and Odin are next to the *skelter*, with Fraya now wide awake in the middle of them, and Ivar stands close to Jade. Hauke makes eye contact with Stefanie, an unspoken conversation happening through their *almaove* connection. Ulf glowers at Jade one last time before prowling in between everyone.

Twenty seconds.

Silence blankets over our strange group and crackles in the space between us like static. I hold my breath, waiting for something to jump out and scare my soul straight out of me. Nyx breathes sharply through his nose, causing a few tendrils of my hair to move on my shoulder. Daru curves his wing along my shins and Zaya's claws latch onto my coverings. There are too many sensations and movements to keep count of, too many possible outcomes whirling around in my head. *Something's coming. What terror is coming?*

Thirty seconds. CRACK.

The sound of a whip shatters the stifling silence. I can't see where the sound came from. We're all searching until the cause becomes painfully obvious, and I don't know whether I'm sick with gratification or heartbroken. The cracking sound was not a whip—it was Eliina's chains exploding and her bones snapping. They pop and splinter, sticking out of her ripped humanoid skin at odd angles.

At the same time, the *skelter* that's been tied down starts straining against its makeshift chains made of Hadwin's snake's skin. It's unfazed by Nyx's shadow daggers still looming above it or my blue flames.

Forty seconds.

I don't know where to look, but the way my flames rise tells me I need to take action. Without second guessing myself, I squeeze Nyx's arm and hope I convey the need for him to trust me. Our bond solidified even more while down here, and while we don't have matching soul bond markings, I still send my thoughts and emotions through my *maji* and into his.

Fifty seconds.

I lunge out of my chair, causing Zaya to go scrambling on top of Daru while hissing and growling like the vicious little beast she is. Dissimilar to the healing quarters, she doesn't jump in front of me. *It's okay, little heathen. Go find safety, or ruffle Daru's gleaming feathers.*

Jade, Stefanie, and Ivar are gaping at Eliina, whose blood is being sucked out of her and funneled through the air toward the *skelter's* cavernous mouth. She's turning into a skeleton with a withered coat of skin, but I don't see any signs of her soul disintegrating into stardust or even leaving her now frail body. Athena and Hadwin still appear the same as they did before, yet the way their bodies are twitching is harrowing. My eyes dance from them to Eliina to our friends to the thrashing *skelter*. Then I see it.

The purple substance oozes its way out of Eliina's parted, cracked lips. Panic surges up from my stomach, dimming my fire. My mother's voice curls around my senses. *Run, Eira. Don't let it take your precious, sweet blood.*

Sixty seconds.

I shrug the voice off as if it's a physical presence. *No. Once was enough. I've now had a taste of darkness, and I'll gorge myself on it if it means I can protect my friends.*

Screaming, I jump *at* the purple substance. I won't let myself be afraid of it, not when I know there are purple flames prowling under my skin. It appears less as a liquid and more as a sludgy, moldable clay this time, which means I can touch it. If the gods favor me tonight, maybe I can lure it out and capture it. With the way Zaya is responding to it, I don't think it's a mere material passing through. I feel it in my tired bones that I'm coming face-to-face with a new creature, especially with the way it's twitching and coming to life. *Is it poisonous? Is this why Eliina's recent actions have been so abnormal?*

I take another step toward Eliina's body. Nyx calls my name, and I can see the others gawking at me. The purple substance has made them all freeze in agony, similar to a few days ago, but I won't let myself stop. Ulf is the only one moving with me. The dark eyes of his wolf assess me, slightly taken aback by my ability to keep going. I bare my teeth at him. My blue flames twist into purple and red fire, no longer afraid of what the others will think of the change in colors or what they mean.

Squatting in front of Athena and Hadwin, my crystalized fox pounces behind me and covers them with the blue and white healing fire. *Good luck getting through that, you purple scum.* The substance is billowing like smoke above Eliina's corpse, and I swear to all the gods, it's mocking me with the way it waves its grimy tendrils at me. *Is this a fucking parasite?* Jade, Stefanie, and Ivar are clawing at their heads and trying to scratch at the purple mist hovering around them. When I look closer, ringlets of the substance curl inside their noses, mouths, and ears.

First of all, I want to throw up. This is revolting.

Second of all, why is it not affecting me? On second thought, it doesn't matter. I can't heal Eliina at this point, but I can take down that skelter *or destroy this purple parasite shit. I'm the Queen of Light, but I'll drown anything in darkness the second it attacks my friends. So I guess the parasite made its choice tonight, and I made mine.*

I try to weave my hands through the purple and red fire. Some of this *maji* is charring me, making me cry out in pain. If my fox and the blue and white flames are healing and protective, then these must be ravaging and destructive. They're ready to rot layers of skin in the same painful way my chronic pain has harmed me. Breathing deeply, I imagine with each exhale that these new flames form into barbed cords. If I'm going to get hurt in the process, then I'm bringing the parasite down with me.

Ulf goes to bite Eliina in the neck, but when he sees me, his eyes widen.

"Go take down that monster," I growl.

Blue and white flames coat my back. Red and purple flames cover my front. Scaled chunks of my flesh peel off me, exposing some of the darkness in the core of my soul. While my fox spirit is standing guard behind me, a second creature emerges before my eyes.

An oversized lioness made of the same brutal flames prowls out in front of me from my solar plexus. My gut tells me this creature has *fim* energy and is full of feminine rage. Her eyes are smoldering coals, and each giant paw imprints smeared markings made of ash on the library floor. Bits and pieces of her body are sheathed in hardened, shiny scales, and they only accentuate her fiery form. My fox is icy fire and absolute stillness, the piercing silence in the woods during a snowfall. She can peel back the layers of pain someone swears don't even exist. My lioness is frenetic fury and passion, the overflowing lava that will scald you if you're not careful. I can already tell she will incinerate the negative energy that sticks to one's soul.

With these creatures, parts of my own spirit, I'm a firestorm. "This substance is *mine*."

My lioness bares her onyx teeth, and Ulf doesn't even remotely push back. His wolf disappears in a flash of shadows and then reforms as he runs in the opposite direction toward the *skelter*. Glaring at the substance still coming out of Eliina's body, a red haze falls over my vision. *Is that my darkness in the form of fire?*

Good.

I raise one of the barbed whips and slash away at the substance. One of the sharp ends nicks Ivar's arm. *Oops.* He doesn't notice, not with the purple mist distracting him. My arms go back and forth, slicing through the air as I try to curl the whip around this substance.

This isn't going to work. If I want to contain it, I need to set up a net, like the one Nyx threw over Fraya.

I weave my hands, imagining a net of flames forming in the space before me. A high-pitched whine steals my attention, and I stumble forward slightly at the sight of the purple parasite coiling around my fox's legs. Some of it escapes through my blue and white fire and surges toward Athena and Hadwin. *Fuck.*

Throwing the net I've managed to make over Eliina, I focus all my energy on burning the substance out of her and into this net. *I don't know what I'm doing. I have no fucking clue, but I'm boiling over with fury that this substance and mist could kill us.* My lioness lunges at the substance still seeping out of Eliina and lets out a vicious roar. I should be afraid of such a violent creature, but I'm not; she's only an extension of myself and embodies my desire to rip this substance to shreds.

I throw both my arms up and with a strangled, piercing scream, I hurl my hands forward, curling my fingers as I imagine the net tucking more around the parasite. My lioness leaps on top of the net and merges with the fire, effectively crushing the parasite onto the ruined rug. Within seconds, I pull the blazing net toward me. The purple substance solidifies a little more the second I trap it and squirms. I'm still screaming and am struck with the realization that I'm more heartbroken than anything at this point. It makes me sick to see Eliina's body not only dead but covered in burn marks.

Sometimes that's the natural consequence of defending yourself and your loved ones— someone gets hurt. *But this parasite made a mistake. It's fucked with the wrong soul.*

The purple mist from the substance floats up to the ceiling, dispersing into nothing. I wrestle with the net for another moment, concentrating on tying it up securely and keeping this fucking leech trapped. The way it pushes out of the net's holes tells me this is *definitely* alive and fighting to break free. One of my hands latches around its slimy body, and for a moment, I imagine squeezing the life out of it. I try to reel in the flames still covering me. The more I consider how much pain this one minuscule creature has caused us so far, the harder it is to get a grip on my emotions.

Out of the corner of my eye, I see Ulf lock his jaw around the *skelter* and rip its head clean off. A mixture of purple, black, and red liquid sprays out of its butchered neck, splattering Hauke, Odin, and Fraya's shocked faces in thick spurts of blood. Ulf's wolf doesn't give a shit what kind of grotesque mess he leaves behind. He went in with the goal to kill, no matter what it took. A small part of me wonders if he has been lost to the blood lust, or if there is a piece of him that kills to protect.

Not all monsters are sheer evil, right?

Looking down at what I've demolished with my fire, I hope not. I might truly be a monster myself.

Ulf's wolf bounds toward where I'm kneeling over the captured parasite, and the thirst for blood still glimmering in his dark eyes makes it difficult to calm my feverish emotions. I'm burning up from my attempt to heal and protect my friends and taking down the purple substance. Going on both the offense and defense was too much for my system, and dense smoke begins to choke me.

Each breath is suffocating, and the room tilts as my vision tunnels. *Will my healing attempts backfire? Will I burn all the way down until I'm nothing but stardust?*

"Sweetheart," Nyx murmurs behind me.

Nyx wraps his arms around my waist, flames and all, and pulls my back flush against his chest. He angles his mouth next to my ear and bites down. "Give me some of that fire, little firefly. Envelope me in your sweet heat." His gravelly voice races through my veins until I gasp and manage to take in a full breath of air. The blazing flames simmer down to a thin coating of fire along my whole body. My chest is still being smothered, and with each stroke of Nyx's fingers down my arms and back, I swallow down any air that makes its way through the smoke.

I fall to my knees and lean my head back against Nyx's body. The coating of fire is soon replaced with sweat, and tendrils of my damp hair stick to both my clammy skin and Nyx's black coverings. My fox is back inside of me, as is my lioness, and any leftover purple and blue *maji* nestles into my soul. Light eyes meet opaque orbs oozing with shadows—telling me his beast is also at the surface, wanting to care for me—and I can't bring myself to look away.

His darkness is my anchor in this current reality. I'm scared of where I'll go or what my *maji* will do if I focus elsewhere.

"That's it, sweetheart," Nyx rasps. "Keep breathing. Send

any smoke and fire my way. I'll keep them safe and far away from you."

I have the sudden urge to climb up his body until I'm wrapped around him and his shadows. When I try to stand, though, my legs give out, and I land in a heap next to the squirming parasite by Nyx's feet. He chuckles darkly. "There are still some embers in those eyes. Save your energy—we'll have time to play later."

My brain short circuits at the way my *almaove* is gazing down at me. It's a mixture of mischief and relief and lust and something else I can't identify right now.

"Eira."

I hesitantly lower my face to whoever is in front of me, and I'm met with both Stefanie and Daru on their hands and knees. They have identical expressions of panic as they search my body from head to toe, unbothered by my muddled state. Zaya slinks in between them and forces her way onto my lap. I try to ignore the way her fur clings to my skin.

"You'll need a healing session, but you seem to be okay," Stefanie murmurs to herself. She grabs one of my hands and turns it over, sparks of her healing powers traveling up my arms. "The bear marking is throbbing again."

I frown down at my forearm. It did that the last time I was near this purple substance. Now that we have it contained, maybe I can get some answers about why it's impacting me so much.

"Eira, you were *incredible*," Daru breathes. He pushes a jar of *lipva* into my mouth. I allow myself to stare into his green eyes while I swallow the restoring liquid, and I'm met with nothing but wonder and awe. Zaya arches her back and nudges my chin with her head as if in agreement.

"Why could I move while the rest of you were frozen?" I whisper. My voice cracks from the thick smoke still trapped inside my throat, the *lipva* only partially healing me. I lean my head down and give Zaya a little peck between her ears.

Daru tucks a strand of hair behind my ear. His hand lingers, and his finger strokes down the curve of my ear to the earlobe. The swarm of butterflies this ignites in my stomach takes me by surprise. I've gone from viewing him as a birdbrained magical creature to slightly tolerable to a potential ally, and now... is he my friend? That can't be the right word for him.

Daya, Del, and Daru were the ones to greet me in Majikaero and apparently used *maji* to bring my soul over to this world. They're similar to long-lost family members, the kind I didn't know existed but have craved their care and affection for so long. The way Daru is peering into my soul right now doesn't feel like a friend or family member, though. Those stupid butterflies flutter their annoying wings—quite similar to Daru, actually—and I'm hit with the sensation that we could have a deeper soul connection than the others. *No. Absolutely not.* I'm already with Nyx and still navigating that chaos. Besides, I don't do more than one relationship. I'm a basic monogamous kind of girl.

A voice I'm starting to think isn't my own presses against the inside of my head.

Except you're not simply a girl, it whispers in a hoarse voice. *You're a* solliqa *with healing powers and now live in a world of magic. You don't get to dictate what kinds of connections your soul needs here.*

An unexpected scene flashes before my eyes.

I'm in scraps of lacy black coverings, nothing that could truly be considered actual clothing. The tulle texture cups each of my breasts, leaving the nipples exposed, and wraps in skimpy straps down my abdomen and hips. My body stretches out along an intricately woven rug, the colors bright silver and gold in the pattern of a sun. Smooth marbled flooring is beneath the rug, illuminated by red and orange flames in the stony hearth behind my head. I gasp as thick smoke binds my wrists together while another burst of darkness slithers around each ankle until they're both shackled to the floor. The only soul I'd trust to chain me up peers down from behind my shoulders, having added more fuel to the flickering flames.

"Are you ready for us to feast on you tonight, firefly?" Nyx purrs into my ear before licking the spot just under my ear lobe. Those crackling eyes make my heart flutter in anticipation.

Another presence crawls in between my legs, pulling my attention away from my almaove. I'm greeted with the swirling dark green eyes of Daru, his blond hair longer and braided out of his face as he places open-mouthed kisses up my thigh. He rips the thin fabric from around my slick folds. With a flick of his wrist, a small funnel of wind trails around my hips and hits my clit in one sharp gust. My body tenses from the sudden pain and releases as a coil of pleasure tightens in my core. Oh, gods.

"We had to skip dinner tonight, my queen," Daru rasps against my pussy. "I'm starving, but lucky me, my favorite meal is laid out right before me."

Daru hums, bringing me back to the moment. My face flushes from the scene that came to me unbidden, yet I can't deny I'm open to seeing where it ended.

I'm still sitting at Nyx's feet while he runs his hands through my hair. The purple substance writhes in the net next to me, and Stefanie and Daru are crouched before my exhausted form, blocking my view of the others. I can hear them all groaning from the pain they were in. Odin is laughing with Fraya about all the blood on them. Ulf is arguing his point about killing the *skelter* with Jade. *What a bunch of disturbed souls corralled together.*

"I'm not sure," Daru mutters. "None of us know. The only thing we do know is that both you and Ulf were able to push past the influence of the purple mist."

I chew on my bottom lip. Daru's eyes dart down to the action, and those swirling forest-green eyes grow even darker.

"That'll have to be one of our missions when we split up," Stefanie says, her voice thoughtful. "One of us needs to figure out Eira's connection to all of this, since she's clearly being targeted. Do you think it's possible that substance *wanted* you to fight? To see what you're made of?"

Nyx growls in response. I scowl at him for acting like a caveman. "I don't know," I mumble before heaving into a coughing fit. Daru takes my hand, and Nyx rubs soothing circles on my back. "I have a theory that the substance is a parasite and could be a creature, but it's not clear if it's that intelligent or not. Where should we even begin?"

"You should begin with taking a gander at Athena and Hadwin. Our friends have woken up," Hauke interrupts.

As if on cue, the soul bond marking flares to life, heating the bruised and sensitive skin of my upper arm. I sway and almost fall forward into Stefanie. My vision tunnels, and without further warning, I'm traveling a green path full of earthy magic in my mind until I'm planted firmly in Athena's soul.

"Athena," Hadwin breathes.

I force myself to open my eyes, but it takes so much effort. My mind is still connecting with what my spirit learned, and I'm struggling to reorient myself to my physical form. Eliina and I communicated in that tent through the earth. I was expecting that, not whatever the fuck that was, pulling me into an actual memory.

"Zamia, look," Hadwin whispers.

The hazy film placed over the library gets clearer, pixel by pixel, until I can see my own lap and feet. Hadwin's body is right next to mine, and our friends are hovering around us with expressions of horror. Eira especially appears shocked out of her mind. Stefanie is propping up her body on the floor and is making animated hand movements around her body. My attention shifts up toward the ceiling. The rain has stopped pounding against the windows—I'm guessing by Odin's face that he's no longer sending his maji *to the clouds. They're all watching us intently. I can prac-*

tically feel their anxiety. My gaze circles to each of their faces, the bookshelves behind them, Zaya hissing, and settles back on Eliina.

When I look at her, I expect to see the same trembling solliqa. *Instead, her body is slumped over. Eliina's skin is leathery and shriveled up, as if she's been decaying for days, and her hair and nails have disintegrated into ash. My breath hitches when I focus on her eyes. They're still swirling black and green, but ruby red tears are falling down her hollowed cheeks. Her soul is no longer with us, but I don't think she was set free and scattered across the universe as stardust.*

No, part of her is trapped somewhere torturous, and I know in my heart that we'll never again see this magical spirit.

I suck in a loud gasp. My best friend... I was just in her mind, in her *soul*. My heartbeat was her heartbeat, my thoughts were hers. *How did I do that?*

My eyes blink impossibly fast, and I finally become fully present in the moment. Nyx is shaking my shoulders slightly, and Daru is gripping my right knee with enough force to break it. Stefanie's hands flitter back and forth across my face and down to the tops of my shoulders. We make eye contact, and she blows out a breath soaked in relief. Hauke is standing tall above Stefanie with his deep purple wings out. He has a hardened expression and looks ready to fire questions at me. I regard the rest of his body and flinch when I get to the blood and viscous, light purple liquid caked onto his arms. *Gross.*

Athena coughs, snatching my attention quicker than if someone announced there was chocolate and coffee on a silver platter. *I'll just have to deal with why and how I flowed into Athena's soul later.*

I try to push myself up again, but my body is still too weak to move on its own. Nyx swiftly lifts me by the waist with one arm and grabs Zaya with the other, throwing her over his shoulder as she releases a muffled meow. His eyebrows furrow when he glances at me, but he doesn't say anything. We shuffle our way around Hauke's winged form while Stefanie and Daru scramble to either side of him. One of his purple wings drapes around Stefanie's shoulders, keeping her tucked into his side. Ulf and Jade abruptly end their argument over the *skelter's* body. Fraya lets out a squeak when she realizes the physical state of Eliina, causing a wave of grave and horror-struck faces across the others.

Eliina is nothing more than a shattered corpse. What's left of her flesh was burned to a crisp by my flames, but I can't bring myself to feel guilty over it. *Perhaps my* maji *put her out of her misery.*

My eyes meet Athena's. A sob works its way out of her. I flounder like a fool until Nyx places me down next to my best friend. *Does she know what I just did?* It doesn't matter right now. We lean into one another, neither of us having the strength to lift our arms for a full hug, and I heave a sigh of relief that she's safe. I peer over her shoulder to assess how Hadwin is doing, and I'm greeted with a haunted face. He appears unsettled and his expression turns grim when he takes in Eliina's corpse again. Hadwin stares at her for one more minute before twisting to the side and retching up the little food in his stomach.

Athena's eyes widen when she looks over at the smashed chains around Eliina. There's a sheen to her eyes, yet no tears fall down my friend's face. She raises her hand as if she's going to reach out toward Eliina, but then she pauses and places her hand on mine instead.

"She said they'd know she told us," Athena whispers.

"They?" I breathe. The longer I stare at what was once Eliina's face, the more lost I become.

Athena doesn't respond. She squeezes my hand and glances at everyone around us.

"Athena," I murmur, trying to hide the borderline hysteria in my wobbly voice. "Please, who are *they*?"

Those stunning green orbs fling back to me. Our soul marking pulsates against my trembling skin, and I can already sense her agitated panic squirming down our soul connection.

"Eliina shared so much," Athena rasps. "*Too* much. I-I have a million questions and now can't even ask her. She didn't say exactly who would know that she shared information with us. From what was shown, I believe it's the Sairn or... or her mother, the Queen of Cudhellen."

Hauke curses at the same time Nyx snarls.

"She could also have meant the Council," Hadwin interjects. "In a way, they all are connected to one another, but I doubt any of us can figure it out right now."

"But she said there's darkness on the other worlds," Athena blurts, dragging her attention over to Hadwin. "This must be bigger than a Council on—"

"Whoa, back up," Ivar interrupts. "Let's focus on Majikaero. Does this mean *all* the Council members have betrayed our world?" Ivar asks.

"What did Eliina even *do*?" Fraya pushes her way into the conversation. She's gnawing on her fingernails as if they're her last lifeline.

Athena and Hadwin glance at one another. There's usually an undercurrent of hostility mixed with denial of their obvious feelings for one another whipping back and forth between them. After their experience with using their earth *maji* to communicate with Eliina, there's only a shared sense of dread.

"Sh-she wanted to give all *our* souls over to the Sairn. As in Nyx, Hadwin—all of us. Eliina's mother is the Queen of Cudhellen, and she has sway with other worlds and this horrible group called the Sairn. Her sister is even with them."

"I remember her telling me that," I whisper, nodding.

"Eliina shared memories with us," Hadwin continues. "All sorts of memories of her communicating with certain *solliqas* about these plans and events. She said her mother could get the

Sairn to take away all the darkness in our world. They have powers connected to such devastating darkness, but the Council would need to give them certain *solliqas* they've been searching for in exchange."

"No..." Odin mutters. "No, they *didn't*."

Hadwin's lips press into a thin line. "They did. The Council agreed to this request. They said they'd give the Sairn *our* souls in exchange for removing the plague of darkness in Majikaero. Apparently, some plans changed, though, because the Sairn used portals to send horrendous creatures to our world in order to capture even *more* innocent souls. And fucking Eliina assisted in opening portals in Rioa, since the divide between multiple worlds is thinnest in this region."

"Fucking Eliina," Nyx growls. "May she *not* rest in peace."

"May she rot in Cudhellen," Ivar adds.

"I just..." Athena wonders out loud. "I don't understand all the *solliqas* Eliina was connected to and what they were talking about." She raises her eyes to peer up at Hauke, who gives a subtle shake of his head. I look around quickly to see if anyone else saw this exchange, but I think I'm the only one.

What does Athena know? What is Hauke not telling us?

"Perhaps that's a conversation for another day," Hauke suggests smoothly. "We might want to focus our intention on what the Council members did and how that's going to impact our plans to meet with them."

Stefanie's auburn eyebrows furrow. "Will it still be safe to go searching for them? Would it be better to research more information before fleeing Rioa?"

"Safe?" Daru scoffs. He's managed to get close to me again while I sit next to Athena, holding her hand on my lap. "I'm more worried about if it's a waste of everyone's time."

Hauke raises an eyebrow at him in response, a silent invitation to continue.

"We all saw what this *skelter* was capable of doing," Daru

spits. "If the Council aren't even showing their faces at this time, and their deeds have gotten darker and darker, who's to say they're even the actual Council members? Are they just a bunch of *canielor* or other monsters standing in their place?"

"Surely, there must be some kind of explanation," Stefanie mutters, her face going white. "That would be a nightmare on a whole other level."

"Things might begin to make more sense once I gather all the memories from Hadwin and Athena," Jade says while chewing on her bottom lip. She turns her attention to my best friend. "I'll need time to sit with the both of you for even an hour of peace."

"That's not going to be now," Hadwin rasps. "I don't think we have much time."

"Then it can happen after you, Athena, and Ulf leave this library," Stefanie suggests.

Athena looks between them, not completely mentally here.

"Do you have any questions?" Stefanie asks her quietly. "We made a concrete plan while you were both communicating with Eliina, so we'd be ready for our missions as soon as you came back to us."

"I said we don't have much time," Hadwin barks louder.

"I'd reckon we don't have any time at all," Jade mutters. While the rest of us have been focusing on each other or on Eliina's body, she's staring straight above at the expansive windows. Not too long ago, there were still a few of her crows gathered on the branches, their feathers sleek in the maroon and gray moonlight.

Now, a single crow lies on top of the curved window, its neck broken and surrounded by burned feathers. The rest of the sky is obscured by the fog of purple mist swelling before our very eyes.

TWENTY-FIVE
Tryq

Due to the layered effect of veils between worlds, there are thousands of species still unaccounted for in the realms surrounding Majikaero.
-Page 3860, Index of Realm Species, Volume II

Eyes, dozens upon dozens of them, stare at me as I dangle over the side of the *drekstri*. The bear paws my hands shifted into were useful for a moment. I committed to the idea that I can save myself if I *focus* on the task of breaking through my chains. Yet when I got to the last one around my left ankle, I stopped. Of course I fucking hesitated when freedom was a mere slice of one of my lethal claws away. One, two, three seconds went by where I froze in place, and that was all it took for my demons to slither back out from where Daya had scared them to. She called my name, and a swell of flames zipped up and down her arms in preparation to frighten the three demons, each more slippery in my grip than the last.

Daya was too late.

With an ear-splitting roar, the *drekstri* beast swooped against the oncoming winds barreling toward us. The sudden motion knocked me off balance, and I tumbled off the side of its massive body, each iridescent scale passing by me in a flash.

One black cord of shadow remains fastened around my ankle. Now as I sway from side to side, bouncing against the beast's hardened scales and up against its thick underbelly, I jerk uncontrollably from the shadows' effect on my skin. They continue to send electrical waves through me, effectively paralyzing me in a state of perpetual pain.

I swing like a hanging corpse, a noose I allowed to stay looped around my body, my arms dangling in the chilled air. Breathing in the pain of each electrical shock, I exhale and find I'm relieved. *Is this the end?* My body is still twitching from the cord, but the rest of my senses are numbed out. *I thought I wanted to live, but do I really? Is living worth the effort it'll take to break down these demons?*

Luminous flames whoosh above me against the cord still attached to the *drekstri*. They don't break or unravel from the scorching fire. Its heat is a warm caress, yet it's unable to reach who I am at my core. The world tilts on its axis again as the beast surges down to the forest below us, folding its wings against the sides of its body and narrowly missing my leg.

It bellows in what could be rage. I have no idea what this monster is screaming about, only that the sharpness of its cry resonates with the part of me still thrashing, still wanting to live. Daya descends next to me, more fire whirling around her petite form, and folds her arms around my torso as we plummet toward the trees. Pinks and oranges and colors that remind me of spring awakening surge up to meet us as we fall to what could be our deaths.

The cackling of my demons has taken over the rest of my headspace, and any emotions I might feel as we ready for impact are muted. All the other flying creatures and *solliqas* are diving right alongside us into the earth, as if they're eager to face death.

I close my eyes and imagine Eira's fiery gaze peering back at me. Whether it's crystallized blue or the red flames I saw in the dungeons doesn't matter. I'll take her in any form. She's all I've ever wanted, and I don't care how selfish it makes me anymore. In this moment, I don't care if it means I have to share her soul with others, even with that arrogant, darkened *solliqa*, Nyx.

We're all the same color of darkness, placed on different spectrums. Mine comes in three different shades—four, including my own soul—and I'll give Eira anything she wants if it means I can even see her one more time. She's a balm to what could be a century-old wound. Maybe if I bare all these parts of who I am now to her, she'll take what I can give. Surely, Eira can find *something* worth saving inside of me.

My eyes crack open for a second, and I watch as the white grass comes into view. I brace myself for the crash, keeping Eira's face in my mind until the last second. Breathing out one last time, I wonder where I'll end up next or if my soul will finally be shattered into millions of pieces, each more insignificant than the last. *Will my spirit be set free to mourn in another life, another world, another timeline? Will Eira find me there?*

All thoughts eddy out of me as the ground expands out from under us, yawning as we enter a circular golden mouth. *No, there are no teeth.* There's just never-ending gold and darkness thrusting at me from all sides. My demons screech in agony as they push against my skin, clawing in desperation to leave my body. All three vicious creatures tear through my flesh in an attempt to funnel out of what's left of my physical form. Bright red colors fly past me in a rush of fire and feathers. Screams echo from every direction until my mind splinters with a loud *crack*.

Dark spots swarm my vision, and everything fades to black.

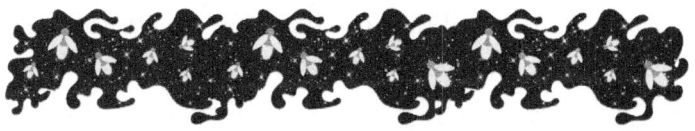

"Think he'll wake up anytime soon?"

"It'll be better if he doesn't. The more rest he can get, the better. I was hoping he'd heal some of what those vile demons have corrupted in him."

A male snorts. *At least, I think it's a male. I can't remember what they call men and women on Majikaero. Something about energies.*

"Turns out you misjudged this one, sis."

A female heaves a sigh, full of irritation.

"I did my best," she murmurs. Slender fingers push back my wind-blown hair and trail down the side of my face.

"It would have been easier if we told him the truth," the male says quietly.

"Which truth? There are many faces to the same coin here. He would have panicked," another voice murmurs. It reminds me of a person I once knew in Sweazn, but there's no way they're here with me now. No, they went missing. "We could only do so much with such little time given to us. None of us thought he'd travel to the Realm of Souls this quickly after Eira arrived."

"He shouldn't even be alive," the male snarls.

Multiple voices hush him, but it makes no difference. My mind is already wide awake—it's my body that refuses to catch up. Every bone under my skin is stiff and weighed down. Breathing is difficult at best, a low raspy sound whittling around in my chest. My eyes beg to stay closed and for me to keep sleeping, but there's something prodding at the back of my mind, keeping me in a state of restlessness. A pounding sensation in three distinct points of my head throbs, the pain worse than one of my fucked hangovers. Groaning, I force myself to peel one eye open and then the other. I'm greeted with utter blurriness, as if someone took a greasy thumb and smudged my entire vision.

"Tryg?" a female breathes.

Tryg. That's right. I have a name, and it's Tryg. How did I forget that?

Someone places pressure on my hands and uses a finger to move gentle circles across my skin from my hands up to my forearms.

"Tryg, can you hear us?"

I blink. Nothing in my vision changes, but I can raise a few fingers off the surface I'm lying on. I urge my mouth to open, to cough or groan or speak, but it refuses to budge.

"I don't know if he's healed enough to interact with us. We might need to breathe more life into him," a husky voice mutters.

A hand massages each shoulder and the sides of my neck. Each muscle flares in mild pain, but I notice I can roll my right arm slightly.

"That's it, Tryg. You've got this. We need you to wake up now."

"I thought you wanted him to sleep?"

"I was wrong. Happy now?"

"Potentially. I'll feel better when I hear you admit that a few more times today."

My head twitches in the direction of these voices. I can tell they're close by, but they aren't attached to whoever is kneading each muscle. Those fingers are now rubbing tight circles along my face, coercing the knotted pressure around my mouth to release its hold on me. Licking my lips, I gradually open them and am hit with unbearable dryness.

The female hums and presses a circular item into my mouth. "Easy does it."

Chilled liquid pours down my throat, and I eagerly gulp it down, welcoming the way it soothes the drought of my insides. With each swallow, the numbness coating my body gives way to tender aches, and my vision clears enough to take in the soul above me. Scarlet orbs peer down at me, and there's no mistaking which *solliqa* is working on my body, not with the stunning white antlers with their shimmering crystals. Her chocolate-brown hair falls in waves down her back.

"He's with us," she whispers.

Familiar souls crowd in around her. I blink a few more times and sweep my gaze from face to face.

"Thank you, Isa," Daya croons. "Those healing powers of yours work even more miracles now."

Isa turns to face Daya and loops an arm around her shoulders. A genuine smile spreads across her face, making her deer form glow even brighter.

"They are, aren't they?" Isa beams. "The benefits of us finally being home."

Daya hums and gazes down at me with those hazel eyes. Her dark red hair is still cropped short, and one side is pinned back with a small braid. Different colored earrings, each in the shape of tiny feathers, travel up the curve of her ear. They match her thin dress that fits snugly against her breasts and along her wider hips, emphasizing her hourglass figure. I hate myself for admiring her physique, yet I can't tear my eyes away.

"Of course you can't, Trygster," Daya clucks. "I'm a goddess in the flesh—most can't keep their eyes or hands off me."

"Don't mess with him," a male chides from behind her. "Not yet, at least. Let's get him up, first."

Daya rolls her eyes. "If he didn't scream his thoughts so loudly, I'd have an easier time controlling myself."

"You have the self-control of an animal in heat," the male laughs.

Her eyes glint with mischief. "Maybe that's exactly what I am."

"Oh, stop," Isa murmurs while knocking Daya with her hip. "Time to introduce Tryg to his new home—for now, at least."

"New home?" I croak.

Daya's lips tug up into a smirk while Isa grins. Another

female that I don't recognize claps excitedly next to them. Her white-blond hair covers her face with the jumping movement. My eyes flare wide when I see the male step around to join them.

"Oh, yes." Del nods. His now shoulder-length auburn hair swishes as he walks closer. "We have to go into hiding while we figure out our next steps. It only made sense to remove ourselves entirely from Majikaero."

"Removed..." I mumble. I groan as I stretch out my fingers and toes, my ankles and wrists cracking with the movement. I try, and fail, to push myself up to a sitting position. Weakness has needled its way into me, and I'm stuck feeling like a dead man on this table.

My eyes dash from one item to the next around me. I'm lying on a slightly padded table in the middle of a medium-sized room. The walls are painted a mixture of bright blue and gray, reminding me of how the sea and sky would meet back near Sweazn. This room expands into a semicircle with large windows lining the curve of the outer wall. Lush cushions and small bookshelves sit under the windows, clearly a space one can sit to read and watch the vast hills and dynamic ocean far below. Isa, Daya, and Del stand closest to me, while another *solliqa* perches on the edge of a small sofa, facing the window.

"W-why remove?" I rasp.

"We've got a lot to chat about," Daya chirps. "The first being that, as much as it pains me, it wasn't safe for any of us to be on Majikaero right now. We had to travel back to our homeworld, Chironant."

I gape up at her.

"We portaled you with us," Daya continues. Isa leans down slightly to monitor my eyes. "It was the only available option with what Eliina did. My only regret is we couldn't afford to go back to Rioa before leaving. Eira is with trusted souls, though, so she should be fine. It'll give us enough time to prepare."

"For?" I hesitantly ask.

Del's eyes match his sister's almost identically. Standing next to each other, they're two halves of a whole. I admittedly haven't spent much time around him, but his expression morphs into one of harsh severity, a single look that has me slinking into the table as much as I can.

"War," he hisses. "One we didn't ask for. Now, due to the impulsive decisions of a few, we're *all* part of this. Each of our souls are inevitably bound to these realms, and it's up to us to set things right."

A wave of nausea rushes through me until I'm turned on my side, throwing up the remains of my sanity.

"I have so many fucking questions, I don't even know where the hell to begin," I mutter.

I'm still in the same room, one I learned is one of many turrets in a damn castle of all places, and am currently nestled against the plush black couch. Blankets of wool and velvet curl around my still aching body. Daya, Del, and Isa sit in front of me on tall floor cushions, each matching the dark tones of the blankets I'm bundled under. Daya is still wearing a dress made of colorful feathers. Del is in a lightweight shirt and loose gauzy pants. Isa is covered in a gold and white lacy bodysuit. Isa and Daya have such similar body structures, it doesn't take me long to put together they're also related. *Cousins, I believe Isa told me.* One wouldn't guess it from their hair or eyes or skin tones, especially with the patches of white that cover Isa's brown skin. Having all three of them sitting next to each other, each with the same intense look in their eyes and mannerisms, makes it obvious they're family, not close friends.

Friends. I long to be with my own friends who've become my family over the years.

Honestly, my biological parents and siblings from Earth can get fucked for all I care. They weren't there as I trained to become an investigator or drank my body weight in liquor. No, they provided the basic care required of them—a house, food, clothing—and did nothing to foster relationships between my brothers and me. When I went off to become an investigator, empowered by the way Eira and the others strived to help those in need, I was effectively dropped from the family who raised me. We all dispersed on our own paths, and I never heard from my parents again.

I haven't thought about my biological family in ages. It's always been Eira, Athena, Ruse, and me. We picked Jace, Astira, Liv, and Lyk up along the way, adopting them into our created family. These memories dance along the edges of my mind. I can't get a full image right now, not when my head is still pounding. And the more information these three share with me, the worse it becomes. *Fuck*.

"Are you even listening?" Daya asks, crossing her arms below her chest.

"Yeah," I mumble, rubbing my eyes and the pressure points above them. "It's hard to listen when this fucking pain won't stop hammering away. *What* is happening to me?"

Isa purses her lips and the others remain silent.

A low growl builds in my chest at their silence. I want answers. *Now*.

"Can you tell us what you understand so far?" Isa asks.

I crank my neck to the side and roll back my shoulders, trying to relieve some of the pressure in my head. Swallowing, I make eye contact with Isa's still glowing red eyes.

"A shit ton of lunacy," I mutter.

Daya arches a delicate eyebrow, clearly unamused by my comment. What'd she call me before? *Obnoxious*.

"That's because you *are* obnoxious," Daya chirps. "We'd love to answer any and all questions, but it'd help if you could share what you *do* understand."

I roll my eyes. One of these days, they're going to get stuck up there.

"The three of you are some kind of royalty here. There are others, too, but some of them had to stay behind on Majikaero. You either weren't able to get to them in time after the festival or decided it'd be best if they stayed there for Eira. A number of other souls traveled with us through... through a *portal*." I pause, still baffled that they opened a large-ass portal, that this even exists. "This portal took us to your homeworld, Chironant, which means none of you are originally from Majikaero. Since you took me with you, that means *I'm* now in a different world when I could barely process the idea of Majikaero existing outside of Earth."

Daya nods her head. "Good." She reaches her hand into a glass bowl that's on the floor near them. Her fingers dig around until she scoops up a few morsels of what I believe is similar to chocolate, plopping them in her mouth one at a time.

They wait for me to continue, but I don't know what to tell them at this point. None of this makes sense to me.

"I don't understand *why* you had to take me with you. I mean, me of all people, and—"

"*Solliqa*," Del corrects me. Now he reaches for one of the small pieces of sugar. They had offered me some earlier, but my stomach is still roiling from traveling through that portal.

I stare at him before continuing. "Right, me of all *solliqas* because I'm not a fucking human anymore." I sigh and readjust myself against the back cushions of this couch. "So, why did you bring me here? And why were you on Majikaero to begin with?"

Isa glances at Daya, and Daya looks over at Del. He chews on his bottom lip for a second before responding.

"I'll start with your second question," he begins. "It's a story of despair and sorrow, one that could go on for many hours with all the details. I know that will be too much for you right now, so I'll give you the shortened version."

Daya and Isa visibly stiffen. Their eyes are downcast and expressions immediately turn sullen. Tension winds itself around us that wasn't here moments ago.

"The exact timing of what happened depends on where you're at and which timeline you follow," Del begins, his voice just above a whisper. "For those of us on Chironant, this started a few centuries ago. On Majikaero, it was a century, and on Earth, it was a good 400 or so years in the past. There was a battle raging across the worlds of gods and spirits surrounding Earth, hidden from view behind the veil that separates each world from one another. The realms engaged in this battle were connected through different portals. Humanity was spared the brunt of it, mostly because humans weren't involved in the fight. How could they be, with their limited minds and inability to connect with the worlds a thin veil away? Alas, violence still found its way into Earth due to the influence of the Sairn. You might remember this as the First Nuclear War on your own homeworld."

Swallowing, I nod in confirmation. "This is the name of that first war. We learned about it in school growing up," I mutter. "I wasn't personally there to remember it, and it was never clear why it started."

Del cocks his head to the side. "You likely *were* there. Remember what Eliina had shared with you after you first arrived in Majikaero? In that tent? We all have hundreds of past lives, many of which we don't recall. It would take a number of healing sessions to connect with those past-life memories."

"Even you have these?" I ask.

"*Especially* us," Del says earnestly. "Whether you're connected to Chironant or Majikaero or any of the other worlds, your soul can't be on these planets for very long, if at all, if it's corrupted. These worlds are meant to be places of general peace, where mischief might flare up here and there, but there's no talk of wars or heavy violence corroding the soul. If we're not fit to be in the lands of gods and goddesses, then our soul is sent to Earth. That's why that world was created, so the High Gods and Goddesses could teach corrupted souls life lessons. When those lessons are finally learned and internalized, the soul can cross over to the world they belong in."

"Whoa, whoa, whoa," I hold up a hand. "You're telling me that the only reason my world even *exists* is to give souls a place to learn a fucking lesson? That's fucked up."

Del shrugs, his face still tainted with sadness. "That was the way of things for many years, Tryg. When you'd finally learn what was meant for you, you could cross over to what humans often believed to be Heaven."

"And if you couldn't ever learn your lesson?" I ask.

"Then you'd be stuck on Earth," Del rasps. "Or be sent to the lands of Cudhellen, or Hell as you know it as, to receive more direct punishments for your actions. Consider if your soul was corrupted in Majikaero, how many are now, and you murdered another soul. Sent it scattering into stardust, to places unknown. The High Gods and Goddesses who watch over *all* our worlds would decide whether you're sent to Earth or to Cudhellen and when you could cross back over."

I mull this information over while the three of them sit in silence. Daya and Isa still haven't budged from their rigid postures. I can tell the story is about to become more twisted with cruelty.

"Why do you keep saying *'would'*?" I ask.

Del heaves a loud sigh. "That's because the group of High Gods and Goddesses who've looked over our worlds has fractured. They were originally called the Chiante, but some of them broke off into another group called the Sairn. It's believed that the immortal gods who formed a second group were wounded beyond repair, but the question still remains: What was able to harm them? The Chiante maintained relative peace for thousands of centuries across worlds and timelines. After the Sairn was formed, a wave of darkness flooded each world in its own way. I don't mean the darkness associated with night. I mean the darkness of evil that hides in the shadows, in our own minds and in broad daylight, that's nearly impossible to completely eliminate."

I shake my head and sink back further into the cushions, letting the blankets rise to cover part of my face. This is mildly overwhelming, yet I'm eager to learn more. It's better than remaining isolated and disoriented, left in the darkness of my own demons.

"What did this Sairn group want?" I wonder. That sliver of who I was on Earth flickers to life at the prospect of solving who wounded the Chiante, and in general, putting the puzzle pieces together of what Del is sharing with me. *It's one giant mind-fuck that my investigator side craves.*

"Absolute destruction," Daya whispers.

"The freedom of chaos," Isa adds.

"For each world to govern its own self, whether evil prevails or not. For the High Gods and Goddesses to either be left to immortal lives, on a world far away, or to be slain for trying to maintain control over millions of souls," Del finishes. "So, as the Chiante and the Sairn fought one another with magical abilities only they have, other worlds were shaken up in the process. While some of the gods frantically kept the order of things, those that broke away from the norm traveled from world to world. They either kept the souls corrupted on their home planets or caused their own form of trauma on different spirits."

"That's so..." I struggle to find words. "Gods, that's fucked up. I'm not sure how I feel about being controlled, knowing each of my human lives was designed with the sole purpose of teaching me a fucking *lesson*, of all things. I'd certainly prefer that over anguish and destruction spreading left and right."

"Naturally," Del agrees. "We all would at this point. The truth of the matter is those of us in positions of power on these different worlds were not included in such discussions. Our own natural abilities were also warped along the way."

"It's been horrendous." Daya's voice catches in her throat. "Half of Chironant has been razed to the ground. We had no choice. It was either burn the spirits that have been manipulated and distorted or let them spread even more darkness to other souls. Majikaero is very similar to our world here. Think of it as a sister world, except we're known primarily as the Realm of Light and Shifters. We're meant to be a world of tranquility, beauty, and where a spirit can come for deeper healing than anywhere else."

"This is why we came to Majikaero," Isa interrupts. "Some of those in power remained here to put out any fires—quite literally—that have come up. The rest of us have been in between Earth and Majikaero for just under a century. Well, most of us. Del here had to learn how to not only portal into Earth from Majikaero, the veil separating the two worlds having a distinct pattern to memorize, but how to pinpoint specific souls across the whole world. There was talk of a Queen of Light that could banish all forms of darkness, who was said to have the same healing talents as those in Chironant. We thought if we found her, she could help us put an end to the battles of these gods. While she originally was on Majikaero, we learned her soul was stuck on Earth and would require support crossing over to the Realm of Souls and *Maji*."

"Eira," I breathe.

"Unfortunately, the Sairn got to her first," Del mumbles bitterly. "They meant to kill her, and it's said they manipulated a soul close to her to do this."

All three of them peer at me from under shuttered eyes. *Oh, fuck.*

"Me."

A piercing silence follows, adding another layer to the tension already suffocating me in this room.

"Why did you want to keep me alive, then?" I rasp.

Daya, Del, and Isa all glance at one another. It's clear they've had this discussion many times before and are silently debating what to share with me.

"Come on," I insist. "There's nothing I can do to harm you. If my demons rear their ugly heads, Daya can use her flame-throwing magic to knock them back down. I can't even cut through the last shadowed cord around my ankle."

Daya snorts, the first sign of her usual exuberant self. *Why do I miss that annoying side of her?*

"On the contrary," Del muses. "You have more *maji* abilities than you can possibly imagine."

"We needed you alive because while you were manipulated, we thought we could undo that," Isa chimes in. "You obviously have a deep love for Eira, and if you choose to take down your demons, we believe your powers could contribute to our overall goal."

"You see, we don't only need *you*," Daya continues. Her eyes are now shining as bright as a fire, unknowingly melting my heart in the process. My stomach churns, realizing what she's about to share is important. "We need any of the souls connected to Eira's, such as Nyx and Athena. Through our research in the library of Rioa and conversations with *solliqas* like Eliina, we are confident that Eira and those closest to her have the sole power to end this war between the gods. To restore healing light to all our worlds."

"Why *us*?" I ask quietly. "What do you mean if I *choose* to take down my demons?"

"Only you have the power to take down your own demons,"

Del murmurs. "*Only* you. By the looks of it, you're well on your way to learning how to do this. If you continue to make the choice of actively fighting back against them, you should be able to cut them loose. At the very least, you can tame them until they work to your advantage."

I raise an eyebrow and decide against responding. Del lets out a slow breath, understanding dawning on his face that I'm not going to say shit until he answers my question fully.

"We need all of you," Del says slowly, as if admitting this to me will expose him. As if it will change everything by putting this out there for others to know. "I—I believe, as do many others, that Eira and her closest companions are direct descendants of the Chiante, meaning they have abilities that normally only a god or goddess would be able to use. This would include you, and uh, we have concluded that you're not just a direct descendant of the High Gods and Goddesses. You're a product of the Sairn, and your purpose was to become attached to those with healing light and eliminate them or persuade them to let chaos reign."

What fucked up shit is Del on?

"Eh-fucking-scuse me?" I growl. "What do you mean I'm a *product* of the Sairn? So, not only does my homeworld exist for the purpose of life lessons and atoning for sins people aren't even aware they committed, but you're saying I was solely created to wreak havoc and destruction?" My chest is heaving, and even though I'm still fucking freezing and can barely move my body, I'm ready to punch something. "No, I don't believe you. I refuse to accept that my soul was created for something evil. I won't let that happen."

I dip my chin in Daya's direction. "Are you also a descendant, since you're so connected to and in love with Eira?"

Daya's face flushes pink while Isa and Del subtly glance at her. A shiver racks down my entire back, as if I have some damn virus.

"And why the fuck am I this damn sick while the three of you are fine?"

"We're not," Isa murmurs. "But traveling through a portal isn't something new to us, let alone going to a new world. We also don't have demons clawing at our minds the second they realize they're on a planet known for healing. It's natural for you to be sick after first arriving here."

"And you don't have to accept it," Del cuts in. "The full purpose and journey of your soul will soon be revealed to all of us, including yourself. However that's accepted is up to you."

I bite down on my cheek to keep from lashing out again. I'm a sad, brittle piece of shit of a soul, and I know this about myself. My friends made sure I was aware over the years of my inability to control my temper. Even when nowhere near them, I yearn to draw on the strength and compassion they'd typically give me.

"I don't know if I'm a descendant," Daya whispers. Her eyes dart to mine, and I'm physically hit by how gutted she is by this. "I've been referred to as a goddess more times than I can count, and my soul sings when I've been near Eira. I can't be certain that I'm a descendant, though, or what my role will be in what's yet to come."

Thick silence rests on us like a quilt, and no one says anything for a few moments. The wind howls against the glass windows, where I watch the ocean waves grow more restless by the second.

"How will we know our purpose?" I rasp.

"We'll go to J'marie," Del confirms. "The Star and Queen of the Sea. She has the gift of being a *seer* and will guide us along to the next stage."

A harsh laugh spills out of me. "One soul will be able to determine my purpose?"

"She can do more than that," Isa warns. "Mind yourself when we visit her tomorrow. She'll give any spirit a chance and will summon every ounce of magic she possesses for you. The moment she suspects your ill intentions... you'll be crushed into stardust before you can take another breath."

"Sounds like my kind of lady," I say with a smirk. A thought presses down on me, and I cut these three souls a look. "Everything you're telling and showing me—why didn't you tell Eira?"

Daya appears visibly pained. "We couldn't," she mumbles. "We wanted to, but we couldn't take the risk."

"We had to stick to a story of how we ended up in Majikaero if we had any hope of escaping the dreaded plague of darkness and figuring out how to defeat the source of it," Isa adds, her voice drenched in sorrow. "The more souls who know what we're up to, the greater the chance the Sairn will find out through the whispers and the quicker the darkness could spread to another planet. I have no doubt some of them have camouflaged themselves to blend in with the *solliqas*. If Eira knew, and they were to capture and torture her, there's a chance everything we've built will come spilling out. She won't find out the truth of everything until we're positive she's powerful enough to hold her own and has the rest of us to support her. We might as well have been truthful, though. It was a hard lesson to learn, thinking we could trust Eliina when her own mother is leading the hunt for Eira. She wants to be on the Sairn's good side, claiming it's what's best for her people and world. If other *solliqas* knew what we were going through and our plan, perhaps we'd have even stronger alliances in Majikaero."

"It'll be okay," Del whispers to her. He squeezes her hand in comfort. "We have a number of *solliqas* who also desire to find the Queen of Light to rid their world of the plague. If the rest of our team guides her as planned, and she tells the world they need to support her while she fights with her healing light, everyone will do it. I know they will."

Daya sniffles and stands up abruptly. "We should let you rest a while longer," she murmurs. "Don't worry, we can talk more when you wake up again."

"I'll get him some tea to help with the sickness," Isa tells her before walking swiftly out the door that's behind me.

I blink rapidly. My body might be spent, but my brain craves any and all bits of knowledge they'll share with me.

"Wait, I—"

"There'll be time to talk more," Del tells me while resting a hand on my covered shoulder. "You've had quite the voyage. It's best to give your body the rest it's asking for. That's one of the first steps to healing your inner demons, Tryg. We must always listen to what our bodies are trying to communicate to us and follow our breath in the process. When we're connected with the core of who we are, we can more easily dissect the issue that's consuming us."

I nod slowly, trying to make sense of his words.

"I'll go get that tea from Isa," Del continues. "Don't fret, it won't do anything harmful to you. It's meant to be soothing, a tonic we only have the materials for here on Chironant."

He steps over to the far corner, just out of my eyesight, and starts a low fire in a hearth I didn't realize existed.

"Del?" I ask, my eyes starting to droop even without the tea.

"Hm?" he hums. I watch him stand up straight after coaxing the fire a little higher.

"Why'd we come back here if half the world is burned to the ground?" I mumble.

His hazel eyes find mine, tinted with regret. "Chironant was deemed safer than Majikaero now that the Sairn realize Eira is there. It saddens me greatly. That world of souls and *maji* has become our second home. Eira has the protection she needs, though, and if we're going to help her and the others, we need to flee for now. Hopefully that splits some of the Sairn up, since they'll be after any of her supporters, and gives us a chance to regroup."

I blow out a long breath. It unsettles me knowing I left Eira on Majikaero, yet being with Daya, Del, and Isa so far has felt... so *right*.

"Why are the Sairn doing this, truly, Del?" I whisper, on the brink of sleep.

Del's hovering right above me. He gently tucks in the top of the blanket around my arms and shoulders. If I was more awake, I'd be more reactive to this moment of care that I haven't often received in my lifetime.

"Why wouldn't they?" he murmurs softly. "Some souls find the simplicity of existence or improving any dark deeds as dull and repetitious. They wish to rule the worlds differently, and the reason is quite unremarkable. Life can be cruel and unjust. If the gods and goddesses can seize that as an opportunity for control, they will, Tryg. Simply because they can."

TWENTY-SIX
Nyx

Being able to fly doesn't make one free.
Detaching from what you think you want and need does.
-Duncas, God of Air

"Can you hold on to me, sweetheart?" I pant as I hurriedly dash toward Eira. Zaya has her claws sinking into my queen's back, and Athena has one hand on her forearm. Fear winds its way around the black markings on my neck, tightening its hold like a noose. "I know I promised we'd see the streets of Rioa when we first arrived here, but I'll be postponing that yet again, little firefly."

The energy in the library has shifted into a frenzied rush of movements. It's a good thing we spoke of a plan while Athena and Hadwin were communing with Eliina, or we'd be as fucked as the poor *solliqas* stuck outside under the purple fog. There's no time to consider alternative options. We have to pray to the gods that have never listened to me that we made the right decision—especially with the turn of events playing out before my eyes.

Stefanie is barking swift orders at Riker and Esen, who are

scooping up as many materials as they can into already overpacked leather satchels. A few scrolls tumble out of the bulging bags, and Hauke squats to pick them up on his way to grab Stefanie, all in one seamless motion. He throws them at the manipulators and pulls his *almaove* into his chest, murmuring something into her ear that only she can hear. Her face remains focused, yet her eyes betray her true emotions: She's petrified of what's to come. Hauke dips his head down to steal a scorching kiss from her, his purple wings enclosing them in a brief few seconds of privacy.

It rattles me to see their pained goodbye, and I grasp Eira's arm even tighter. She looks stunned, in a catatonic state. I can't let her fear bind around her, freezing that tantalizing fire. Not when she's managed to thaw the parts of me I thought were frozen in shards of ice. Our growing relationship over the past month has changed me from a wallowing soul, seeped in his darkness, back to a fucking prince who won't back down from a challenge, no matter the risks. Eira breathed life back into me the second our eyes met in that dream of a past lifetime. She didn't just raise me from the dead—she showed me her own monster and threw herself into my grave, ready to face the underworld together.

I *refuse* to lose her, to watch as she loses herself in the midst of this chaos. I stoop down, gently prying Zaya's claws off her mother's back. Zaya hisses loudly and latches onto one of my legs instead. I run my hands down Eira's stiff, motionless shoulders, back, and the curve of her ass, urging my shadows to wake each of her muscles up.

"Firefly, can you—"

A monstrous scream curdles the blood roaring in my ears. My shadows snake out of my body in their dagger forms, ready for an onslaught of violence. Before I can even take a step, it's clear what the issue is, and there's nothing I can do to stop it. The *skelter* I thought was dead wraps its headless body around

Eliina's corpse like a blanket. Hauke and Stefanie both lunge to stop it, but a number of *canielors*—the ones Eliina has kept hidden down here—come slinking out from the bookcases in a matter of seconds.

They all have different skins, ranging from leathery to gaping holes in a floating body to oozing unknown liquids, but they all emit the same stench of corruption. They're all *monsters,* and I'm not sure what Eliina thought could be saved in them.

Athena breaks out of the daze she was in and, pushing herself off Eira, leaps out in front of the *canielors*. Her green *maji* glows brightly along her palms and wrists. Hadwin manages to push her down at the last second, sending spurts of her powers along the floor as scattered lightning. She squirms in his arms, tearing part of her pastel-colored robes and screaming to let her fight. He only constricts his body around her, pushing her flat against the ripped rug beneath her.

"Let me go!" Athena yells. "I won't let them take another soul's body."

"She's already gone from this world," Hadwin grunts. My best mate has partially shifted into his python, encasing Athena's thrashing legs. "It makes no difference what they do now. We shouldn't touch any of them. They could be venomous."

"I don't care!" Athena sobs. "You know what she showed us. She doesn't deserve this ending."

Ulf's shadow wolf bolts straight at Hadwin and Athena and grows large enough to clamp his jaw around both of their now stilled bodies. The *canielors* shrink back at the cloud of darkness that rises out of his wolf—for some reason, more afraid of *him*. They, too, were innocent souls who've succumbed to their pain and trauma. From my understanding, Eliina has allowed a number of these harmless *canielors* into the safety of the library in the hope that she or someone else could save them one day. They spend their days lurking in the back shelves, wallowing in their misery. Even if Eliina could sense some kind of light in them, that doesn't mean they won't act like the monsters they've become. They're drawn to the distress in others, eager to taste their sadness.

Ulf growls at the foul creatures, making them back away until they're cowering behind the nearest bookshelf. He sets our companions back down, turning to face the rest of us.

"A corpse is a corpse," he booms. "Nothing more, nothing less. A body is nothing without its soul. Let's move."

Jade swiftly shifts into her crow form and glides close enough to my face, the tips of her silky feathers brush against my cheek. A harrowing sensation squeezes my chest the second we make contact.

Danger. Predator. Terror.

There's that voice again, and it's gone with the next flap of Jade's wing. *Who's voice is that? Does anyone else hear it?*

I sweep my gaze around the room, and no one is moving except for Jade. *Is it about her? No, she's never given me reason to suspect her of treason.* She flies in a fluid motion around Hadwin and Athena before landing on top of Hadwin's shoulder, her green eyes flickering under the purple fog pressing against the library windows. Ulf's wolf snaps his wide jaw around our companions and, without another word, bounds away toward the library door.

"You better keep them safe!" I yell at Ulf's wolf.

He stops suddenly right before the towering, wooden doors, his eyes of endless darkness staring right into my own. He gives a curt nod, his only signal that he heard me, and dives through the closed doors as a mist of shadows. Eira's new marking from her soul connection with Athena blazes a bright white. My queen looks up at me with silver lining her eyes. I can tell she's swallowing a sob now that her best friend is traveling far from here in the maw of Ulf's wolf—a terrifying reality that I'll have to trust is safe.

"I'll come back for Eliina's body," Stefanie tells my now shivering Eira. Her *maji* must be bottoming out. We have to get out of here *now*. "Esen and Riker know where to go with the tomes and scrolls we were able to find. I need to get to the healing quarters to help any *solliqas* trapped out there, okay?"

"No, please—" Eira chokes while Zaya scrambles to burrow herself in her chest. "Don't go out there. I can't lose another friend."

Stefanie's gaze hardens in determination. "We'll see each other again," she insists. "In one way or another, I know we will. The healing quarters have a protection spell on them too, remember? Eliina cast it on both the library and the healing area. Regardless of what she's done recently, she's always prioritized knowledge and mending trauma. I'll be safe there, I promise."

"Don't make promises you can't keep," Hauke bites out from behind her.

Stefanie raises her emerald-green orbs to stare at her closest soul connection. She doesn't look away as she says, "I don't." She leans down to kiss Eira on the cheek. I don't miss the soothing, golden *maji* she sends into her face and then a spark into Zaya, smoothing out her puffy fur. A parting gift meant to ensure Eira survives the oncoming journey. I watch as Stefanie plucks the net containing the purple parasite off the floor and ushers Esen and Riker toward the library's doors. With one last glance back at Hauke, she pushes the doors open enough to slink out into the havoc of Rioa.

Hauke's body morphs into his raptor, his dark feathers vivid under the purple fog. Those swirling eyes of orange and yellow are blazing.

"The rest of us need to scatter," he growls. Turning to me, he asks, "Think you can portal all of us out of here?"

"As soon as we leave the library doors," I grunt in confirmation. The more solliqas that travel with me when I portal, the quicker my *maji* drains. I don't tell him this, though, because as cocky as he can be, I'm not about to leave him and my companions to *gods-only-knows-what* under this purple shit.

Odin holds onto Hauke's giant legs, the whetted tips of his talons scraping against the already torn rugs where we've been gathered. Ivar shifts immediately into a similar raptor, but his feathers are deep blue and black with tips the color of amethyst. He pins Fraya with a no-nonsense look, and she heaves an overwhelming sigh before wrapping her arms around one of his talons. He bends the other few to clutch Fraya's slim body, her thick, blood-stained coverings doing little to hide her near skeletal form.

I shift my attention to Eira and have to swallow the irritation I feel seeing her in Daru's arms. He's muttering something too low for me to hear, worry clearly etched across his face. Zaya jumps off my leg and bounds for Eira. She sits on her stomach, watching Daru closely as he speaks. Gritting my teeth, I force myself to take a breath, so I don't shred his arms apart for holding what's *mine*.

"Daru, I need you to hand Eira over to me. You can fly through the portal in one of your bird forms," I grumble.

His dark green eyes glare at me. The single black marking on his neck pulses in warning.

"No."

Groaning, I take a step toward him. "Yes. We have to go before the purple fog makes its way down to the library doors. *Now*."

Daru doesn't budge a muscle. "I'm going with you. I'll hold Eira as we portal."

"You're supposed to fly in search of Daya and Del!" The vein in my head is throbbing in rhythm with my accelerating breath.

"Change of plans," he snarls. "I'm not letting Eira out of my sight. Agree or I'm not moving with you. I'll find another way out of this lost city."

My blood simmers for a moment, and part of me wonders if

those red flames will make an appearance again. I don't wait to find out if they will. "*Fine*. Now come on!"

Daru cradles Eira closer against his chest as he jumps to his feet, not remotely hindered by carrying my queen and her feline in his arms. My hand goes to my dagger, ensuring I still have it with me, and I stomp ahead of the others. I have yet to use it in combat, but I was taught from a young age how to wield all variations of weapons in case my *maji* was drained to nothing. I'm hesitant to keep this specific dagger, since Eliina was the one to gift it to me long ago, but that gut feeling flares in warning at the mere thought of chucking it somewhere in the library.

The thread connecting Eira and me hums as Daru jogs to walk at my side. No, not a simple thread. We broke that when we bared our fears to one another. There's a whole tidal wave of *maji* that connects us, and it churns in excitement as she appears at my side. Hauke and Ivar flap their wings, hovering off the ground behind me. We quickly approach the doors looming ahead of us. I give half a thought to the tomes Eira has stashed away in one of the other rooms, but we don't have time to stop for them. We'll just have to make do with the text pages I stuffed in Eira's boot and the library of Drageyra—assuming we can arrive there without issue.

I steady my breathing. Ulf found his own way out of Rioa using the warped *maji* of his darkness. Stefanie has the ability to shield herself with healing light, and it's not a far walk to the healing quarters from the Council building. Eliina... Ulf's right. There's nothing to be done about her corpse or the *canielors* now lurking under the expansive windows, right where we were a moment ago. It's now time to flee the city that was always a second home to me, as fucked up as it's been lately. I have to hold on to that hope Eira instilled in me that we'll make it out of here alive, that my darkness won't inhibit my ability to portal *all* of us.

"Okay," I breathe. Nervousness that I don't typically experience works its way through me, forming a solid pit in my stomach. This isn't only about me now. The prospect of one of these *solliqas* becoming stardust under my watch unnerves me—even if it's Daru, the asshole. If he's keeping my *almaove* safe while I form a clear gateway to Drageyra, then I have to do everything in my power to guard him from the fuckery that's about to greet us.

"Ready?" I ask no one in particular.

Ivar presses his beak into my back, a silent reminder that I'm not alone in this. Eira shifts in Daru's arms next to me, her eyes glazed with fatigue, and reaches a hand out to hold mine. Our fingers interlace, and for a fleeting moment in time, it's just her and me against the world. Those silver eyes connect with my heart.

I let it beat once, twice, three times before I squeeze her hand, and I force myself to let go. *She'll be right next to me. Eira will walk with me through the darkness.* Daru's hand latches onto my bicep, the other keeping my firefly securely against him. *She's only weak from that purple parasite and is in a state of shock. That's it. She'll survive, she'll be okay. She has to be.* Zaya purrs loud enough for me to hear, the usually ferocious cat keeping herself small in Eira's arms.

I inhale sharply, and as I push a strangled breath out of my lungs, I use one hand to push the wooden door open. The other is swarming with shadows and calling forth the *maji* that allows me to portal to other regions in Majikaero. We all nearly fall over one another in our hurry to leave the cryptic library and its *canielors* behind us. As soon as my foot lands on the corridor floor, a surge of power rushes through me as a black and red portal opens before us. It swirls violently fast in a small sphere in front of my face, and I feed it more *maji* to grow large enough for us all to step through. It only expands marginally.

"We've got to get to higher ground," I yell. "I can't portal all of us out of here from so far underground."

I don't wait for confirmation from the others. I sprint up the winding corridor, and Daru is keeping speed with me, much to a hissing Zaya's dismay. There's a fluttering of wings that echoes off the chilled, stony walls. I pump my arms, going fast enough that my shadows smother the floating orbs meant to guide us up the narrow passage. Keeping part of my attention on the portal steadily expanding in front of me, I strain my eyes in search of any signs of danger or that purple substance shit.

We round a slight curve, none of us missing a beat. Each of us powers through faster and faster, the fear of the unknown nipping at our heels. *Were we better off waiting things out in the sacred library? What's ahead of us? If we come into contact with the purple fog, will it take us down?* The questions float aimlessly around my mind until we stumble at the end of the hallway. We shift left and then quickly right until we're nearly out in the open of the broken-down entrance of the Council building. A stone from the partially collapsed ceiling cracks in half and falls over the edge. I push Daru and me out of the way as it nearly misses hitting our heads. I can see the purple fog surging up ahead—a living monster—as it rapidly encloses in on us. My *maji* flares to life and the portal whips out of my soul, forming a tunnel of winds through time.

"All of you hold on to me somehow," I growl. "This is going to be choppy."

I take the first step into the portal. Daru half-shifts and latches his fucking sharp talons around my leg, causing me to grimace in mild pain. *Birdbrained fucker.* Zaya leaps onto my shoulders and curls around the back of my neck, effectively becoming a furry scarf.

"Ambra?" Eira croaks from Daru's arms.

My gaze drops to hers, and I shake my head once to the side. "We can't. I trust in her to find us. Don't underestimate creatures like the *drekstri* and *alklen*, sweetheart. There are plenty of others where they came from, and they've survived centuries in this world for a reason. They'll survive this, too."

Eira has a stubborn look in her eyes, ready to argue that we should take the animals with us. We *can't*, and I have to hope they won't die.

Ivar bites down just hard enough on my other arm to tell me his beak is connected firmly to my body. I'm only waiting for Hauke. I can't leave with the others until he's holding on—it's too dangerous. There's a high chance that he could get lost in the portal or land somewhere unfortunate in our world. *What the fuck is he doing?!*

"Hauke!" I bark over my shoulder. "Let's go!"

I catch a dark movement in the corner of my eye. Tilting my head as much to the side as I can, I frantically search for where Hauke went off to. He has Odin, and I refuse to leave without Erika's brother. I *know* she's alive out there, and I won't give up on the soul who might as well be my little sister. There's no way I'm leaving my soul sister's brother, and soul brother by extension, out on death's doorstep. Ivar loosens his grasp on me at the same time I see where Hauke has gone.

Stefanie is lying in a pool of blood and purple sludge on the now tinted white grass beside the healing quarters. Her eyes are flared wide open while her chest pants in jagged movements, telling me she's barely hanging on by a thread. The net with the purple parasite squirms under her hand, where she's putting the last of her strength to keep it contained. Stefanie's dark red tresses fan out behind her like a halo. She's the very image of an angel perishing in the shadows of the enemy, a fading light we didn't realize was our beacon in the storm.

Not her.

Daru shifts next to me with my *almaove* struggling to break free. She's picking up on what's happening, which tells me she feels it, too—we *can't* lose Stefanie.

The warrior in me locks down all my senses as I take in the

different scenes before me. I'm guessing we have one minute, at most, to jump into my portal and get the fuck out of here.

That's sixty seconds, and we can't waste any of it.

"Hauke, we have sixty seconds!" I scream, my voice carrying from the smashed in entryway down the small hill to where he stands over Stefanie's body, half a minute from the healing quarters' front doors. Riker dashes out with a blinding speed, his shadows writhing above him as the fog starts to settle just inches above his head. Odin rolls out from Hauke's talons, his eyes coming to life for the first time in days. He sends a spurt of water at Stefanie's failing body, encasing her in liquid protection. Hauke tries to send healing *maji* into her body, but each time it gets close, the parasite leeches through part of the net to consume it instead. Eira kicks her legs out in an attempt to escape, as weak as she is, while Daru sends a gust of wind at the fog creeping in on us.

45 seconds.

Hauke looks around at us wildly. I can see it in his eyes that he's both distraught and doesn't know what can be done for his *almaove* before him. Riker yells something at him and doesn't hesitate before scooping Stefanie up in his arms. Odin sprints directly toward me, accepting there's nothing that can be done in this city right now and is ready to follow wherever my portal takes us. Ivar frantically beats his wings, causing a cyclone of wind to keep the fog at bay, only for it to push back even harder against his *maji*. He yells out in pain, and I reach out with one of my hands to steady his shoulder as he falls into me. *Fuck.* Daru curls one arm around Eira's flailing form, screaming at her to be calm, and uses his other arm to wrap around Ivar's feathery neck. I've never felt so helpless. I can't move without this portal diminishing, and no matter what happens with the *solliqas* around us, I will not leave Eira here under any circumstance.

30 seconds.

Riker stumbles back toward the healing quarters' barely

open doorway with the trapped parasite in his shadowy hand, while Hauke starts to run back up toward me. The grip of his fist is tight enough to crush stone. Silent tears roll down his bronze face. Those orange and yellow eyes speak of unbearable agony as he leaves his strongest soul connection behind, not knowing if she'll live or die. We all know what'll likely happen, even if we don't want to accept it yet. Daru sets Eira down on her knees, and she crawls until she's wrapped around my leg. Her silvery eyes are flashing bursts of ruby red, a clear signal that her soul is distressed. My queen's *maji* is too weak for her to do anything other than hold on, and it breaks my heart that there's nothing else I can do about it. Not with such little time. Daru lunges to get a better hold on Ivar's bird form, which results in Ivar opening all his talons as his body becomes fully unconscious. Fraya rolls out onto the withered grass. Hauke goes to pick her up, but she dodges his hands at the last second, leaving him to stumble forward into my side.

We both gape at where Fraya is heading. Riker's shadows are grappling with the heavy fog. He's unable to fight the toxic substance *and* carry Stefanie's unconscious body and the purple parasite inside.

15 seconds.

Fraya pushes Riker fully into the doorway. It doesn't take much considering his attention is divided. A few healers open the large door made of stone and drag both Riker and Stefanie inside. He calls out to Fraya, but it's no use. She saw that he wouldn't make it in time, and of all the fucking *solliqas*, she risked her life to make sure Stefanie even has a chance at surviving. Fraya peers back at me. Odin, Hauke, Ivar, Eira, and Daru are all gripping different parts of my body. My portal swirls fast enough to blow my hair behind me, a few strands falling in front of my face. Fraya's hazel eyes, typically overwhelmed with darkness or fragments of every nearby soul's emotions, erupt in dazzling white and gold flames. She smiles. It's a blithe smile, the kind associated with sheer relief. Her cropped dark hair dances out of her face and all that inner beauty shines brightly.

0 seconds.

Fraya parts her lips to speak one last time, but nothing comes out. The purple fog crashes into her still wounded body with the force of a wave. Tears I didn't realize I'd have after all her vile actions stream down my face. She desired me to the point of obsession and took what she could from my beast without my permission. I didn't know her empathetic and brave soul would persevere in the end, that any of the healing sessions she's gone through recently held any merit. Fraya meant what she said about wanting to support Eira, to keep our Queen of Light safe. *How could a soul so corrupted by the plague also hold such softness, such selflessness?* The last view I have before the portal envelopes us in its darkness is Fraya's soul drifting out of her body in the form of stardust, only for the filthy, oozing hand of a *canielor* to smother it.

The rest of us are swallowed up by the portal and depart from Rioa. We leave Stefanie's fate in the hands of the healers and know beyond a doubt, Fraya's sacrifice might not matter. Trial after trial with the plague of darkness, starting from the moment her own father laid his sordid hands on her young body, has not resulted in restful days or peacefulness or for her soul to start anew.

No. Her soul is *never* coming back to us. The plague buried beneath the healers' light was her ruin, as it might be for us all.

TWENTY-SEVEN
Hauke

Clipped feathers are nothing compared to a clipped heart.
-Correspondence from Jade, Prince Nyx's Lead Council

I thought I knew how easily something so fragile could shatter into thousands of pieces. It just didn't occur to me that it'd happen to *me*.

When it comes to Stefanie—my beautiful, selfless, precious love—how was I to know that all she'd have to do is let go of my heart? Of the way our *maji* intertwines with one another in our souls? And it'd be me falling to the ground in too many pieces to possibly pick up.

I didn't get to tell her the truth of where I am from.

I didn't get to tell her how much I love her one more time.

I didn't get to stay long enough to confirm whether the pulse of her soul was too weak to survive.

Who... the... FUCK... sent this carnivorous purple fog into Majikaero?

Why?

Why stab their dagger into my broken heart?

Why slash down as pure a soul as Stefanie's when there are plenty of fucked-up *solliqas* here, willing to die in her place?

I'm fucking willing to take her place. I want to scream this to the gods and goddesses, but why should I bother? What else has the kind of power to spread a mist or fog or oozing, destructive liquid into a world? There's no way they'll listen, not if Stefanie is right and they're connected to this.

I want to find each Council member and bring them to their fucking knees. But is there a point? What if Daru's right? Are there even actual members anymore, or are there a bunch of *canielors* sitting in their places in plain sight?

Oh, Stefanie.

My poor, poor Stefanie.

All she has done is serve, serve, fucking serve this world.

What did she figure out that the gods and goddesses, the fucking Council members, and the gods damn enemy didn't want her to share with the world?

A tear trails down my cheek as Nyx's shadowed portal starts to close around us. I hesitantly touch the path it makes down to my chin. Angrily wiping it away, I snarl and form a tiny ball of my *maji* in the palm of my hand.

I have to get a message to the others that this world is no longer safe for us. They need to leave, if they haven't already, and find us help from somewhere else.

There's no fucking hope here. And we can't count on the gods and goddesses, let alone our own leaders, to protect us. I form the ball of *maji* into the shape of a tiny bird and send it hurtling through the last small opening in the portal and into this realm's wind until it reaches its intended receiver.

Del and the others need to escape... *again*.

I yearn to go with them, but I can't leave until I can confirm if my connection with Stefanie breaks or not. She's the only reason I'll stay. I know she believes in Eira, our Queen of Light, and thinks the healers can find a solution, a way to fight back against this plague of darkness.

But are we too late?

Will it matter if I can't live in a world with my Stefanie, my strongest soul connection?

TWENTY-EIGHT
Athena

*Our souls are more than mere
threads connecting to one another.
We're all steps in the dance of starlight.
-Dilay, God of Solar*

All I know is that right now, I'd kill for some espresso or enough pain meds to knock me out for days. One or the other. Either wake me the hell up or send me to the land of dreams because this *hazy-unable-to-fully-function* shit is not cutting it. I know I'm not the only one. My heavy eyelids open just enough to peer at Hadwin, who's curled up on his side across from me. He's staring at me with the same drowsy expression, his eyes glazed with the elongated pupils of his python. Jade is still latched onto his shoulder blade with ruffled, black and gold feathers. Of course, *she's* on high alert, since she didn't use up most of her *maji* to travel through the earth and communicate with Eliina. I'd be crouched and ready for trouble if my soul wasn't so drained.

Looking beyond Jade's twitchy head, a gap momentarily

opens in Ulf's jagged teeth, giving me a front and center view of the horrors outside of his shadows.

His wolf manages to lunge and deflect each *canielor* with precision while a purple haze rains down in the background, completely hiding the city of Rioa in a cloud of murderous fog. One of the *canielors* jumps up onto Ulf's snout. Its deformed body is divided into two. The front half is a swirling, chaotic bundle of tendons in different colors, the face matching this design with a strained, too-wide smile. This one actually has eyes, unlike the other *canielors* I've seen, and they're flashing with sickening levels of glee. In my next breath, its face swivels to the back of its body, now giving me a good look at its other side. This is held together by tendons of black and gray with a mouth turned down in a perpetual frown. Its eyes are black pits with silver tears rolling down its knotted face. Any embers left of my healing *maji* flicker with recognition. I'm painfully aware that this monster now gripping onto Ulf's black gum is a soul overwhelmed by what some of my patients endured back on Earth: bipolar disorder. Its heavy presence drains my powers a bit more, and fortunately, Ulf's wolf snaps his teeth and the *canielor* drops down below in pieces.

If anything is keeping me awake somehow, it's the fact that I'm honestly lying in this wolf's fucking jaws. I didn't even think shadows *could* hold something tangible, yet here I am—stuck in the mouth of death itself, praying that he doesn't have a taste for a soul with earth magic.

"Stop worrying," Hadwin grumbles. My eyes snap back to his, and I move a shaky hand in his direction. He's only a few inches away from me. I can't tell if I'm going to flick his nose with my sharp nails or grab his top gray covering and pull him closer.

"Easy for you to say," I croak.

"You think you're the only one who spent almost all of their *maji*?" he asks with a raised eyebrow. *Argh, put that eyebrow back down, you infuriating male.*

My fingers curl around his serpent pendant that's dangling down his chest. I make the mistake of brushing against his toned pecs, not at all hidden by the dark covering he's wearing. A shock of warmth travels up my arm at the brief contact, but I refuse to acknowledge it. I'm too damn exhausted to give this connection between us another thought. I instead focus all my attention on the way the golden serpent swirls, as if it's a living creature tied down to a piece of jewelry he wears. It has specs of dark green woven through its scales that's similar to the color of my powers. Well, *our* powers. There's no point in asking Hadwin about this pendant. He barely answers me on a normal day, let alone when we're magically spent and at the mercy of Ulf, of all *solliqas*.

Hadwin hums, the sound traveling through his body into the pendant, making me want to shift closer in his direction. *Damn him.*

"It was a gift," he rasps.

I risk looking back into his eyes and am surprised to see no mask set in place. My eyes must reflect his own weary expression, especially when Ulf's wolf jerks to the side and causes the three of us to jumble around. Jade caws and shakes out her feathers in the process.

"My aunt gave it to me as a small child," Hadwin continues, taking me by surprise. "She claimed it was passed down through the different *solliqas* in my family, given to them by one of the High Gods himself. She told me it was never meant for the others, no matter how badly they wanted to claim it. This pendant was passed down until it arrived to the chosen soul and glowed brightly on its wearer, finally being called home."

I lick my parched lips, not missing the way his gaze homes in on the movement. "Chosen soul for what?"

He stares at my lips a moment longer. Raising those golden

orbs, I can feel the power of his python just under the surface. "I'm supposed to—"

BANG.

A scream tumbles out of me as Ulf's wolf dives to the ground. My body rolls into Hadwin's, and Jade frantically flutters between us and the roof of the wolf's mouth. Darkness still ripples around us and Ulf's shadows keep us contained in his jaw, but there's a splinter of pain that racks throughout his body. It trembles all the way to us, making me gasp as it causes Ulf's wolf to come to a full stop.

No matter how sapped he is, Hadwin flings his body toward me and angles his torso in such a way to keep me covered. From what, I can't be sure.

"What are you doing?" I pant.

"Ulf doesn't stop in the face of danger," Hadwin murmurs. His eyes are flared wide in alarm. "He *is* the danger. I won't leave you exposed to what's out there."

"Yet you have no trouble leaving me," Jade clucks from in front of us.

He scowls. "*You* don't need protection."

"And I do?" I scoff. His mouth is barely an inch from my own.

"Of course you do," he whispers. It's so quiet, I don't even think Jade can hear it. "You're a healer. You'll always need a protector to keep your soft heart safe."

My breathing hitches. "Just any protector?"

Hadwin growls, the mask he usually wears still nowhere to be seen.

"No. You need *me*."

My heart flips in endless circles at his statement. His eyes glow a fraction brighter and are nearly throbbing as hard as my heartbeat, as my core. They're begging me to see something, but I can't see through my own mask I've put in place.

"It doesn't seem like it," I breathe into his mouth.

"It's often easier to live in the darkness than to accept what's buried beneath it," he breathes back.

"Funny," I hum. "I've always thought it easier to live with a mask than to accept what's buried beneath the light."

"That, too," he growls. Jade bristles behind him, but her words fall on deaf ears as his voice takes up my entire awareness. "If we keep what's buried a secret, *zamia,* the others won't see how much we struggle, how deeply we wish to end it all."

"*Zamia?*"

"The whole word is *zamiaten,*" Hadwin whispers, his lips brushing against mine as he speaks. "It means the holder of my heart, my mind, and my soul."

Hadwin pushes his mouth against mine, and I forget every reason I've been upset with him. Our lips twist and mold to one another, and my tongue greedily reaches out in an invitation. Each second our lips touch sets my soul aflame and has remnants of my drained earth *maji* rising to the surface. Hadwin encases us in a swarm of shadows, effectively blocking everything else out that's not the crackling sexual tension I've been drowning in. He reaches a hand along my neck, squeezing his lithe fingers until the pressure borders on pain and has me whining for more. One of my hands snakes along his exposed bronze pecs while the other travels south to where his pants cinch—to where he keeps the goods. Hadwin grunts when I wrap my hand around his balls, giving a gentle tug. His golden eyes shine brighter, and a shiver of excitement winds down my spine at the clear hunger on his face.

Hadwin moans into my mouth, the sound traveling straight to my core, and deepens the kiss until my back arches and my toes curl against the wolf's tongue.

Wolf's tongue. Oh, gods. NO.

Hadwin pushes off me the same moment I jump back in disgust at where we're sharing our first kiss. What are we doing inside what's basically *Ulf's body*? Bile surges up my throat that *this* is where our magical moment happens. As if on cue, Ulf's body shudders, and not a second later, the three of us are tumbling out onto a blackened patch of grass.

"If you're both awake enough to do all of that, then I'll be taking those memories from you right now," Jade snaps at us.

I don't respond. I can't. I'm lying on what might be Hell's ground, all shards of stone and dead turf, with my pastel-colored robe flattened out around me. My hair is bunched up in a long braid tucked into the hood of my robe, and I'm breathing hard. I hesitantly touch my lips with a finger, still soaking in the electric way Hadwin kissed me. He's on his hands and knees right next to me, matching each of my breaths. The way his eyes remain wide and focused on my lips tells me he's thinking the same exact thing.

We just did that. In the most revolting of places. And fuck, I don't know why he was fighting so hard against our connection. I want *more.*

"At least some of my team kept up with us," Jade mutters. Sure enough, a few smaller crows soar above us in the gray fog and then dive to where we're splayed next to Ulf's smoking wolf, looking and feeling like roadkill. They land across from Jade and stare intensely into her eyes, their purple irises shining bright against the dreary environment, obviously communicating in a way none of us can hear.

Hadwin blinks quickly and tears his focus away from me. He groans as he stretches out his arms and pushes himself up to his feet. Patches of his loose, gray coverings are torn from our landing, but from what I can see, the wide bandages around his torso are still glued to his body. Turning in half a circle, he marches up to Ulf's wolf, unfazed by its gruesome face or the various stains of blood coating its shadowed form.

"What the fuck happened?" Hadwin grumbles. Grimacing, he brings a hand up to cover his heart and rubs small circles over the area.

Ulf's wolf glares down at Hadwin and, in a blink, shifts back into Ulf. I'm almost surprised to see him looking haggard. He coughs a few times with his hands on his knees, spurts of shadows coming out of his mouth, and he wipes his mouth with the back of his scarred hand. I first thought Nyx had the most black veins from the plague, but Ulf has him beat. The black markings coat him like a second skin, a fact that can't be hidden by all the black coverings he wears. His eyes are the color of night, and they look... crestfallen? *He's showing emotions?*

That's unnerving.

"Did you feel it snap, too?" he asks Hadwin, his voice all gravel.

Hadwin swallows once and nods his head. I can tell he's trying to stuff down a bigger reaction, but he's not fooling anyone. Jade, her two crows, and I are all staring at these two ornery souls, our gazes flicking back and forth between their rigid stances.

"Fucking Cudhellen," Ulf growls. He shoves a hand through his dark, shoulder-length hair and kicks one of the tiny, sharpened stones across the dead grass. His eyes sweep over to us before he barks a laugh. "It's only us who'd know."

"That's right," Hadwin murmurs. "We're the only ones here who were apparently connected to them."

Ulf laughs again, the sound harsh. "Guess that confirms some of our soul bonds. I didn't think us darkened fucks would get to have them."

Hadwin's eyes immediately find me. "We do. Another one of fate's games, I think."

"What's going on?" Jade demands. "There's no point keeping secrets right now."

"Says the *solliqa* who only speaks with her crows telepathically," Ulf growls.

Jade glares daggers at him, but Hadwin interrupts their brewing argument.

"We lost one of our own," Hadwin rasps.

My eyebrows furrow. "One of your own? As in, one of the *solliqas* in your group? Ivar?"

He shakes his head. "It wasn't him."

"We lost Fraya," Ulf adds. "She's gone from this world."

I can't help the emotion that pinches my heart. I've only known her for the weeks that I've been here, but time moves differently in Majikaero. Each day goes on like months here. Perhaps it's because part of me is still set on the way time works on Earth, and gods, it's *exhausting*. It doesn't feel as if I just met Fraya and the others, though. While I thought her suspicious when I first arrived, with her all-consuming obsession with Nyx, she's grown on me. How could she not when, at the core of her soul, she's empathetic and endearing?

In another timeline, she was meant to be a healer—just like me. If she was tied to Ulf, Hadwin, and the others in their group, and Ulf is mentioning a soul bond, then their connection ran deeper than convenience or through shared trauma. *They were all soul mates in some way.*

"I'm so sorry," I mumble. "Do you... do you know how?"

Ulf shakes his head. "We're not *seers*. There's no way to know the specifics right now. Knowing her, though, she probably did something fucking stupid. Wanting to protect Nyx or Eira or some shit."

I close my eyes to hide my emotions. Nothing about that kind of death is *stupid*. It's self-sacrificing, a trait so many healers have. I was right about thinking Eira is a blazing sun and those surrounding her will get burned eventually. My poor best friend. She wouldn't want this to happen, but when she's as bright as fire itself, there's no way it can't. Fraya is only the first companion to be killed. We're all going to die at some point. Guilt sluices its way through me when I consider how relieved I am that it wasn't Stefanie or my best friend. There's no doubt I would travel to the afterlife with Eira. If it was Stefanie, I'm not sure there'd be enough time to pick up the pieces of my heart—not when she's shown me such grace and love as a healer already. Having her by Eira's and my side is too right to have her taken from us.

At least Fraya is out of her misery now. There were such tragic, uncontrollable waves of pain always coming off her. She'd go from fiery in one moment to fatigued and broken in the next. Whatever she's experienced and has felt from other *solliqas* certainly weighed heavily on her heart. Her soul was always attacking itself, and she couldn't escape the cycle. Now, she's been set free. *I hope she's found peace.*

I'm still depleted of energy, but I find the healer part of me surging forward.

"What do you both need right now?" I ask Ulf and Hadwin.

Ulf stares at me, as if he's trying to solve a puzzle. *Good luck, buddy, I lost most of the pieces years ago.* Hadwin has part of his mask back up, wanting to hide his pain, yet another part of him is begging to be held.

"We don't have time for what they need," Jade sighs.

I cut her a glare, and she scoffs. "I'm sorry, but we don't. Ulf, where the fuck did you land us? Is it safe?"

"It's safe enough," he grunts. "We're on the cusp of the veil between Majikaero and Earth."

"All the way down to Sayfters, where we're supposed to go?"

"Yeah," Ulf grumbles. "I said I could do it. Still don't know why I had to drag your feckless asses with me."

"Feckless?!" I ask, glaring at him incredulously. "I've taken plenty of initiative since being here. I'm the one who busied myself with ways to connect to our friends still stuck on Earth."

He snorts. "Sure, but you didn't help with getting us out of Rioa through that maze of *canielors*."

"You backward, pig-headed—"

"How *did* you get us out of there so quickly?" Hadwin interrupts. He swings his gaze back to Ulf and crosses his arms over his chest. I try not to ogle his lean muscles but fail miserably.

"You know how," Ulf barks.

"Yeah? The rest of us don't," Jade mutters.

He sighs. Deeply. "I can't use this power often because of the plague weighing my *maji* down, but I traveled through the veil itself with my shadows. By doing that, I was able to weave through the timeline in a matter of hours instead of days."

"I don't understand," I groan.

"I wouldn't expect you to," Ulf quips. I instinctively push myself off the ground and start stomping my tired ass over to him.

"Alright, enough," Hadwin says and steps in between us. I don't miss the way he angles his body into mine or how one of his fingers latches to one of my own. "So, we're here. Where exactly are we in the veil of time?"

A vein in Ulf's jaw ticks a few times, and he doesn't respond.

"Oh, so it's a surprise?" I huff. If I thought Hadwin made me irritable, Ulf takes it to a whole new level. "Anywhere we can sleep around here? All I can see is thick fog and dried up grass with sharp rocks. I'm bone-tired and need to rest."

"We all do," Jade snaps.

Hadwin fixes his python eyes on Ulf. There must be an underlying threat in there somewhere because Ulf finally sighs and tugs on his hair again.

"My wolf took us to a place near Earth. We're in the future by a good four years here."

My heart seizes. *No.* Hadwin and I glance at each other, and I swear he can taste my panic. I told him I couldn't go back to my homeworld with the state it was in, and I meant it. Memories of what Eira shared with me flow right through me. She'd said Tryg shoved the most awful images into her mind in the dungeon. She spoke of bones and fires, of our friends bound together with corpses, of squirming children and humans forced into underground tunnels. I blink tears away and shake out my head and shoulders, forcing my breathing into slow, shaky breaths. I can't panic right now. There'd be no point.

Hadwin surprises me by fully grabbing my hand. I think the panic stops more so because I can't believe he's intertwining his fingers with my own, that he would even know what that gesture is. Yeah, he kissed me before, but a kiss is one thing, and a romantic gesture that's meant to keep my heart safe is another. I gnaw on my bottom lip while watching his thumb trace an unknown pattern on the back of my hand. The black veins along his wrist almost match the black floral tattoos on mine. *So fucking poetic.*

"We don't know that he brought us to the same spot," Hadwin murmurs to me. "Let's see where he brought us first."

Jade flutters in between us and looks up at me. For a split second, I see a kind soul peering up from the gravel. *This is the one who is loyal to Nyx.* She then snaps her beak up at Hadwin and makes a guttural sound at the two smaller crows nearby.

"Let's go see, then," she orders.

Ulf glances at us and he... *shit,* is he *nervous*?

"What don't you want us to see?" Hadwin asks.

"My wolf has attached himself to a certain human on Earth," he grumbles. "She's a thing of beauty and from what I could see in my dreams, she's in an underground city."

Hadwin tightens his grip on my hand. I scream internally.

"Okay?" Jade prompts.

"My wolf is just protective of the female," Ulf continues. "Nothing more, nothing less. He's a lovestruck beast. While I think it's pathetic, I'm unsure how it'll impact what we do here. He's already restless."

Hadwin hums. "We'll cross that road when we see her. Let's at least get somewhere out of this veil. It's disturbing here, even for me."

"Right," Ulf sighs. He steps forward and holds out his blackened arms. "Each of you hold on to me, then."

Jade and the other crows fly up to his shoulders. Hadwin grasps one meaty hand, and I hesitantly place mine in the other. It's disconcerting how Ulf's palm is the size of my whole hand.

"Time to take you to meet someone you might be familiar with," he mutters, glancing at me. "She has waves of golden-red hair, a mouth that always has something to say, and a heart that's been shredded beyond repair. My wolf *adores* her. He has met her often in our dreams, and the lovesick pup has found ways to travel to her world, always listening in on her conversations. He's heard her mention your and Eira's names, even in passing, when she speaks to one of her companions. You might know her by the name Astira?"

My eyes fly wide open, and a wild squeal escapes me. If this was any other situation, I'd cackle at how distressed Ulf and Hadwin look at my reaction. I squeeze both of their hands as hard as I can, silently urging Ulf to travel through the veil. *Now.*

His shadows snake up from his feet and travel around the rest of us in thick puffs of smoke. They're cool to the touch and almost relaxing, although that could be some of my tension loosening up at the very thought of seeing Astira. *My friend, I'm coming for you.*

I can't see what's happening outside of the shadows, and the sensation of movement is so subtle, I wouldn't notice if I wasn't paying attention. We're inside the veil between our two worlds and then we're breathing in the scent of soil. Ulf cocks his head to the side, but I can't hear what he's listening to. All I can see is him pushing us flat against a surface, a wall of some sort, and he mutters a few unintelligible words to himself. His shadows turn impossibly darker and press against us, reminding me of a thin shield.

"Don't move," he breathes. "They'll be able to see us here. Just stay right where you are, and my shadows will keep us camouflaged. The second you move, Athena, we'll be vulnerable."

"Why are you only addressing *me*?" I whisper back.

"Because if that high-pitched noise that left your mouth is anything to go by, you'll have zero self-restraint the moment you see your friend."

I scoff and choose to ignore him.

"Okay, I'm thinning the shadows so that we can see where we're at now," Ulf mutters.

All the breath funnels out of me. Hadwin is still holding my hand and squeezes hard enough to cut off any circulation. I'm not sure I feel it. *No, how can I?* Not with the spine-chilling scene before me.

I don't know what I was expecting. I'll admit a sliver of me was hoping to dart out and throw myself around Astira's body. Another slice of me thought we'd watch her go about her normal day from the shadows, and Ulf's wolf would share how we can communicate with her. Zero part of me thought I'd see not one, not two, but *three* of my friends shuffling down a curved staircase that leads even deeper into the earth. My brain is barely comprehending that there are other humans walking around in the distance, as if existing in a city of steel far below the earth's surface is *normal*. The earth *maji* that's been drained sighs in contentment that we're surrounded by colossal walls made from dirt, but the rest of my soul is crying out in alarm. Something isn't right down here, and I have a terrible feeling we're all about to find out why.

"Do you know the others?" Hadwin breathes next to me.

"Two of them," I whisper.

Jace, as charming as ever with his laid-back walk and those blond waves pulled half up in a knot. He's wearing dark clothes with a blue armband. His smile immediately sets a handful of other people walking up the stairs at ease, which is so normal for him. *So Jace.* I want to fall under that same spell as our friends always have around him, but a knot forms in my stomach when I watch him pause on one stair. He doesn't turn or say anything to our two friends following behind him. It's the way he tilts his head to the side, though, that makes me uneasy. His ear is turned in the direction we're standing. I don't let go of the breath I'm holding until he rolls back his shoulders and continues down the curved pathway of the stairs. Hadwin rubs my hand with his fingers, a silent indicator that he saw that, too.

I watch as Jace mutters something to another male worker before turning back to say something to Astira... and *Liv. Gods, my heart is going to burst*. I don't get any inkling of foreboding with these two. Every muscle in my being is strained, aching to spring toward them. I want to get a closer look at Astira's curvier form and the simple cotton clothes that she's wearing. Her dark red hair is in a simple braid, but maybe I could weave a new style for her. My fingers want to play with the ends of Liv's cropped hair and see what we can do about dying it again. Maybe tease her for choosing all black clothes instead of something lighter. I'm absolutely *dying* to ask where Lyk and Ruse are and why they're not all together. And where's Morgan? Any of our family members we still manage to talk to? *Why are they all underground and what's happened?*

I'm practically buzzing with anticipation. The room we're in is dark with minimal lighting. There are no colors or furniture or plants or families. It appears to be one immense pit in the ground that has a trail of stairs winding down in a circular pattern. *It's a spiral, just like Hadwin's pendant.* Jace is guiding Astira and Liv further underground, and my senses go haywire.

"Ulf," I whisper.

He grunts. *Typical.* "We need to follow them."

"You want to get caught?" he asks.

"No, I have a sinking feeling. Something isn't right. We *need* to get down there," I insist.

I can see Ulf scowling, even in the shadows. "It'll be tricky. I can't determine if we'll land where you're hoping. I don't have as much control over my *maji* down here and outside of the veil and Majikaero."

"Have your wolf follow Astira. Or don't. I don't care."

"Don't be a brat," Hadwin snarks.

I glare holes into the side of Ulf's head until he gives in. "Fine. Don't say I didn't warn you."

His shadows slink in around us, forming an even tighter barrier, while additional darkness blooms against the wall of dirt. The earth shifts under my feet. I'm left dangling midair for a few seconds before we plunge through the soil and into a space large enough to be a stadium. *Fuck, this is why I hate being up high and in the air.* My brain and stomach are still catching up with one another as my eyes sweep across the vastness of where we're standing. An unexpected green glow coats my wrists, startling a gasp from me. Hadwin's body is glowing, too, and we look at each other, the sound of a siren going off in my head. I'm not quite feeling well enough to use any powers, but it's more like my *maji* is trying to warn me of impending danger. Glancing over at Ulf and the crows, I see he's crouched in a defensive stance and Jade is flaring with light gold light along her wings.

"Where are your other crows?" I ask, trying to keep my voice low.

"Look around you," Ulf growls. "I think we're in a more concerning situation than where two fucking birds flew off to."

The knot in my stomach flattens out and empties into its own pit. As my eyes adjust more to the dimness down here, I have to fight the urge to vomit. We're standing on the outskirts of piles upon piles of human bones. Some of them still have decaying flesh suctioned to their surface. Gagging, I pull on Hadwin's arm and point a little farther ahead of us toward the center of the area. A few men are huddled, muttering together as they walk next to a second stairway, wearing the same simple clothes I saw on my friends. They have the same blue armbands that I noticed on Jace. Luck might be on our side because none of them notice us standing against the dirt wall. As they slowly, unknowingly approach our space, my heart starts to hammer.

"We have the next one ready," one of the men says way too loudly. *They must think they're all alone.*

"Is it fresh?" the second man asks.

The first man scoffs. "Of course. I doubt Risha would accept it otherwise. Only the younglings with the thicker blood will do."

My face pales. *Where the fuck is Jace taking Astira and Liv?*

A few robed figures approach these men, seemingly appearing out of thin air. Their robes are woven with a darker material, and I can barely make out the colors that they're wearing. One of them lights a candle, the flickering flame only drawing my attention to the darkness lurking under their hood, while the other hums quietly. It's soothing in a way that's too familiar. The hairs on my neck stand up, and I subconsciously lean closer into Hadwin's side. I can't be sure if this new mood of his is a permanent change, and I'll take whatever affection he's willing to give.

Hadwin must sense my apprehension. "You can stay close to me," he breathes.

"Why now?" I whisper, earning an elbow to my ribs from Ulf.

"When we were all in death's clutches, it clicked I could lose you. Sometimes that's what it takes for a soul to realize what they can't live without, to accept they might deserve love."

I swallow down the snarky reply I instinctively want to dish out. It shouldn't take death to bring life to a relationship. Yet the way Hadwin tilts his mouth into the side of my head in a silent kiss has some of my bitterness melting away.

Seconds later, I freeze Hadwin out of my thoughts as another robed figure shuffles out at a steady pace. Their movements are labored, and as they approach the others, it becomes clear they're dragging an object along the dirty ground. A broken whimper echoes against these walls, and it takes every power inside me to keep my mouth clamped shut. *No, these people are absolutely not dragging a child like a sack of ruined meat.* As the third figure steps closer and closer, my body breaks out into a cold sweat. This child is very much *alive*, and for reasons I don't understand, that makes this situation even worse to me. They're squirming—a panicking caught fish, still breathing and desperate to be released back to its home.

"P-please," the child sniffles. "Le-et me go-o."

The robed figure who's humming stops abruptly. They take small steps until they're standing in front of this poor child, who's being held up by corded rope. The other figure with the candle sways closer, bringing the light down to the child's face. Their hair has been shaved down to a light layer of fuzz along their small scalp. Round eyes peer up at whoever these adults are, frightened yet tainted enough to know better than to speak out against this person. Their bottom lip quivers and gives away how horror-stricken they are. The first robed figure starts to hum again, and this time they grip the child's chin and turn their face from side to side. Not a moment later, the child's frail body is tossed to the ground in a heap, as if tarnished goods. I grind my teeth together to keep from sprinting out there.

The humming robed figure bends down to where the child is lying. New dirt covers their unwashed body. "There's no need to fear," the figure rasps. "It'll be over before you know it. Then you'll be in a realm called Majikaero, where you won't remember a single second of this."

Every muscle in my body tenses. I *know* that voice.

"Why?" the child cries.

"Because humans have already corrupted Earth beyond repair," they say easily, as if speaking in a classroom. "We're just ensuring that humanity can't encroach on other worlds, that they can't continue to live."

A fourth robed figure carries a large sack out to this repulsive grouping. Their hood falls off as they dump something out of the cloth bag. *Gods*. Hadwin, Ulf, and Jade all jerk uncontrollably at the sight of the fucking *solliqa* in front of us. Even I'm taken aback, and I barely know the guy.

"Namid," Hadwin whispers next to me. At some point, his arm trailed around my back until his hand is now snugly against my hip, keeping me pulled close into his side.

"Fuck," Ulf grunts. Jade clacks her beak at him in warning to stay quiet, but even she can't hide the distress in her green eyes.

"Hold him down," the leader, I'm presuming, commands.

"Yes, Risha," the other three obediently respond.

Risha? Who the fuck is that?

We all watch in dread as the robed figure holding the candle places it on the ground before putting all their weight onto the child's arms. The other one who dragged the child in here places their hands on each of the child's tiny legs and applies pressure. Namid, one of the prodigious Council members, turns to face them all. *Fuck, I knew he was sketchy, but harming a child? Really?* My jaw drops as I watch Namid use his *maji* to funnel the spirit—or essence or lost soul or whatever the fuck these psychos want to call it—from a damn *canielor* into the child's body. A cracked scream pierces my ears, and for a single breath, I'm grateful for it, so I can let a sob break free from my chest. This is *wrong*. Another wail of torment surges over us, and I'm clutching Hadwin's torso with a death grip—I'm barely holding on, being forced to remain silent in the shadows.

I sniffle as the child's soul drifts up above their body in particles of gold dust. One of the robed figures—perhaps they should be called demons, if I'm being honest with myself—collects the soul in a small jar and pockets it.

"We'll send this back to Drageyra to create the next *canielor*," Namid murmurs to Risha. "This little one suffered significantly for being so young. They were a victim of their mother's hands, quite a lot of abuse, and should be formed into that type of creature back home. I'll get the—"

Namid pauses. A stocky man in black and white clothes jogs out from a second hidden stairway. *Was it there before?* He pants after sprinting over here and places an arm on the leader of these robed figures. The man leans in to whisper something into her ear, and Risha cackles happily.

"That's excellent," she laughs. "I had no doubt they would come, just as planned. As soon as Eliina opened her virtuous mouth, she got what she deserved for betraying our secrets."

I'm no longer breathing. *All of us* are holding our breaths at the mention of Eliina.

Risha gazes around the empty space until her eyes land on me, her face still mostly hidden under her hood. *No, no, no. I know those eyes. No.* Depleted or not, my *maji* flares to life under my skin. It's telling me we need to move or accept our death.

"Don't worry, child," Risha says with a smile. "You don't have to keep hiding in the dark over there. I already knew you'd come and were standing in the shadows. Did you enjoy our little demonstration? It's a pity you didn't jump in to save the child. I was *really* hoping you would."

Purple fog billows and whirls like the beginning of a hurricane high above us. My breathing picks up speed and the vastness of the space we're all standing in starts to close in around me. *I'm going to suffocate in here without seeing Eira again, without saving our friends from being subjected to this.* Someone's calling my name and shaking my shoulders, but I can't look away from Risha's full smile and the way it extends too widely on her narrow face.

Two crows caw loudly while swooping down the wall to the right of us. My vision is tunneling, and my limbs are heavy and glued in place. I'm flipped onto my back, so all I see is that purple fog churning. Someone is holding me, their arms a vice around my sagging body. My *maji* is fluttering under my skin like a dying bird, and each breath I inhale sends shards of ice scraping against my lungs. One of the crows dips into my vision, their jet-black feathers now a vibrant lavender.

"It's a trap," Jade snarls.

My body curls deeper into whoever is holding me. *Hadwin.* It's Hadwin. I know it's him by the rich scent of pine and earth and the intoxicating spice intertwining with it. Trying to inhale that smell again, my breath gets caught in my throat. I'm coughing, an oily black liquid dripping down my chin. Hadwin's face comes into view, and even with his nearly full python shift, he can't hide the panic in his eyes. A long, forked tongue flicks out of his mouth, and I wonder if he's tasting me. *Would I taste sweet, or would he taste the darkness I hide so well?*

There's no time for me to find out. Ulf growls as he shifts into his shadow wolf, the sound morphing into a roar. He snaps his teeth at Risha and the others. I'm tilted slightly onto my side while Hadwin's tail winds itself around me, keeping me secure as the rest of him transforms into his massive python. Opaque liquid gathers at the tips of his fangs, and he swivels up and around to get into a striking position.

"Pythons aren't poisonous," I mumble to myself. I'm startled when Hadwin slinks his face right in front of me. He blinks twice.

"*My powers aren't from Earth,*" Hadwin's voice slithers in my mind. "*I have many talents you wouldn't know,* zamia."

In the blink of an eye, Hadwin shifts his attention back to Risha and pulls us closer to where Ulf's wolf is prowling, his hackles raised. I don't see Jade, but I hear multiple crows cawing, the sound sharp and intense. *Is she okay? Will she die here, too?*

Just as Ulf is about to pounce on Risha, that hair-raising smile never leaving her face, Jace enters from the original stairway we were trying to follow before. He claps his hands in what could be delight, and Astira and Liv stumble to a stop right behind him. They both gasp when they notice I'm here, but I'm too captivated by the differences in Jace to give a reaction. His gray eyes are boring straight into mine. There's no joy or friendship to be found in them. The irises slowly transform into a bright turquoise and splashes of sparkling pink. Jace's cheeks become more gaunt and the texture of his skin ripples until it's leathery.

No, no, no. No, he can't be the canielor *I saw out in the field. Jace, what have they done to you?*

He grins as if in response to my thoughts. I'm too weak to shed any tears, but they're building behind my eyes as I continue to watch him. The dam will surely break, just like my heart.

Hadwin bites down on one of the robed figures, missing Risha by an inch. Their hood falls back, exposing a male with short red hair and ashen skin. Black and purple blood pours out of their wounds and the life drains from their translucent eyes. Risha screeches in outrage, that smile finally wavering. She bares her teeth and, firmly rooting her feet on the ground, starts weaving her hands in different directions while muttering under her breath. *This* will be it. She'll strike back in retaliation, and my soul will drift off in the wind. I'll return to the earth, to the place that my spirit calls home. *Is this what I want? Such a fleeting life on Majikaero? Has the weight of my depression, the illness I conceal, become too much to bear? Can I finally let go?*

As if sensing the direction of my thoughts, Hadwin curls around me with the rest of his cylindrical body and flicks his tongue out along my arm. It's subtle, but I see the way his python shakes his head from side to side, clearly telling me *no* to whatever I'm thinking. *Would he care if I wasn't here? Would it matter?* Hadwin glances back at Risha, who's still muttering away, and dives right in front of me. The top half of his body shifts back into a humanoid form, and he grabs each side of my face with his calloused hands.

"My *maji* allows me to pick up on your emotions, since we have such similar powers," he murmurs. He takes in my whole body, still wrapped in the confines of his tail, and scowls. "We'll discuss those melancholic and morbid feelings later. We're leaving. I'm not letting either of us die down here, *zamia*. One of those fucks is emptying out your energy, so we're going to have to hurry. I've got you."

Hadwin throws himself onto Ulf's wolf's back and grips onto the glimmering shadows rising along his spine. I'm pulled with him, not giving me even a second to process the full force of his sweet words, until his tail winds around the wolf's belly and situates me right next to where he's latched onto Ulf. My eyes find Astira and Liv again. I can't yell out or do much of anything. They're going back and forth between gaping at the dead child to the robed figures to Jace transforming into a monster. They land on *me*—a close friend who's supposed to be dead but is being held by an enormous python and now on the back of a wolf made of shadows. I have no doubt they think this is a nightmare and they'll wake up any moment now. *Jokes on them.* This is indeed a nightmare that they're going to be hauled into.

Because I'm not leaving them here. I can't let the darkness of this room and these creatures cloud my mind. I won't let the gloom dim my light. Not yet, at least.

In a handful of seconds, this current nightmare comes to a close. The two crows that came with Jade are attacking her as she plummets down to Ulf. There are plenty of missing feathers and one of her eyes has been scratched out, but the look of fury in her other one tells me she's not accepting death today. Her battered body is caught with one of Hadwin's hands, barely breaking her fall, and he tucks her in between my arm and the curve of his tail. In one swift movement, Ulf's wolf launches himself up in the air, narrowly avoiding both purple crows and the fog that's starting to descend upon us. He arches until he's diving directly toward Astira and Liv, their mouths going slack in shock. Risha shrieks and throws her hands onto the ground, causing it to crack and bubble up below us.

Fuck, she's started a series of explosions deep in the earth.

Jace turns to grab both Astira and Liv's wrists, but they fall backward as the soil ripples underneath their feet. I watch as our friend—*he's supposed to be our fucking friend*—makes a quick decision and chooses to save his own life by jumping to the patch of earth Risha is kneeling on. Namid is nowhere to be seen now, a thought I'm trying to ignore in case he's waiting for us elsewhere. My head sways back to Astira and Liv, just as Ulf reaches them and swallows both of their petrified forms in his shadows. We dive straight into the dense weight of darkness that only Ulf can travel through.

My head tilts backward, as if pulled by a thread, and I make eye contact with Risha as we plunge into the veil of time. This time, I don't only *think* I recognize her, not as her eyes become a deep blue, as blue as the sea. Her hood falls back and long gray hair spills out over her shoulders. The tawny skin I'm used to shrivels up into patches of decaying flesh. Even though we're escaping out of her clutches, the realization of who she is shatters my spirit.

It's Shira, and she's coming for us, one by one.

TWENTY-NINE

Ceira

*The spirit is not able to be contained.
It wanders extensively based on
the other spirits it craves to find.*
-Speech from Council Member Lesak, Grand Spirit Reader

One of the most devastating sensations a healer can experience is the death of a distressed soul. It's especially difficult if they have the willingness to defeat the pain holding them down, yet fate has other plans. I expected the onslaught of grief the moment Nyx led us out the front entrance of the Council building. Daru had seen me spiraling after Stefanie disappeared through the library's doors with the manipulators. I *knew* her spirit was heading straight into the mouth of danger, its teeth sharpened and ready for new blood, and there wasn't anything I could do to stop it. There was no proof of what was to come. Only a gut feeling that scattered throughout my nervous system, alerting me that Stefanie is not only a strong soul connection but that she was going to be in immediate danger.

Hauke must have sensed it too, if the hopeless look in his eyes was anything to go by.

What took me by surprise was the way Fraya's actions yanked a piece of my soul downward. She sprinted to push Riker and Stefanie into the healing quarters before the purple fog could suffocate their souls. She voluntarily sacrificed herself to ensure Stefanie even has a chance of survival, something that might not be possible. Watching her so easily switch places with my favorite red-headed healer, a true *friend*, tugged on my heartstrings, and the second her soul turned to stardust, I felt *pain*. It might be an extension of what Nyx is experiencing, since our souls continue to weave themselves together and Fraya was a part of his group.

She was, whether I like it or not, a *solliqa* who saw him with the plague and didn't flinch back. She loved him, and in a way, he loved her back. There's more than one way to break a heart, and Fraya—a soul meant to be a healer with her empathic abilities and sensitivities to others—just broke mine. *Were we meant to have a stronger soul connection? If we can have more than one* almaove, *could she still have been connected to Nyx? What will this mean for our group going forward?*

A tear slips down my cheek and blows away with the wind as Nyx closes the portal. I yearn to hold him and to be held. My hands stroke the outline of his gauzy dark pants, and I watch in awe as his shadows snake out and blend in with the portal around us. One of his tendrils slinks around my neck in a brief caress, letting me know he's aware of my mournful heart and is here. I know I'll be able to collapse into his protective, dark embrace. *We just have to get out of Rioa first*. Daru is balancing his weight between holding Ivar, who's hanging limp in his bird form, and gripping Nyx's shoulder. There's a slight pressure against my lower back, and when I glance back, I see it's his talon. It's another nudge of affection, in his own way, and an indicator that he sees my reaction and will be there to pick up the pieces that shatter.

How will he do that when I might burn those pieces of my heart to ash?

Nyx presses more of his weight into the balls of his feet, and grunting, we all clutch on as our bodies surge forward through his portal. My body is flung and twisted in all sorts of directions as time and space rush past us. *I fucking hate portals.* Bile bubbles up, and right as I'm about to be sick, Nyx slams us to a stop—except we're still in the portal.

"Nyx, what—"

"*FUCK!*" Hauke roars.

Zaya leaps down onto me from Nyx's shoulders with all her claws unleashed. Daru pushes the curve of his talon deeper into my back to keep me from moving between him and Nyx's lower body. Crying out from my cat sinking her little murder claws into my chest, I twist my head around as Nyx turns at his hips, keeping his feet firmly planted next to me. Daru is panting above me, trying to keep a tight hold on Ivar's body that's starting to slip out of his grip. My gaze sweeps from them and back over to Hauke, and a strangled scream escapes me.

Hauke has his hands around the neck of a *canielor* while Odin has one hand around Hauke's arm and the other practically glued to Nyx. *Gods, help us.* This creature is hard for him to trap down or direct any *maji* to—it's smaller and fluttering around at an overwhelming speed. This one has black wounds oozing dark blood, but its shriveled body is bright with nauseatingly bright colors. *Oh, its eyes.* They're all white and are swiveling around and around like a spinning marble. The *canielor's* mouth is a wide, gaping space that's panting unbelievably fast.

I don't need my *maji* to tell me what happened to this soul. I'd recognize these symptoms anywhere, like the back of my hand. *Anxiety*. It's overcome with serious levels of anxiety, but *why? What happened to it?*

Golden light shoots out from Hauke's hands, trying to injure it enough to slow it down. I can see in Nyx's eyes that he wants to slice its throat, but he can't move his shadows without risking us falling out of the portal. We don't even know where we'll land at this point. That dark purple darkness builds inside of me and slithers past the rest of my soul, a sweetened, toxic reminder of what lurks beneath the surface. It tries to coax a reaction out of me, wanting to convince me to reach out to this *canielor*. That I shouldn't be afraid, and with the right spark, I can set what I fear in a burst of colorful flames.

I can't attempt anything with my *maji* right now. I simply *can't*. I'm too scared. How can I know where my powers will go? What will they do? Why don't I know who I'll die trying to protect within Nyx's shadows?

"Hauke," I rasp. It's futile. No one can hear me over the roar of the portal. He won't be able to destroy this *canielor* with blunt force or blasts of his powers. That's only going to make the soul more distraught and enter a state of panic. We need to soothe it into a false sense of calm and security. "Hauke," I whisper. "This isn't the way."

He wrestles with the *canielor* for another few seconds and gets in a good punch to its chest. It wails, high-pitched enough to drive anyone to madness, and tugs Hauke into it. With wide eyes, we watch as he tumbles out of the portal with the monster, and Odin slips away with him. He manages to glance back at Nyx and mouths, "Erika!" Then, they're gone, as if they were never in this portal with us.

Nyx screams and lurches us forward again, and the remaining five of us land on heated black sand. My vision clouds with black spots, and then I'm gone.

Tufts of fur tickle my nose. I wrinkle it in an attempt not to sneeze, and a groan escapes me as a heavy pressure kneads the skin above my chest. Coughing, I raise my right arm to shield my eyes as a gust of humid wind blows loose strands of my hair across my face. I keep the back of my hand against part of my face, and taking a deep, ragged breath, open my eyes enough to squint up at the sky. Dark, billowing clouds are above me, each bloated with moisture and ready to burst with rain. I haven't felt the splatter of rain on my skin in weeks; I'm ready to soak in the brewing storm around me.

Blinking my eyes open wider, the tips of my eyelashes kiss the area above my cheekbones. I groan again and my tongue darts out to lick my lips, realizing in the process how chapped and dry they are. My gaze shifts from the sky down to the creature pinning me down and making it so hard to breathe. *Zaya.* She purrs loudly as her golden eyes take in my waking form, and she brushes her head against my chin to mark me in greeting. I want to lift my left arm and push myself up to a sitting position, but my muscles are still leaden with exhaustion. Clearly, I was knocked out for some amount of time, and it appears my soul requires more rest and a healing session to recuperate from yesterday.

Was it yesterday?

Low voices drift with the black sand in the wind. My eyes snap open when it hits me that we traveled through a portal, and now I'm lying in a bed of sand next to the sea. *Where are the others? Are they hurt? Did the rest of us make it here safely? Where even is here?* Questions bombard me from every angle, and I have to physically shake my head to stay centered in the current moment. *What would Morgan tell me all the time? Ah, yes. A fox needs to focus on their hearing if they wish to catch their prey. They listen before making a decision.* She has such a sweet, maternal soul and always knows what to say. I don't know where she's currently at on Earth, but if anyone can find her, it'll be Athena. Gods know that I need her support now more than ever.

For now, I put my energy into listening. If I slow my breathing down, the rest of my senses settle down enough to make everything I hear clearer. There's the sound of the wind that naturally opens up my sense of smell with the way they carry the salty scent of the sea. I hear multiple men speaking to one another, and from what I can gather from their tones, the conversation is laced with pain and dispute. A lighter tone, one of a *fim*, softens the sharp notes of the argument. Outside of these voices, it's easy to hear Zaya's purring and feel the way it vibrates between my rib cage and wraps around my heart. The roar of the sea muffles everything in the most comforting way possible. It's soothing enough to lull me back to sleep. My worn-out body pleads with me to succumb to more rest, but a sense of urgency tugs on my soul. I don't think it's my own, which leads me to think it's—

"Nyx, darling, is this really how you chose to make an entrance?" that feminine voice asks.

"He's always had quite the flair for drama," a different *solliqa* mutters.

That sense of urgency crackles as a living flame into a sense of agitation and a throbbing ache. It's the kind that can only come from a familial betrayal, when you realize those who are supposed to love you choose to mock and belittle you instead. Immediate resentment for *solliqas* I haven't even met yet surges upward and pushes any lingering fatigue back down. I might collapse at any moment, but I'll be damned if I just lie here while my *almaove* experiences emotional whiplash.

I move my right hand from my face to Zaya's fur and scratch

behind her neck. She meows and snaps her mouth at me, probably asking for food, before leaping off my chest into the divot of sand next to me. Placing my weight onto my elbows, I sigh and stretch out my upper back. I'm about to pull myself up when Daru crawls on his hands and knees to my left side.

"Eira," he breathes.

My eyes dip into every nook from his head to his toes. His blond hair is disheveled. There's a handful of bruises blooming up his arm and neck, nearly covering up the single black vein crawling from right below his Adam's apple. The thick, protective coverings that he was wearing are partially ripped, especially along his upper body. Other than all of this and the look of blatant strain in his eyes, Daru seems to be okay. I release a breath I didn't realize I was holding and force myself to push all the way up to my hands to be at eye level with him.

Daru stops a few inches from my face and appears to be doing the same assessment of my body. His gaze pauses on the tattoo I share with Athena, watching as it shimmers even under a cloudy sky, and continues to inspect my torso. I don't miss the way he lingers on my chest, with how exposed it is after my bodysuit was torn from such a tumultuous landing. He swallows and raises his eyes to meet mine, and I can see the relief break through the clouds of stress in his green irises.

"You're okay," he confirms.

I clear my throat. "I'm okay."

Daru nods to himself and scoots a little closer to examine my hands and feet. I apparently lost my shoes somewhere along the way and have scratches littering the areas still touching the rough sand. He does a quick search of Zaya, much to her dismay if her low growl is anything to go by. Once he's satisfied that she's still in one piece, he settles back on his heels. Daru stares out at the sea beyond us, and as I follow his gaze, I notice how the water is a dusty pink instead of the blue-gray waves I'm used to on Earth. We don't speak, and I'm so disoriented, I nearly jump with the realization that I can't see Nyx.

My head whips back and forth along the dark coastline. I squint and try to make out any movement in the gray fog, but only the swirling points of the volcanic mountains are visible. Looking back to my right, I notice a blue heap of feathers in the distance. The pink waves are dangerously close to touching it, leaving a layer of sea form in its wake. *Fuck, that's Ivar.*

The panic must be obvious on my face. Daru grips my forearm, his slender, tawny fingers squeezing the skin where Tryg's bear marking still resides. A rush of warmth and affection flows through me, instantly putting me at ease. I recognize it as the same *maji* he used on me after I first arrived in Majikaero. What once made me irritated now gives me the feeling of rightness.

"Nyx was taken inside," Daru rasps while pointing to a towering stone structure behind us. Its black with molten-red crystals resembles the surrounding mountains. "A handful of protectors sheathed in all black coverings took him a while ago. They took one look at me and stated they'd come back for the uninvited visitors shortly."

"Uninvited?" My heart sinks at the realization this won't be the intimate and fuzzy family introduction I was secretly—and *naively*—hoping for.

Daru grimaces. "They wouldn't even take Ivar, who still hasn't shifted back from his bird form." He lifts his head into the wind that's picking up speed and glances around the beach that the three of us—four, including Zaya—have been left on. When his eyes find mine again, an unwelcome pit of anxiety settles in my stomach. "Danger is on the horizon, my fire queen. The wind carries many secrets and hasn't yet lied to me. We aren't safe here."

I open my mouth in protest, a scowl already forming on my face. "I refuse to—"

"I know," Daru cuts me off. "My *maji* that comes from the

wind itself is urging me to flee eastward. It tells me to fly us until we cross the violent sea and seek safety with those who are truly allies. I don't know which of the Council members are innocent or safe, but if the wind is urging me east, then I imagine it could be Lesak or Rakiana. Or even leaders underneath them. I can't be sure yet. But even if I did know, I know you won't leave Nyx, as you shouldn't. He's your *almaove*." Daru leans forward and tucks some of my hair behind my ear. "I won't deny my feelings for you, and if they're even half of what you have for Nyx, then I don't blame you for needing to stay. Just beware, my dear, that we might not all make it out alive if we remain."

The seriousness of his words bleeds through me and causes me to choke on my next inhale. Daru has lifted that reassuring veil of tranquility that only he has been able to feed into my soul. There's no influence from him. It's me... and the pieces of myself that are as scattered as the tiny particles of sand whirling in the wind. For the briefest of moments, it's just Daru and me. I'm lost to his dark green eyes and the way they pull me into their depths, as deeply layered as the *maji* he wields. His soul reaches out to me, yearning to connect with my own, yet hesitant to make any sudden movement. That low murmur of voices rings like an alarm in the back of my head, and I flinch. *I will never leave Nyx, but why do I still want to fly with Daru away from here?*

"It's okay, my fire queen," Daru whispers. His eyes are as wide as mine, watching my every reaction. My senses are in overdrive. The rumble of thunder in the distance, the way the pink waves are getting higher, the combination of earthy tones mixed with the freshness of spring air that makes up Daru's scent. Zaya scratches at my ankle, and I hear Ivar moan in pain behind me. All the while, those low voices and that higher tone are a constant in the back of my mind, pulling me toward wherever Nyx was taken. My nostrils flare as I take in the different smells and sounds and sensations running through me, and it all starts to become too much.

"I won't leave you," Daru rasps, grabbing my shoulders. "I promise. The moment you want to fly east with me, we'll leave immediately. But I won't leave you while we're here. No matter what they do to us."

I gasp as fresh tears fall down my face. "What will they do? Why am I feeling *everything*?"

He reaches a hand up to my face and wipes the pad of his thumb across my right cheekbone. Daru frowns down at his hand. My tears are thick and purple, that hidden darkness growing restless now that Nyx is no longer by me. That power is too near the surface, threatening to break free.

"As your *almaove* connection strengthens, you'll be able to pick up on one another's senses. Your soul is experiencing whatever Nyx is going through right now, or honestly could be reacting to something Athena has done. Either way, it's likely waking up again. We're always waking up in some way or another here," he murmurs. "I don't know what they'll do, but I do know that we aren't on the part of Drageyra that Nyx tried to portal us to. There's a great deal these *solliqas* living in the southern royal lands can do to us, especially to their banished prince."

A tremor racks its way through me. Daru is physically holding me up at this point, and the more Zaya paws at me in distress, the less I know what to do. I've been learning about *maji*, how to heal others with powers, and the intricacies of this new world. Most of my focus has gone to learning about the plague of darkness that's stemmed from trauma and is overtaking Majikaero more and more each day. I've thrown myself into understanding *canielors* and what it takes to not only destroy them but hopefully save the souls suffocating inside of these monsters. Now, as I take in the never-ending coastline and the fact that the four of us have been *left* out here, this dark beach feels barren. The rose-colored sea nudges unsettlingly closer, eager to swallow us up until whichever creatures lurking under the surface devour our souls.

"What do we do?" I ask.

"Well," Daru sighs. "If we aren't flying away from here, then we can either wait until someone comes back for us or take matters into our own hands. It's up to you. I'll follow you straight into the fires of these mountains, Eira."

An unhinged laugh spills out of me. "You can't mean that. I'm not even the *solliqa* or Queen of Light you view me as. *Look*." I make quick work of spreading the shredded material covering my abdomen, exposing an area usually concealed from everyone. Daru quickly assesses my skin, his mouth parting when he realizes what I'm showing him.

"Don't you see?" I laugh bitterly. Not even Nyx saw this since it was covered up by my fire and those puckered scars. And I was already baring the monster within... I couldn't show him *this*, too. "Clearly, none of us are safe from the plague."

Daru places trembling fingertips across the dark blue vein stretching across the skin over my uterus. It's not the same as the others' black markings, but the design couldn't be more obvious.

I've caught the plague of darkness in one way or another, the very disease I'm meant to destroy.

"No," Daru murmurs softly while tracing the length of the vein. "None of us are, but that doesn't mean I view you any differently. Listen very carefully to what I'm saying, Eira. Just like there's light in everyone, there's also darkness. This must be what's waking up inside of you, and we will have to learn how to work with it. It's not only the light within us that matters. It's what's buried beneath this light that we have to learn to love and accept."

I clench my jaw until it hurts. "I'm diseased. Tarnished. Infected," I spit.

"My fire queen," Daru says sadly. "You make this wretched darkness beautiful. I watch it growing inside of you, and all I see is your strength." His eyes sear into me, and for one heartbeat, I fully allow myself to embrace what it'd mean to have *both* Nyx and Daru. "This vein," he mumbles while placing my coverings back over the marking. "It's just proof that you've faced trauma and found the courage to keep on living. That's all these markings really are. We have to keep our focus on banishing the plague from this world, to show it that we won't accept what it's doing to our souls. The moment we succumb to all the pain is when we've truly lost, but not yet, Eira. We haven't lost quite yet."

Adoration as rich as honey blooms in my heart. *Could he be right? Can even those of us with signs of the plague still fight against it?*

A buzzing, crackling sound fills the air, and there's a faint touch of static along my legs and arms. Orange lightning flashes silently in the distance, high above the crashing waves. A storm is imminent and could very well be coming for *us*.

"May I be of some assistance to you all?"

I'm abruptly broken out of my thoughts, out of the trance of Daru's words. I fall out of his arms with a shriek loud enough that Zaya hisses and scrambles in the sand, circling me until she's positioned right in front of us. Her fur rises in a giant poof, but she must determine whoever spoke to us is not a *canielor* or related to the purple parasite she loathes. She grows as tall as a *drekstri* and bares her teeth at our visitor, blocking them from my view as her tail swishes out and nearly topples me over.

"Zaya!" I growl. Her tail brushes sand right into my mouth. *Maddening furball.*

"Oh, I'm sorry for scaring you," the *solliqa* chuckles, their voice muffled by the sound of the wind and from me still positioned behind Zaya's fluffy butt. "That wasn't my intention. I, err, saw you all out here alone and thought you'd prefer to come inside."

Sighing, I push myself up to a standing position, wobbling slightly before leaning into one of Zaya's back legs. Daru has been staring at the *solliqa* with his mouth gaping open and hastily makes his way to stand next to me, shoulder-to-shoulder. My eyebrows furrow at the way he presses against me, but one look from him keeps my mouth shut. Daru is studying whoever is in front of us with an intensity that reminds me of Athena, which I've learned the hard way that I usually shouldn't interfere or push back against. The key word is *usually*. I hear Ivar shift and moan again behind us. Without a second thought of what could happen, I pivot back and stoop under Zaya's tall leg and rush over to where Ivar's bird form is splayed out on the sand.

"Ivar?" I breathe. I fall to my knees, momentarily hoping that I don't have to get up again, and place the palms of my hands around Ivar's large head. His golden beak is cracked from the tip up along the side. Some of his blue and black feathers are velvety and smooth, while others squelch with moisture. Hidden in between each feather is a frothy purple mixture, and I swallow back a gasp. *Is he even able to heal when this damaged?*

"I assure you we can restore him back to good health once inside."

My neck snaps up to see the mysterious *solliqa* standing behind me. Breathing in and out slowly, I take in their appearance. Brown curls frame an almost childlike face with bright gray eyes peering down at Ivar with worry. With each breath, the little *maji* that's still working inside of me is able to read his aura. I think this one has mostly *misn* energy, but it's not the same as Nyx or Daru or some of the others I've become close to. All black coverings frame this *solliqa's* lean and wiry form, and the very act of wringing his hands reminds me of my mother. *It's not her, though, I'm sure of it.* He shifts his gaze to mine, and I'm struck with the oddest sensation. There's a familiarity I wasn't expecting mixed with such purity and innocence I haven't felt in ages.

"My name's Dahviid," he says while crouching to kneel next to me. A few other *solliqas* in matching dark coverings advance on either side of us, putting me on edge.

Dahviid tsks. "I didn't request their presence yet," he mutters.

I turn my head around, not letting go of Ivar's face, and find Daru with one hand on Zaya's back. He's walking them closer to where I'm kneeling, his eyes not wavering from where I'm located. "Are these the ones you saw earlier?" I call out, not caring what this Dahviid *solliqa* thinks of my question.

Daru shakes his head from side to side. Puzzlement is etched on his face. He chews the inside of his cheek and comes to a stop directly behind me. His shoes land on either side of my hips, caging me in. Zaya's body lights up as she shrinks down to a smaller size and jumps onto my lap.

"Ack, *those* souls," Dahviid scoffs. "I'm not sure how much you know about Drageyra, but there's been quite the divide over these last ten years. It all started when Prince Nyx was banished from his homeland and taken as prisoner in Rioa. Many of us were against this decision, but there were some—especially distant relatives of the royal family—who sought to use his tragic situation as an opportunity to seize any power for themselves. Barbaric, I personally think. I believe they might have gotten to you before we could."

"Who's *we*?" Daru asks.

Two of the *solliqas* clad in all black lift Ivar's enfeebled body off the sand. He's placed onto a stretcher made of colorful wooden poles and the same gauzy material most *solliqas* wear. They work their hands in circular motions, and with what must be air *maji*, raise the stretcher until it's levitating in the air. Particles of sand drift off the wooden poles and are carried away with the forceful wind. Zaya chirps and pounces onto the piles of sand still moving from where Ivar was lying, her claws peeking out from those brown, furry paws. I extend my hand out to her, beckoning her closer until I can wrap my arms around her antsy body. Daru clears his throat and crosses his arms over his chest.

The *solliqas* march their way toward the colossal building with Ivar floating in between them, the black and red crystals incised on each stone glimmering under another flare of lightning in the sky. Dahviid steps to stand in front of us and offers me a soft smile. There's such raw goodness and light in those gray eyes. I know instinctively that I can trust him, yet that unsettles me. *Is this a trap? Are we being lured to our deaths?*

"We're the Neleh of the Isle. You can think of us as the torches used to light the way to safety in these calamitous mountains. Not that the rivers of lava can't help you see in the dark, but our light is different. Safe. Secure. Come, we have much to discuss, and hunkering down on Drageyra's coastline during a storm isn't ideal."

"I need to see my Prince of Shadows," I blurt out. With Daru at my back and Zaya in my arms, my breathing is more measured than I'd expect. I'm starting to shiver, though, and my enervated soul craves rest and... and *Nyx*.

Dahviid nods adamantly. "We all do," he insists. "He might be your *almaove*, but he's still our prince."

"How do you know what he means to me?"

"The eyes never lie." Dahviid hums and bends down, so his face is directly in front of me. "Yours seek a repose. There's a heaviness that strains your eyelids. A restlessness and crazed yearning that can only mean one thing: You've lost or have been separated from one of your strongest soul connections. Fear not, Eira. We'll reunite you shortly."

My lips part in surprise. *He knows my name?*

Dahviid gives me a knowing look before sweeping his gaze along the shoreline and up into the clouds. I follow the direction of his eyes, where dozens of *drekstri* are soaring alongside the sparks of lightning. Drops of rain the color of snow splash onto my face. They're warm, yet I shiver nonetheless. I hardly notice the temperature as the *drekstri* fly closer and closer, one as dark as night leading the way. *Ambra*. Daru shifts and places a hand on my shoulder, squeezing slightly.

"We're all drawn to the prince," Dahviid mutters while staring at the herd of *drekstri* gliding on the blustery winds. His voice is so hushed, I barely hear his next words. "Just as we're all drawn to you, Queen of Light. We need you both now more than ever before. *All* of us."

My fox and lioness are too drained to make any major movements, but they both uncoil at Dahviid's words. These *solliqas* need us. I crush Zaya closer to my chest and her tail swipes against my lower abdomen. *All of these souls need us.* I'll do everything I can to wreak havoc on this plague that's ravaged so many in Majikaero, starting with healing myself even more and finding where my Nyx was taken on this volatile island. For him—to find him, to keep him safe—I'll do *anything*.

What will these *solliqas* think of me when they find I'm willing to set myself on fire for those I love most?

Yes, love. I love him. My heart is filled with this emotion, and it blazes with a passion I didn't realize I could have for another soul.

I'll do what needs to be done, even if I burn myself until I'm buried deep beneath the light.

A beacon of hope for many. A soul turned into embers and nothing more than a corpse.

And all of it will be worth it if it means I've driven away the plague of darkness from this world.

THIRTY

Astira

Intelligence is nothing without action.
Action is nothing without commitment.
All of this will cease to exist if we
allow the stars to override sensible thought.
-Ove, God of Intellect

Worlds collide in an explosion of colorful shades. Fragments of earth spiral past suspended asteroids, taking the screams of disheartened creatures with them. The pain of their cries—their endless, rupturing cries—slice into me as I dance across the stars. They cut as deep as a whetted sword, and pieces of my soul are splintered into unrecoverable shards. I welcome the pain and the way it throbs like a heartbeat in my chest. Each speck of stardust I turn into, the freer my soul becomes, finally untethered from the reality I was shoved into.

Yes, this is where I belong. Destined to only myself and who I wish to become. I open my mouth, my tongue darting out to taste the starbursts and see if they taste as sweet as they feel.

"Astira," a voice rumbles. I leap from star to sun to moon to planet, taunting it to follow me if it can.

A presence of shadows twists and turns, matching my movements leap for leap, until it's cradling me in the silky confines of its soul.

"My starburst," the voice echoes around me. "It's time for you to wake up."

My thoughts become muddled. I'm already awake, rushing through the galaxy without need of rest.

"Wake up. It's time to seize the energy trapped inside of you," it murmurs. "It's time to devour what belongs to me. What's MINE."

Coughing up rancid bile, my eyes fly open as I launch myself up into a sitting position. An aching sensation carves into my chest as my mind tries to catch up to my body. There are four walls around me, and they are wide enough apart to ease any simmering hysteria. Each wall is made of a smooth clay material with the scent of moist soil, as if I'm being sheltered by the earth itself. I don't see any metal, though. My fingers curl into a plush blanket, the fabric unfamiliar to me. I realize the bed I'm sitting in is twice the size of the usual tiny bed frame I cram myself into every night. The lack of harsh steel, a comfortable bed, and the size of the dim room confirms I'm not in Nedrazon anymore. *But where am I?*

A small hiccup from the darkened corner of the room snags my attention. Squinting, I persuade my body to move each shaky limb, so I can get a closer look at who made that sound—or *what*. Memories of what Liv and I witnessed flare behind my eyes, images dropping like stones into my mind. I try to shake my head to get them to stop, but it's no use. There's no use pretending that Jace didn't bring us to a creepy as fuck lower level where the most unbelievable scene was playing out before us. I can't rip up the image embedded in my heart of Jace's face, with that too-wide smile and sparkling, otherworldly eyes brimming with malignant intent. It doesn't make any sense. None of it, especially witnessing *Athena*—our dead fucking friend—

huddled up next to some python monster. It must have been a nightmare, and while I'm no longer in my room in Nedrazon, I'm somewhere else underground. Jace might have brought me here to rest in isolation, clearly delusional. This is easier to accept than whatever the hell that fuckery was.

Except I also saw my wolf, and I'm no longer sure if he's just a dream. Not when he closed his jaw around my paralyzed form, and the second I made contact with him, my soul cried out in honeyed bliss. Even the trauma I wear like a second skin was near nonexistent, dulled by the overwhelming presence of endearment I've rarely been allowed to feel.

"Astira," a vague voice whispers.

No, not vague. It's *Liv*. I push myself more until I'm in a crawling position on all fours. *Right hand, left knee. Left hand, right knee. Keep going. Get to Liv.* "I'm coming," I croak.

I shuffle forward toward the sound of Liv's voice, and then I see her. She's still wearing the dark clothes from... from I don't know when, yesterday? A week ago? *Who the fuck knows—obviously not me.* I notice the way her pale skin nearly glows as I slump down next to her, leaning my back against the even texture of the wall. I'm wearing the same simple clothes, too, and I'm concerned about how long it's been considering how rumpled up they appear. *Fuck.*

Sighing, I lift my heavy arm, now exhausted after making my way to Liv, and intertwine my fingers with my friend's. We're both hidden in the darkness, and I bask in this fleeting moment of safety, but I can't be certain who we're concealing ourselves from.

"Astira, I'm scared," Liv sobs. "My heart is breaking, and I don't understand *why*."

I watch as her shoulders shake with more tears and the way tension radiates from her slim body. My mind processes that she's having a normal reaction to whatever we're going through, but I can't seem to latch onto that same response. Instead, I'm distant and peering into this scene of two friends, battered and bruised, leaning into one another for strength. There's no telling what strength Liv will receive from me. I'm operating on autopilot and am stuck between what's happening and where my dreams take me.

"I think I'm scared, too," I rasp. "I'm just not sure of what."

"If that answer isn't evident, then I'm not doing a good enough job."

Liv and I both jump. Our hands clutch one another tighter, and then I see *him*. Liv's body begins to shake uncontrollably, yet I settle into a fathomless peace that I didn't know existed.

"Azrael," I breathe.

My wolf stalks toward us. He snaps his teeth, and Liv flinches into me, but I don't have fear. For some reason, I'm under the impression that he's showing off, trying to impress me with how lethal he can be. Azrael is at least four times the size of a normal wolf and is entirely made of shadows. Smoke swirls up from each step he takes, and his very being reeks of night terrors. All I can focus on is the way his eyes smolder and how the darkness inside them is similar to the everlasting skies of the galaxy. I find I want to reach out to touch that fur made of shadows, to know how it feels against my skin.

Then reality sinks in, and the horror Liv has been experiencing finally crashes straight into me. I open my mouth right as Liv screams, the sound winding around me like barbed wire.

Nothing comes out of me, though. How can it when Azrael shifts into a mass of shadows and swarms into a man right in front of me? My mind is trying to tell me that the existence of a shadow wolf and a man being able to shift into one are both equally abnormal, but my heart doesn't give a shit. It's beating wildly as the most beautiful creature I've ever laid eyes on strides toward me. He's all delicious muscle wrapped up in darkness, and when his thick hand whips out to squeeze my throat, I nearly faint with anticipation.

A primal desperation sparks to life, and *oh, daddy*, I can't wait to see what he'll do to me.

He applies a startling amount of pressure to restrict my airflow and lifts me up by the neck. My feet dangle in the air as he raises me until we're at eye level. *Damn, he must be seven feet tall.* Each muscle in my body twitches and *wants* to tremble with fear. Yet *surprise, surprise*, something is wrong with my fucked-up soul because I'm ready to let this man made of shadows do whatever the hell he wants to me.

As those dark eyes bore into mine, his nostrils flare. *Is he smelling me? Whatever, don't care. Smell me and then fuck me. Do as you please, thank you.* A wicked glint shines in his eyes. I'm simultaneously delighted and enter a state of shock when it hits me: Azrael is this man, and this man is my wolf. *What the what?*

"Ulf, enough!" Athena barks from the doorway into this room. My gaze locks onto her hollow-eyed face, but this man—*werewolf?*—keeps me hanging in front of him like a rag doll. *Athena?! Is it her?*

Another man with blond hair slides in beside Athena. He has a partially shaved head with a small braid pulled up into a knot on his head. He's also muscular, with tight, gauzy clothing that matches his gold eyes. With the way he's angling his body toward Athena, I get the distinct impression that they're an item —or well on their way to becoming one. His hand finds another part of her to touch when she tries to bat him away. There's a possessiveness in the way his other arm curls around her and leans against the doorway.

"Ulf, come on," Athena's man grumbles. "It's been a long enough day as it is. Let's recoup while we can."

There's his name again. Ulf. He tilts his head to the side, a predator assessing their prey, not breaking eye contact. I play along with his staring contest and let him see that no matter what he is, I won't let myself be intimidated.

"I heard crying," he grunts. "And then this one wanted to play."

Athena glares daggers into the back of Ulf's head, and laughter sputters out of my choking throat.

"Doubtful," she grinds out. "Put my friend down. *Now*."

My eyes widen when I see a green light pulsate from Athena's hands with green and golden vines winding up her arms. Ulf sighs, and while I'm expecting to be tossed to the ground, he lowers me gently until I fall onto my knees, greedily swallowing down air. He glares down at me with those dark eyes and raises a hand. Instinctively, I flinch back but keep my head held high, wanting to show strength while bracing myself for the incoming pain.

Yet it never comes.

I peer back up at Ulf, and he narrows his eyes. When he brings his hand down, layers of what must be clothes drop onto the ground next to me. I don't believe my eyes, but as I watch his raised hand, shadows flow out of it until another clothing item is created. It's *magic*. Even Liv has stopped sniffling near me. Ulf has both of our attention as he continues to fabricate more pieces of clothes and what might be a blanket. When he swiftly lowers his hand, both Liv and I shrink back marginally. He gives me that assessing look again while Athena bustles her way over to us and hastily picks up the pile of clothes.

"My friends," she says, her voice thick with emotion. Peering over her shoulder, she huffs and mutters to herself. "Can either of you do something useful? Like get some light in here?"

Even with the dimness, I can see Ulf's scowl. "Useful? I just fucking used my *maji* to make them new coverings. I'm the one who brought us to Sayfters. And remember, I—"

"Yeah, yeah." Athena throws her hand to the side. "We get it. You're powerful. We need to get some light, *lipva*, and food into them. Honestly, into all of us at this point, especially Jade."

Ulf scoffs at her and looks ready to argue, but blondie man

pulls up behind Athena, squaring his shoulders. I can't see where Ulf stomps off to, not as Athena brings shaky hands up in front of her and with her next exhale, a rush of green light floats out of her in tiny spheres. With a flick of her wrist, she sends them up to the ceiling, giving me a clearer view of the simple room we're in. Similar to Nedrazon, there are plain walls without any artwork or personal effects on them, as well as a simple bed and an attached smaller bathroom. Unlike Nedrazon, or Earth for that matter, magic continues to unfold before my eyes, and I'm hesitant to believe if it's even real.

Athena mutters something to blondie, and he grunts in confirmation before jogging out of the room. She turns her focus on me and Liv, who's now scooted right next to me, and the dam breaks. My friend looks unsure whether to hug us or give us the new clothes or speak. Liv makes the decision for all of us and throws an arm around me, pulling us both in to tackle Athena. She grasps us back and tugs us in close to her chest. I'm not sure which one of us starts crying first, but it's only a few seconds before we're all blubbery messes.

I break out of the hug first, allowing myself to take in Athena. Liv reaches her hand out and touches our friend's long dark hair. Her fingers trail down Athena's face and one of her arms until they're clasping hands. Liv cries once more, the sound heartbreaking, and mumbles incoherent words to herself. I play with the green material wrapped loosely around Athena's lithe form and marvel at the way it sparkles under the lights above us —the light that she *made*.

"How—"

"It's a lot to explain," Athena rasps. She swallows and tosses her hair over her shoulder.

"We thought," Liv begins, her voice cracking. "W-we thought you *died*."

Athena nods, silent tears falling down her cheeks. "In a way, I did."

"Does that mean we're dead, too?" I whisper. Who the fuck knows where we're at or what the fuck is going on, but I don't want to ask too loudly. *That might make it true.*

"Not exactly," Athena states slowly. "It's just, we're sort of, um—"

"You're in a magical realm of souls called Majikaero," her man states simply. *Ah, yes, as if anything magical is simple.*

He plops down next to her with a curvy jug and a plate piled high with food. *Fuck yes*. My stomach grumbles eagerly, ready to inhale what looks to be brightly colored vegetables and meat dripping in grease. *Meat. It's back on the fucking menu.*

Athena elbows him and huffs in annoyance. "Way to throw them into the deep end."

He shrugs. "Sometimes that's the only way to do it. Best to get it over with instead of sniveling like a youngling."

"Hadwin..."

Liv and I couldn't care less which world we're on right now or if we're dead. What we *do* care about is the mouthwatering smell that's drifting off that plate of food. An unsettling growl escapes me and, as if in sync, Liv and I dive for it at the same time. *Potatoes and roots. That's all we had for days. Now we're sinking our teeth into glorious steaks of who knows what.*

Moaning, juice from the piece of meat I stuffed into my mouth trickles down my chin. I sigh in contentment. If we've died, then at least we're in Heaven. That's the only place we could be with such delectable, juicy meat in our rapacious hands. Liv makes eye contact with me, and we both giggle from the thrill of eating something with so much flavor after *years* of bland food, day in and day out.

Ulf steps back into this large room, appearing irritated and quite provoked. He raises an eyebrow as he makes his way toward where we're all huddled in the corner. With a smirk, his eyes home in on my mouth.

"Enjoying the food, are you?" he observes.

Licking my lips, I smile brightly up at his towering form. "Mhm, we *love* meat!" I chirp. Liv hums in agreement, her body buzzing with just as much excitement as mine.

"All kinds of meat?" Ulf asks.

I lick some of the grease off one of my fingers and blink up at him. "Is there a kind you'd like to show me?"

Athena throws her head back and laughs at Ulf's open mouth.

"You have no idea what kinds of souls my friends have," she chuckles.

"I very much want to know," Ulf responds, not taking his eyes off me.

Athena's expression sobers up, that weariness in her eyes sneaking back in. "You will, as will many others." She sighs and glances between Liv and me. "I expected you two to be much more freaked out right now."

"Oh, we are," Liv says around a mouthful of a hot pink, leafy vegetable. "We'll both be breaking down into hysterics any moment now. You spend enough time underground, though, and hot meat quickly changes everything. Our questions and breakdowns will just have to wait until we're done eating."

"She's right," I agree. "We were buried under the earth for too long. Gods only know which emotions we're capable of processing anymore."

Liv snorts. "Yeah, remember when that one woman asked where you came from? You casually shared how you were born as a creature of the night inside one of the tunnels, and Damon locked you up in chains in fear you'd eat them all?"

My teeth tear into another piece of meat. "Mhm. Her face was priceless. You'd think she'd have some darker humor having lived underground, but chaining me up was a bit too much for her."

Athena's eyes are bouncing back and forth between us, a mixture of alarm and concern flaring in them. Hadwin, I think she called him, furrows his eyebrows, and Ulf looks downright menacing.

"What?" I ask.

Athena touches my forearm lightly. "It appears you also have a lot to share with us."

I blink. A wave of fatigue washes over me. Athena grabs the clothing items and sets some of them in front of me and then a few next to Liv.

"Tomorrow," she murmurs while removing the plate of food. A cup is placed into my hand, the liquid sloshing around similar to water. "We can talk about all of this tomorrow."

I look from the cup to the clothes and back up to her. "If you're into horror and monster stories, then you'll be in for a treat."

Ulf makes a sound. *Was that a laugh?* "We know all about monsters here, little star. You might just be sitting with some of them."

My hand automatically moves to my neck. When my fingers wrap around my star pendant, I let out a sigh of relief. No one has taken this from me yet, and for a reason I can't explain, I know it's important.

Raising my amber eyes to Ulf's dark ones, I smile faintly. "Then it seems we're in good company," I whisper, my eyelids becoming heavy. "We're all just monsters wearing different skins."

He stares at me hard enough, I swear he touches my soul.

"And we're all just monsters stuck on different worlds. Sleep well, little star. You'll need your energy for what's to come."

THIRTY-ONE
Tryg

*Those who dismiss the qualms of
the sea will soon be at its mercy.
-Deniz, Goddess of Water*

"Come along, Tryg!" Eira calls out to me. She giggles like the little girl she currently is.

This isn't the version of her I typically dream about. Eira is wearing a lightweight dress with little foxes adorning it, her childlike face free of the tightness stress causes. She twirls around in the field of wildflowers, her long white hair trailing behind her, a flag signaling ceasefire. Her laugh reverberates in my chest, the same as everything about her does. Eira's a part of who I am, no matter our ages. She continues to dance around, each bright flower adding a splash of color to her pale features. The sun is peeking out behind one of the mountains in the distance. It's the start of a new day, a fresh beginning.

Eira pauses with her back to me. I take a step toward her, but my movements are sluggish. It's as if I'm wading through translucent quicksand, and my limbs are stuck and being pulled under an imaginary surface. By the time my foot presses into the soft dirt, the *sun has risen directly above us. There's no more laughter, no twirling, and the flowers have lost their shimmer. Eira continues to stand still with her back facing me. I go to take another step, but my right foot sinks deeper into the soil below me.*

"Eira!" I yell. "I can't move!"

Her young body stays still as her dark dress flutters in the oncoming breeze. The little foxes all over it pulsate a bright blue. Static white noise surrounds me, making it impossible to hear my own voice. Eira's body glitches, disappearing and reappearing in mere seconds. Is she just in my mind? This is a dream after all, isn't it?

Eira disappears again into thin air and reappears right in front of me. She turns her head slowly over her shoulder, the movements jerky and robotic. When those eyes face me, I'm still sinking into the earth, being held hostage by a force I can't stop. Will I drown? Is that how I'll awaken?

"Tryg," Eira whispers, her voice raspy and warped. Those small eyes that captured the innocence of childhood earlier as the sun was rising are now... gone. Pits of darkness stare at me, making my breath hitch. I instinctively try to scramble away from her, but the soil continues to pull me under until Eira is looming over me. Dark red tears fall out of where her eyes should be, and when she opens her mouth, glowing fireflies funnel out from inside her. They're each pulsating with small blue and purple flames. As they trail out of her cracked lips, usually as soft as a rose petal, I watch as blue veins flare to life up and down her fragile arms.

"Tryg," she whispers. Her fireflies swarm around my head, keeping only my eyes clear to see her. "I thought you said you'd love me in any form."

Her bones push out of her thin flesh until she's crumbling into the same earth that's swallowing me up whole. Those empty eyes stay focused on me, and her head turns into a mutilated skull with red tears still streaming down her cheek bones.

"You said you'd love me." Eira's gravelly voice whirls around

me. "You're already awake, Tryg. So, come give me your love. Tryg, please—"

"Tryg, wake up!" Daya yells in my face while shaking my shoulders.

Startled, I shout a slew of profanities while tumbling off the sofa, one of the plump cushions coming with me and knocking me in the head. Daya is still leaning over the side of the sofa from where she woke me up, cackling like a fucking hyena.

"What the fuck is wrong with you?" I grumble into the floor.

Daya screeches in laughter again. "Oh, plenty!" She stoops down to help me turn over, and then she offers a hand to pull me up. I suppose that's the least she can do. *Fucking psycho.*

"I'm actually not one of those, Tryggy," Daya chirps while tapping my nose. "I *do* have a conscience, thank you very much."

Groaning, I swipe a hand down my face. "Then why did you wake me up this way? I didn't even realize I fell asleep."

"I mean, I *tried* waking you up the normal way," Daya mutters while smoothing out the material of her pants. She's wearing a maroon laced-up top that shows off her toned stomach. Her pants are black and flowy with lacy designs along the sides. "You're the one who wouldn't listen and open your eyes. With the way you were practically screaming your nightmare to me, I thought you wanted to wake up immediately."

"Fuck, you can even hear my dreams?"

Daya shrugs. "Most of them. I've noticed that you mostly have nightmares, dreadful ones at that."

I scoff. "Yeah, that adds up."

Isa pops her head through the doorway next to us. "Ready?"

Daya's eyes blaze like simmering coals. "Oh yes. The time is now, Trygster. Hope you're at least a little rested after that nap!"

Not giving me time to respond, Daya hooks her arm with mine and pulls us through the doorway. Isa smirks at me and follows right behind us as we make our way down the winding staircase. She guides us down a few hallways, each decorated with art pieces of varying styles. We're walking fast enough that my eyes can't keep up with each image, and they blur together in a swirl of colors.

"What's the rush?" I pant. I narrowly bump into a *solliqa*, who gives me an intrigued glance.

"J'marie isn't known for her patience," Isa chimes in, now keeping step with Daya and me. "If she gives the all clear that we can see her, then we need to see her *right* at that second."

Another few *solliqas* walk past us in the opposite direction carrying a stack of tomes, some of the dust brushing off as one of them cracks a spine open. They look vaguely familiar, but naturally, we zoom past them without even acknowledging one another.

"If this meeting is so damn important, then why did you let me fall asleep? Rather than getting me at the last moment and now sprinting through this castle?" I huff.

"We'd normally portal and be there right away," Daya says as we take another stairway out through an arching open door.

"But then we realized you'd probably feel sick, and that just wouldn't do," Isa finishes.

I roll my eyes. *Women. They probably weren't ready on time and are using me as an excuse.*

Daya throws a small ball of fire at the side of my head. An embarrassing shriek leaves me as I duck out of the way, which only makes both Isa and Daya giggle with glee.

I'm dragged down a stone path that leads directly away from the castle, its dark presence towering behind us, and straight to a large glass building that backs up to the shore. There's no sand anywhere to be seen, only a long beach full of rocks and what could be sparkling gemstones. The ocean waves trickle over onto the pathway, the sea foam a bright turquoise. This color glistens with darker shades of blue and gray throughout the rest of the ocean. As I peer up at the sky, a singular sun shines down upon us, the color a pastel pink that reminds me of the strange colors in Majikaero. Also reminding me of that realm of souls, I spot a few *drekstri* in the distance, looking at home in this new world.

"Are those—"

"Mhm!" Daya chirps happily. "We're the ones who brought them over to Majikaero." She tosses me a saucy wink.

In a blink, we're entering the glass building. The ceiling is a dome that gives an unobstructed view of the sky and dazzling sun. It's unsettling to walk beneath walls made completely of glass.

"What is this place? If the waves crash hard enough into the glass, won't it break?" I ask no one in particular.

"This isn't glass," Del responds. I jump slightly, not realizing he was here with us. "It's a special material made from the sea itself. J'marie has many talents and wanted to construct a space where she could meet with those of us on the surface while she still has easy access to the ocean, her home."

"Oh," I breathe out. This place certainly gives me quite the view of the water, especially as we descend more stairs to a lower level. All around us, the ocean is brought to life. A group of smaller fish swim past with glittery scales, their eyes a jet black. They weave in and out of a vibrant coral reef that's tall enough, it could be mistaken for a city.

"You'll want to be careful around those," Del nods his head toward the last of the glittery fish. "They're tiny, but they pack a real punch with those venomous fangs."

"Sounds like someone else I know," I mutter.

Daya slings an arm around my shoulder. "You wouldn't be referring to me, would you?"

I give her some serious side-eye, and she merrily laughs. The sound is rather carefree after all the talk of war. Daya raises onto her tiptoes and gives me a quick peck on the cheek. I touch the spot she kissed, and turning to her, I'm unable to hide my surprise.

"What, no one's ever kissed you before?" she asks with a hand on her hip.

"I, no," I mumble, keeping my eyes down and avoiding direct eye contact. "I've kissed plenty of people. Just no one's shown me that type of affection in quite some time."

Isa frowns at me. A booming sound rattles the walls, jolting me out of the self-deprecating spiral I was heading toward. Daya hooks her arm with mine again, and Isa does the same on my other side. For some reason, a sense of calm washes over me. I don't question it and let it settle over my muscles as Isa and Daya walk us toward a room at the end of the hall. It's unnerving walking with the ocean around me on all sides, as if I'm pushing through the water itself. I try to keep my gaze straight ahead, but it's hard to do that when a snake-like creature with white fins traveling down its spine slithers right underneath us.

"You'll get used to it in time," Isa murmurs while patting my arm.

As we approach the end of the hall, I realize this is the only part of the building that has any kind of normal walls. A few *solliqas* greet us at the doorway, one with strawberry-blond hair with gray eyes and the other with long, curly dark hair and even darker skin. Daya and Isa both smile broadly and unhook their arms from mine. They lean over to hug these females that, yet again, feel familiar.

"This is Naeva and Paloma," Daya says with a smile. "You might remember them from Majikaero. We all trained as healers together in this world before departing to the Realm of Souls."

It's staggering when they offer me warm smiles. *Why's everyone being so fucking nice to me?*

Daya scowls and lightly flicks the side of my forehead. "I can't wait to sink my talons into those demons in there," she murmurs. "Plenty of souls have been kind to you. They're messing with your perception."

"Not surprising," the dark-haired beauty nods. "If he has

three of them in there, it's likely they each come out to play at different times."

"Sometimes all in one day," Isa confirms.

What?

My gaze sweeps across the four of them in alarm, and honestly, morbid intrigue. "You're saying my demons interact with others without me knowing?"

"Of course, hun," the strawberry-blond female says, pity shining in her eyes. "They all have their own personality that wants a chance at life. We'll have to meet them where they're all at right now, which might be in a few different places."

"What else can you tell me about them?" Even I can hear how desolate my tone sounds, but I don't care. I've been spinning into a tunnel of madness for weeks now, and no amount of clawing or screaming has gotten me anywhere. I'll do *anything* to make it stop.

BOOM.

That sound scatters the few thoughts I just pieced together.

"That'll have to wait until later," Daya shouts over the clanging that won't fucking stop. "We'll go over everything about your demons, the other parts of our world, and anything else you want to know. I promise."

Those determined hazel eyes stare at me until I nod in confirmation. Del places a hand on my back, and the four of us follow Naeva and Paloma further into the dim, closed-off room. A nebulous glow makes it even more challenging to see where the fuck we're going, but the others don't seem to have any issues. I shuffle along in the middle of these healers, feeling very much like a trapped disease surrounded by their healing light, until we come to an abrupt stop.

"Bow with us," Isa whispers, so quietly I can barely hear her.

I plant my feet firmly on the glassy material beneath me and lower my head in a low bow. My eyes widen as I take in what's lurking under this room: creatures with metallic, scaly tails as their bottom half and humanoid torsos with flowing long tresses of hair. Hundreds of them. Males. Females. Breasts with shells covering up the important bits. Whirling, intricate designs that travel up and down their arms. Nearly translucent skin with plush lips, barely containing rows of razor-sharp teeth. *Are these... what the fuck are these?*

Daya leans slightly into my side as we continue to keep our heads and chests lowered to the floor. "You might know them as merpeople," she whispers.

Merpeople? Seriously? I'm looking at fucking mermaids?

Daya elbows my ribs, causing me to cough. Loudly.

"You may all rise," a deep, alluring voice resounds.

Standing up straight, I'm already scowling at Daya for hitting me. I don't even have to open my mouth before she shushes me. She, Del, and Isa are all gazing ahead of us with a look of deference in their eyes. *No, not only that.* They *adore* the creature before them, and as I take in her appearance, I can already feel my own soul being drawn toward her.

On a throne of shells and coral and pearls, a curvy woman with wavy, long hair perches. Her eyes are a remarkable deep blue, the kind that entices you until you're being pulled into an undercurrent. Her hair, a mixture of auburn and blond and gray, cascades in loose waves down her exposed back, barely concealing the milky tones of her skin. Threads of pearls are woven through two thick braids that start at the top of her head and flow down her back with the rest of her hair. She's wearing a dress that cinches at the waist and accentuates the way her chest swells and her hips curve outward. The material ebbs and flows like an actual ocean wave. I typically go for the small and athletic types, but her thicker-set body is doing it for me right now. This soul commands your attention, and damn it, she fucking has mine already.

"Tryg," she sounds out my name, her lips rolling as if she's tasting the flavor. "So, you're the one everyone's talking about."

I open my mouth, and nothing comes out. I'm left speechless as her eyes pull me into a vortex.

"That's J'marie," Isa whispers. Daya steps on my toe, effectively snapping me out of my reverie.

Swallowing, I bow my head again. "Greetings, J'marie," I mumble, my words sticking to the roof of my mouth.

J'marie snorts, and those pink lips pull up into a smirk. Her eyes dart over to Daya. "I can see why you enjoy messing with him."

Daya smiles softly and glances at me.

"I understand you've come to request my services," J'marie croons. She rises from her throne and takes delicate steps toward where I'm standing. Del, Isa, Daya, Naeva, and Paloma all slink off to the side to give J'marie ample room around me. My throat squeezes closed while my breathing quickens, feeling skittish at best and unsure what to expect from this gorgeous, yet menacing, creature.

J'marie places the tip of one of her fingers under my chin and lifts my head up for her to examine. "You've come to see the Star and Queen of the Sea, have you?" She lets my chin go and walks in a circle around me. A sharp, stabbing pain starts at my shoulder blades and works its way down to my lower back. J'marie grins. "The symbol of your powers is breaking through your flesh, aching to bare itself to me."

As she continues her slow pace, a shiver and line of sweat breaks down my back. "You want to see your role to play in these games of war?"

She pauses to my right, and I turn my head to face her, catching the ghost of a smile on her lips. My muscles uncoil, the tension leaving my body for a brief few seconds as I observe that smile. I realize too late that it was a false sense of security, and now I'm trapped.

Quicker than a pistol, J'marie snatches the back of my neck, her fingers a vice around my skin. I scream out in pain, but I'm unable to move even an inch. I'm at this queen's mercy and can only pray that she doesn't take advantage of my most vulnerable emotions.

Blue mist billows around us, the colors blending in with J'marie's dress and the ocean surrounding this building. She yanks my head backward and brings her face close enough that her breath fans out over my mouth. Those deep blue eyes churn until they're a creamy, opaque mixture. I physically recoil from the way she scratches and tears at the outside of my soul until she has me in the palm of her fucking hand. One wrong move, and she could squeeze the life out of me.

J'marie's laughter fills my mind. *"What a shame it would be to throw away such potential. I won't be the one to kill you, Tryg."*

The sensation of water inundates me until I'm convinced I'm drowning.

"Your demons' poisons are addicting," she murmurs. *"You still have an ambitious journey ahead of you."*

I refrain from rolling my eyes at a super powerful ocean queen.

J'marie laughs again. *"What can I say? I love the sweetness your demons give me. The ones you need to fight through aren't the three you think, Tryg. You have more to dig out from under here if you truly desire to aid the others. Your friends wish to erase the trauma spreading through souls and spirits everywhere, across the bridges between our worlds."*

Is that what I want to do?

"It will be," J'marie sighs. I swear I can feel her breathe right through me and touch all the spots I prefer to keep covered. *"Your thirst to please Eira will overpower other thoughts of despair."* An electrical current surges down my back, and my body seizes. *"All that strength and wisdom and healing medicine of your bear magic will flourish as you peel back all these layers. They're all buried beneath the aggression and solitude you've used*

as a brace all these lifetimes, so you wouldn't have to face the untreated pain that chafes against your soul."

So, this is my path?

"No." Her voice reverberates as loud as rumbling thunder, pounding against all of my senses. *"I cannot see your destined path through the sludge you refuse to heal after all these lifetimes. The gods should have sent you to Cudhellen—there's not enough time on Earth to make a stubborn soul like yours see the ways you've wounded those around you, especially the harm done to yourself."*

J'marie pulls her essence out of me with the force of a waterfall. I fall backward, expecting to crack my head on the floor, but cushions of sea foam catch me before I hit the surface. My coverings are soaked in the salt and water of the sea, and with heaving breaths, I push myself up onto my forearms. I blink multiple times in an attempt to clear the sting of the salt from my eyes and watch as J'marie floats back to her throne, her body at ease.

She throws me a hardened look. "Come back to me when you've done the necessary work on yourself. Only then will you be able to complete the passage already laid out for you. And bring our missing stardust back with you."

My eyebrows furrow. "How do I find missing stardust? I should come back here after some healing sessions?"

J'marie nods at Daya and the others, and without hesitation, they line up and leave me alone with this queen who I'm terrified to admit might actually be a goddess.

"Leave the stardust to the healers. You'll complete your healing with one of my own." Her words travel along my skin like satin. "It needs to be with a *solliqa* who personally understands how the plague of darkness works and knows the ways it sticks to a soul for centuries."

"And who would that be?"

One of the creatures—*gods, merpeople*— swimming below us shoots up through the glassy material, unaffected by the barrier between this room and the sea. Their metallic tail shifts into flowy pants, and the shells adhered to their body shimmer into a sheer long-sleeved top. Each intricate design on their arms breaks apart into inky black veins. Black and blue hair falls just above their shoulders, and when they turn their head, cerulean eyes peer at me under thick lashes. A *solliqa* I barely knew, yet she connected to Eira and all the others with immediate ease.

"That'd be me," Erika announces. She smiles broadly, showing off all those serrated teeth. Daya squeals behind me in elation, and Erika's gaze sweeps around the room until they land on the healers who brought me here.

"Miss me?"

THIRTY-TWO
Hadwin

The earth can sense when danger arrives,
but we refuse to listen.
-Correspondence from Council Member Weke,
Grand Commander of Earth

My jaw tics as I watch Athena from the shadows, camouflaged behind one of the deep-rooted trees. The moons above us are mere shards of light. They make the bright blue and yellow leaves of each tree appear as shades of gray, almost completely engulfed by the darkness of night. I hadn't planned on spying on Athena—not even now that she has miraculously broken my shield and holds my soul like wet clay in her hands. Yet I couldn't resist when I saw her padding silently out of the secret home we're all sleeping in. Since Sayfters is the region in Majikaero that can most easily take any of us to the country Eira and her friends resided in—Sweazn—I was informed that there would be simple homes we could use. Not that I'm pleased about this. For reasons I can't decipher yet, my earth *maji* is resistant to this humid, swampy area. It's agitated, coiling in the same way as my python form inside of me, and the way it curls under my skin has me on edge.

We completed part of what we came here for, though, which is more than I thought we'd do already. There's no mistake—when it comes to my fortune, it'll run out before I can fully grasp it, if the gods have anything to do with it. For now, we've managed to learn bits and pieces of what Namid, and probably others on the Council, are doing on Earth. I chew the inside of my cheek while I consider the possibilities. These fucks want the souls of innocent children, and my mind is still reeling from what was said: *their thick blood*. There's now a *canielor* inside a dead child's body. We had to flee before we could see what the fuck they'll even do with it now—let alone what will happen with the child's stardust. It's maddening.

There's also still the question of why Ulf's wolf feels so damn connected to one of Eira and Athena's friends from Earth. *Is she his almaove? What do we do now with her and the other friend, Liv? Why does Astira's aura permeate me like the night sky?*

Athena steps onto a twig and hesitates before moving forward. She gingerly sits on the edge of one of the massive tree roots winding through the tall white grass. My jaw tenses again. Athena is still recovering from traveling between the veils of time and should be sleeping where Jade currently is. We have to get them both to another healer, so Jade doesn't lose *both* of her eyes and Athena can recuperate the rest of her powers. Instead, the soul I'm undeniably crazy for is sneaking off deeper into the woods in the middle of the night. *As if anything good ever comes from that.* Fortunately for her, the plague has brought me even closer to the darkness in this world, and I can follow her through the pitch black of night with ease.

I step on a twig myself, and holding my breath, I wait for Athena to realize I'm here. Her back stiffens, but she relaxes a few seconds later and digs her hands into the soil surrounding the tree she's sitting on. The green light of her *maji* glows around her robed form, the color as dark and green as her eyes. She's whispering muddled words that dance on the breeze flowing past me. *What in Cudhellen is she doing?*

I'm lifting my foot to go ask her and drag her back to the clay house—desperate to feel her skin against mine again, no matter if she's still recovering—when a dark mass appears in front of her. I instinctively shift into my python form and glide in the grass to get a closer look, bracing myself to strike at anything that might harm my *zamia*. The mass of shadows bends and twists until it takes the shape of an *alklen*. This one has the same streaks of maroon and starlight throughout its shadowed form that I've seen on other *alklen*, but instead of only having black antlers, there are flickering flames on the tips of each one. Those same flames match the color of its eyes. I study the way this creature is bending its head to Athena and nudging the palm of her hand with its dark head. *After what we went through today, this shit is too bizarre.*

My python slithers in a frenzied way, and I'm essentially letting this part of me take the reins of where we go and what we do. We get closer and closer until Athena and the *alklen* are a foot away. Winding up and opening our mouth, we prepare to strike out and wrap our body around Athena's pliant form, keeping her safe.

Yet I can't move. One of the tree roots has lifted upward, chunks of soil crumbling off the edges, and has twisted around the body of my gold python. It squeezes around me, almost as if it's inhaling—this tree is *alive*. It's a living, breathing soul with crystalized eyes that are slowly opening.

The *alklen* and Athena snap their heads to look at us at the same time. My thoughts ping back and forth between the fact that a tree is actively curling around me, that there's a shadowy *alklen* communicating with Athena, and the million questions I have for my *zamia*.

What secrets is she keeping from me? From everyone?

Those questions will have to wait for now. There are no longer flames in only the creature's eyes. Athena is staring at me while her *maji* still flares luminously around her, except those stunning green eyes aren't there. All I see are golden-green and black flames, ready to set me on fire.

Maybe I'll let her.

She'll have to burn away what's still covering my soul if she wants to find what's buried beneath the plague of darkness.

And perhaps I'm looking forward to the way only Athena can set fire to the parts no longer serving me and how she'll scorch me with not only her *maji*... but with her love.

I don't break eye contact with those eyes of green fire, content to let the earth strangle me if it means I'm with her. She stays focused on me, not even blinking as she raises one of her muscular legs to stand on top of the *alklen*. I shiver. The humid air of this swampy land swirls around me until it turns abnormally bitter and delicate frost travels down my golden scales. Athena stands tall on the *alklen's* shadowy back, so many feet above me as the creature has grown within seconds. Her forlorn gaze is full of longing and what-ifs that I don't understand.

Athena's lip quivers. It's the only warning I'm given that something is terribly wrong. Dread scoops out my heart like a shovel digging a grave. Any good fortune I've been blessed with has run out. I knew it would come. I just didn't think it would happen in this way.

A scream bursts out of me as I break free from the tree's twisted root around my python's body. I surge forward, but I'm not sure I can reach her in time.

Not as a trail of her *maji* disguised as vines falls from a tree branch above her. It takes the form of a noose around her slender neck—a beautiful necklace of death.

With a flick of her wrist, the vines tighten their hold on my *almaove*. She leaps off the *alklen's* back in an attempt to end it all before we've even begun.

THIRTY-THREE
Nyx

*Fire can heal us if we let it,
or we can burn those we love in the process.
-Valencia, Goddess of Fire*

Love is not an emotion I've entertained in years, not since I was a youngling learning how to wield my *maji* for the first time. It remained a slim possibility, appearing only as sparks and cinders during the moments when my soul family showed affection, or rather, their approval. I gave up on being able to love another *solliqa* and to be loved in return.

The revelation that I didn't tell Eira that I loved her before we left that library and dove into Majikaero's new reality is not simply shocking—it's disturbing. And the fact that I crave hearing those words from her delectable lips, more than the air I breathe? *Unfathomable.* She's truly my *almaove, and fucking gods*, I'm going to tear apart anyone and anything that gets in the way of me fixing this mistake. Eira *must* hear the full extent of my love for her. I'll just have to hold on to that fickle hope she's instilled in me that her own feelings have grown equally strong in such a short amount of time. She deserves nothing less than a *solliqa* worshipping her very existence—even if it means I haven't been fully healed and still have the plague of darkness congesting my soul.

I didn't think I was worthy of her healing light, but as I've thought about everything I wish I told her sooner, it's become clear that only she will get to decide what's worth her time. It was never about me or my shadows or the darkness I've resisted yet am so at home with. It is *always* going to be about her. She's healed me enough that I can see the path forward leads straight to being buried beneath her light and her own darkness that's starting to make an appearance. *Yes.* Both will put me into the ground, but I know my soul will be born again, and she and I will be free together.

We'll be far away from this fucking trap.

SMACK.

"He's daydreaming again," the voice I wish I didn't recognize mutters.

Another *solliqa* snorts near them. I don't know them. "He thinks he's going to survive this. How cute."

"Nyx isn't supposed to die. That wasn't part of the deal."

"No, the deal is that his soul won't be *purposely* killed. They never said anything about what'll happen to him when we take what he values most."

The first voice sighs. "Right. *Eira* and that special feline of hers." A hand tugs at the sapphire dagger still strapped to me. "And perhaps this as well. We wouldn't want that prophecy coming true."

Hearing Eira's name come out of their mouths has me writhing against the shackles binding me down to the muddy floor.

"See?" says the second voice. "He can't even stand us mentioning her."

Grinding my teeth, I force my eyes to open. Blood trickles

into them from the wound on my forehead that's still pulsating in pain. Fresh bruises are blooming down my torso, but that doesn't concern me. If anything, I'm used to unbearable torture —*these souls can't torment me more than I've done myself.*

Just as my blurry vision becomes clearer, my head is swinging back. Someone has sliced a cut down my jaw, and the sensation is excruciating. Dark *maji* flares in the corner of my eye and swarms the top half of my body.

"I'm going to prevent you from fully healing, Nyx," that second voice rasps. "The plague will already make it difficult for you to change your physical form while your soul continues to suffer. Let's see how much Eira wants to be with you when she sees how much we've carved up this pretty face of yours."

I scream in outrage, the sound echoing off the dark stony walls.

My face is pulled forward. "Open those crackling eyes, *Prince*."

Rough fingers press down on my eyelids and fling them wide open. My vision is marred by the still dripping blood, placing a gruesome filter on anything I look at. Blood or not, I can see fucking perfectly who's inflicting this current anguish on my body. I don't know their name and definitely haven't seen them before, but *I know* who the fuck they are.

Cropped white hair. Pale features. Blue eyes of crystals with streaks of silver and gold like lightning.

My captor is the spitting image of my *almaove*, and he's more of a monster than I am.

But he's not as much of a monster as the *solliqa* peering down at me from behind him. Her face and soul are imprinted on me forever. Those long waves of black hair with equally dark eyes. She has sharp features, from the arch of her nose to the black claws curving out of her fingertips. She's the reason the Council imprisoned me to begin with. The reason my heart shattered into too many pieces to put back together. The reason I spiraled down into the tunnel of guilt and self-loathing.

Yet here she stands before me, watching on as I'm tortured and held prisoner in an attempt to lure my firefly into a fucking trap.

Danger. Predator. Terror.

"Mother," I breathe.

THIRTY-FOUR
Hauke

Our worlds are interconnected more than we know.
It's a pity it'll take destroying them to understand this.
-Correspondence from Ambassador Zhuayla of Chironant

Darkness surrounds me, devours me, slices down through where my wings should still be connected to my body. The wind is roaring in my ears. I'm in a tunnel of black smoke that spirals down and down until it's impossible to know where the ground meets the air.

My soul is detaching from who I think I am. It won't completely settle again until I know in my heart that Stefanie is very much alive. Our *almaoves* are supposed to strengthen us, to make us into better versions of ourselves. That's not my little *luxriel*. She *is* my strength. Without her, I don't see a reason to continue existing. Not as the *canielor* latches its filthy mouth to my ribcage, its black, oozing poison smearing my skin with my own blood.

Another hand tugs on my ankle. I can barely feel it, though. It'd be so much easier to succumb to the grief that's crashing into me over and over again. This tidal wave might be able to wash away the tears that are still trailing down my face. I've failed. I didn't just fail my Stefanie, I failed this world. I don't even want to think about my homeworld or the fact that I'll never get to show my love all the beauty it holds.

"Hauke," a voice grits against my ears. "Come on, we have to get out of here."

My eyes peel open. Everything I see is bleary and soaked in endless surges of darkness.

"Hauke."

I try to move my head to that voice. It sounds familiar. Is it the *canielor*?

SLAP.

Blinking, I shake my head rapidly. What the fuck slapped me?

"Hauke, wake UP!"

My body is half-dragged across the ground. Each bump along the rocks jerks me in and out of consciousness. Then it all stops. The movement. The deafening wind. The heavy weight of the *canielor* against my side.

Just that voice hovers above me, and I force my eyes to fully open this time.

A half-shifted Odin glares down at me. His eyes are the same cerulean blue as his sister's with thin, vertical pupils, reminding me of a sea monster. Yet massive, webbed wings are expanding out of his back, growing wider with each breath that I take.

"Get the fuck up," Odin barks.

"What's the point?" I mumble.

"What's the point?" Odin repeats. His clawed hands—each with streaks of black and blue scales on them—grab the collar of my ripped covering. "We all have our missions, remember? Let's get you cleaned up and we'll plan out which Council member to hunt down first."

I gape up at him, at this quiet soul who's been burying his rage and heartache beneath that solemn exterior.

"Get up. We've got some worlds to save."

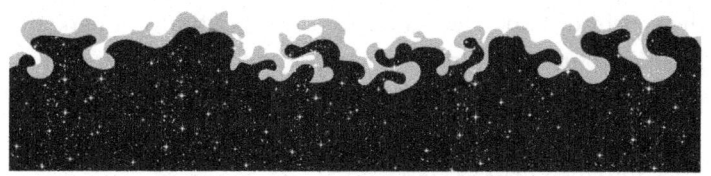

THIRTY-FIVE
Unknown

We'll laugh at their destruction.
After all, they started it.
-Unknown

Mother of Gods and Goddesses, do I silently watch on and do nothing?

Souls dance around one another, as if they aren't already bound to their designated realms. They think this is a battle they can win when there's a war raging they know nothing about. They all believe they have a choice and are choosing to strike down the evil in their midst.

Little do they know each action, each step, each insignificant thought and emotion are all part of a larger game, one of which they don't even know the rules.

They're so buried beneath the light of their queen, beneath the weight of hope, they don't see the other forms of darkness lurking around the corner—ready to snatch their meager dreams of a peaceful future and sink them down further.

Sink them into their chaotic minds, into their devastating fears, into their marked graves.

To Be Continued...

Thank You for Reading!

I'd be so grateful if you could please leave a review on one or all of the following places. Reviews are SO important for indie authors and are one of the main ways to create visibility, sales, and trust with new readers.

Scan to leave a review on Amazon - these matter A LOT!

Scan to leave a review on Goodreads - this can also help!

Scan to leave a review on B&N - this helps if you go to this bookstore!

Note from the Author

Dear Reader,

Thank you for reading my book! Readers are everything, and without your beautiful energy, trust, reviews, and hyping me up during the writing process, this second book wouldn't even exist.

I gave all of the attention I could to this book during a time when my physical health wasn't in the best place. Fatigue, body aches, GI symptoms, and endometriosis pain turned swiftly into chronic migraines and depressive episodes. Learning I have fibromyalgia, amongst other personal issues, sent me down quite the spiral at first, but I took one step at a time and have made it to the end of book 2. There were days when my body was SO exhausted, I could barely function or even speak. I mean this from the bottom of my heart: Knowing that readers loved The Light Within kept me going. I knew that Buried Beneath the Light had to be shared with the world—especially as my characters basically shouted their stories at me—and I needed to push through the draining symptoms whenever I could.

Of course, there were certain mental health themes in this story that rattled me. I work with kiddos and teens throughout the week as a therapist—I cried when I had to write what some of the characters are doing to these poor souls, especially knowing that it's essential to the end of the storyline. Astira's hatred of her body and what's been done to it against her will breaks my heart, but her story deserves to be shared. Her journey will soar to incredible places, and I'm already outlining where she'll go in Book 3. Eira's raw emotions when she was coming to terms with how chronic pain has deeply impacted her and what it's like to always be the healer—this was challenging to write. Lastly, all of the suicidal ideation... my fucking heart could barely take it. Some of the scenes would send me tumbling back to each time I've experienced those same thoughts.

Each of my characters needed to tell their story. They have a right to do this, just as I do, just as we all do. If you're reading this and feel it in your heart that your story hasn't truly been shared or heard, and you desperately want it to— then write it, sing it, draw it, paint it, shout it, share it in any way that you want.

Your story is worthy of being heard.

You're not alone.

Love,
Carliann

Acknowledgments

The amount of people and love I've been surrounded by is unbelievable. I'd argue that writing the second book in a series is even harder than the first one. There's an unspoken—and let's be honest, some very loudly spoken—expectations about how the story should continue. A million comments about the writing style, formatting suggestions, and the list goes on and on. The following people made *Buried Beneath the Light* possible—I love you all so much!

To my husband, Daniel. Our grumpy x grumpier trope has never been more real than these past months. Even as you transitioned into your most challenging year of teaching, you were my constant the entire journey. Thank you for your daily encouragement, brainstorming sessions, walks, treats and food, saying yes to many author events, and everything else that you do. So lit, so chill!

To the one and only Hayley. I adore you so much. Thank you for taking my books to the next level, organizing my street team, hyping me up, reading my rambling messages, making all those remixes, connecting me with a bunch of remarkable humans. You're just the best.

To my editor, Maddi. My fellow raccoon lover. Thank you for making me laugh with all of your comments throughout each draft—*Sir, this is a Wendy's (dungeon)*. You're able to see the holes in my story that I cannot, and I'm full of gratitude for your hard work. You're amazing, and I'm never letting you go.

To my alpha reader, Melissa. Thank you for such detailed feedback and pushing me in the right direction for this story.

To my beta readers, thank you for taking the time to read the unpolished version and for hyping me up.

To my final proofreader, Rachel. You've been with me from the very beginning and gave me love and encouragement when I wasn't giving it to myself. Thank you, friend.

To my street team, thank you for sharing such love for each idea and update. Each comment kept me going when times were rough.

To my pets. You'll never read this, but without you, I wouldn't have been able to write. Your companionship made each day better.

To my friends, thank you for your excitement about my books and cheering me on. You know who you are, and I love you.

To my parents. Your enthusiasm and love helped me feel supported throughout this journey.

To Emily McIntire. Your journey of pain and ability to share with the world such raw emotions kept me going. Thank you. You inspired me to push through, no matter how significant the physical pain was or how low I emotionally plummeted.

To the indie authors who've helped me along the way. Thank you. I'm fortunate enough to know so many. I don't want to name only a few when each individual has helped in their own way. May our journeys continue to cross—I love you all.

To the artists who have helped my characters come to life. Art is *everything*.

To my readers, *thank you* from the bottom of my heart for reading my books.

PART ONE
A Guide to the Regions on Future Earth & Majikaero

Regions on Future Earth

Previous Earth was a planet once thought to be doomed after nuclear war nearly erupted and destroyed many innocents. While total carnage was avoided, the impact of poverty, trauma, and threats of war wreaked havoc across each country. Violence still bloomed like wild poppies the color of fresh blood. Much of humanity fell to the reprieve drugs and alcohol offered, hugging them in a tight embrace until they were left choking the life out of themselves.

The world fell, no longer flourishing with abundant nature or thriving cultures. Not in the frigid north, nor in the heated south, nor in the beckoning warmth and chilled winds found in between. Citizens were left with a lukewarm version of what was once a land of hope. All of them left to reform what little remained, to construct new country lines, to merge languages and beliefs and colors of people who previously clashed like silver swords in the moonlight.

Another world war is imminent. Grievously unstoppable, and trauma has the world in its clutches once again.

New Africa Territories

Conea Nigoon (Coh-nee-ah Nih-goon)
Previously Nigeria, Cameroon, Equatorial Guinea, Northern part of Republic of the Congo

Guinegalia (Guh-ing-eh-gah-lee-ah)
Previously Senegal, The Gambia, Guinea, Sierra Leone, Liberia

Niya Tunypt *(Neye-yah Toon-yi-p-t)*
Previously Egypt, Chad, Niger, Libya, Algeria, Tunisia

Sahliocco *(Sah-lee-oh-coh)*
Previously Morocco, Western Sahara, Algeria, Mauritania, Mali

Sumalpia *(Suh-mahl-pee-ah)*
Previously Somalia, Ethiopia, Sudan

Tonihana *(Toh-nee-hah-nah)*
Previously Cote d'ivoire, Ghana, Burkina Faso, Togo, Benin

Ugenya Danican (You-gen-yah Dah-nih-cahn)
Previously Northern part of DRC, Central African Republic, Uganda, Kenya, South Sudan

Zambiana (Zahm-bee-ah-nah)
Previously African countries south of the equator but were obliterated after a nuclear attack

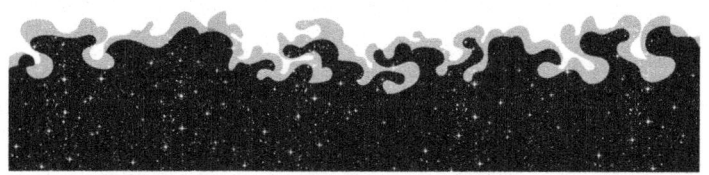

New Antarctica Territories

Antica (Ant-tih-cah)
Large parts managed to survive with little to no habitants.

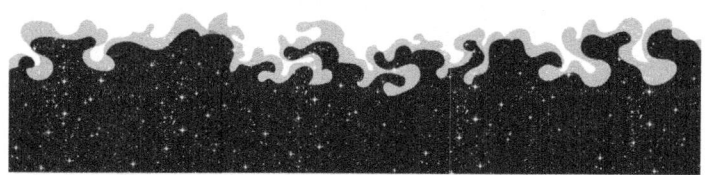

New Asia Territories

Innmartana (Een-mahr-tah-nah)
Previously countries of Asia east of Pakistan but were obliterated after a nuclear attack

Irtukistan (Irr-tuh-kee-stahn)
Previously Iran, Turkmenistan, Afghanistan, Pakistan

Kopania (Koh-pah-nee-ah)
Previously South Korea, North Korea, Japan, Coast of China, Coast of Russia

Kyazssia (Kee-ah-zee-see-ah)
Previously parts of Russia, Kazakhstan, Uzbekistan, Kyrgyzstan

Yemania Arabia (Yeh-mah-nee-ah Ah-ray-bee-ah)
Previously Saudi Arabia, Yemen, Oman, the United Arab Emirates

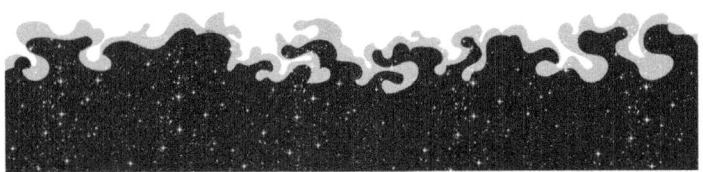

New Europe Territories

Belaity (Beh-lah-ih-tee)
Previously France, Belgium, Spain, Italy, Netherlands

Griclin Edinales (Grih-sih-lihn Ed-ih-nah-lays)
Previously Iceland, Greenland, the UK

Hungatia (Huhn-gah-shee-ah)
Previously Croatia, Slovenia, Austria, Slovakia, Hungary, Czech Republic

Kosnia (Kohs-nee-ah)
Previously Bosnia, Serbia, Montenegro, Kosovo, Albania, Macedonia, Bulgaria

Nedrazon (Ned-rah-zon)
An underground city built below Sweazn.

Sweazn (Sway-zhn)
Previously Norway, Sweden, Finland, Denmark, Germany, Switzerland

Syreean (See-ree-ahn)
Previously Greece, Turkey, Syria, Lebanon, Israel, Jordan, Iraq but did not survive war attacks

Ukuanova (You-kuu-ah-noh-vah)
Previously Estonia, Lithuania, Belarus, Ukraine, Moldova but did not survive war attacks

New North America Territories

Dakourin (Dah-koh-uu-rihn)
Midwestern United States that survived war attacks

Guaoaera (Gu-wah-oh-air-ah)
Previously parts of Mexico

Idada Calana (Eye-dah-dah Cah-lay-nah)
Western United States that survived war attacks

New Virlina Yorkshine (Nu Virr-lee-nah Yorh-kah-sh-ine)
Previously North and South Eastern United States but was obliterated after a nuclear attack

Riuba Haican (Reye-oo-bee-ah Heye-ih-cahn)
Previously Cuba, Puerto Rico, and other islands but was obliterated after a nuclear attack

Torinarry (Tohr-ih-nair-ee)
Previously southern parts of Canada and Alaska

Zonicoma (Zohn-ih-coh-mah)
Southern United States and parts of Mexico that survived war attacks

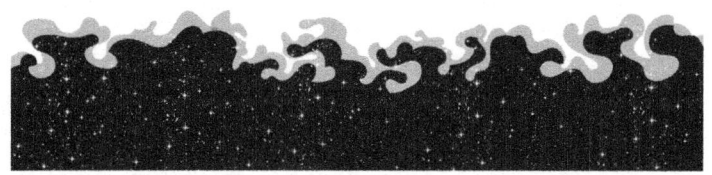

New Oceania Territories

New Taszealia (Nu Tah-zee-ah-lee-ah)
Previously New Zealand, Tasmania, parts of Australia

Phindonea (Fihn-doh-nee-ah)
Previously islands surrounding Australia but were obliterated after a nuclear attack

New South America Territories

Bochentuay (Boh-chehn-too-ai)
Previously parts of Argentina, Chile, Uruguay, Paraguay, Bolivia

Guizeuras (Guh-eez-eh-oo-rahs)
Previously Guatemala, Belize, Honduras, El Salvador

Guzuelail (Guhz-uu-ay-lah-eel)
Previously the eastern half of South America but was obliterated after a nuclear attack

Panicaga (Pah-nee-cah-gah)
Previously the southern countries of Central America but was obliterated after a nuclear attack

Zilbia Perador (Zihl-bee-ah Perr-ah-dohr)
Previously Peru, Ecuador, south parts of Colombia, western parts of Brazil

All other countries and locations did not survive.

Regions on Majikaero (Mah-jee-kair-oh)

Drageyra (Drah-gair-ah)
Land of Fire
Bold, Ambitious, Competitive, Direct

Eikenbien (Eye-kehn-bine)
Land of Woods
Relaxed, Calm, Dependable, Receptive

Lagunit (Lah-goon-iht)
Land of Many Waters
Intuitive, Sensitive, Empathetic, Dreamer

Myrellden (Meye-rehl-dehn)
Land of Darkness
Innovative, Progressive, Revolutionary, Builder of Worlds

Reykashin (Ray-kah-shihn)
Land of Smoke
Elusive, Mysterious, Powerful, Ruthless

Rioa (Ree-oh-ah)
Land of Natural Cities, The Capital
Balance, Harmony, Justice, Variability

Sayfters (Saif-tairs)
Land of Clay and Buildings
Patient, Dedicated, Persevering, Motivated by Duty

Shymeira (Sheye-mair-ah)
Land of Tropics
Spontaneous, Erratic, Playful, Comical

Skugvaytir (Skoog-vai-teer)
Land of the Shadows
Logical, Practical, Systematic, Attention to Detail

Sunnadyn (Suhn-ah-dihn)
Land of Sunlight
Passionate, Loyal, Fiery, Loving

Viorfelle (Vee-ohr-fell)
Land of Mountains
Intellectual, Adventurous, Curious, Grounded

Wyndera (Wihn-dair-ah)
Land of Wind
Highly Intuitive, Layered Personality, Moody, Perceptive

PART TWO
Gods & Goddesses, Council Members

Gods and Goddesses Worshipped

*The following include the most
prominent names found in the
Head Council Library located in Rioa*

Of Water
Deniz (Deh-neez) and Derya (Dair-yah)

Of Fire
Edan (Eh-dahn) and Valencia (Vah-lehn-cee-ah)

Of Earth
Abarrane (Ah-bar-aine) and Neta (Neh-tah)

Of Air
Aapeli (Ah-peh-lee) and Duncas (Duhn-cahs)

Of Spirit
Cajsa (Cah-shah) and Faramond (Fahr-ah-mohnd)

Of Shapeshifting
Nixie (Nih-ksee) and Perogus (Pair-oh-guhs)

Of Manipulation
Nitika (Niht-ee-kah) and Wrathiala (Ra-thee-ah-lah)

Of Solar
Lahahana (Lah-hah-hah-nah) and Dilay (Dee-lay)

Of Healing
Eliina (Ehl-eye-nah) and Berlind (Berh-lihnd)

Of War
Cairo (Cai-roh) and Dabria (Dah-bree-ah)

Of Intellect
Ove (Oh-vay) and Oaxa (Wah-ha)

Of the Soul
Namid (Nah-meed) and Nicola (Nih-coh-lah)

List of Council Members

Council Members of Majikaero
*The following include the current
Council Members of Majikaero.
They come from different regions,
but they all meet at the Council building of Rioa.*

Eliina
*Grand Healer
Eikenbien, Land of Woods*

Elio
*Grand Commander of Sunlight
Sunnadyn, Land of Sunlight*

Enya
*Grand Commander of Fire
Drageyra, Land of Fire*

Haliean
Grand Commander of Water
Lagunit, Land of Many Waters

Lesak
Grand Spirit Reader
Viorfelle, Land of Mountains

Mohi
Grand Manipulator
Reykashin, Land of Smoke

Namid
Grand Soul Reader
Myrellden, Land of Darkness

Neoma
Grand Commander of Moonlight
Skugvaytir, Land of the Shadows

Nova
Grand Commander of Travel and Space
Rioa, Land of Natural Cities, The Capital

Rakiana
Grand Commander of Wind
Wyndera, Land of Wind

Waneta
Grand Shifter
Shymeira, Land of Tropics

Weke
Grand Commander of Earth
Sayfters, Land of Clay and Buildings

PART THREE
Character Names & Pronunciations

Main Character Names & Pronunciation Guide

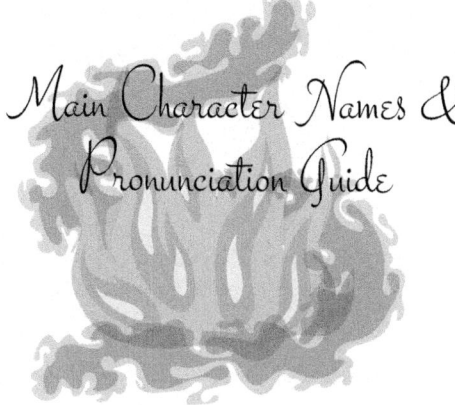

Future Earth

Astira (Ah-stir-ah)

Athena (Ah-thee-nah)

Eira (Air-ah)

Jace (Jays)

Liv (Lihv)

Lyk (Leek)

Morgan (Mohr-gahn)

Ruse (Roose)

Shira (Sheer-ah)

Tryg (Trihg)

Zaya (Zeye-ah)

Main Character Names & Pronunciation Guide

Majikaero

Ambra (Ahm-brah)

Azrael (Az-ray-all)

Daglo (Dah-gloh)

Dahviid (Dah-veed)

Daru (Dah-roo)

Daya (Dye-ah)

Delano (Deh-lah-noh)

Eliina (Ehl-eye-nah)

Erika (Air-ih-kah)

Fraya (Fray-ah)

Hadwin (Had-whin)

Hauke (Hawk)

Isa (Ee-sah)

Ivar (Eye-vahr)

Naeva (Nay-vah)

Namid (Nah-meed)

Nyx (Nihks)

Odin (Oh-dihn)

Paloma (Pah-loh-mah)

Rada (Rah-dah)

Stefanie (Steh-fah-nee)

Ulf (oolf)

Main Character Names & Pronunciation Guide

Chironant

J'marie (juh-mah-ree)

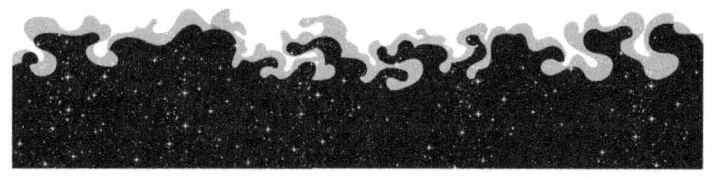

PART FOUR
Common Majikaero Terms

Common Majikaero Terms & Pronunciation Guide

Alklen (Ahlk-lehn)
Akin to a deer made of shadows, smoke, and other elements of nature

Almaove (Ahl-mohve)
The deepest soul connection and love a solliqa can have

Bholei (Buh-hole-aye)
An unidentified monster that is similar to a canielor, but it is much larger in size and has the capability of portaling between worlds and wielding maji.

Canielor (Cahn-ee-eh-lor)
After a solliqa has caught the plague of darkness, this is the creature they can turn into before they evolve into a monster specific to their pain and trauma

Chiante (Chi-an-tay)
A group of High Gods and Goddesses who've looked over the worlds. They maintained relative peace for thousands of centuries across worlds and timelines.

Chironant (Chi-roh-nahn-t)
A realm closely tied to Majikaero, typically referred to as its sister world. It's primarily known as the Realm of Light and Shifters.

Cudhellen (Cuhd-hell-en)
A realm closely tied to Earth and Majikaero, typically referred to as Hell by people on Earth.

Dayre (Dai-air)
A small mammal with velvet antlers, hooves, and a long multicolored tail

Drekstri (Drehk-stree)
A dangerous and loyal creature with characteristics of a horse and a dragon

Einral (Eyen-rahl)
A liquid that awakens the mind and body

Fim (Fihm)
Energy that's described as more feminine
A term used to describe souls with feminine energy

Lipva (Leep-vah)
Hydrating water

Maji (Mah-jee)
Magic powers connected to the elements, creatures, and souls

Misn (Mih-sin)
Energy that's described as more masculine
A term used to describe souls with masculine energy

Sairn (Sair-ihn)
A group of solliqas that believe in gods from another world and believe Eira's powers to be bad for Majikaero

Solliqa (Sol-ih-kah)
A soul that exists in Majikaero

Veina (Vai-nah)
A liquid that is similar to a mixture of wine and dark, sweet liquor

About the Author

Carliann Jean has always loved reading, writing, and throwing herself into anything creative. Her path took a turn into the fields of education and social work, where she thrived in the classroom and as a school social worker. She has a passion for helping those impacted by trauma and mental health issues, and in general, she loves to build deep, healing connections. While Carliann adores her current work as a licensed clinical social worker in private practice, she wants to fuse her mental health specialization with one of her favorite things: fiction stories.

She currently writes fantasy romance that focuses on mental

health, trauma, and darker themes. Her goal is multi-purposed. Carliann wants to continue aiding those who have experienced trauma and mental health issues through the art of storytelling. She also wants to bring readers the joy, laughter, tears, and many other feelings experienced from immersing yourself in a character's life.

When Carliann is not writing, she thoroughly enjoys spending time with her husband and pet children, reading more books than she has room for, spending time outdoors, traveling and exploring, stress baking with music, and laughing with her loved ones. She's an Illinois native who felt drawn to the West. If you can't find her cuddled up with her feisty two cats and excitable pup, you'll see her hiking in the mountains or at one of the local shops with a new treat and shaken espresso.

Let's Connect!

I'm all about building connections!
Follow me on Instagram to stay up to date about my books, upcoming events, art and merch, and more. Send me an email or DM if you're interested in working together or have any questions at all.

My website: www.authorcarliannjean.com

- instagram.com/carliannjean
- amazon.com/author/carliannjean
- threads.net/carliannjean
- goodreads.com/carliann_jean

Printed in Dunstable, United Kingdom